John Seymour Wood

College days. Or, Harry's career at Yale

John Seymour Wood

College days. Or, Harry's career at Yale

ISBN/EAN: 9783337056827

Printed in Europe, USA, Canada, Australia, Japan

Cover: Foto ©Andreas Hilbeck / pixelio.de

More available books at **www.hansebooks.com**

OR

HARRY'S CAREER AT YALE

BY

JOHN SEYMOUR WOOD

Rewritten and reprinted from Outing, May, 1891—March, 1893

WITH ILLUSTRATIONS

"We aint no thin-red heroes, nor we aint no blackguards too,
But single men in barracks, most remarkable like you."
—KIPLING

THE OUTING COMPANY, LIMITED

239-241 FIFTH AVENUE, NEW YORK. 170 STRAND, LONDON, W. C.

1894

PREFACE.

The author's object in this story of College Days is to give a picture of student life as it was twenty years ago. The Yale of to-day is more cultured, less democratic, less boyish than in the Seventies. In this story the public student life has been treated rather than the private life, and it may be added that the period covered was the close of what has been termed Yale's "barbaric era." The attitude of students to the faculty and to one another, the relations of classes, have all materially altered for the better these latter years. The student enters college at a more advanced age, feels himself much more of a "man," has already experienced some of the delights of secret societies at Exeter or Andover, and is altogether about as experienced as a junior in the old days.

But a Yale student of to-day has much the same old hardy spirit of his fathers, and the glory of Yale is always his cherished thought. He will die for Yale gladly, in his athletic contests; such is his patriotism. So will an Oxford or Cambridge oar pull his heart out for his 'Varsity, if called upon, from Putney to Mortlake. Love and devotion to Alma Mater are the same with Harry and Jack as with Tom Brown at Oxford. With the hope that this story will bring some agreeable reminder of college life to old "grads" of every college, and may interest the undergraduate as a picture of older times at Yale, the author relinquishes to them what has been to him a pleasant task.

J. S. W.

New York, *April*, 1894.

I DEDICATE

THIS VOLUME TO MY CLASSMATES OF YALE, '74.

J. S. W.

CONTENTS.

ILLUSTRATIONS.

COLLEGE DAYS;

OR.

HARRY'S CAREER AT YALE.

CHAPTER I.

" IN THE BEGINNING."

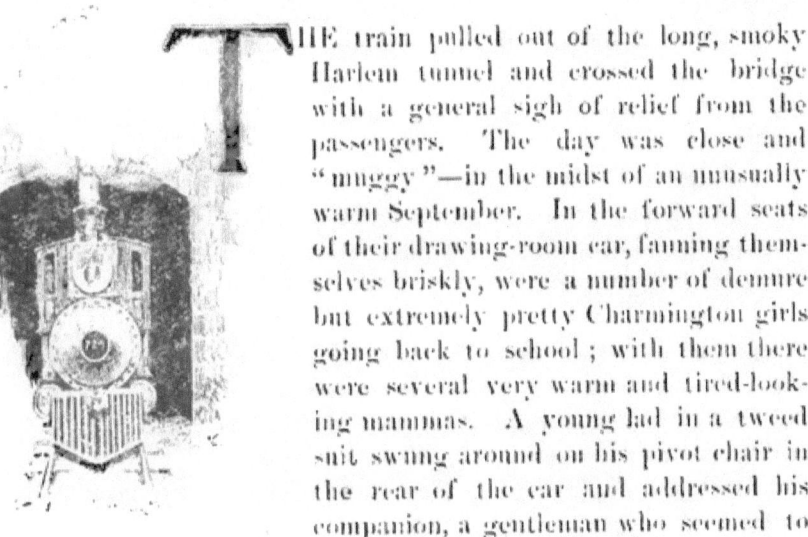

THE train pulled out of the long, smoky Harlem tunnel and crossed the bridge with a general sigh of relief from the passengers. The day was close and " muggy "—in the midst of an unusually warm September. In the forward seats of their drawing-room car, fanning themselves briskly, were a number of demure but extremely pretty Charmington girls going back to school ; with them there were several very warm and tired-looking mammas. A young lad in a tweed suit swung around on his pivot chair in the rear of the car and addressed his companion, a gentleman who seemed to make some pretensions to classical attainments, for he held an open Homer's Iliad on his knee. The young fellow was well built, strong, his skin clear as porcelain. His laughing boyish eyes had already made several futile assaults upon the Charmington girls, and especially one of them, a pretty brunette, the initials of whose traveling bag he observed were " C. H." He wondered who " C. H." could be. He met his companion's frank gaze very coolly.

"Do put up that book, Uncle Dick," he said, laughing. "I refuse to be examined. I know I shall pass all right. Mother and you will be the death of me."

"But your mother would feel so dreadfully if you failed."

"I shan't fail. *What* an idea!" he replied quickly.

His uncle, who was a man of about thirty, ran his eye over a few lines of the Iliad in silence. It was more than he could do to scan it, and so he closed the book discreetly and laid it by the window.

"I am very sorry your mother took you abroad with her this summer, Harry. You ought to have gone up in July. Then by this time you would have been through with everything—but the conditions——"

"Conditions! I'm not going to be conditioned!"

"Now, don't be too cocksure. I got six when I entered Yale."

Harry opened his eyes very wide.

"Yes—but you never went to Andover——"

"Let me tell you, my boy, that Andover never could hold a candle to East Hampton." Uncle Dick pulled the ends of his mustache violently, as if with some irritation.

"East Hampton—oh, pooh!" laughed Harry contemptuously.

Uncle Dick frowned.

"I tell you we have turned out more men of reputation——" Uncle Dick was thoroughly in earnest.

"Andover—George Washington was at Andover—with his army!" laughed Harry.

"Oh, be—serious!" said Uncle Dick. It was evident that they were about to come to blows over their preparatory schools. Fortunately the conductor happened along, and in the diversion of showing their tickets the dispute was forgotten. Harry spun around for another glance at the Charmington girls—such a strangely circumspect lot he had never seen before, and his uncle buried himself in his morning paper. The express swung with a rush and a roar through a charming little seaport town embowered in the deepest greenery. As it did so his uncle leaned forward and whispered :

"They very unkindly rusticated me here, Harry, in S——, when I was in college, for stealing the clapper out of the college bell."

"I'm afraid you were terribly bad in those days," the boy laughed. "Mother must have worried awfully about *you*."

Uncle Dick smiled, and relapsed behind his paper in silence, his mind reverting to the memories of other days. They reached

"DO PUT UP THAT BOOK, UNCLE DICK."

Bridgeport presently, and, as the train came to a full stop, outside, on the platform of the station, a band of rakish-looking, well-dressed young men gave a shout in unison, "Delta Kappa! Delta Kappa! Kappa—Kappa—Kap!"

They seemed to shout their cry as it were by way of defiance. They were evidently students, and as they got aboard the train and walked through the car Uncle Dick observed that they were possessed of all the insolent air of sophomores. They made a great deal of noise and loud talk. They stared at the pretty girls and were entirely unmindful how they carried their canes. As they reached Harry's seat one young man, in a loud, flashy necktie and diamond pin, bawled out to the rest : "Where the mischief are they? I say! I guess all the freshmen will come up by boat."

Harry rose quickly. "I am going to Yale," he said politely, touching his hat. It was sometimes difficult to tell exactly when Harry was in earnest and when not.

"Hold on, fellows, here's a sub,"* said the swell young man, whose name they found out afterward was Caswell. Some of the sophomores came back. There was a pleasing odor of cigarettes, perfumery, and an air of high life—the life of very great swells—about them, which to Harry was extremely fascinating.

"Pledged?" asked the swell young soph, with a half contemptuous size-him-up-at-a-glance stare.

"No—sir—I——"

"Well, you're not going to risk going to New Haven *without* being pledged, are you?"

"Why not?"

"Great Scott! fellows, look here!"

Several of the sophomores, who had gone on into the smoking compartment, turned back. They all stared at Harry with the same impertinent disdain. It may be admitted that the "sub" stared back at them with an equal effrontery.

"Here's a fresh who isn't pledged to Delta Kap."

"Good Lord!" said one. "Impossible!"

"Now, then, just put your name down here, and it'll be all right. It may save you a peck of trouble."

"I'm an Andover man," said Harry, "and I want to go where my friends go."

"Why, they are all going our way. Where were you when our delegate was in Andover last June? It's the only way to go. The

* A sub-freshman, one who has not matriculated, or passed his preliminary examinations.

faculty are down on Sigma Eps, and of course no one would be seen dead in Gamma Nu."

"What shall I do, Uncle Dick?" whispered Harry. "Shall I sign? I know Delta Kap is where I want to go."

"Wait till we get to New Haven."

Uncle Dick was a great wag in his own serious, circumspect way, and he dearly loved a college joke. He whispered to Harry, "Make them think I'm a freshman, too, and don't call me Uncle Dick."

"Why don't you pledge my classmate?" said Harry boldly to the sophomores.

"He isn't going to enter, is he? Lord, fellows, he looks as if he might be thinking of a professorship!"

"I'm not too old to learn, am I?" Uncle Dick asked solemnly.

"But you're old enough to know better than enter Umpty-four."

"Well, we're going to lay you fellows out!" There was a smile of derision on Uncle Dick's face.

"Will you pledge?"

"No," said Uncle Dick timidly. "Father wants me to go to Gamma Nu."

There was a shout of derision.

"Well, go there and be hanged to you!" said Caswell, moving off vexedly and entirely out of patience. "I'll haze that old fellow out of his boots before the end of the term!" he said wrathfully. Luckily for Uncle Dick's welfare he never had the chance.

The other sophomores, each wearing a blue-ribbon badge, indicating that they were on the Delta Kappa campaign committee, now took up the running with the two freshmen with serious insistence. But Uncle Dick gave them so many good and virtuous arguments against freshmen secret societies* that they hardly knew how to answer him; in fact, they couldn't answer him.

"See here, you!" burst out one fellow, leaning over the seat,

---

* The freshmen societies were abolished at Yale by the faculty a few years after Harry graduated, as were the sophomore fraternities also. Those which exist now, and we are told that several do exist, are only "tolerated" by the faculty, not "encouraged."

while the passengers on all sides laughed, "we want you! You're dead sure to take the valedictory! You've got it in your pocket! We'll give you a chromo and a pound of tea if you'll pledge and say nothing more about it!"

"Gamma Nu forever!" replied Uncle Dick, laughing. "Still, gentlemen, I'm open to argument. My friend and I are not pledged anywhere, as yet. We'll think it over."

As the train approached New Haven the sophomores grew much more conciliatory and more polite. They persuaded Uncle Dick

"N-N-NEW HAVEN! TEN MINUTES FOR 'FRESHMEN!'"

to go back in the smoking car, where they offered him an expensive cigar and labored to convince him. Presently the train seemed to run into a sort of dark tunnel and stop. It was the famous old underground New Haven depot. "N—N—New Haven!" shouted a huge, smiling darky in a white apron, coming through the car. "Ten minutes for 'freshmen'!"

Everybody laughed. It was the thing in those days for all classes in New Haven to guy the poor freshmen when they first came on, and everybody, even the "cullud brother," seemed to take generous advantage of it. "Well, it's four years for you, Harry," said Uncle Dick, who had returned to his seat for his bags and umbrella. "Now, mind what you do. When we get out here in the crowd, the Kappa Sigma Eps men will be after us. You keep mum. They'll do anything to pledge us. Let us hang off as long as possible."

"It's such a joke your palming yourself off as a freshman—you!—old as you are!"

"Why, I'm not thirty yet, my boy! I feel as young as you

do. Besides, I feel as if I were going to join Umpty-four myself!"

"*I'm* in for it when they find you out!" Harry laughed.

"Oh, I guess you can take care of yourself. You'll have a hundred and thirty or so friends the minute you get through with the examinations at Alumni Hall. If they haze you you haze back, that's all. Remember retaliation is the thief of time!"

They made their way to the platform of the dimly lighted underground station. Here students were crowding and jamming, and all sorts of people were struggling for the train. There was a pale youth, with a long, thin face and colored spectacles, standing near a pillar. He looked so green that Harry thought he would try and have some fun out of him. "Hello, freshie!" he called out to him. "Pledged yet?"

He thought the pale youth was about to explode. "Sh-sh!" laughed Uncle Dick in a whisper. "Don't you know who that is? Why, what a freshman you are! That's Professor Cube, the famous author of Cube's series of arithmetics."

Harry tried to hide himself by diving in the crowd. But thinking it was probably one of Uncle Dick's jokes, he returned to him.

They watched the row going on at the end of the platform. There seemed to be two crowds of students doing battle against each other, one lot shouting in unison "Delta Kappa! Delta Kappa-Kappa-Kappa-Kap!" and the other "Sigma*reps! *Sigma*reps!* Hooray, Sigmareps!" They were hustling a poor meek freshman between them, and it appeared that the poor freshman was getting much the worst of it.

While they were watching the fun the members of the committee from the rival fraternity, that of Kappa Sigma Epsilon, got hold of them, their bags and umbrellas, and were for immediately hustling them off into hacks and hurrying them up to college. Fortunately the astute Caswell, with a great shout of dismay and re-enforced by a dozen Delta Kaps, rushed to their assistance. For a moment it was very like real war. Then there was a hasty flank movement, and they all climbed the depot stairs pell-mell and poured out into the street. The two fraternities pulled and hauled each other about in the most fraternal spirit imaginable. It seemed like a football game. Harry thought it great fun, and Uncle Dick, who had been an old rowing man himself in days gone by, pulled and hauled as hard as the rest ; he seemed to enjoy the sport very well.

"Now see here, you confounded Sigmareps men!" shouted Caswell, his hat smashed over his head, making him look extremely idiotic, "these freshmen don't want any Sigmareps kindergarten! This man Lyman—is that your name?—before Lyman quite made up his mind he was in need of a college education he had at least six grandchildren!—he's much too old to go into Sigmareps kindergarten, you see, so he'll send on his grandchildren next year!"

The ridiculous allusion to a kindergarten seemed to make the Sigma Eps men furious. They caught hold of Harry and his uncle by one arm, and Caswell and the Delta Kaps caught them by the other. They tugged and hauled, until Mr. Lyman, perspiration pouring down his face from every pore, determined upon strategy, dark and mysterious.

"Gentlemen!" he shouted, "isn't there some comfortable place near here where we can get a—er—lemonade, and talk this thing over?"

"Oh! come along over to Brood's," said Caswell hotly, leading the way. The whole noisy crowd of students followed toward the entrance of a small, highly respectable, old-fashioned, brick dwelling house.

Brood's was then in the full prime of its glory. On hot summer nights it was where the Yalensian of those days took his lexicon and Latin grammar, his Tacitus and his Herodotus, and sat till the small hours pouring over his books, in company with a catawba cobbler of the most mellifluous character. Ladies, you little know how studious your sons and brothers become in such a purely classical atmosphere! Brood's!—ah, me! how easily the old fellow surpassed the Parnassian recipe for nectar!*

* We trust that parents and guardians will kindly take this *cum grano salis.* Students of Harry's time rarely studied aught but truth—*in vino veritas*—in the bottom of a cobbler.

They entered the door of the dwelling house and passed upstairs in Indian file. Caswell called out to the jolly barkeeper, "Ned ! send us out fourteen catawbas—Sigmareps can pay for their own ! "

The barkeeper, in a neat white apron, smiled and nodded. They filed past the bar, down a short flight of steps to a charming, cool,

DEMURE BUT EXTREMELY PRETTY CHARMINGTON GIRLS.

vine covered arbor. A musical fountain was playing into a shallow iron basin. Here and there were little tables at which students were sitting, sipping their sherbets and lemonades out of long, fascinating glasses through straws.

While the cobblers were coming, and after, the debate waxed high. The merits of the two fraternities were discussed in no measured terms, and with loud approving applause and disdainful hisses Caswell trotted out the great and eminent Delta Kaps of his class—Dobson, a big boating man ; Steele, the pitcher of the nine ; McCutchin, the great single sculler and winner of the Southworth Cup. Harry was greatly impressed. They wore Delta Kap pins on their waistcoats and square sophomore society pins on their scarfs. They ordered a second round of cobblers. They were very mild, but insinuating, the cobblers.

"Harry, you'd better take a lemonade this time." said his uncle. "Remember that examination to-morrow ; keep your head clear, my boy."

"Oh, I guess I'll go just one more," said the lad. Uncle Dick fell into a discussion with some Sigma Eps men and Harry was left to be "stuffed" by Caswell and his friends. Cobbler No. 2 loosened his tongue a little and deprived him of his usual caution. He forgot that he was in the presence of his natural born enemies !

"Of course you know of Professor Brood," said Caswell, "head of the scientifs ?"

"No," said Harry. "What of him ?"

"Oh—he runs this place to help eke out his salary."

"What—a professor ?"

"Why, Professor Brood is the hydrostatic professor on liquids, you know, in the scientific school. He conducts most of his experiments here."

Harry wondered if he was being chaffed, but Caswell and his friends were so serious that he thought it impossible.

"You generally meet most of the faculty here every night. Prexy always has a warm lemonade before going to bed. Now, by the way, almost all the faculty are Delta Kap men."

"Well, I want to be in with the faculty," said Harry sagely.

"You'd better pledge, Mr. Chestleton, before it's too late ; you may get left," said another. "The faculty are down on men not in Delta Kap."

It seemed so nice to be called Mr. Chestleton ! What fun it was already ! He felt he was being made so much of, and he wondered if this was what he was to expect his entire college course to be. How jolly of the faculty to be convivial and all that ! At Andover "Old Unk," as the boys irreverently called Dr. Taylor, looked with a sinister and terrible eye upon all sorts of conviviality, and no saloons had been allowed to approach Phillips Academy nearer than Lawrence, which was miles away. Perhaps it was because the boys had now grown to be "men," and were to be treated by the professors as equals and out in the world. "Why was it you weren't pledged with the rest of the Andover men at Andover last summer?" asked Caswell.

"Because I was in Europe; but even if I'd been here—mother doesn't approve of secret societies, you know."

There were several ill-concealed guffaws of laughter.

"Perhaps your mother would prefer you not to join now?"

"Oh, hang it," said Harry, reddening, "I don't believe she will care. When a man gets away from home he's got to do as others do. I'm going to go in for all the societies I can—one each year. What does a man's mother know about these things?"

"Are you going on the 'varsity crew or ball nine?" asked a mild-looking soph pleasantly, as he lit a cigar.

"Or both?" asked a third.

"Oh, I don't know," said Harry—the second cobbler made him feel strangely confidential. "I was short stop on our nine at Andover, so I guess I'd better go in for baseball. Say, how is it, fellows, can a man go in for athletics and take a high stand at the same time?"

"Well, that depends. Do you feel inclined to take the valedictory?"

Everyone was silent now, awaiting his reply.

"I should like to show my family I *could* do it. My sister's an awful tease. I'd like to show *her*. She thinks she knows more Latin than I do—the idea!"

"The idea!" laughed the sophs. Harry laughed too; the cobbler made him see the funny side of everything.

A slim, mild-looking gentleman with a huge watch chain and watery eyes, and a very fat, seedy-looking gentleman, with creases in his cheeks and little piglike eyes, came out from the house.

"Why, here are Professor Brood and Professor Sadley, now!" exclaimed Caswell. The fat gentleman wiped the perspiration from his forehead and took a seat near them. Harry could hardly believe he was really in the presence of the faculty.

"What sort of a freshman class have you got this year, Professor Sadley?" asked Caswell, tipping him the wink.

"Not much—pretty poor pickings!" said Professor Sadley. "They're superlatively and vividly green this year."

"Let me present Mr. Chestleton, of the incoming freshman class," said Caswell. "He's quite ripe——"

"Wal, I hope he aint a-goin' ter be plucked," laughed Brood.

"What! not *Chestleton?*" exclaimed the "professor."

"Yes—the great and (thank Heaven!) *only* Chestleton," answered Caswell.

"Why, how do you do, sir? I've heard of you." He extended his hand gravely.

"At Andover he was famous," said Caswell. "He was their short stop."

"Oh, my friend Dr. Taylor has written me all about him," said the fat gentleman. "Wonderful talent! wonderful mind! Yale College is to be congratulated, sir, on its acquisition." He bowed graciously, and Harry, not knowing what to do, bowed too.

Professor Sadley bowed low again gravely, and there were cigars all around. The two professors, winking at the sophs, drew their seats up to the table.

"Have you—er—had occasion to look into my grammar?" asked the fat gentleman affably—"Sadley's Greek Grammar?"

"Oh, yes!" said Harry. "We studied it at Andover."

"Hope you looked upon it favorably?"

"Yes, sir."

"Hope you enjoyed the irregular verbs?" and he quoted half a dozen Greek words.

"I had to, sir. Unk made us like them before we got through!"

"I made them as easy as I could," he laughed. "And now I know you, Mr. Chestleton, I shall enjoy so much hearing you recite—er—er. Won't you please repeat for me now the second aorist of τύπτω?"

"Professor" Sadley closed his eyes as if about to listen to the

most delightful music. " Go on, go on, please. I often hear my
recitations here, in connection with my old friend, Professor Brood.
Go on!" Harry turned red, while " Professor " Brood looked on
with a grim but kindly grin. He was used to student jokes.

" I'd rather not, sir. Oh, come on, Uncle Dick," he cried suddenly, " let us be going up to college ! "

The latter was busy talking with several students of the glories
of old Mother Yale. He seemed to know a good deal about them.

" Yes, we must be going," said Uncle Dick, rising. " Good-day,
gentlemen—er—the dinner at Gradley's, at seven, did you say,
Mr. Caswell ? "

" Yes, prompt seven, Mr. Lyman," said Caswell, who had invited
them to meet " certain prominent Delta Kaps " at dinner that night.
Mr. Lyman, who was fond of good living, as he was of a good joke,
had promptly accepted the invitation. They took leave of their
friends at Brood's, and as they walked up Chapel Street toward the
colleges, Harry asked :

" Was that fat gentleman Professor Sadley, *really ?* It couldn't
be possible ! "

" No, my boy ; he was an alumnus by the name of Hetherington ; an example of a man who never survived his college course.
He's been hanging around New Haven for the last ten years. He
was a very promising senior when I was a freshman. He was a
Greek wonder. They prophesied great things of Hetherington,
but look at him now."

" I should think he had all run to fat," said Harry, laughing.
The boy was, as yet, a curious mixture of blissful ignorance and
audacity.

" So he has—an example of a man who could have made a great
reputation as a Greek scholar, but who got too fond of good living,
and who'll end up by drinking himself to death, probably. But
even to-day I hardly know whether he's fonder of the bottle than
his favorite Greek."

They walked up the left side of the street and passed many
pretty girls, all of whom had, as Uncle Dick said, " the historic
New Haven stare." They never dropped their eyes as they passed,

and Harry (poor innocent "freshy") actually found himself blushing and being almost stared out of countenance.

When they came to the famous green, with its smooth grassy lawns, its straight paths, and its line of stiff churches, and the mildewed Greek Parthenon of a State House—long since, alas, destroyed—in the distance, Harry thought they had arrived at the college campus. He was for turning in past the old Washington elm, but his uncle held on his course. "There is old Trinity," he said, pointing out the vine-covered old stone church, "and this is the famous Temple Street. See how the elms arch above it, and form a Gothic roof. Isn't it beautiful?"

"Do they have their baseball matches down there on the green?" asked Harry irrelevantly.

"Oh, no; they go out to Hamilton Park, I believe, for baseball; it is about two miles out toward West Rock. There are two famous hills—East and West Rock—you know. Some day you must walk out and climb them. There are plenty of beautiful walks around New Haven, and you must take them this fall and get acquainted with the general lay of the land. You must go out sailing, too, and get an idea of the harbor and where the lighthouse is and the Thimble Islands. How I wish I was just going to college! There is no more delightful four years in a man's life. It's a world by itself, with its joys and sorrows; but you have no such struggle as goes on in the great world. The chief worries of life are bills—and *your* bills will generally be met and paid. And, by the bye, Harry, you must be careful and not spend too much—not over one thousand dollars a month, you know."

Harry laughed with a jolly air. He was a deliciously frank and confiding youngster, and he had a zest and relish for everything he heard or saw. Though three years at Andover, the school life had not sophisticated him.

They arrived at the New Haven House, which seemed to be crowded to the doors with students, most of whom belonged to the incoming class.

"Hello, fellows!" cried Harry, shaking hands with one or two of his Andover friends. They had Latin grammars or text-books

of some kind in their hands. They dreaded the entrance examination of the morrow, but they could not be persuaded, any of them,
to go to their rooms in the hotel and work. They preferred to be
out on the street and in the front of the hotel, seeing what was
going on. A fat, well-dressed sophomore stood on the corner of
Chapel Street, conversing with a number of students. Some of
Harry's friends pointed him out.

"That's the great Billy Holland," they said ; "he's the president
of Delta Kap, and there is Gifford, the stroke of the university crew,
talking with him."

Harry went into the hotel with his uncle and registered. The
proprietor greeted him with a paternal smile.

"Don't you think you'd better go to your room and study ?"
Uncle Dick asked jokingly. "You will have two good hours
before our dinner."

"Oh, no ! I want to see the 'fence' and walk about over the
campus first," replied the lad eagerly. "I want to see everything
I can as soon as possible."

"Very well, come along, then, and bring your friends with you."
Uncle Dick lit a huge cigar, and they followed him out of the hotel
across Chapel Street.

CHAPTER II.

THEY strolled over to the fence where, along Chapel and College streets, were little groups of students, some talking, some singing, and almost everyone smoking pipes or cigarettes.

"This is the famous fence," said Uncle Dick. "It is very convenient to sit on. You can just catch your heels on the second round very nicely. It's as comfortable as an easy-chair. This is where the social life of the college centers. I hope it will never be removed, though the disposition on the part of the faculty is to remove it and disperse these daily gatherings. In my opinion the splendid democracy of old Yale will receive a blow the moment the fence is gone. Here a man shows what's in him, forms his lasting friendships, and shows what he really is to his classmates."

Harry and his friends perched on the fence, and the former felt a secret thrill of joy as his Uncle Lyman went on :

"We are now sitting on the senior fence. Below that gateway there is the junior, as far as the corner. Then around the corner comes the sophomore fence. Freshmen have no fence."

"Why not ?" asked Harry, apparently much grieved. "There's lots of room for them ?"

"Well—er—you see, it would be dangerous. You are too young to roost on it. You'd only fall off and hurt yourselves," laughed his uncle. "Toward the end of the year the sophs move over to the junior fence and the freshmen have a chance at it, but it is always a matter of favor to them and depends, I believe, on whether they beat Harvard at baseball."

They roosted for a while longer, and Uncle Dick met one or two old friends who happened along and whom he shook by the hand warmly. They laughed when he told them about the dinner the Delta Kap men were going to give him that night in order to persuade him as well as his nephew Harry to go "their way."

IN UNCLE DICK'S TIME.

One of Harry's Andover friends, Jack Rives, nudged him and said in a whisper, "That's Professor Ritchie talking to your uncle." "Is it?" said Harry vaguely. "I think he's got such a pleasant face. I wonder if he goes down to Professor Brood's much, and if he will have us in Latin?"

Then they found out how he'd been guyed by Caswell and his sophomore friends and laughed at him.

"Caswell is a very popular man in Umpty-three," said Rives.

"He's rich—drives a dog-cart, and rents a house on York Street; and they say actually keeps servants. He's a regular howling swell ; he and Billy Holland."

Harry told them how he and his uncle were going to "play" it on Caswell.

"Look out, Harry ; he'll haze you to death for it later, old boy !"

"Then I'll haze him back," said Harry stoutly. "'Rah for Umpty-four !"

His uncle soon joined them.

"This first brick building of the old brick row," said he, acting as *cicerone* to the new boys, "is South College. Many famous men once roomed here in their senior year. Chief Justice Waite and Mr. Evarts had that second-story back room. Chauncey Depew had that one in the south entry. Judge Howland had that middle front room. I had that north corner room," and he smiled with pleasant recollection.

They passed along the stone walk before the building. On the trees were nailed advertisements of furniture to sell, and notices of meetings, etc. One startling advertisement of furniture read as follows, at a distance, to their astonishment :

PREXY STOUT

WILL WEAR

A WOODEN LEG

To Chapel To-morrow Morning !

But on a nearer approach it read : " *Prexy Stout* has won the respect and admiration of all who know him. We predict that he *will wear* as well through his term of service, and that his retirement will be *a* cause of regret. But it will cause no such remorse as a failure to attend the great sale of *wooden* and iron furniture now in progress. If you would get what you want, O Freshman, just *leg* it to 202 Durfee, even if it makes you late *to chapel to-morrow morning !*"

"Well," laughed Harry, "I should think the faculty would sit on that."

"Well, they sit on almost everything," sighed Uncle Dick, "and I dare say the day will come when they will sit on the fence!"

"This old building is South Middle," said Uncle Dick, pointing with his cane. "Here are the sophomores' dens. Here they conceive their villainies. Listen, and you will soon understand."

"Oh, *fresh!* Oh, Fr-e-e-e-sh!" came out of the open windows of a third-story front. A crowd of sophs were standing about the door of one of the entries and echoed the cry, "Oh, my, poor *freshy!*"

South Middle seemed very dilapidated and old. The brick front was weather worn, and the entire building seemed to be in need of repairs. The boys paid no attention to the sophs and passed on, feeling rather proud of being dubbed "freshy" by men in college. It made them feel as if they belonged there, too.

"I wish I was back in college myself," said Uncle Dick with a sigh. "What fun I've had in that old building! What midnight suppers! What peanut 'bums'! What narrow escapes! Ah, me—*Postume, Postume! Eheu Postume, labuntur anni!*"

"He was 'wooden-spoon' man of his class and awfully popular," said Harry, in an awed whisper, and there was a respectful silence as the old 'grad' mused over the long-forgotten memories of other days for some moments. "Here is the chapel," he said, "with these tall, gloomy pillars in front of it. It is about as unpleasant a house of worship as Puritan ingenuity could make it. The backs of the seats are bent forward and the seats themselves very narrow, so that you can't be comfortable if you try, and if you do try you fall off. Then they fire at you two-hour sermons, and they compel you to listen to them, for you've got to be present or they will fine you eight marks. In my day they had chapel every morning at 7.30; on Sunday they had church at 10 and 2. I frankly admit that I had too much of a dose then, and it's been hard to get me inside a church since. But perhaps you boys will like it. I used to like to hear the anthems at Easter. The best singing in the world. Perhaps I am prejudiced—I used to sing bass until I found I had a tenor voice."

" Uncle Dick, why did they give up the wooden spoon ?" asked Harry.

" A great mistake," he replied. " But I suppose it got to splitting up classes too much, on account of the politics involved. You will find Yale the best school for politics in the world. The wooden spoon was given to the most popular man in the class. Then there were eleven spoon *cochleauruati*, who stood next in popularity. Oh, I don't know ; we used to have great fun out of it, but it has died out at last. The spoon exhibition was always the great event of the year. Now they have theatricals all the time, I'm told— especially the Thanksgiving jubilee. I remember Professor Blinks, now one of the most severe, glum, and solemn-looking spectacled members of the faculty—I remember Dave Blinks acted the part of a billy goat in my day, and did a double clog on his hind legs, to the edification of an audience which filled Music Hall from floor to ceiling. Great days those ! But they are all past and gone. There is not so much fun in college life now as then. Do you see the dark-brown stone building over there at the end of Durfee Hall ?"

" Yes."

"That is Alumni Hall. There are held all the examinations. It is a terrible building for some. That is where you are going to-morrow, Harry. Do you notice how easy it looks to go in and how hard to come out ?" And Uncle Dick went on to tell them some amusing reminiscences.

They walked over to Alumni Hall and then back past Farnam College, just then completed. " I suppose in time they will have a great quadrangle with dormitories around the edge of the campus, and flower gardens and fountains in the center. But for me, give me the ' old brick row.' The rooms are comfortable and are not too fine or fancy. Why, they tell me they have lace curtains and upholstery and pianos, and all that sort of thing in these new buildings. I don't believe in it ; it will ruin Yale College—the boys will get to be Sybarites !"

They walked on a little way " 'neath the elms of dear old Yale," and Uncle Dick continued :

"In my room I had a cheap carpet, a table, a kerosene lamp, three or four wooden chairs, a pair of dumb-bells, an old lounge that came over in the *Mayflower*, and perhaps a set of shelves for books, and an old Franklin stove. We used to black our own boots and make our own beds, some of us. Now, every entry has its ' sweep,' who acts in place of a valet. How many changes are going on here! These new buildings alter the campus very much. I can't say I altogether like it ; it doesn't seem natural to me, and every building that goes up necessitates cutting down an elm."

They returned to Chapel Street and sat on the fence. Jack Rives was a sturdy, wiry young fellow, with a frank, honest face. He and Harry were to room with each other, and Jack told his friend he had found good quarters over on York Street, in a remarkably quiet boarding house, where only *ten* other freshmen had taken rooms, and they would take their meals in an eating club hard by.

" Why, I thought we would live in one of the big dormitories," said Harry disappointedly.

" Freshmen must room wherever they can," said Uncle Dick. " Next year you can get a room in college, and I advise your going into South Middle, which is generally given over to sophomores because it is too noisy for upper-class men."

After another stroll through the campus and seeing the "gym," in which half a dozen men were at work running and jumping, Harry and his uncle went back to the New Haven House and prepared for their dinner.

" Oh," said Harry delightedly, " I am going to enjoy college life—I know I am. It's all so jolly ! Singing, fun,—faculty nowhere in sight,—and all New Haven for a playground ! Oh, it's grand ! though I do think that freshmen ought to have their building, just as the other classes."

" Well," laughed his uncle, " that is easily remedied. Just die and leave the college a dormitory."

CHAPTER III.

ROOD'S, Mrs. Moriarty's, Charlie Gradley's, and Gus Lager's are names familiar enough to Yale graduates of ten years' standing. *Horresco referens* —but our story shall be nothing if not true to the life of those college days. Let others tell of the immaculate youth who went straight from his mother's apron strings to college and passed through its jolly four years without having been acquainted with that genial old piece of respectability, Mrs. Moriarty! To know the good old soul was an education of itself.

The Gradleys catered to the student appetite for late suppers, game dinners, and swell college society feasts. Located on a side street in the center of the town, "Gradley's" was then the bohemian Delmonico's of New Haven. It was a hotel, restaurant, and bar room, and down below, out of sight, was supposed to be a dog and cock pit and a twenty-four-foot prize ring. Policemen and members of the faculty rarely ventured within Gradley's precincts, and many a student, suspended and rusticated for cause, has passed a week in hiding there, under the very eyes of the college and the noses of the faculty. Here, too, at many a champagne supper college politics waxed rife and logs were rolled and plans laid for future conquests.

It was here (if anywhere in those days) that the upper-class man allowed himself to unbend to men of a lower class, and to treat them as if they were actually to be permitted to breathe the same air of heaven with him! In fine, the old hotel was a place where bohemianism with a spice of the improper prevailed—so delightful to the student mind! Here were seen the "sports" of the college with their bulldogs; the flash set, the "hard" lot. If you passed along the narrow little street at a late hour some jolly college song could have been surely heard coming out of an open upper window, and you knew some students were dining and wining there, regardless of chapel and early recitation the next morning.

When Harry and his uncle arrived at Gradley's it was just dusk and the barkeeper was lighting the gas. Harry amused himself by looking at the sporting pictures hung about
the walls. There were
ladies of the ballet standing on one toe, and hunt-
ers in red coats leaping
five-barred fences. There
were pictures of emi-
nent trotters and brightly
painted cuts of cele-
brated fighting cocks.
His uncle approached a
large, heavy looking man,
whose face beamed with
a fat, benevolent smile,
and shook him by the
hand.

"Why, Mr. Lyman, I
remember you very well,"
said Gradley, for it was he.
"You used to own a first-
class dog."

"Don't let on you
know me. The sopho-

GRADLEY'S PICTURE GALLERY.

mores are giving us a dinner to pledge us to Delta Kap!"

"No!" laughed Gradley. "Well, that's a good joke on them!"

"Well, keep it mum!" laughed Uncle Dick. "This is my

nephew—Harry Chestleton—just entering college." They shook hands, and Gradley beamed pleasantly.

"I've got a good dog for him, as gentle as I ever see. Cost one hundred dollars. Want a dog? Sell him for seventy-five dollars."

"What kind—a Newfoundland dog?" asked Harry. Mr. Gradley looked at him contemptuously for a moment, while Dick laughed.

"He means a bulldog—a fighter," said he.

"Well, what should I want of such a beast?" asked Harry.

At which Mr. Gradley looked down on him more contemptuously than ever. "Why every gent as considers himself a gent has a dog," said he.

Harry wondered if this were true.

Presently Caswell, Billy Holland, Gifford, and three or four other sophomores entered.

"Where are those confounded freshmen?" asked Holland, who, though somewhat fat, was as handsome as an Apollo, and dressed in very swell evening clothes. He didn't observe Harry and his uncle. When he did he said rudely:

"So you're making our committee have a devil of a time pledging you, are you?" and he laughed. "Well, from what I can see, you're hardly worth a dinner, either of you. No, sir—and you look old enough to be Mr. Methusaleh. Are you this young chap's father?"

"Oh, let up, Billy, be decent to the fresh gentlemen!" said one of his friends, and he walked away, talking to Charlie Gradley.

"He's been working very hard this week in the campaign, and he's had to drink hard to keep up," said another to Harry confidentially. "The Sigma Eps men have made it very hard for us. They've kept us on the drive, and the work's all come on Caswell and Billy Holland."

They went upstairs shortly after, and entered a rather shabby room, hung with a tawdry chintz. The table was laid for twelve, and at each plate were several wine glasses.

"Many a dinner have I eaten here." whispered Uncle Dick. "It's the same furniture—the same old chintz."

Caswell introduced his friends. They were all nothing loath to spend the D. K. campaign funds in giving a dinner in this way and having a good time, and they were as polite and affable to Harry and his uncle as possible. To be sure they talked a good deal of the prowess and victories of Umpty-three, but they told Harry a good deal of what he wanted to know about the crew and the ball nine and about the junior and senior societies.

"The junior societies, you know," said Caswell, "are B. K. E. and Phi U., and the senior are Spade and Grave and Book and Lock; now if you join Delta Kap you are sure of Spade and Grave, d'ye see? And let me tell you once for all—you'll find it out soon enough yourselves—that your one aim in college will be to get into a senior society. That's what we're all here for, and as there are but thirty vacancies and a hundred and forty odd in your class, why you and your friend want to hustle and make a right start *now* in the freshman year, if you want to reach them, d'ye see? Now, if you get into Sigmareps Lord knows what will become of you; you'll sort of waste away and get forgotten; dry rot will set in, and you won't amount to anything; and you'd better commit suicide at once rather than join Gamma Nu."

"But mother doesn't approve of secret societies," said Harry, laughing inwardly.

"Well, your mother's all right, of course," said Caswell airily; "but she doesn't know the advantages of Delta Kappa—she isn't a member, and how can she know?"

"That's so," said Harry, yielding a little.

"Now, Mr. Chestleton, I'll fix it all right with your mother. Professor Jones was in Delta Kap. I'll get him to write her; I know *he* approves of it. He said once that Delta Kap had been the making of him. He got such a start there that he's gone on all right ever since."

"Has he?" said Harry, looking round the table. There were nine sophomores, with a seat vacant for Holland, who was busy writing campaign letters in the next room. Two or three had on their dress suits and talked about going out later to a reception and dance on Hillhouse Avenue. It all seemed very fine indeed to him. The champagne was iced to a nicety. The oysters were delicious,—his first venture on the dainty New Haven bivalves,—and what birds ! How jolly college life was indeed, and what an auspicious beginning ! to know all these great men already !

"I believe I'll take all my meals here," he said to Dobson, a huge, manly looking sophomore who sat next to him. Dobson rowed on the 'varsity crew.

"Oh, no," said Dobson, "the food's too rich. You'll want to go in training, probably. Gradley's is all very well once in a while, but it's not to be thought of for common. Holland and Caswell dine here too often. You don't want to get in with the fast crowd ?"

"No," said Harry, "I'm going in for athletics."

"That's right."

"I want to play on the freshman nine, and have a try for the 'varsity."

"Well, they are after good men, whatever class they happen to belong to. A new era is dawning for Yale. For four years Harvard has had it all her own way. But things are going to change, and there's a man in our class going to change them."

"Who is that ?"

"Well, it's Bob Clark. He's that modest looking man at the end of the table on the other side."

"*He* doesn't look as if he was going to do much," said Harry dubiously.

"Well, just wait and see. He is really very strong, the best boxer and wrestler in the college, and he takes to rowing as a duck does to water. He is an ideal boating man, and he strips at a good weight—158. We're making up a purse now to send him to England to learn the English stroke."

"I'd like to have a go at him," said Harry, who felt his champagne a little. "I used to wrestle at Andover. Why, yes ; Bob Clark was there a year, I believe. I remember him now. But I never knew him to speak to."

"Well, you wait and see. I believe that Clark is going to revolutionize rowing in this country before he gets through—he's so full of ideas about it."

Then Caswell started up the song "Jolly D. K.," and followed it up with one or two other college songs. Holland came in sleepily, and seemed to have got rid of some of his bad humor. He took his seat at the head of the table and ordered a "thick porterhouse, and broil it underdone, mind." Then he proceeded to make a little speech.

"We're here on serious business," he said with a yawn. "Delta Kappa is the largest college secret society in the United States—I mean has the largest active membership in one chapter. Why, there are over seventy members in our class, sixty in Umpty-two, and about sixty in Umpty-one. That makes—how many does that make?" he asked, turning to Bob Clark.

"It makes about 270 altogether in college at one time."

"Two hundred and seventy—all in Delta Kap. What point was I going to make, Bob? My head is so full of the champagne —I mean campaign—I don't know what I am saying."

There was a laugh.

"Why," said Clark, "if there are so many in Delta Kap, it shows that it's the most popular society in college, doesn't it?"

"Oh, yes," said Holland. "That's it. I knew I had some sort of an idea." And everyone laughed and talked of the coming college year.

They came to coffee and cigars. Uncle Dick told a number of good stories, and there was more singing. Holland got his beef-steak and began eating it. "Now it's time we heard from the young Lord Chesterfield, who is here with his royal dad," he said. "Mr. Chestnut, please rise and address the chair."

There was loud applause and Harry rose. He had never made a speech before. The room swam around him. "Ge-gentlemen of Delta Kap," he said, "I—I like your society first-rate. I think I'll pledge—and so here's my hand for Delta Kap."

"Rah! rah! rah!" shouted Caswell, waving his napkin around his head. Harry couldn't think of anything more to say, so he sat down covered with blushes and confusion.

Uncle Dick got on his feet. He began to talk very quietly and reverently of Yale in the past and of its future glories. As he did so he unbuttoned his coat as if by accident, and disclosed on his waistcoat a senior society badge. The effect was magical.

Holland, Caswell, Clark, and all the sophs turned a greenish, sickly hue and said nothing.

"Governor Yale," he orated, "when he gave his name and library to that little school at Saybrook was doing more to make his name famous than Shakspere in writing 'Hamlet,' or Napoleon in winning Austerlitz. Oh, gentlemen, here's to good old Yale! May she live forever! From her first class—a little Indian boy of one—she chooses now from every school in this vast country. Sir—I——"

"This isn't the alumni dinner," remarked Caswell _sotto voce_. He was disgusted at the turn things had taken.

"Here's to the class of 1795!" said Holland, rising. "We have with us to-night, unexpectedly, an old graduate—in fact, the oldest living graduate. But I move we initiate him into Delta Kap just the same, since he has expressed a desire to pledge——"

"I'm going to Gamma Nu," laughed Lyman.

"Well, you have a good one on _us!_" laughed Dobson. "It is the best grind I ever saw! So you're an old hand at this business, I suspect—here's to you, sir!"

"Here's to Umpty-three!" shouted Harry, enjoying the joke at the sophs' expense.

"Oh, you young rascal!" said Caswell, with a warning finger. "We will have to get even with _you_ some way!"

Then Uncle Dick said: "I've had my fun, fellows, and now I'm going to insist on paying for it. My nephew is just coming on, and I am not going to let him be a mark for your hazing proclivities, Mr. Caswell. So, if you please, I'll pay for this dinner, and you will consider it as given to Umpty-three by a worshipful freshman."

"Oh, no; it's too good a joke on us," laughed Holland. "We'll pay the shot ourselves. Delta Kappa doesn't get fooled often, but once in a while even Homer nods, eh?"

But Lyman would not have it. He paid the bill, and all said he was a mighty good fellow. Then they went up to college, locking arms, and walked up Chapel Street, singing as they marched to the fence. Some juniors at the fence were singing "Mary Aileen" and "Nelly was a Lady." It was beautiful. The moon poured its light down through the magnificent elms and bathed the New Haven House in a flood of light. At the windows could be seen, here and there, the face of some fair maid, to whose listening ears, probably, the juniors were directing their warbling. Harry wondered if any of them were as lovely as the Charmington girl he saw in the train, the one with the dark gray eyes. To him it was all romantic, fascinating, delightful. The sophomores who were at the dinner in dress suits jumped into a hack and rode off to the dance on Hillhouse Avenue. Harry and his uncle sat on the fence and listened to the singing. The great trees above them made a vast dome, through which the moonlight percolated as with a shower of silvery light. They were singing "Ah me, magnovem te."

Then out from the shadows of the elms above the junior fence came the pretty song :

"Stars in the summer night
Far in yon azure deeps,
Hide, hide your golden light,
She sleeps, my lady sleeps !"

"This is old Yale at its best," said Uncle Dick. "As someone has said, it would be the most delightful place in the world for a fellow to live were it not for its religious and literary exercises. That is its more serious side—what you are really here for, I suppose. But I believe, on the whole, the social life is the most valuable. The classics and mathematics fade out of your life, but the friends you make remain forever."

"I only hope," said Harry solemnly, "that I'll live through the whole four years, and that I'll never be dropped and compelled to go to Harvard !"

"Well, just be—yourself, my boy, and no such calamity will befall you."

They sat on the fence a while longer, listening to the music, then went over to the hotel, where Uncle Dick mysteriously disappeared. It was rumored that he stole over to his Senior Society hall. Harry chatted a few moments with some Andover men and went upstairs to bed. He had begun his career at Yale.

CHAPTER IV

THE next morning Harry rose with the first ray of the sun that penetrated through the blinds of his chamber, high up in the top floor of the crowded New Haven House. It was a warm morning, and before he dressed he thought he'd just look over a few of the propositions in the first book of Euclid. Mathematics were not his forte. He had no fears of his Cæsar, his Xenophon, or his Vergil or Iliad. They came easily to the boy, and Dr. Taylor's faithful and heroic drill in the grammar during his senior year at Andover had made second aorists, ablative absolutes, and pluperfect subjunctives and the absurd *reasons* for using them a matter of indifference.

Euclid, algebra, and arithmetic, however, were different. In the classic shades of Phillips Academy they were left to take a second place. They were slurred over and considered a bore by Harry and most of his friends. Fractions were all vulgar to *him!* They tormented him. It was before the days of electives, and it was not considered that the brain of one boy differed much from another. He could choose at Yale, as at Andover, the academic or the scientific course, but once he had made this election he must perforce be prepared to accept the cut and dried curriculum allotted to him.

The object of education was "mental discipline," not culture. This was the keynote of the system of those days at Yale and Andover, and is, we fear, much the keynote of the system at the present time. "Drill" was the word, and mental gymnastics the object of recitations.

Harry sat on the edge of his bed, poring over his *pons asinorum* and trying to discover anew the real reason that the angles of a right-angle triangle equaled two right angles. The underlying point in his mind seemed to be—well, and what if they did? Of what benefit was it to the world in general? To render the study more useful to him he thoughtfully drew the figure of a triangle on the white wall of his room with a lead pencil, and stood off a few paces with his book behind his back, demonstrating the problem.

He found that it helped him a good deal to have the diagrams on the wall in this way. In the course of half an hour he had four more displayed upon the wall. "It's as good as a blackboard," he said to himself.

Just then came a tap at his door. "Come in," said Harry, wrapping himself like an old Roman in his toga-like sheet. A tall, lank youth entered the room, looking pale and miserable. He held a Homer in one hand and a translation or "pony" in the other. Around his head was a wet towel. He had the awkward beanpole look of a boy who had shot up and got his growth too rapidly. His legs were too long, his ears too large, his hands seemed to reach down too far; he had a sickly grin on his face as he crept into the room and glanced at Harry.

"Been up all night," he said, "and I feel like a faded flower. I say—it's no fun reading Homer while every cock in New Haven is crowing in the morn! It's awful dismal work. Guess if the faculty knew how I've crammed to get in they'd say 'we haven't the heart to condition you!' What are you doing? Say, they'll charge you for spoiling those walls! A B equals C D. Let the angle B C D represent—oh, it's all a blank to me now. This Homer has driven Euclid out of my head, and when I've got Euclid in Xenophon and Homer walk out. Oh, Lord! I wonder who invented examinations?" and he yawned dismally.

"Say, Jim, for Heaven's sake, go to bed and get a few hours' sleep! My uncle Dick says that it doesn't pay to get frightened beforehand. He told me that a good sleep was the best preparation. It keeps your head clear—see?"

" Yes, but you know where I stood at Andover—I led the foot.
I tell you it's going to be hard work for *me* to get into Yale.   Oh,

DEMONSTRATING THE PROBLEM.

what will father say?"   He sat on the bed and buried his face in
his hands.

"Jim Danforth, brace up, old man!   You're all broke up.   Go
to bed now, and then go and get your head shampooed before
breakfast."

"I tried it once, you know, last July, and they said that I could have one more trial this September. I only failed in—in everything but arithmetic, and so I've been cramming all summer."

"Well, you're sure to get in now. They always let in Andover men. Don't get discouraged. If you sit near me I'll try and help you."

"Father graduated in 1844, and he was salutatorian. You can see he is prejudiced in favor of the faculty and against me. He thinks I am a fool."

"You're not a fool, Jim. You were the best second base that ever was at Andover. Do you remember that high fly you caught on a backward run in the Exeter match? Your long reach was just the thing. It saved the game. A fool! By Jove! You may not have the knack for study, but you're no fool. You took second prize in the Philomathean prize debate, and you know you were class marshal. The faculty ought to know that, Jim." Danforth looked a little more cheerful.

"I haven't any head for study," he said. "But, Harry, you do the best you can for me in the examination, and shy the answers over to me on a bit of paper. I only scraped through Andover because you sat next to me and whispered up when I got up to recite. Old Unk never suspected."

"Well, I'm going to pull you through this time, too, old man! Now, you go and get a sleep, and then get a good shampoo before breakfast and you'll be all right."

Jim Danforth silently shook him by the hand and left the room, whistling a lively air.

"Poor Jim," laughed Harry, putting another figure on the wall. "It's absurd how scared he is. If the faculty only knew what's what they'd let him in free and give him a medal to boot. Unless I'm very much off he'll go straight on the 'varsity nine—he's a dandy second base, a Jim dandy. Reach? Phew! how he can reach for a ball!"

Then he fell to thinking over some old exciting ball matches at Andover in the past. A boy's life passes rapidly, and the days of the Andover three years already seemed so long, so long ago.

But he soon brought himself up with a round turn. "Let A B C equal a right-angle triangle, then let K L M equal——"

Then came another knock. His uncle Dick entered, looking very seedy and cross. He had a shawl wrapped about him.

Harry burst out into uncontrollable laughter as he glanced at him. Uncle Dick scowled.

"What are you up to, you rascal? Diagrams on the walls? They'll raise Cain over that!"

"I'll rub 'em out," said Harry. "But tell me, where did you disappear to last night, Uncle Dick?"

Harry stood grinning knowingly.

"Never you mind, you scapegrace!" he said grimly.

Harry laughed again.

"Go down and tell them to send me up two bottles of soda water and a lemon, that's a good boy. I feel like a 'biled owl,' as Artemus Ward says. I can't make the servants hear. They pay no attention to the bell. Get dressed, Harry, and go down. You'll save my life!"

And Uncle Dick returned to his room.

Harry good-naturedly did as he was told. He dressed and went downstairs. Selecting a Vergil and a small Latin lexicon for his *vade mecum*, he sent the soda water up to his uncle, whom he suspected of being out all night at his senior secret society "spread," and strolled out in the fresh dewy morning over to the campus.

No one was on the fence and so he sat down, his Vergil on one knee and his lexicon on the other. He saw students on their way to breakfast looking at him askance, and heard some of them make unsavory remarks about him.

"Why, it's only a sub-fresh anyway," said one young man; "let him sit there."

A little after a number of sophomores came along.

"Git—freshy!" they cried.

"Git—where?"

"Get off the fence! It's no place for you. Only gentlemen are allowed to sit here. Git!"

At first Harry refused to budge, but at last sullenly obeyed.

He strolled into the campus and walked over to the Art building meditatively, and reading his Vergil and conning the lines.

He was a handsome, well set up lad. As he made his way along, book in hand, two or three pretty shop girls came down Chapel Street on their way to their store. All smiled and nodded in the most familiar manner.

Harry bowed politely and took off his hat. One of the girls— the prettiest of the three—looked back at him and smiled again.

THEN CAME ANOTHER KNOCK.

He took off his hat again to her. One could see the innocence and the gentleness of his act, as compared with the naughtiness and forwardness of the pretty shop girls.

When he went back to the hotel his uncle was awaiting him to go in to breakfast. After the noisy meal was over he said :

"Are you frightened ?"

"Oh, no."

"Well, I'll walk over with you. I'll speak to Professor Sinister—one of the dearest, nicest men—after graduation—I ever knew."

"Oh, I'm sure of passing in everything. Don't bootlick any-one for me, Uncle Dick. There was really no need to put you to the trouble of coming on with me. It was mother's being worried."

"Well, you can't start too well with the faculty," said his uncle. "You want to try and get them prejudiced in your favor. They are generally prejudiced the other way. They regard a boy as bad until he proves he's good. Now that's just where I come in. I'll steer Professor Sinister and Professor Black the right way. I'll make them think you're a sort of a hardworking dig, and all that sort of thing. I'll try and persuade them that you are a natural student—but a little timid in recitation—afraid to let out all you know of a subject."

Harry laughed. "They'll soon find out I've got the check of a rhinoceros—then they'll flunk me right and left!" They fell in with a number of Andover men, and walked over to Alumni Hall. Before this awful, gloomy building, with its twin forbidding towers surmounted by wooden moldings to look like stone, were gathered that morning about sixty trembling sub-freshmen. A majority of the incoming class had entered in July. Some of the boys were accompanied by tutors who were cramming last instructions into their heads, but most of them were alone.

Standing over by Durfee was a fellow working away at his Xenophon and "pony," with pale face and anxious eagerness. It was poor Danforth. He had several books under his arm, and now and then he would take a peep into one and the other in turn to refresh his memory. On the ground before him was an open Cæsar; he kept the book open with his foot, and on either side were text-books and grammars. He looked brighter and fresher than he had done at six o'clock that morning when he went into Harry's room, for he had gotten some sleep and had a shampoo, but he was dreadfully worried, poor fellow, and he was much too engrossed with his book to notice the laughter he excited.

Talk of the delights of Yale to Danforth! He was undergoing then—as he underwent all through his college course at examination periods—the pangs of Hades.

A little way over by North College was a curious couple walking to and fro. They excited little attention because they were far out of the throng of busy, talkative young "subs" who were eying one another with great interest as members of the coming class of "Umpty-four."

One of them seemed to be a tall spectacled New England old maid, the other, quite as tall, a slender New England over-studious youth. He was pale, but his eyes were bright; he had the acute air of an intellectual "smart boy." He carried no books, no implements. He had a very sweet, yet amused, condescending smile. He chatted and laughed with his maiden friend, and every now and then he glanced over at the crowd before Alumni Hall, as if impatient to have the fun begin. If one could have overheard them—

they were gossiping upon the state of Rome under Marcus Aurelius! Presently they came nearer the Hall, and stood idly watching the young fellows, who were now rapidly increasing in number.

"David, be meek; don't be too impatient," said the spinster. She had taken his arm.

"I will be meek, but I'd like to show these classical Pharisees that a man doesn't need to come down from Andover, or Exeter, or East Hampton, or St. Paul's, to know Greek and Latin, or even mathematics——"

"But you can show them later. First impressions count, you know."

"I know it, Aunt Sarah, I will be meek. What a lot of children!" He glanced about. "I mean intellectual children. I suppose every man-child here could physically thrash me! Why, I believe there are some here who may fail."

"Oh, impossible—Xenophon—Cæsar? Nonsense. Infantile minds perhaps, and fond of foolish sport and play—but they can't help *passing!*"

"Aunt Sarah" speedily became an attraction. She wore a curious up-country dress, but her glance was keen as lightning. "Here's a milksop's brought his mother to college with him!" laughed a friend of Harry's, in an aside.

At a distance was another group in which this was literally the case. A young, soft-looking boy was kissing his mother and sister good-by. His father stood by and whispered encouragement. His mother was in tears. His sister clung tightly to him. It would appear that they believed he was about to undergo some sort of horrid torture. The chapel bell tolled. Every stroke seemed to fall with crushing weight upon the boy, as indeed it did also upon poor Danforth opposite. Several professors and one or two tutors appeared, and with a curious celerity slipped through the crowd and threw open the great doors of Yale to Umpty-four with the bland smile Danforth thought he had often seen on the face of a dentist. "Gentlemen," said they, "it is necessary first to pay to the treasurer a fee of ten dollars."

CHAPTER V.

BUT the results of the examination, which lasted two days, were not as painful to Danforth as he had imagined. He got a table next to Harry's, and the latter snapped over to him small bits of paper containing the answers to some of the more difficult problems in algebra and geometry. He had the luck to hit just the passages in Xenophon and Vergil he knew. As for Harry—it was child's play to him. He loafed through the morning and devoted himself chiefly to steering Danforth through his difficulties. It was hard work, and once he thought Professor Sinister's eagle and detective eye was fixed upon him, but it wasn't fixed to his detriment. Once he gave up all hope; he was sure he was caught. Professor Black got slowly down from his desk and marched with terrible tread straight across the room, down the aisle to his table. His heart stood still. The glum portraits of the former presidents of Yale on the walls swam before him. When he reached him Professor Black said with a keen incisiveness:

"Your uncle was a classmate of mine."

Oh, what a relief!

"Yes, sir?"

"He says you are one of the best boys that ever came to Yale. I'm afraid you are given to mischief."

"Oh, no, sir."

"Well, I wouldn't fire paper balls at my fellow students," and he passed on with a certain deadly smile, while Harry shivered.

Professor Sinister was kind and genial, with a gently amused smile. Harry felt that he would be a good friend always. Professor Shepard was the kindest of all and had the most sincere smile. How different they seemed from the scowling severity of Dr. Taylor! The several tutors seemed so pleasant and jolly. Their smiles were even affectionate! He was a little afraid of the keenness of Professor Black's sharp little black eyes, but Professor Maynard (the distinguished author of Maynard's Arithmetics) was, though stiff and prim, and carrying his head above his high choker collar, the best smiler of them all. He reminded Harry of a print of an old beau in an old magazine. The boy wondered if the great man was solving arithmetical problems in that courtly old head of his. "Fractions are plain figures to him," he thought. "I'd like to hear him talk about his rule of three." There was a vague idea in his mind that he was the author of it.

After the examinations were over the second day, Jack Rives, who had passed in July, met him at the door with his uncle and they walked over to their rooms on York Street. Harry had been too busy to go over and see them.

"Why, the examination was nothing at all," said Harry lightly, "and I had lots of time and helped Danforth through the hard places all right. You ought to have seen Dan this morning, Jack ; frightened to death! Now he's in, he's sure of the 'varsity, I guess."

"Oh, lord, yes," said Jack Rives. "He could feel around in the air after a fly ball with his eyes shut and pull it down. I've seen him talking to a man an' hear a ball coming an' reach out backward an' not look at it, and haul it in. In your day did they have baseball, Uncle Dick ?"

All Harry's friends got to calling him "Uncle Dick" unawares.

"No, we had cricket—a little."

"A beastly stupid game, isn't it ? Takes all day and part of next week. You never know for a week of Sundays how the game came out."

"We used to take long walks."

"Long walks ! yes—with girls, I suppose ? "

"Oh, no ; we walked, three or four of us together, climbed East Rock, or sometimes got a fast nag and drove over to Bridge-port to a dog fight. I was the best billiard player in my class."

" All that sort of thing has gone out now," said Harry. " Fast trotters and billiards and all that."

"Oh, no ; billiards are as popular now as in my day, but you don't see men betting so much on billiards now. I've seen one thousand dollars depend on a stroke. There were two great players in my day, myself and—and a man by the name of Allick, from Cincinnati, since dead. He and I fought many a match in those old days. He paid his way through college by billiards ; it was as good as a scholarship."

"Say, is Uncle Dick a 'sport' now ? " asked Jack Rives, in a whisper, of Harry. " Is he an old gambler ? "

" Heavens, no ! He's a sober, rich, steady lawyer in New York. He never has any fun except when he comes back to New Haven. But I guess he must have had all his good times here ; he likes to talk about it so much."

They came to a wide, two-story frame house on York Street, where Rives had got rooms. The landlady was a sad-eyed, middle-aged woman, with her gray hair done up in fronts. She looked as though she had been through considerable trouble in her day for and on account of freshmen. Her little eyes were steely gray and snappish and suspicious. She suspected any and every male being under twenty and over fifteen of an inordinate love of tricks and all manner and kind of wickedness. She opened the door on a crack at first, as if it were a usual precautionary measure ; then peeped out and saw who it was, and let them in.

"Oh, it's Mr. Rives. Oh, I thought mebbe it was some o' them softmores, not knowin' yer faces all. I never allow none of them in my house. My friend Professor Shepard told me not to. My friend Professor Shepard says that I keep the quietist and best house in New Haven in consequence."

" All right, Mrs. Gimly," said Rives, leading the way in, and they passed upstairs.

" I've been here two days fixing up," said Jack, rather proud of what he had done, as he glanced round the large, low-ceilinged room. He had arranged four new boxing gloves, in the way of plaques, over the mantel. On either side were two sporting pictures of Messrs. Dooney Harris and Patsey Sheppard, the then ornaments of the prize ring. Then see this," he said, pointing to a dog kennel in one corner of the room, out of which was emitted a low, angry growl. "Here, Stamp! come out, you rascal! I got him in New York of a friend, and we'll have to pay Mrs. Gimly three dollars a week extra for being allowed to keep him. Oh, he's a dandy! I'm going to name him Stamp because I have to lick him so much; but he's a dandy!"

"Mr. Gradley wanted to sell me a dog last night," said Harry thoughtfully.

"Well, our dog can lay out any New Haven dog of Gradley's or anyone else's. He's a terror. He never lets go. He's got my best trousers in his kennel now, and I can't get 'em away from him."

Uncle Dick burst out laughing, and the dog, hearing a new voice and feeling provoked at it, made a rush out of the kennel, still holding the trousers in his strong, ugly mouth.

He had the beautiful ugliness, the ugly mug of a full-blooded bull. Harry fell on his knees before him and petted him. Strange to say Stamp dropped the trousers and licked his face, wagging his stumpy tail affectionately.

"You've got a good room here," said Uncle Dick, "and you're right in the center of freshman life. Most of the rushes are on York or High Streets, behind the colleges. When you're in college *be* in college—be in the thick of it. But from this dog—and all—to protect you merely, Mr. Rives—do you know I'm afraid that—I'm afraid you have come to college with a wrong purpose."

Uncle Dick spoke very earnestly, and looked solemn.

"Why?"

"You intend to study too hard—to shut yourself up here and pore over your books too much."

"Oh, no, sir," said Rives innocently.

"Yes, you do; and that bar on the door—you mean to sport the oak, I see."

"Oh, that's in case we get chased in by the sophs, that's all," said Rives. "It's something the fellow that had the room before me put on the door. First-rate idea, isn't it? With that on you can't break in."

And Jack shut the door and pulled the heavy oaken timber into place.

There came a thump, and he opened it again. In rushed five or six friends—Thornton, Coles, Ritch, Nevers, and others, all Andover men, who roomed in the house.

"How did you get through, Harry?"

"First-rate. Easy as mud. Look out, fellows! Stamp may object." He introduced his friends to his uncle — "an old grad." Harry sat on the floor; the dog and he had suddenly developed the most interesting friendship.

"Boys," said Uncle Dick, "won't you all smoke with me?"

He offered around a handful of fine cigars; all but one

JACK RIVES' PET.

came back to him. He seemed rather surprised, but he said nothing.

"Professor Sinister told me you would have a very large class. Perhaps 150; you ought to have it pretty much your own way with Umpty-three. They'll snatch your caps. Well, snatch theirs, then! I'm a thoroughgoing Yale boy myself. Fight fair, but fight like the devil, is what I say. There is no part of a man's life so pleasant as the four years at college, and I'm not prepared to say that the first year isn't the best."

Thornton was a stocky big fellow, with muscles of iron. Uncle Dick looked him over admiringly.

"You ought to go in for the crew," he said. "We've been beaten every year but one since '66. Harvard has got it all her own way. Oh, it's terrible for an old graduate to pick up a paper and read about the Harvard crew winning by six boat-lengths every summer! It makes me feel like going into college again and taking hold. By Jove! sooner than see Harvard win the way she's been doing, you, Thornton, and you, strong, young fellows, all of you, ought to go in and pull your hearts out."

Uncle Dick had risen in his excitement and there was an impressive silence.

" By all that's true, it rests with you to do it! You can if you will. Don't let this disgrace go on year after year. Put some of the old Yale spirit and Yale sand into your boating and baseball. Confound it, Harry, you are all new to it and don't feel the disgrace! I do. I get chaffed by Harvard men every day in New York. I—I—I can't stand it. I care so much for Yale it's—it's just like my family to me. I'd give every cent in the world— when I die every cent is going to Yale anyway—but we must have a victory next year, I—I——"

These impressionable, honest, hearty young fellows each shook his hand. It seemed as if a sudden intelligence had dawned upon them, a sudden awakening into the Yale spirit.

When he went out, agreeing to meet Harry at dinner, the latter said : " He's the best old fellow in the world. I believe the only thing he thinks of is his law and Yale. It's queer how excited he gets ; it's a religion to him."

" And he's right," said Thornton warmly. " I like him for it."

" He was the bully of his class—and wooden spoon," said Harry. " A Yale man to the core. I believe he'd like to be buried in the campus under the old elms !"

He bade his uncle good-by that evening after discovering, to his chagrin—Mr. Lyman got one of the professors to tell him—that he would probably be conditioned in Latin and arithmetic, but that he was otherwise through his entrance examination creditably enough.

Harry was so surprised he was unable to speak. " You were so cocksure," said his uncle, " I was afraid you'd slip up."

. " Latin !" exclaimed Harry, provoked, " my stronghold !—and Vergil of all things !"

"Oh, well, go to work now ; study hard, and work the conditions off. Play hard, fight hard, be a man, and you'll be popular. You're a Delta Kap man, remember."

"So are you, you dear old fellow !" said Harry, shaking his hand at the station. They both laughed, and the bell rang for the cars to start.

"Well, Harry, you know I've never married, and, my dear boy, you're *my* boy. If you want extra money send to me ; don't badger your poor mother. I've arranged to have all the faculty's letters sent to my office. Oh, don't start ; they'll come, and I dare say you'll be suspended and all that. But your mother mustn't have any of these worries. Now, if you get in a scrape you know whom to come to. Good-by !"

Harry stood a moment as the train went off, and made his way thoughtfully back to his room in York Street. "*I* get into any scrape !" he repeated disdainfully. "I guess *not!*"

CHAPTER VI

DELTA KAPPA INITIATION.

EVERY hour of the day carried an engagement. There was much to do getting acquainted with so many new fellows, seeing so many new things of interest—the boathouse, the harbor, the town, Hamilton Park, where the ball ground was, learning the ropes about college and the recitation rooms. The class was to be divided into four alphabetical divisions. He was in the first and his chum in the third. He consoled Rives with the remark that in the ensuing term they would both be together, probably in the fourth division, for then they were to be divided according to standing. He found with surprise that he would be obliged to study, and study pretty hard, too.

His first week was one of disenchantment in the recitation room. College life was not to be all glees and good suppers, moonlight and romance, oh, no. Professor Black had flunked him dead twice in Greek. His stand in that must be 'way below zero. Four was perfect, but no one ever was known to get over 3.40, at best ; two was average, and if below that at the end of a week or so, a fellow was warned ; then if he didn't improve, or his other studies did not bring him up, he was incontinently and mercilessly dropped !

Harry thought that once in college—through the entrance examination—all a fellow had to do was to look wise, study a little, and amuse himself a great deal. By George ! "it meant a lot of mighty hard study !" he wrote his sister, "and with small room for any fun." The boys were both scared after the first few days of Professor Black's keen and scathing sarcasms and Professor

Walker's snappy recitations in Euclid. It was so deuced easy to flunk ! It had never been so easy at Andover, even under Dr. Taylor. He became a faded, fat old angel to them. Yet at Andover—how they feared him !

" How good he always was to us," said Rives one night, as with coats off they were boning down to their work and Stamp was lying in his kennel, blinking out of his one never-closed eye, and wondering if he was to be owned by a damned " dig " after all and never to have any fun ? " How good and kind Unk was in recitation. He was terribly severe, but never got off any sarcasms on a fellow. Black is so icy cold ! He takes all the life out of a man. He tries his best to flunk you, not to teach you anything."

" He has the ingenuity of the devil ! " groaned Harry, looking up, " he flunked me to-day when he had no business to. I knew the lesson, and, by Jove, he saw it and he jumped back and asked me a lot of questions on our first day's grammar lesson ! Of course I flunked, and he smiled like a fiend at me."

Harry dug away at his lexicon vexedly.

" There was a good grind on *me* yesterday," said Jack, in a melancholy voice. " He asked me what was the difference between οὗτος and οὕτως—pronoun and adverb. Of course, if I hadn't been fascinated by his dreadful eyes, I would have answered all right, but I stammered like a fool, ' one's singular—the other plural ! ' The whole class laughed, and Black remarked, in his cutting way, after everyone was quiet : ' Possibly, Mr. Rives, you have only your *English* translation before you.' "

Harry laughed.

" And Latin prose is beastly stuff, isn't it ? Unk never gave us much of it—it isn't fit for gentlemen ! "

" And to think," said Harry, "that I've made that grand old man many a night chase me down Andover hill lickety split, he gaining every stride, for he could run like the wind—downhill. Then, when I was afraid he'd lay his hand on me. I jumped a wall, and I had Unk dead, for he couldn't climb for a cent ; and then I would hide in the grass and chirrup to the dear old fellow. Ah, dear old Unk, *you* were a gentleman ! "

" He *tried* to teach, but here they try to flunk you. Well, I hope it won't be so as we go on. Perhaps it's only because we are freshmen."

" I wonder if it was so in Uncle Dick's time? I guess he forgets the recitations and thinks only of the good times he had."

The usual freshman rains set in for two days, and beyond a

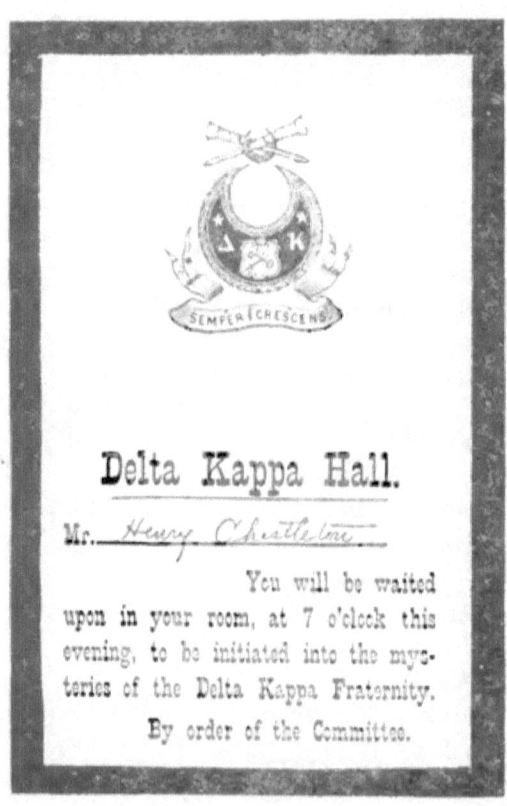

Delta Kappa Hall.

Mr. *Henry Christletine*

You will be waited upon in your room, at 7 o'clock this evening, to be initiated into the mysteries of the Delta Kappa Fraternity.

By order of the Committee.

certain amount of cap-snatching everything was very quiet. Caswell, Holland, and a lot of sophomores had a swell eating club near by, and walked down four abreast, in lordly swagger, past their room every day. Once Harry bowed to Caswell out of the window. Caswell stared and cut him dead. He had known one or two sophomores at Andover and also several juniors. They all cut him when they happened to pass him. He was undergoing the "discipline" of first term freshman year and becoming properly chastened.

At the end of the week they were notified of their election by solemn invitations printed in deep black borders, and advised to attend Delta Kappa Hall at prompt seven o'clock the following day. The day was Saturday.

When Harry and Jack presented themselves, by advice of friends, in their old clothes, at Delta Kap Hall, then on Chapel Street below Church, it was a quarter to four. They were at once taken up on the roof, where they found at least fifty Umpty-four men in waiting.

"Do you know why they herd us up here so early?" said Thornton. "It's because they're afraid the juniors and seniors will steal us. Any freshman who will put up a dinner at Gradley's can get in without being initiated. The juniors or seniors will rush him right in. I had a chance to, but I refused. I'm not afraid, and I'm so big they can't hurt me, though they do say a man was killed in Delta Kap two or three years ago."

It is presumable that Thornton threw this out merely to encourage some of the weaker neophytes. No death, oh, fond parental heart, has ever been known to occur at Yale, purely from an initiation.

It grew dusk, then dark. The number of freshmen now amounted to about fifty-eight. There were about twenty absent. These had probably been "stolen," Thornton said, by upper-class men.

They were ushered presently down into a dark garret under the roof, and made to sit there in hot, sweating suspense for an hour. Then it was evident the fun was about to begin. They fancied they could hear below them horns blown and shouts of fiendish glee. Names were called out of the darkness, and freshmen began to disappear to their doom. It was actually terrifying. The initiation had begun in earnest. One by one their ranks were thinning out. A soph in the costume of Mephisto stood at the door and kept order.

Harry, Rives, Nevers, Coles, Danforth, Thornton, and a lot of fellows were all sitting close to each other on the floor in the dark, waiting. The door opened quickly, a blast of hot, gassy air came up.

"John Carrington Rives," bawled out a gruff voice into the darkness. It sounded a little like Caswell's, disguised.

"Present!"

"Henery Walcot Chestleton."

"Present!"

"Come this way!"

Then in an aside to someone outside:

"Let 'em go up together, Bill. Two such cats I never saw. They'll claw each other to bits in the blanket—more fun for the boys!"

"All right. Men whose names are called come forward faster, will you!"

The two terrified, boyish freshmen went to the door, where there streamed in a brilliant light. Within the room whence they came was darkness, typical of the intellectual chaos before entering "Jolly D. K." The light flashed into the garret and lit up the thirty or forty who were left. A beautiful ultramarine hue pervaded the very darkness about them. "Men!" They were fair, beardless boys, most of them, fresh from loving mothers and gentle homes. Here and there was an incipient mustache. A few had beards. All were pale with the heat and expectancy, stifling in that miserable den under the hot roof; but it didn't matter, they were soon to be hustled into "Jolly D. K.," and all would be well! They had kept their spirits up by telling awful stories of men who had been killed while undergoing the ordeal of the gridiron. "Roasted to death by accident is no fun," said Danforth, who was a wag in everything but baseball and examinations. "Sometimes they let you go by accident, and your flesh smells of burnt steak for a week. I had a cousin who had a brother-in-law who was compelled to live the rest of his life in a flour barrel after a D. K. initiation."

"Silence! Freshman!" growled Mephisto at the door.

Poor freshmen ! you could almost hear their teeth chatter.

Harry and Jack, as soon as they stepped to the door, were seized from behind and walked quickly into a little room lit by a single candle. The candle stood on a desk, in front of an open book. Behind the desk sat a huge blinking owl, with great yellow eyes. It was more than enough to frighten a saint.

"Sign !" chanted the owl.

They each signed the book tremblingly.

"Raise your right legs !" cried the owl.

They tried to ; it was awkward, but they succeeded. The owl then read off a lot of rigmarole promises to obey the orders, to keep secret what transpired, to pay dues, to do all they possibly could to injure all other freshmen societies, and chiefly to worship the glorious class of Umpty-three.

"Swe-e-e-a-a-r !" cried the owl.

They swore and kissed the book, being warned to still stand and hop about on one leg, under the most grievous penalties.

Then the candle was blown out and a door opened. Some inner mystery was about to be unfolded. They were blindfolded and then led out on a narrow platform. They could hear below them a great crowd of students, shouting, blowing horns, and keeping up a terrible din. The great hall was crammed with upper-class men.

"Make a speech, freshy !" bawled a strapping big soph in Harry's ear. "Tell the gentlemen you're glad to be here !"

Harry began in a weak, timid voice :

"Gentlemen—am very glad on this auspicious occa——"

Swash !

A spongeful of dirty water is flung straight in his face ! Then he felt himself grabbed by his ankles and his collar, he spitting and protesting, and with a one, two, and three ! swung and hurled into space as though flung out of a catapult.

Oh ! Ugh !

What a sensation ! His bandage fell off his eyes. He found himself landed in the center of a great canvas blanket or sail ; up he went again, head down and legs flying. He saw he was surrounded by hundreds of leering, grinning faces. He had nothing

to catch hold of. He clawed the air. Down, down he went, striking so softly ; he rather liked it. Then he became aware that
someone else was in the thing with him.

"For God's sake, hang on to me !" cried Jack, as they bumped
together, and "Now with a will, boys !" up they soared together
again like twin aëronauts. They seemed to dally close to the
ceiling for a moment, and then down "like a thousand o' brick."
They clung to each other with the frenzy of despair. What a gone,
sinking feeling, and then up again, while the crowd roared. Again
—and again—and again ! Would it never end ? They were sore
with bumps on the floor, and bumps against the plaster ceiling, but
they clung to each other still, as one senior remarked to another
who was watching the tossing, "with an affection produced only
by mutual calamity."

At last it ended. They had time to glance about at a hundred
grinning fiends and have horns blown in their ears, when they
were blindfolded again.

They were hurried along, conscious of a howling, angry, yelling
mob of sophs, to the several ordeals. They were thumped down
on seats and fell into tubs of ice water. They were guillotined—a
frightful ordeal ; for their bandages were removed and the execu-
tioner, in a black cap, made it all the more frightful by never fail-
ing to whisper, "The knife is broken, and so, if it should slip and
really cut you, have you any last message, freshman ?" But as
they attempted to speak the awful thing fell with a jerk, and as it
descended a piece of ice was drawn across their bared, upturned
throats, and hot water gurgled down their backs. Not Marie
Antoinette or Louis XVI. had more realizing sense of their
untimely end ! Then they were dragged away and made to crawl
through a piano box filled with sawdust. They were rolled in
flour and were slid down planks into tubs of water. Men pulled
and pushed and hauled them. They were sore from head to foot
and wet and dirty, and their hair matted. Sweat and grime
poured down their necks in rivulets. Their clothes were torn and
ruined. In such a condition were they at last admitted to membership of "Jolly D. K.," and had their coats promptly turned

"NOW WITH A WILL, BOYS!"

inside out for them to prevent their being initiated over again by accident.

"Go to work now, freshy, and help put through some of your friends!" roared a big soph. It was Bailey, who pulled No. 4 on the 'varsity in the race of the summer before. "Oh—my—poor—fre—e—sh !" shouted the sophs in unison, and Bailey shouted, too.

"Umpty-four! Umpty-four!" shouted back Harry and Jack and a crowd of freshmen, who were gazing about the crowded hall, in a very dazed and hopeless condition, like kittens with their eyes just open.

It was a great room, about sixty feet square, carpetless and filled with dust and smoke. What a crowd! Here were seniors jamming and rushing about with juniors and sophs. It was great fun seeing their classmates put through. But the din and the noise were terrible. The Yale boy is primarily a good fellow ; he is no "dude," no Miss Nancy; he likes honest roughness. But he can be pleasant and amiable enough if he tries. Some juniors came up and talked with Harry, and asked him how he liked it as far as he had got. Then some sophomores' made themselves agreeable. They told him that the initiation was not so rough as usual, and that in their year three men were killed. "Generally," they said, "six or eight men are lamed for life."

"Why, some of these sophs are very decent sort of fellows," said Harry to Rives, who stood near him.

"I don't trust 'em—they're our natural born enemies. The juniors are our friends. They hate Umpty-three as much as we do."

Then they caught hold of the blanket and heaved with the rest. What fun it was! Fifty men all pulling at once. It was grand! It repaid them for all their trials ! How they heave, O ! heave, O ! Up went the poor freshmen, head down, heels up ; then feet down and head up, now here, now there. Sprawling—clutching—oh, it was great fun after all !

At last there came a lull. Dobson and Farley, two enormous men, stripped to their undershirts, came down from the scaffolding, where they had assisted freshmen into the blanket, stood on a box and proclaimed "Order! Order!" Silence ensued. "Is President

Stout present?" asked Dobson, looking about anxiously, and pretending to spy him, and then to lose him in the crowd.

There was a roar of laughter at the idea of calling for the president of the college.

"PROFESSOR MAYNARD."

"Are any of the theological faculty here to-night?" again asked Dobson, with stentorian lungs. "If so, I ask them to come forward and make a few remarks suitable to the occasion."

No one responded.

"Is Professor Maynard here?"

When this distinguished person was called upon a bustling

gentleman in high choker collar, and looking just like the beau from an old fashion plate, pushed forward. Harry shouted with laughter, for he saw that someone had copied the manner and dress of Professor Maynard to perfection. There were the spectacles, the buff waistcoat, the long watch-guard and seal, the high choker and stock—it was an admirable imitation of the "old beau."

"Professor Maynard" clambered up on the platform and stood a moment with folded hands, waiting for the noise to subside.

"Gentlemen of Umpty-four."

His voice was squeaky and like the professor's own.

"In the absence of the president and of Chauncey Depew, it is my duty as a member of and a representative of the faculty to welcome you to the glories of Delta Kap. [Cries of 'Hear! hear!' and hootings.] I am speaking for them when I say that it is their wish to be present here in a body to-night, for they regard this great institution as the one grand bulwark of dear old Yale. [Catcalls and shouts of laughter.] Unfortunately they are detained. President Stout has a swelled head, owing to his great pride in having the very largest freshman class that ever came to Yale. ['Umpty-four! Umpty-four! Whoop 'er up for Umpty-four!' The freshmen yelled themselves hoarse over this.] Professor Black is busy filing away at a new sarcasm [laughter]; Professor Walker is busy dropping freshmen into Salt Creek off the *pons asinorum* [shouts by the sophs]; Professor Sinister is busy—smiling—at Brood's, and all the rest are overcome by the size, the beauty, the intelligence, the bumptiousness, and the magnificent—er—stupidity of the freshman class. [Great laughter.]

"There never was such a class. ['Hear! hear!' from the freshmen.] There never will be such a class again—thank *the Lord!* [Laughter, and many freshmen, who started in to applaud, kept silent.] Why, the very grass in the campus has turned yellow with envy, and I am credibly informed that yesterday a freshman was eaten by a cow at Hamilton Park. She couldn't make him out exactly, but she knew he was something mighty green! [Laughter.] But a word in my own behalf. I want to say to you how much Delta Kap has done for me and the faculty.

Here, gentlemen, in these halls, that vulgar fraction of your class which has gone to the oblivion—nay, the purgatory of Sigmareps—and the Hades of Gamma Nu—[Loud groans, hootings, shrieks, and yells of derision]—they may never enter here to 'sully your pure prayer,' and the faculty are glad of it. [Laughter.]

"Here, gentlemen, you are given (provided you pay your honest dues) [applause] these magnificent halls, decorated by the old masters at vast expense. Here you will cultivate those powers of speech which will make of you second Websters and will cause the fame of Demosthenes to grow dim. Here, in jolly D. K., you will, I trust—and the faculty always get trust here [laughter]—find that *home* life which you have left behind you with your mothers and sisters. Ladies, to be sure, never enter here, but very good, manly imitations of them are often found in D. K., tripping the light fantastic, and whispering soft nothings in the dance. To you, members of Umpty-four, the faculty look to keep these sacred mysteries inviolate—mysteries such as you to-night participated in—with the hope that you will transmit them to the freshmen of another year the same as when you received them. Gentlemen, the faculty propose to close up that nest of vipers, Sigmareps, very soon. Gentlemen, three times three for dear old Delta Kap!" [Prolonged cheering.]

The bustling old gentleman in a high collar—the exact imitator of, if not the real Professor Maynard—got down off the platform, and then followed songs, other speeches, and a general jollification. A keg of lager was carried in. "Here you—have some beer, won't you?" Harry was standing gaping about with his hair in his eyes. It was Jones, who played second base on the nine, who spoke. Harry took the glass of beer and thanked him. "Do you play ball?" he asked, scrutinizing Harry. "Come out to Hamilton Park Monday afternoon, won't you?"

Would he? His eyes beamed with delight.

"Where did you play on your Andover nine?"

"Catcher sometimes, and short stop."

"Dale was a slow pitcher, wasn't he?"

Harry bridled, but he said nothing. The inference was that he couldn't catch swift pitching.

"We are anxious to have a few substitutes in training in your class."

Substitutes! Oh, merely to be a substitute in the 'varsity!

"I've been playing all summer, sir," said Jack Rives. "I'd like to go out, too."

"Very well," said Jones. "Come out; we want you." Then he turned away.

The first thing they had learned so far at Yale was to revere upper-class men. There were certain seniors whose names Harry already knew who filled him with abject awe. Such great men! Such tremendous intellects! They were members of the Spade and Grave and the Book and Lock. There was the great Hawley standing by the window and looking on the crowd with solemn senioric dignity. How could the great man bring himself to patronize Delta Kap? He wore a mysterious golden badge upon his necktie. Harry and Jack looked upon it askance, in holy awe.

They drank some more beer and felt on very good terms with the whole college. Harry saw a junior whom he formerly knew in New York, Tom Bixby.

"Hello, Bix!" he called out briskly.

Bixby gave him a frightful stare. "Oh, it's—young Chestleton, is it? How de do, young Chestleton—er—glad to see you here——"

Then Bixby turned abruptly, and made a remark to his friends upon the dashed impudence of these dashed Umpty-four men. Harry felt hurt, but it renewed his respect for upper-class men. Caswell and the men he met at dinner with his uncle were much nicer to him. Even Holland laughed and talked pleasantly with them. Holland was the great man in Delta Kap. He had beaten Sigma Eps out of sight, and he could strut about with his friends and "lug it" as he liked. "Oh, he's sure to go into a senior society," said one of Harry's friends, "and he can take his friends with him—anyone he likes."

It seemed to invest Holland with a new romantic interest.

After the "exercises" were over, on the way home there was

a rush. The freshmen of Delta Kap formed on the sidewalk outside their hall four deep, and marched along up Chapel Street by the green, keeping step as they marched and waking the echoes of midnight with their "rah—rah—rahs for Umpty-four." They were about seventy in number, and they presented a delicious mark for the sophs, who were skirmishing about here and there in the darkness after "scalps." The Sigma Eps gang came up the street singing presently, and joined them. It was an open secret that up about the colleges the sophs would try their mettle *en masse* in a rush.

The freshmen, nothing daunted, advanced up Chapel Street with locked step. About opposite old Trinity the sophs were waiting for them, a hundred strong.

It was midnight, and the bells were just tolling out the hour.

"Umpty-three, Umpty-three!" shouted the sophs in a hoarse roar, which made the hearts of the freshmen tremble, and reverberated in the still night far under the old elms.

"Umpty-four, Umpty-four!" bawled the freshies, keeping step. Then the two cohorts came together. All was tumult and confusion. There was no striking, only wrestling, pulling, and hauling. Everyone tried to roll everyone else in the mud. Harry and one of his own class wrestled, in their excitement, and rolled over and over on the wooden pavement. There were some blows, too, very few. Coats were torn into shreds. Pretty soon most of the freshmen were in the street and the sophomores on the sidewalks. They began to crow and shout for Umpty-three and their glorious victory, and poke fun at the freshmen, who, whenever they tried to regain the sidewalk, were ignominiously thrown out into the street.

Meanwhile, however, scouts had been sent on the run up to the college to awaken sleeping freshmen and urge them to the fray. Twenty big fellows came down from a freshman hive on High Street. Their ranks began to fill up rapidly.

They formed again four deep and charged. This time they had the larger force. They rushed the sophs pell-mell up the street toward the colleges. Then there was a halt at the fence. The sophs made a last stand. It was of no earthly use. They were rushed into the Street. Then came the cry—that cry so ominous to the midnight student marauder: "Faculty! Faculty!"

Everyone ran. Harry was in the midst of throwing a heavy soph in the mud. He paid no attention to the warning cry. Someone had grabbed him by the collar.

"*Name!*" came down to him in a solemn voice which made his flesh creep and his heart stand still.

"Jones," he replied, quaking.

"Jones," said the voice, which seemed to come from the airy space above him. "Disperse to your room!"

"Yes, sir!" said Harry.

"At once!"

"Yes, sir."

Off he sped until he got behind Old South College, when he skirted around the building and came out on the street again, joining a number of freshmen he met.

"Who was that tall professor?" he asked. "He told me to ' disperse ' to my room, and I'm going—if the fun's over."

"Oh, he was only joking," laughed one of the freshmen. "I guess he didn't mean it—one fellow can't '*disperse*.' "

"By Jove! he was, was he?"

Someone who looked very like the tall professor came charging down upon them, along the fence, at full tilt. He could run like the wind. Off started the freshmen, but, run as fast as they would, the demon professor kept gaining on them. On, on, on—up to High Street. Harry jumped the fence, and so did the professor.

Harry put on a burst of speed and ran down High to Elm. The professor "followed fast and followed faster." Harry turned down Elm and so into the campus again by Durfee, the professor ever after him.

Harry ran like a deer down by Farnam, and made a dive into North Middle, and so upstairs three steps at a time. His blood was up; he made for the second story window and jumped out. The fall shook him up a little, but he straightened up and laughed as he saw he had stumped the professor. He did not dare follow.

"Jump, professor!" he called out.

"Jones, is that you?"

"Yes."

"I think you are telling me a deceitful bonnet——"

"A what, sir?"

"A falsehood."

"Well, who am I, then?"

"Chestleton, of Umpty-four."

Harry trembled. "Don't report me, sir; I didn't mean anything."

"I shall be obliged to—unless——"

"What, sir?"

"You set up the champagne for the faculty." Harry could not believe his ears.

"What, sir?"

A peal of hearty laughter followed, and the professor said:

"Youngster, I think I'll try you for the nine. You've got pluck, and lots of it, and you can run like—ahem! You ought to make second every clip!" The professor disappeared, and Harry then knew it was Harding, the captain of the 'varsity nine!

He went trotting home in the rain. He was soaked, dirty, frowzy, but in good spirits. He had had lots of fun for one evening—and—if—if—was it true that—he—a freshman—would actually be tried—for the 'varsity?

When he reached his room on York Street Jack Rives and half a dozen classmates were regaling themselves with crackers and beer, waiting up for him. He told them of his adventure.

"Jack," he cried, "if I get on I'll make it all right for you, too, old man!"

Stamp was seated on the table, gravely catching the crackers they tossed to him. Things were beginning to go as he wanted them to. He was better natured than he'd been for a week.

"Well," said Jack, "you're in luck, and they say Umpty-four is the best class that ever entered Yale!"

"Oh, shoot it!" laughed Coles.

There came a knock on the door. Mrs. Gimly, in nightcap and doublegown, stuck her head in.

"Air you aware of the noise you are making, gentlemen?" she asked. "Air you aware it is the holy Sabbath day, though only one o'clock in the morning?"

"Come in, Mrs. Gimly, and have something with us!" called out Jack cheerily.

A hasty slam of the door, and Mrs. Gimly vanished.

Almost the entire freshman class cut early chapel the next morning. But what a smile of victorious content rested upon their fresh, honest, boyish faces at church!

They had met the sophomores—and they were theirs.

CHAPTER VII.

THE DAILY LIFE.

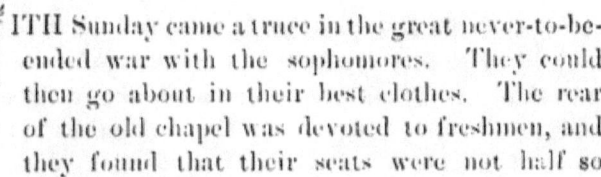

ITH Sunday came a truce in the great never-to-be-ended war with the sophomores. They could then go about in their best clothes. The rear of the old chapel was devoted to freshmen, and they found that their seats were not half so bad as Uncle Dick had told them. Up in the high galleries sat the "snab"—as they were called—the pretty daughters of professors and visiting cousins and sisters. At the close of service it was great sport to see President Stout walk down the middle aisle between the ranks of bowing seniors. The freshmen were supposed to bow and keep bowing while the upper classes passed out,—a reminder of the old fagging days at Yale,—but the freshmen usually refused to bow to anyone except the dear old president, for whom everyone seemed to have so much affection.

It was rather hard being obliged to attend the afternoon service in addition to the morning ordeal. The sermons were long and "knotty." The president generally had some keen, hair-splitting theological point he wished to prove out of the Old Testament for the edification of the theological faculty, who sat up in the gallery and were the only persons in the chapel who appeared at all interested. There was rarely anything said applicable to the especial needs of young men, except to keep up as far as possible the general weekday notion that students were all particularly sinful as a class, unworthy of anything more than a cold toleration.

The week succeeding the D. K. initiation their York Street room was pleasantly adorned with more than a dozen "scalps." It was great fun, this carrying the war into Africa. The sophs thought it tremendously impudent. It was their prerogative to steal freshman caps. Several of them went to Thornton and com-

plained. "Umpty-four" was carrying things with too high a
hand. All the good old customs of the college were being upset,
etc. But the freshmen persisted, and the rowing began to be
noticed by the faculty. A sophomore by the name of Bunsby got
into the Euclid recitation room while the freshmen were reciting,
and stole over twenty hats. In retaliation a freshman by the
name of Best stole into the soph recitation room while they were
reciting their Agamemnon, and tried to get away with all the caps
on the hooks. He had his face carefully blacked, and looked like a
darky. He dressed for his part, and corked his hands, his neck,
and wrists.

A sophomore caught him by the ankle as he was making his exit,
and dragged him into the room before the entire division. Then
Best braved it out as best he might. He had the "gall" to talk
darky lingo to good old Professor Sadley, who was hearing the
recitation and who was imposed upon. He pretended to cry, and
told them that he had been paid a quarter by some "gemmen" to
get the hats, an' was mighty sorry he done it. He couldn't tell
the names of the gemmen. Dey was gemmen though, an' showed
money.

A soph, who was a candidate for the 'varsity nine, pretended he
believed Best *was* a darky, and led him out of the room and gave
him a "boost" that sent him flying downstairs. Best was
"spotted" for hazing purposes and he was well roasted later in
winter term, but the faculty never "rowed" him.

The house on York Street soon began to have a reputation.
Jack and Harry on the second floor front; Thornton, the great
freshman heavy-weight, on the floor above them; Nevers, Coles,
Ritch, Steele, and others in the rear rooms kept things very lively.
Mrs. Gimly they discovered — very much after the manner of
Harry's Andover landlady—was always on the *point* of "going to
see" Professor Shepard, but never did.

The noise they made at night—the wrestling and heavy falls in
Harry's room, just above where she and her "darter Samanthy,"
who was studying to be a teacher, sat round their study lamp
every evening—was not calculated to soothe her feelings. The

boxing, too, disturbed her. It made the whole house shake like an earthquake from garret to cellar. The everlasting sophomores she was able to bar out of the house; but her inmates were a "terrible bad lot" she told Mrs. McGuiness, who kept a boarding house across the street. Mrs. McGuiness was a swarthy, tall, strong Irishwoman who never relied upon Professor Shepard or the faculty in *her* intercourse with freshmen. No, indeed!

"What do you do, Mrs. McGuiness, when them freshmen make sich a noise? It gives me an' me darter headaches, both of us; an' the winders rattles."

"What does Oi do?" answered Mrs. McGuiness. "I jest fires 'em out, if they're bad behaved. Shure me byes is all dacent an' quiet, student loike. Shure they til me Oi have the fadin' of Mr. Alum, the vallydicatorian. It's him an' his aunt, Miss Alum, boards wi' me; ha' ye sane her? A grit tall spook I call the likes av her! Shure she sez, sez she, she's in Umpty-four hersel! I see her snatch wan o' thim softmore bastes' hats thuther night as shure as guns!"

Mrs. Gimly smiled sadly. The allusion to the sophomores as "bastes" was quite to her taste. She knew Mrs. McGuiness' tendency to draw the long bow, however, and she was not inclined to let the last statement go without challenging.

"Your lady boarder stealing a softmore's hat?"

"Oi sane her!" lied the landlady boastfully. "Shure she thought none was lookin'. It's her nevvy as sneaks along, coward like, fer fear o' thim bastes, to his recitation—him the vallydicatorian! Shure he has none o' thim softmore scalps hangin' in his room but the one she stole. She's no coward. She's fit fer to fight the loikes o' me! She stands by her nevvy, the vallydicatorian, like death to a dead nigger! Thim limbs o' Satan tried to break in his room while the poor lad was larnin' Greek principles—an' what did Miss Alum do? She stood her ground till I come up, an' thim softmores is wearing court plaster till this day, an' she stole the hat sos't her nevvy would be considered as brave as the nixt. Shure I do be expictin' her to be in the big rush next Saturday!"

Mrs. Gimly went sadly into the house. The night before there had been a general caucus in Harry and Jack's room to elect a captain for the freshman nine. About forty freshmen had crammed and jammed themselves into the room. They had wedged themselves in so tight—for it was the first class election and the "Andover crowd" wanted to work things their own way with Harry as their candidate—that the boy who was crowded up on to the top of the bookcase was unanimously elected the chairman of the caucus, and the boy in the center of the room nearest the inkstand was elected secretary. Several had baseball bats in their hands and naturally hammered them on the floor at every opportunity given them for applause, besides stamping and ' 'rah, 'rahing' at the top of their lungs. Mrs. Gimly got mad. Her daughter Samanthy, in ringlets, ran upstairs to protest four times. It was of no use.

The next day Mrs. Gimly announced, with tremendous solemnity, that nothing would or could ever soothe her feelings except "seeing" Professor Shepard! To Professor Shepard she would go! Nothing should prevent her telling him about the noise, the beer, the cigars, the boxing matches, the wrestling, which the rules of the house forbade, as they knew! Harry, who had had experiences in Andover of a similar nature, hastily passed the hat around through the rooms and collected five dollars. This he placed in an envelope and in the presence of all the freshmen in the house, who invaded Mrs. Gimly's parlor for the purpose, and with a great deal of oratory and fulsome eulogy presented to her in due form.

"It was a token," he said solemnly, "of their esteem and love. They had learned in the few weeks they had been at Yale to love Mrs. Gimly like a stepmother. They had no mother there at college [pathetic pause]; they needed someone to love them, to care for them. Mrs. Gimly could act *in loco parentis*. She could love them even if by accident there was more noise than they could otherwise wish." Samanthy wept; Mrs. Gimly grew less stern. She accepted the five dollars and did not visit her dear Professor Shepard.

"Umpty-three!"

"Whooperup! Whooperup for Umpty-four!"

These were the cries to which the facetious sophs and freshmen clubs marched through York Street and kept step by nearly every night. It was hardly safe for a "fresh" to go about alone those first weeks. Already Jack and Harry had had many a cap snatched from their heads, but as they had a collection of five very much damaged soph hats, or "scalps," as they were called, hanging in their room, they felt they had made adequate reprisals, and their collection had only just begun. It got to be so that sophs and freshmen went to recitation in the queerest old straw hats and broken down beavers, so that if in the *mélée* they lost them they didn't care.

One of the sophomores who gave the freshmen a great deal of

THE CHAIRMAN.

trouble was named Joe Briggs, or "Lambda Chi" Briggs. He was a tall, red-haired chap from the wild and woolly West. They called him "Lambda Chi" because in the previous year he was initiated into that society as the greenest freshman in his class. "He had no idea of anything at all," said a friend in Umpty-four who had known about it. He would do anything they told him. He went about the first week he was in college slapping professors and upper-class men on the back, and saying, "How are you to-day?" because the sophs put him up to it. He slapped President

Stout on the back and threw the kindly old gentleman into a coughing fit. He tried it on Professor Walker, but the latter turned on him and gave him an indignant and powerful box on the ear. They got him to leave off wearing a collar and necktie, which he did for a week. They invited him to faculty meetings, and got him into all sorts of scrapes, and then they "Lambda Chied" him in earnest. They stole him out of his room one night and carried him out to East Rock in a hack. Then they had a grand powwow up there, dressed like Indians, they tied poor Briggs to a stake and made ready to roast him.

The poor fellow was stripped down to "*pueris naturallibusque,*" as he said afterward, and had to make his way back to his room in an undershirt! Naturally when Briggs came to be a sophomore he wanted to keep up the "grand old custom" of "Lambda Chi" for the benefit of Umpty-four. Harry fully believed that Caswell, Storrs, and Holland, and the rest of the campaign committee of D. K., had not condoned and would not forgive him for Uncle Dick's dinner at Charlie Gradley's. He felt that trouble was brewing for him. Jack Rives, too, got himself quickly into trouble. He snatched Caswell's cap one night. It had "Umpty-three" on it in white patent-leather letters. Jack persisted in wearing it to recitation, and of course it made the sophomores perfectly furious. It was such a "dare" and showed so much "gall," they said.

Twice Caswell and his friends tried to get into Mrs. Gimly's and haze those "cheeky freshmen," but Mrs. Gimly knew the "softmores" by instinct, and refused to open the front door, and threatened, if they persisted, to call a policeman. Harry and his friends sat in the open window of their room on the second story and jeered at them. Caswell shook his fist at Rives, who wore his cap. "You're too d—d sassy!" he bawled out; "it's time you were in heaven! You know too much for this earth."

"Caswell, it's a pity you don't know a little *more*, isn't it!" laughed Harry. "Then you wouldn't be pledging old goods to jolly D. K.!"

"I should like to know what right you have to snatch sophomore caps? It's contrary to every tradition in Yale College," yelled Caswell angrily.

"We're going to establish a new one, then."

The sophomores on the sidewalk below held a consultation. Mrs. Gimly stood peeking out of the front door, holding the fort, as it were. Harry called down:

"See here, Caswell, I'll go out now [it was about 9 P. M.] and wrestle you best two out of three for a dinner for the crowd, or I'll meet you and box four rounds with hard gloves, or I'll back our dog Stamp against any dog in the sophomore class. Come now!"

Caswell and his friends walked off, pretending not to notice him.

And so it went on from day to day. The freshman eating club, which Harry and Jack joined, was not far from their rooms on York Street, and the swell soph eating club, which Holland, Caswell, Guthrie, Storrs, etc., belonged to, was in the next house but one.

There were about a dozen men in each club, and they contained the pick of each class. Hostilities between the two clubs began to grow very bitter. They had had two or three sidewalk rushes. But hard feeling culminated on Wednesday night—the week which ended in the grand annual class rush after the ball game at Hamilton Park on Saturday.

It seemed that Thornton, who knew a lot of New Haven people, learned that there was to be a sophomore german that night at the house of one of the wealthy residents on Temple Street. He mentioned the fact casually at supper (they always dined in the middle of the day) at their eating club, which was located in a house on York Street on a block farther west than Mrs. Gimly's.

"I wish we could go, too," laughed Harry. "It would be good fun to cut out Caswell and the sophomores."

"Let's get through early," said Jack, "and have a rush after supper. They won't want to, and we can have some fun with them. If any of them happen to have on dress suits, why, so much the worse for them, that's all."

"I think we'll get enough rushing at Hamilton Park," said

Thornton. "Besides, Bob Clark told me to look out and not get strained ; our race at Lake Saltonstall comes off in four weeks, you know, Jack."

"You get strained !" laughed Jack Rives.

"Oh, I'm not frightened, but I have to do most of the work, you know ; it comes on me. You, Coles, Nevers, and Rives, light-weights, can go flying off into the darkness any time, but I can't get away. I always seem to have three or four sophomores on my back at once. These night rushes are all very fine if it's only leg work. But you see, when a man like Bellamy Storrs or big Guthrie gets to tackling you, it's deuced hard work. It's business from the word 'go' !"

"But you threw Bellamy Storrs twice last week."

"Yes, and now he's fierce to throw me. He won't be really satisfied until I roll him over in the mud again, and it makes me sore to think of it."

Jack Rives, who had gone out as a scout, ran in again to say the sophs were coming out of their club, and had formed two by two. There were four or five of them in dress suits ready for the party.

It seemed such a good and opportune time to have a little sport with them that even big Thornton reached his cap from a peg with the remark :

"Well, fellows, we can have a little *talk* with them, anyhow."

Thornton put on his hat very tight and they all went out, some with their caps in their belts.

"Now, then, let's form three abreast and go after them on the double-quick," said Harry. "Let's try to pass 'em on the inside. If they get shoved in the gutter it's their own lookout. Come on !"

They formed as he suggested and very soon caught up with the rear ranks of the sophomores. A favorable opportunity occurring they pushed in between the sophs and the fence. The sophs were in no mood for rushing—they weren't dressed for it—and stormed loudly and vigorously at the freshmen. But they could not help fighting for their rights. It ended in being the toughest night row since D. K. initiation night. Nearly everyone had his coat ripped off his back. The sophs, in dress suits, fought like tigers. But Harry and Thornton got hold of one after another and down they rolled over and over in the miry street near the library. Caswell lost his temper outright. He drew off and struck Harry a sounding thwack on the jaw, which Harry returned with interest in the left optic. Caswell tore madly at his dress coat, which he gave some-one to hold. He wanted to fight it out then and there. Our hero, though not so heavy as Caswell, was more than willing. He was in much better training. "You scoundrels," Caswell yelled, "to lay for us when you see we're dressed for a party. But I don't care how I'm dressed—I'm ready now. Come on, Chestleton—I may as well lick you now as ever!"

Harry "put up his dukes," as the sporting phrase goes, but the crowd interfered and stopped it. Captain McKensie, of the football team, a junior, and one of the most influential men in college, came running up to see what the row was about. He read the freshman class a lecture as soon as he learned the facts. "By Jove!" he said indignantly, "you freshmen are getting to be a confounded nuisance in college. You haven't been here two weeks, but you are at it night and day! Here these gentlemen were on their way to their rooms, peaceably minding their own business, and going to a 'shindig' after-ward. What right had you to rush them? You'll get the whole col-lege down on you if you keep this sort of thing up. Rushing is all very well—and you'll get your fill Saturday, if the faculty don't stop it. But you sophs have brought the whole thing down on yourselves. You've tried hazing, and you've tried to keep our class from steal-ing freshmen from D. K. Why, juniors have *always* been allowed to steal a few freshmen, and rush them in without initiation. It always was, till this year, one of our rights. Now there are tradi-tions of the college that you've got to respect." [Cries of "Come off the roof, papa," from sundry freshmen on the outskirts of the crowd.] "One is that rushing shan't take place every night in the week, and cap-snatching ought to stop altogether after Saturday."

And so the crowd dispersed. Harry, Jack, and Thornton, in a freak of boyish generosity, loaned their own dress suits to the sophs who were the most damaged. They were accepted in the right spirit, and none of them cared very much about the damage to their evening clothes. Caswell laughed and said:

"You're the cheekiest fresh I ever saw. But hanged if you're not good fighters, and I don't care. Wait till next Saturday, and we'll do you up in great shape!"

He put on Harry's dress clothes and got a friend to chalk his eye. He had no hard feelings! Harry admired him greatly as he strolled off to the party, a cigarette in his mouth, "like a gentleman," with a haughty, superior swagger, just a boy's "gentlemanly hero!"

Meanwhile, every afternoon, Harry and Jack meandered on the slow horse car out to Hamilton Park, where Captain Harding, of the 'varsity (then always called "university") nine, was arranging some class games for the fall, in order to test the ability of men who wished to get on the different class nines.

Numbers of students walked or rode out to the ball ground every afternoon. The freshmen thus made a number of acquaintances among the upper-class men : Hoadley, the celebrated back stop or catcher of Yale for the previous four years, and who had sworn to stay in college until Harvard was beaten if it took a lifetime; Murdoch, the first base—a hulking big fellow, a Kentuckian with a handsome blond face, who was a terrific batsman, but who was slow in getting around the bases; Stranahan, a capital left fielder, whom they had known when he was at Andover. The latter told them how it was that Harvard had been able to win so many years running.

"They've beaten us since 1864," said he, "and for the last four years it is all owing to Dr. Taylor of Andover."

"Rather to the faculty," said Harding, "who cut their own noses off!"

"You see Bush—Archie Bush—of Albany, one of the finest baseball players ever on a college nine, was at Andover, and so were White and two other men who now make up the Harvard team. Well, a lot of them went over to Lawrence one day, contrary to Unk's rule. I believe they went over to play a match with the local team. It was perfectly harmless, what they did. But Unk got hold of it, and you know what a disciplinarian he is.

"It was just after they had graduated from Andover too, and Unk had really no control over them whatever. The only thing he could do was to withhold their letters to the faculty saying they were 'O. K.' Well, the faculty asked for the letters. There were no letters. What! no letters? 'Then you can't enter Yale College,' said the faculty, and, by Jove, they were just cutting their own noses off, for four of the best infield Harvard ever has had would have all come to Yale straight. Yes, sir! Oh, Harvard took them right in, you bet she did! She knows a good thing when she sees it! But the Yale faculty has seen Harvard, who was behind us in numbers in '65, walk right up and pass us, and I attribute it entirely to baseball."

"Of course!" was the general assent, for the car was full of ball players, who believed the world revolved around the green diamond.

"Yale has been run too long by old fogies living up in the rural districts of Connecticut," said Captain Harding. "It's falling back while Harvard is pushing ahead. Yale isn't any monastery, nor are we all going to be ministers. But I defy anyone to tell me of any institution more behind the age than Yale is to-day!"

"Oh, I can tell you of several!" laughed Stranahan. "There's Union and Hamilton and Princeton and Amherst; they are to a still greater degree run by the old fogies. Yale is at least holding her own, and I believe she's going to take a great leap ahead in a few years."

"Yale goes ahead or falls behind just as the University nine wins or not—it's the best weather gauge Yale can get," said Harding, "and we're going to change things next summer, sure," and he looked at Harry encouragingly.

Stamp, who always accompanied the boys wherever they went, emitted a low fierce growl.

"That's the talk, old boy," said Harry, laughing. And so they reached Hamilton Park.

CHAPTER VIII

HE great eventful Saturday of the annual rush at Hamilton Park came at last. A ball game in which Harry pitched and Jack caught for the freshmen came off at two, and in which the juniors, who had out an inferior nine, were badly beaten, 16-4. They stopped the game in the third inning, and the excitement began in earnest as the two classes stripped and prepared for the great rush.

The day was warm and clear. There were rows of carriages, for New Haven society is always glad to turn out at all these college affairs. Pretty girls who had cousins or brothers in the sophomore or freshman class were pale with fear, for there was always a great deal of danger connected with the rush, especially to small, slightly built men, who were apt to fall down and get trampled on. Far to the north and west loomed up the rugged front of West Rock, and the fresh wind from the Sound gave the air a cool, delicious saltness and put heart into the men. The sophomores, five deep, formed over by first base and the freshmen behind the home plate. The seniors marshaled the sophs, and the juniors the freshmen. A dozen men on either side were deputized to act as "scouts," whose duty it was to pull men out of the opposing ranks and break up the strength of the on-rush as far as possible.

Nearly the entire college was present, and quantities of "townies" and "micks" and some Harvard men down from Cambridge and Columbia men from New York to see the fun.

The soph column, with three 'varsity crew men, and two stout fellows who rowed in their class crew in the front rank, with Bob

Clark as head scout, made a most formidable and terrible array. The freshmen put their tall men in front, and some of them were poor material, with merely length without breadth or thickness, but they outnumbered the sophs, and made up by their numbers what they lacked in strength. Both sides locked arms, and the outside men of each rank had their arms about the waists of the men in front of them. It made two solid masses of men, of about 125 on one side and 150 on the other, going against each other end on, and, as someone expressed it, "Something was bound to give way."

The two front ranks leaned back on a slant, and the ranks behind them stood massed together in a solid phalanx.

"Umpty-three, Umpty-three!" shouted the oncoming sophs, keeping step.

"Umpty-four, Umpty-four!" answered the chorus of freshmen, with their lockstep in unison. "Whooper up for Umpty-four!"

The heads of the two columns slowly and with terrible earnestness came together end on. The scouts had orders not to get in their work until the two classes jammed together. Jack was in the third rank and Harry was a scout.

"Boom, boom, Umpty-four!"

"Come, close up there!" shouted the juniors who acted as marshals, "close up!" and they went skirmishing around the freshman cohorts, pressing the men closer together and advising the scouts or skirmishers how to "hook" out their men by crooking their elbows around their necks and nearly pulling their heads off.

The two opposing armies drew nearer and nearer. A great hush fell on everyone. There was Bob Clark, the best wrestler ever in college, looking like a fiend, in a red shirt, with fire in his eye, crouching as he came along, ready like a tiger to leap upon the freshman ranks. There was the fat Holland, still maintaining the leadership of his class and giving orders which men much his superior in athletic affairs obeyed without question. They said his head was "level." On they came slowly, moving like two huge leviathans on the green, close-cut turf. As the ranks came within talking distance they jeered and taunted and threatened each other with instant annihilation.

"Oh, you poor fresh ! You're done for this time !" "Say your prayers, freshmen, we're going to sweep you into the Sound !" "Say good-by to mamma, freshy," etc. The freshmen answered "Umpty-fooooor !" with a roar. "There'll be no more Umpty-three after to-day !" "Good-by, sophies !"

Now ! They came within five feet, three feet, then an impulse from both sides and from behind, and they were pressing each others' life out !

"Good Heavens ! I'm flat as a pancake !" cried Holland, who was so fat that he could not be entirely "squoze" out of his breath. The front rank were carried up in the air off their feet ; the next rank could just touch their toes to the ground ; the third rank had the hardest squeeze, and all the while each side behind these ranks were shouting cries of defiance and pushing like oxen.

"Shove, freshmen, shove !" shouted the juniors, who had gotten out of the way.

Neither side gave way exactly, but what happened was that they went round and round and struggled as if on a pivot, the scouts pulling out man after man on each side, and as the grand rush melted up into a promiscuous shoving and hauling a number of individual wrestling matches took place. Harry found himself pitted against the redoubtable Bob Clark, and he realized that a ring had been formed around them and that it was to be a decisive battle. Harry had already achieved a reputation second only to Thornton in his class as a wrestler, and Bob Clark was famous as never having been yet thrown in two years. By this time Clark had his red shirt torn half off his broad back, and the perfect oarsman's "barrel" showed itself plainly through it. His arms were small. He had very little "beef." But for strength, wind, depth of chest and splendid power of loins, no such man had ever entered Yale before. He was not quite as tall as Harry, and our hero's agile lithe figure and his good legs would have seemed to an ignorant bystander to be fully the equals of the great Clark.

They "felt" for each other for a few moments, then came

THE SOPHS BROKE RIGHT AND LEFT.

together, then appeared to " teter " for a moment, dancing about on their tiptoes, and then came the crashing fall—poor Harry was underneath, but quick as a cat he twisted as he fell, and Bob had a job to get him on his back. He pulled and hauled and tugged, but Harry would not be turned. The sweat stood out on their foreheads. But it was with Harry as he expected, and he played his game. He stuck to the ground, and Bob could not work him over on his back to save his life! Umpty-four men shouted themselves hoarse. Once Harry nearly had to yield, but he was so spry that he was on his stomach again quickly, and Bob Clark had the job to do over again. He clung to Bob's legs, " like a kitten to a hot brick," as the juniors said, and at last Bob said good-naturedly : " It's an all-day job, freshman ; I'll call it a draw ! "

Then Harry jumped to his feet. He had no shirt on at all, but his flashing eyes, his jolly smile, told the story. It was the proudest moment of his life.

Then the classes cheered and formed again. It was the same thing as before, only harder and fiercer and more earnest. The freshmen were not quite so scared. They realized that they had greater numbers, and if they kept cool they could hold their own. They bumped together as before and the appearance of things was a little changed.

But at this juncture, as the freshmen were winning, there came the dreadful cry :

"MAN DOWN ! MAN DOWN !"

A freshman had fainted in the heat and pressure and had fallen ; the crowd passed over his body. They broke ranks and lifted him out. They thought he was dead. His face was deathly white and his tongue hung out of his mouth. His name was Finck, and he was the boy they had already nicknamed " Baby Finck " because he cried over his entrance examination with his father, mother, and sister. But he had been brave enough in the rush. He was in the fourth rank both times. It looked as if he had had a fit.

Two or three surgeons ran up as he lay flat on his back on the grass. They felt him over and found that he had two ribs broken and his foot was crushed. Presently he came to and called faintly

"Water!" Finck's catastrophe precipitated many others. A sophomore fainted and had to be carried away. Then the crowd of sophs—half of them shirtless and *sans culottes*—made for the park gate on the run. It was their plan to hold the gateway against the freshmen and prevent their return to college.

Bellamy Storrs and "Big" Guthrie led their class toward the side gate. The main gate of the park was about a quarter of a mile distant, looking toward West Rock, but the side gate to the east, which everyone took who walked in from the ball ground, consisted of one large, heavy wooden door about seven feet wide. The high wooden fence was strongly built, and if the freshmen could not break through the sophomore guard they would be obliged to walk away over to the other entrance, amid the jeers and hootings of the entire college.

The sophomores quickly locked the gate and thrust a wooden stanchion through the iron latch. They then formed in front of the gate and awaited the freshmen's onset.

The freshmen halted at a little distance and held a council of war. There was a pile of timber lying at the side of the race track which environed the ball ground, with which some workmen were repairing the track fence. Thornton and several others seized upon a long stick of timber.

"I'll show you how to get through," cried Thornton. "Here! form on this stick, and then make a charge on the double-quick. I'll warrant there won't be a sophomore who will stand up against the gate when we ram this through the crowd."

As the freshmen began to form along the piece of timber there was evidently some commotion in the sophomore phalanx. No one seemed to be particularly willing to be impaled on the end of that formidable looking ram, and as the freshmen moved forward faster and faster there was evidently great consternation.

A body of sophs came out and met the freshmen, and tried to arrest their progress. But the freshmen had learned a thing or two, by this time, and their skirmishers tackled the sophomores and kept them busy, while the main body, led by Thornton, kept on their way.

As they neared the gate with their ram they broke into a fast trot. Nothing could withstand them, except perhaps a stone wall ten feet thick!

Thornton as captain shouted his orders: "All together, now! Let her go!"

JACK RIVES HAD TO GO HOME IN A LINEN DUSTER.

The sophs broke right and left. The ram struck the gate near the lock, and the whole affair broke off its hinges. The freshmen, with a loud shout, burst through and out of the park, shouting "Oh, my poor *Soph!*" It was a great and glorious victory—and the sophs seemed crestfallen.

On the way home, Bob Clark, Storrs, and other big sophs wrestled nearly every strong freshman there was in the class. Storrs was thrown twice by Thornton and once by Harry, but the great Bob maintained his supremacy. It was an eventful day for him, because it gave him a great reputation in college—he had not been present, for some reason, at the rush of the year before. He threw Jack Rives with the ease of a man tossing a child. He threw Thornton after a hard struggle.

"Lambda Chi" Briggs was red-haired and full of enthusiasm, but Jack and Harry both threw him, as they threw Caswell and Thompson and Holland, without much difficulty. All along the grassy sides of the street were wrestling, fighting, and grimy students, half their clothes torn off their backs. Jack Rives had to walk home in a linen duster; he had lost—everything but honor! But he was full of *that!* Everyone—seniors, juniors, theologues, townies—admitted that it was a great day for the new class of Umpty-four. As they neared the city, they formed two by two, and sang:

> Here's to Umpty-four
> Drink her down, drink her down!
> Here's to Umpty-four,
> For she licked the Sophomore,
> Drink her down! down! down!

And so the great rush ended, and poor Finck was carried home in a hack, proud of the glorious victory and happy in the thought that he had given a few ribs and a leg to the cause. As his class saw him carried by, the enthusiasm, as he waved his handkerchief at them, was something tremendous.

Those good old days at Yale! There are no such massed rushes now, no such royal battles for supremacy. Class feeling is to a certain extent dying out. Perhaps it is best so, but college life in those famous days of fighting and dare-deviltry for class honor was something far more exciting and interesting than it can ever be again. These dull modern days are more virtuous, but are they as jolly or eventful?

THEY WENT ROUND AND ROUND.

CHAPTER IX.

LAMBDA CHI.

A FEW weeks after the grand rush at Hamilton Park the two chums were sitting in their room one evening by their study lamp. Harry was just finishing a letter to his mother, as follows:

My Dear Mother:

Now we are all settled in our rooms on York Street at Mrs. Gimly's, and I may as well tell you exactly what is the routine of our daily life. We rise about seven. Mrs. Gimly rings a great bell in the hall, then we bathe, box a little, and dress, and go out to our eating club a little further down the street. At 7.45 o'clock we go to chapel, which is over in about twenty minutes. (It might be over sooner and not be missed.) Then from chapel we go immediately to recitation in the Athenæum—very comfortable wooden benches to sit on! This lasts an hour. Then we go to our rooms and study until 11.30, when we have our second recitation of an hour, then at one we dine. In the afternoon we go out and play ball at Hamilton Park or row on the harbor. At five is our third recitation of an hour, and at six we have supper. After supper we generally walk down to the post office, and perhaps play a game of billiards at Bill Noodle's. Then home and study, and bed about eleven. Saturday nights we have D. K., which keeps us up debating until twelve, sometimes. I'm told this system of recitation hours is the same for all classes. So good-by. Your loving son,

HARRY.

P. S. Please send me fifty dollars. I need it for—lots of things. Tell Kit to work me a slipper case for our room.

Stamp was lying with his head half out of his kennel and one eye open, blinking at his masters, who were grinding away over their Euclid and their Homer's Iliad; the clock had struck 10, then 10.30, then 11. "By Jove! I'm awful sleepy!" yawned Jack. "I can't work any more. I tell you what I'll do, Harry; I'll run down to Brood's or Gus Lager's with you and have something and then go to bed, or I'll go to bed now, or [laughingly] I'll go and get into the chapel and cut the bellows of the organ with you, or I'll——"

Harry did not finish, for Stamp uttered a low growl and began to sniff at a window.

"Hi, Stamp! lie down!" cried Jack. Stamp began to sniff again in the direction of one of the windows. He ran out of his box the length of his chain. At the same moment the sash was thrust up violently and, one after another, half a dozen masked men leaped into the room, holding ropes in their hands. A ladder had evidently been placed against the building, and Mrs. Ginly's faithful surveillance had been thus avoided. Harry jumped for the door quick as a flash, but one of the masked men was ahead of him and stood with his back against it.

"Freshmen! if you resist you will be instantly killed!" said the leader of the gang in a hollow voice, displaying a silver-mounted revolver. Jack answered, laughing: "Then let's die while fighting for liberty!" and he made a rush at the pistol holder and tore his mask off. Beneath his mask he had blackened his face—it was Caswell!

It was a hard tussle with the two wiry, strong young freshmen, but at last they were bound and gagged. They yelled and howled, but the sophs were too many for them. The other freshmen in the house thought it was only an ordinary rumpus with the gloves, which Jack and Harry and their friends were very frequently engaged in. Stamp's barking caused Thornton to wonder a little at the affair as he turned over in bed in the room above; so he got up and looked out of the window. Two hacks were standing in front of the boarding house. A ladder was placed against the house, and the light was streaming from Rives and Chestleton's open window. He could not understand this; he had no light, so he quietly opened his window, partly dressed, and leaned out.

Presently he observed three masked men come to the window bearing a figure muffled in a dark cloak. Two more came up from the hack, holding a ladder, and between them they slowly let down the muffled figure and deposited it in one of the hacks. Then followed another struggle at the window, and a second body was in like manner carried down and the whole party drove off. Thornton could hardly believe his eyes. He raised the cry "Lambda Chi! Lambda Chi! Umpty-four!" and other freshmen came running into the room. Thornton hustled on his clothes, and, shouting for the others to hurry after him, started out in the rain to follow the two hacks. They had, he saw, galloped away down York and up Elm. Thornton was after them on a dead run. He passed a boarding house in which were a dozen freshmen, most of them strong, stout young fellows, some of them up studying. He shouted up to the windows, never letting up, however, on his steady, swift stride:

"Lambda Chi! Lambda Chi! They've got Rives and Chestnuts [Harry's nickname] in a hack! Hurry up! Hurry up! For God's sake, hurry!"

Several freshmen rushed out into the street pell-mell, until there were some thirty strung along, following the sturdy pace of Thornton, who kept the two hacks in sight. For half an hour they kept up a steady jog.

The hacks reached Westville, a small hamlet at the foot of West Rock, where they stopped before a lager beer saloon and some of the men got out. Thornton came up a few minutes later in good shape, but he felt hardly able to cope with six or seven sophs and waited for the re-enforcements.

It was now raining in earnest. In a few moments several freshmen came running up. Thornton told two of them in a whisper to get up on the rear of the hack. He detailed another, Coles, a stout fellow, to slip around in the darkness and mount the hack in front as soon as it started off. Thornton's plan was to climb up over the back of the hack, knock the driver off his seat, and take the reins.

Presently off they started. Coles ran and succeeded in climbing on the rear axletree of the forward hack, which "Barney," a hackman who had often taken part in these student performances before, was driving. He was a stout, smiling, jolly Irishman, with a fat, good-natured face. Old Yale men remember "Barney"

very well, when he had the best "rig" and pair in New Haven
and used to stand out in front of the New Haven House and laugh

"BARNEY."

and joke with his soph friends. He scorned freshmen always, and
regarded juniors as too high toned. But he was always hand and
glove with the soph campaign committees of D. K., and he had in

his day stolen many a young "sub," and before he had done with
him seen that he was pledged "the right way"—to jolly Delta
Kap.

Inside the hacks the sophs, who had provided themselves with
bottles of whisky, began to get very noisy. Each party began to
sing and shout for Umpty-three and the glorious "Omega Lambda
Chi." The hacks rapidly drew out of Westville, followed the
main turnpike eastward for a mile or two, and then turned off to
the right. It looked very much as if the plan was to have the
initiation ceremonies of Lambda Chi on the top of West Rock.

When they reached a sandy hill Thornton, telling his two com-
rades to make as little noise as possible when he gave the signal to
"knock out" the driver, went ahead to assist Coles with the
stronger and more difficult Barney. Coles was ready for him, and
as the horses panted up the hill ran to their heads. Thornton
gave the signal, and leaping on the forward wheel grabbed the
astonished Barney by the collar and had him sprawling on the
ground before he knew where he was. Coles meanwhile had
quietly turned the horses around, and he and Thornton, grasping
the reins, drove off down the hill at a top gallop. The rear hack
was turned in the same way and came flying down the hill after
them.

Inside, the sophs, with their prisoners, kept up their drinking
and singing, and as it was now raining much harder they had the
windows up and were entirely ignorant of their capture. Thornton headed toward New Haven and soon met a large crowd of freshmen, who had been roused from their beds and had come out to
the rescue. They stopped the hacks and held a consultation.
What should they do with their prisoners? They formed a guard
around the hacks and opened the doors. "Now, fellers, tak 'em
(hic) out and let's do 'em. Barney, Bar-ney! Where's Barney,
fellers?" came in uncertain tones from the inmates, who thought
they were on the top of West Rock.

"Stay inside!" growled Thornton to the sophs, as he and his
freshmen friends helped Jack out and untied the cord that bound
his hands and feet. Others had taken out Harry, who was almost

suffocated with the handkerchief gag that was tied in his mouth. The sophs saw the game was up.

"What shall we do with them?" shouted Thornton. "Let's take a vote. All those in favor of Lambda Chi-ing the sophs say aye!"

"Aye!" came with one voice.

There were nine sophomores in all, and the task seemed on the whole too difficult. They then decided to drive in on the campus, and procure sufficient rope to tie the sophs to trees and leave them there all night. While they were in the midst of this discussion one of the sophomores—got away, and made a break for South Middle, where they were well aware he would rouse a rescue party as soon as possible. Most of the captured sophs were by this time half maudlin with bad liquor, and would be capable of no great resistance. The question was what to do with them during the night. Harry and Jack were each fierce to "put them through" in retaliation for the indignity of being dragged out of their rooms and bound and gagged. It was a fair capture, and the sophs were their lawful prey.

"Hoo-ray for Omega Lambda Chi!" shouted one of the sophs.

"Come on (hic), fellers, le's put 'em through, le's have everythin'. Hi! *Bar-nay!*"

It was the ex-Lambda Chi man of Umpty-three, Briggs, who escaped them, and they knew Briggs well enough to expect he would rouse the entire sophomore class and be back again in a hurry if they didn't get their prisoners away. It was therefore quickly decided to carry the sophs off to some out-of-the-way barn in the suburbs and stand guard over them till morning, and initiate them at their leisure on the following night.

CHAPTER X.

F course next day there was a tremendous stir in college over the absence of the eight sophs. The freshmen knew nothing about them, naturally, and the sophs had kept the "Lambda Chi-ing" of Harry and Jack such a secret that only those whom Briggs had roused from bed knew anything about it. But as the day wore on the most wild and exaggerated accounts of the whole affair spread like wildfire. The inflammable Lambda Chi Briggs got out a poster which he plastered over all the elms in the campus. Naturally they attracted considerable attention. But as everyone knew crazy old Briggs pretty well, they believed generally he had been "stuffed" by wicked juniors.

One thing was certain. That was that Caswell, Holland, Storrs, Stranahan, and four more sophs were not to be found in their rooms, nor had they been seen since the preceding night, when they were observed bargaining with "Barney," the hackman, in front of the New Haven House. Then the facts gradually leaked out. The upper-class men laughed and applauded the freshmen. "Served 'em right!" they said. Barney turned up late in the afternoon, very sore and angry, saying that "he'd get even with somebody some day."

Where were the sophomores?

The freshmen, not to be outdone, got out a counter poster in the afternoon, disclaiming all knowledge of their disappearance. It was delicately hinted that the sophs, disgusted at their defeat in the great rush, had driven themselves off the end of Long Wharf into New Haven harbor, or perhaps had debased themselves to such a degree as to apply for entrance to Harvard!

By nightfall every student outside the freshman class and many in it—to whom the secret of their hiding place was not known—were prowling about the outskirts of New Haven, peering into outhouses and barns, asking all manner of questions. Mrs. Gimly put on her bonnet and shawl and went across York Street to see Mrs. McGuiness.

" Did ye hear the news?" she asked, with a gleeful smile.

" Good-day, Mrs. Gimly. Do yez mane about thim bastes bein' suitable come up with?"

" I do. Them limbs o' Satan, Mr. Caswell, Mr. Holland, an' their pals—them softmoores."

" Have they been found yet? Bad luck to them for stealin' away two of yer best lodgers, Mrs. Gimly. Oh, Oi'm not fer sayin' it's not for the best, shure. Axe thim lodgers o' yourn ; they knows. Axe thim ; they can tell a thing or two. Arrah, byes 'll be byes ; they've the softmoores hid away."

" Where?"

" Did yez look in yer cellar, Mrs. Gimly?"

" My cellar?"

" Why fer no? P'r'aps they're there!"

Mrs. Gimly gave a cry of astonishment.

" Mrs. Gimly, Oi tell no lies ; 'twas me see arly this mornin'. Oi woke up an' me bid is forninst the windy in the garrit, an' Oi see two hacks druv up, an' Oi see in the strate lamplight, which they soon turned out—bad luck to 'em !—Oi see there was scufflin' and shovin' an' a fracas. At three o'clock this mornin'—shure—I thought I see them lift the cellar door—but it's in confidence Oi tell yez."

Mrs. Gimly then went, excitedly, flying back to her house as fast as her rheumatic old legs would carry her. She had a horror of sophomores, and the bare thought of their being locked up over night in her cellar, and being hid away there all day, naturally gave her the " shakes and shivers," as she said. She first frightened poor, pale, weak-eyed Samanthy out of her five wits by seizing her arm and whispering in her ear in a low hiss : " There's softmoores in the house!"

Samanthy nearly tottered against the door in a faint. The college chapel bell had just finished ringing for five o'clock recitations, and the house was as still as a church.

"What shall we do? What shall we do?" cried Samanthy, agonized.

"If it is so, it's a time for Professor Shepard, an' him alone," said her mother. "Oh, them limbs —to get into my cellar!"

She lit a candle and timorously made her way down the cellar stairs, and peered around in the darkness.

"Say—air you—there?" she asked.

Oh, unutterable horror! They heard from the further corner a stifled groan. Samanthy flew upstairs and locked herself in her room. In the dark corner of the cellar a dog growled r-r-r-r! It sounded like the ugly but efficient Stamp.

"LAMBDA CHI!"

Mrs. Gimly continued calling into the cellar, but to her repeated "Who be ye?" a feeble moan was the only response. She went back, and having lit a candle went down again. There, on some hay, lay five young men, securely bound with ropes. They were all sound asleep. At one side, guarding them, was Stamp. He seemed to regard Mrs. Gimly as a friend—the giver of former beef bones—and as he came forward wagged his tail in friendly recognition. "Land sakes!" cried Mrs. Gimly, "who be ye?"

No one answered.

Mrs. Gimly went upstairs to call Samanthy, but she was out. The freshmen were all at afternoon recitation. She saw Policeman McCrea across the way and hailed him.

"Come over, an' go in my cellar and turn them men loose!" she cried excitedly. "Them men, five on 'em, tied together an' hid away! Go right down, you, and find out who they be. I suspicion they be softmoores."

"What be I fer to go down an' be shot? I'm a N'Haven police for to do strate duty. Lave the cellar dure open, and wance they're in the strate Oi'll tak' 'em in fer burglary."

Mrs. Gimly returned and called, but Stamp was faithful to his trust. The first sophomore who moved received from him

POLICEMAN McCREA.

a low growl and a fierce snap. "Go up and get him a bone!" called out another soph sleepily. "I say, where are we, fellers?"

"In Mrs. Gimly's cellar," was Caswell's dry reply.

Just then Mrs. Gimly reappeared with a bone, and lured Stamp up outside and so into the house. It was the work of a few moments for Caswell to free himself, and then in turn to free his four friends.

" If we hadn't been—well, if we hadn't dallied too much with the wine cup and fooled too much over mixed drinks, we'd been all right," said Caswell ruefully.

When the sophs emerged from the cellar they presented a most miserable appearance. The clothes they wore were old and well-worn, but now they were in rags, and Caswell's sleeves were literally torn out at the armpits. Policeman McCrea promptly arrested them and hustled them along York Street toward Chapel.

" Where are you taking us, you infernal old loafer ? " bawled out Caswell, who jerked his arm free.

"Oi'm a-taking yez in ; thet's where. To the station-house yez go, and if yez go quiet, all right, but if yez is disorderly Oi'll bat yez all in the heads ; aye, an' carry yez in before the justice feet foremost."

It was, fortunately, during afternoon recitation hour, and there were no students present to see the sophs' discomfiture. They were now thoroughly roused to the situation, and had no idea of being arrested and "taken in." As they passed Library Street—a street leading down to the colleges—Caswell struck the " peeler " a ringing blow square in the left optic and shouted "Break away, boys ! " Each one of the five started in a different direction. Policeman McCrea stood up against the fence perfectly dazed. He wanted to run in five different directions, but did not seem to know how to accomplish it. Then he began to rap on the sidewalk with his "billy" for assistance. It was a laughable sight, and the crowd began to jeer him. Apparently he couldn't stand that, and so set out in chase of a soph up York Street. He had got as far as the D. K. E. Hall when he stopped, out of breath. By this time the sophs were all safely out of danger, and the great affair of the Omega Lambda Chi was over for that time.

CHAPTER XI.

UTUMN is apt to be clear, bracing, and generally delightful all along the pleasant Long Island Sound. There are few wet days after the "freshman rains," or "equinoctial storm" as others call it, which occur about the second week of the college year. October is a genial, mellow month, brimful of luscious fruit, wild grapes, and watermelons, and the air is just right for all sorts of outdoor life. There is a rich, smoky tone in the landscape across the long wide salt marshes. The nights are cool; the days inviting for long rambles in the woods.

A week later they elected Harry captain by about ten majority at the class meeting held in Tutor Smile's recitation rooms. The Andover "crowd" carried the class, as they generally do at Yale, and for several days Harry devoted himself to selecting a nine. The plan was to play a few games with other classes in the fall, and keep the nine in a sort of semi-training through the winter. Some time in June they played the Harvard freshmen, and the record showed that they very generally won. Jack Rives, who was accustomed to the water, had naturally taken to rowing at first. He was strong and plucky, and in the first freshman crew chosen for the fall races at Lake Saltonstall in the ensuing October. Men got on the crew then who afterward were never heard of on the water—clumsy men, thick-waisted men, with narrow chests and scarecrow backs, who never could pull their weight.

The freshmen crew always did well at Saltonstall, however, showing the effect of pure ambition triumphing over obstacles! It was before the days of the new boathouse, and the training had to be done from the old, barnlike structure near the steamboat wharf. The freshmen were taken in hand by Bob Clark, and their first row in the barge made most of them wish they had never indulged in any aquatic ambitions. They came home with sore hands and lame backs. Rowing was a terribly serious business with Bob. "Eyes in the boat there, freshmen!" "Now, all get together!" "Is this the best six men [they rowed sixes in those days] you've got? Why, you'll never move the boat over the first mile!" With that the poor freshmen would splash and splutter, and Bob would say in anguish: "I can call any six men in off the street who will do better than you!"

On one of these mellow, sweet October afternoons the college races took place at Lake Saltonstall. This is a dainty sheet of water a few miles to the eastward of New Haven. It is not two miles long, but it is set like a jewel in the wooded hills. Hither about noon on race day all the population of New Haven betook itself. It was in old days the Derby Day of New Haven. The dusty road was full of carriages and glittered with the bright gowns an sunshades of pretty girls.

In the fall and the spring this laughing, shouting, cheering migration to Saltonstall took place; the thousand students and their friends, their girls and mothers, aunts and sisters. On these days Yale was only aquatic. Everyone more or less "knowing" about "strokes" and sliding seats, which at the time we speak of were something new in America.

The battle betwixt the sophomores and the freshmen was now to be transferred from land to water, and the sophomores were, as usual, sure of carrying the big class race at Lake Saltonstall. They were rowing in good form in their barge over the waters of Quinippiac and the harbor, while every mothers' son of the freshmen, under Captain Clark, who was trying to coach them, rolled out of the boat. Of course they could not aspire to shell form, so they were to row in an old black barge called the *Black Maria*. It was a famous barge, however, and though old and very heavy, was built on capital lines, and when once got going (but there was the rub) was a hard boat to beat. It had belonged to the Yale navy from time immemorial.

Jack Rives went on the crew as No. 2. He had never been on any crew before, but he was used to the water. He knew how to row, he thought. He could "yank" an oar. He had rowed his sister about on the Hudson River. He had rowed, too, on the pretty little Adirondack Lake where his father had a "camp" every summer. He had fished and lived days on the water and could swim like a duck. Consequently he thought he knew everything there was to know about rowing. The freshman crew was a queer lot. Thornton, a tall, handsome, strong lad, with down on his chin, and modest blue eyes, pulled stroke. An old fellow over thirty years, solid and stiff as an ox, pulled No. 5. He wore a long red beard and his name was Grannis, from Kankakee, Ill. He had been a school-teacher in the far West. The sophs jeered at him as they rowed past in the harbor one day and called him "The Lone Fisherman." Grannis dug his oar in the water and grit his teeth. No. 4 was Bullock—a disappointment in the race. Bullock looked like a beautiful oarsman; he was well set up, broad backed, very muscular arms and legs; but he had no grit—he was a coward. He gave up at the slightest pumping.

Their bow oar was a tall, slim fellow, who had distinguished himself the summer before as one of the most graceful dancers at Newport. He could dance—and they found he could pull too. He was light and slender—a city-bred boy of rich New York parentage. He had shot up very tall at an early age; and he was chosen as being of the right size. De Koven was that rare combination—a great stickler for etiquette and good form, and yet at the same time plucky and full of the sublimest check. Such was the great freshman crew of Umpty-four! Long may its glory wave!

The "Gimly gang" on York Street hired three barouches and went out carrying long streaming banners with "Umpty-four, with a roar. Oh, we can down the sophomore!" on them.

They started off from York Street with a great flourish of horns.

The "sophomore crowd" started off on a stage coach and four from the fence corner just as the freshman hacks hove in sight.

Harry was driving the leading carriage. He whipped up, and coach and carriage tore rapidly down the wooden pavements of the incline of Chapel Street almost side by side, to the imminent peril of pedestrians and babes in arms.

"Run 'em down!" shouted Caswell angrily, from the top of the sophomore coach. "Blank their impudence! run 'em down!"

But, unfortunately for the coach, a heavy furniture van came across Chapel at Church Street, and it was compelled to pause in its mad career. Harry drove ahead, amid the shouts and cries of a large body of his classmates who were walking toward the depot to take the Shore Line train for the lake.

On the road out, for some distance past East Haven, on the hard, shelly roadbed, after they had crossed the drawbridge, they could hear the coaching party bounding along behind, tooting their horns and singing their Beta Xi and Theta Psi society songs. The freshmen kept the coach, which had come up, behind them by spreading out across the entire road side by side. Caswell and Holland were in a frightful rage over it. But the freshmen said nothing and sawed wood. To look at them one might have supposed they were on their way to church, or rather to a funeral, they walked along so slowly, and looked so solemn.

They kept everybody else behind, too. Seniors, driving out their "best girls"; parties of New Haven fashionables with coachmen and footmen in livery. Several professors were in the line, chafing at the unreasonable delay ahead. Professor Maynard drove his prim family out in a one-horse carryall, and wanted to be prompt at the lake in time to get a good place from which to see the races. But the freshmen were stubborn, and were bound not to let the soph coach get ahead if they could help it. Ridiculous enough this sounds to you, oh, business-bred reader! but student life is just thus ridiculous, and its free uproariousness and deviltry make it half what it is.

"Drive on there, you confounded greenhorns! You stupid freshmen! You impudent rascals!" How the sophs raved at them! It was awful; but the freshmen, being in the wrong, kept silent and answered not. They just sang calmly, sneeringly, and triumphantly,

> Oh, we meet to-night to celebrate
> Omega Lambda Chi !

Presently they came to a bend in the smooth shell road, and beyond it there was a long hill. It was Caswell's opportunity. He seized the reins from the driver and pried his way between Harry's and the middle carriage, taking the short cut of the angle. Harry had the better team, and he whipped up and got his horses running down the hill ahead of the coach. But Caswell had fire in his eye. He wanted to teach the freshmen a lesson. He tried his best to run them down. He didn't care if he tipped the coach over, not he.

At the foot of the hill, hearing the noise and seeing amid the dust the carriage and coach come dashing down the road in a deadly chase, an elderly lady ordered her coachman to drive to one side of the road, draw up, and let them pass. By the elderly lady's side, in the swell landau, was a very pretty girl, with blue ribbons on her hat; on the box, beside the coachman, a tall, gawky youth, who might have been a theologue, he looked so pale and thin and green.

Harry drove his team straight along the road, but the coach, having the greater momentum, and the horses being better and fresher, dashed between the landau drawn up at the side and the freshmen. Smash ! bang ! the landau was upset and the forward right wheel of the freshmen's hack came off and let them down all in a heap. The sophs laughed and jeered, and rode on. Harry threw the reins on the backs of his horses and ran to the landau. His first thought was, "By Jove, I believe that girl is killed !"

Fortunately no one was hurt. The freshmen helped the ladies out and set the poor, frightened young theologue on his feet. Fortunately the horses were staid old family coachers and had no idea of running.

"I demand instantly the arrest of that miscreant !" cried the elderly lady, pointing with her parasol at the wicked Caswell, who was rapidly disappearing down the road with his jeering friends in a cloud of dust. Harry bowed; he hardly knew what to say—what story to make up.

"Who was it, young man? Tell me his name!" shrieked the indignant old lady excitedly. She was dressed in rich black silk, a high bonnet, and wore a brooch of large and splendid diamonds. Harry glanced timidly at the young lady, who was engaged in brushing the dust off the elder lady with her handkerchief. Had he not seen her somewhere? He felt sure he had; she had a face which was not easily forgotten.

"His name was Dennis! He was a 'towny' from Bridgeport," he said. He wasn't going to let Caswell in for a faculty "scare." A crowd gathered. Some gentlemen—one of them had been pointed out to him as a distinguished New Haven lawyer—got out of their carriage and came forward. "My dear Miss Mulford, I trust no accident."

"Judge, it's a perfect outrage!"

"Ah?" He smiled pleasantly, rubbing his hands.

"I suppose you will call it merely a 'student's prank.' We have been upset, that's all. My niece, Judge Boompointer—Miss Hastings. A nice reception these Yale students have given to a Charmington girl. Eh, judge?"

"A Charmington girl! By Jove!" said Harry to himself. "She's the one I saw on the train—the very same!"

"I'm awful sorry about it. I'm afraid the coach horses were frightened," Harry said in a low voice to Miss Hastings.

"Oh! it's nothing at all. You were very kind to *stop* and help us."

What a sweet, frank, lovely, yet half sarcastic face she had! It was the same girl. It was the one in the train!

"But you will go on and see the races?"

"Oh, certainly! Why not?"

"And you'll—you will like to see us win?" It was a bold venture.

"Who are you?" She gave him an anxious glance.

"Why, Umpty-four."

"Oh! 'Umpty-four.' Certainly, companions in misery—victims of that horrid Mr. Dennis of Bridgeport!"

She looked at him knowingly and smiled.

"You know who it was?" he asked laughingly.

"Oh, everyone but aunt knows Mr. Caswell!" she laughed. "But I can keep a secret, too—I'm not going to 'peach.'"

"You know him?"

"I've danced a german with him. Don't you think he's very handsome?"

"Oh, very!" he said. "But he's no driver."

"No—he's no driver!" she laughed. "He has a 'cousin' at Charmington and goes up to see her quite often."

It was on the tip of his tongue to say: "I wish I had a cousin there," but the landau drove off and she gave him a bow and charming, quizzical smile. "Good-by, Umpty-four!" she laughed.

How he hated Caswell! How pert—yet beautiful she was! He gnashed his teeth! Poor Umpty-four, indeed!

He resolved to search out Miss Hastings among the carriages and junketing parties at the lake. Then the thought struck him: "Oh, Lord! I'm only a freshman! She won't look at me this year," and he heaved a deep sigh.

The long train of well-loaded cars had already arrived at Lake Saltonstall when the "Gimly gang" finally got there.

The whole scene was most beautiful; the colors of the flags and bright dresses along the shore; the spectacle of the boats and the cheering parties on the point. Across the lake, under a grove of venerable pines, a junketing party were already setting out beneath the trees an extensive "spread." There were a number of the New Haven "snab," * and Harry fancied he detected there amid a group the beautiful Miss Hastings. He felt an additional pang to see her surrounded by a number of good-looking juniors with real blond mustaches, one of whom he recognized to be Tom Bixby, who had treated him so cavalierly at the Delta Kap initiation. But now Jack and the crew demanded all his time and attention.

The freshman-soph-junior six-oared race was third on the pro-

---

* A college term for fashionable ladies and pretty girls.

gramme, and when he went into the boathouse the crew were gathered about Captain Bob Clark, of the 'varsity crew, who was stripped for the single sculls. Bob was perfectly free from bias and unfairness in boating matters. He counseled the freshmen with just as much squareness and honesty as if it were his own crew.

"We're going to give you two minutes' handicap," he said, "and you may win if you keep cool and pull in the boat, and keep your eyes on the man's back in front of you. Don't listen to the shouts on the point. There are 150 sophs there, and they'll try and make you catch crabs as you go by. You'd better put wax in your ears, as Ulysses did going past the sirens. You've got some good men in your crew. I've got my eye on you."

Here Bullock smiled, self-satisfiedly.

"You've got an old boat, but she's fast if you ever get her going. Stick to your stroke. Go easy. Don't get rattled and dig your oars in too deep. Don't lose form, and, whatever else you do, don't give up till you cross the line!"

No one rowed in the "buff"—the weather was a little too cool for this—and the white gauze shirts of the freshmen crew had huge "Umpty-fours" on their breasts in blue. Jack Rives was hard and wiry as hard training could make him. He looked rather unusually pale, however, and it made Harry nervous to look at him. The soph crew were out on the float watching the start of the pair-oared race. Presently everyone ran out but Jack.

"What's the matter, Jack?" asked Harry.

"Nothing."

"Yes, there is. What is it?"

"Oh, nothing."

"You're not feeling up to snuff."

"Well, look at my hand."

A painful felon had started in at the root of his thumb on his left hand.

"By Jove! you've kept it a secret."

Jack nodded.

"But you can't row."

"Can't I?"

"The pain will kill you."

"Well, let it!" And he laughed dismally.

"I thought you were not sleeping last night, and it was this thing that kept you awake?"

"Yes."

"Then it is simple cruelty to let you row." Harry started to go out of the door to confer with Captain Grannis.

"Stop, Harry, I'm going to row. I don't care if it kills me. But the fact is it doesn't hurt very much, and in the excitement of the race I shan't think anything about it. Please don't say anything. Coxswain Gifford says we're going to win on our handicap, and if we do—oh, glory!"

"Jack, I'm afraid you will have a frightful time of it."

"I don't mind."

"Jack——" Harry hesitated. "I'm awful sorry for you, but——"

"Well?"

"It isn't right—it isn't fair to the crew—to the class."

Jack Rives' eyes flashed indignantly.

"By Jove!" he cried, walking up to Harry, "do you think I'm not going to pull my heart out?"

Their eyes met. Jack's were blazing with wrath.

"That's just it, old man; you will be crazy with pain, and you will not pull right. You're sick now with this thing. You see my point; it isn't a square deal."

"But I will pull the harder—the stronger. Indeed I will."

Harry walked slowly out of the boathouse, and Jack whistled softly, "And the band played Annie Laurie." It was the first time that the two chums had ever really had a disagreement. Both said less than they felt. A little would have impelled Harry to utter words he would never have forgiven himself for afterward. He hardly knew what to do. Should he confer with Clark and Grannis? He went out and leaned against the boathouse a long time in silence. He wisely ended by trusting Jack, and said nothing.

The first race for pair oars was a one-sided affair, easily won by two seniors, who, after four years of rowing, were past masters of their craft. Then followed a close shell race between the "Sheffs" and the Law School. Then Bob Clark won his single-scull race hands down, beating the great McKinley of the junior class with ease. Then came the great race of the day. Harry stood by his "chum," said nothing, and rubbed his back with whisky, very silent and depressed. Jack's face was pale and determined. He chattered a good deal and cracked jokes, every now and then a twinge of pain shooting over his face. The sophs got into their light cedar barge and pulled prettily under Dobson's stroke and Farley at bow, with Jones, a senior, as coxswain. It was a splendid crew, very beefy and very confident. The fact was they were too confident, and were not trained down fine enough for a hot two-mile sprinting race. The juniors got out next in their light barge; they had a light crew with an ex-'varsity oar at stroke. They expected to "lay out" the freshmen, but practically conceded the race to the sophs.

The three crews lined up in the placid waters of the lake for a moment; then the referee shouted:

"Are you ready?"

Silence.

"Go!"

Of course the sophs jumped ahead in the first ten strokes. But what was the matter with the freshmen? They tore up the water like a steamboat, but the old *Black Maria* acted as if she was anchored. The juniors lapped the sophs up to past the point and then fell away. But see! The freshman boat has got going at last! Now watch her! Gifford's face is stern and set. He knows what he's about. He keeps in deep water and she gains on the other boats a little! Thornton is setting a beautiful regular clocklike stroke, and Bob Clark's keen, admiring eye is on him from a wherry. They near the point. Then the great Jim Danforth turns loose his pack of deep-baying freshman hounds.

"Umpty-four, Umpty-four! Whooper-up! Whooper-up! Rah-rah-rah! Rah-rah-rah!" There is a fearful din, and the dear old tub responds.

"Gee whizz! boys, how she goes!" cries Jim Danforth, knee deep in the lake. "She'll catch 'em yet. You see! Now, with a will! Whooper-up, Umpty-four! Rah-rah-rah!" etc., *ad nauseam.*

And the noise is so great one almost forgets the race. Once going, and once feeling she was in for a good race again, and seeming to hear the freshmen cries, the old barge responded to the oars like a thing of life. She never stopped. Her weight shoved her along. She neared the juniors; crept along, oar by oar; passed them; met the sophs at the stake; they were just turning, and here De Koven "let his jaw wag." His calm, easy, rattling tongue broke them all up. Where he got the wind no one ever knew. It was his pure, untrammeled "cheek," which was supreme in death (he fell over in a dead faint at the end of the race).

"Why—why, what's the matter in your boat, Dobson?" he asked. "Are you well? Here we are almost even with you in this old tub. Are you well, Dobson? Say, Farley, get out of the boat: you're not pulling your weight."

As they turned the stake Bullock cried out: "Oh, I can't row any farther—I'm done up!"

Gifford swore. "What?" he cried. "You loafer!"

"I'm done up—my heart troubles me!" cried Bullock peevishly.

"Well, keep up the motion at all events," shouted Gifford, "and don't put the crew out." Being on the port side, he was not obliged to do any pulling at all going round the stake, but hold his oar deep in the water.

"Throw some water over him, Rives."

Gifford had sent the boys along at a terrific pace, what with his "Now, then, let her go; you're gaining fast. You're sure of the race," etc.

He knew well enough the duties of a coxswain are always to encourage, never to tell a crew they are falling back.

On the home stretch they went slower, and barely kept ahead of the juniors. Gifford kept them at it, however, and the shouts on the bank did the rest. They crossed the line ahead of the juniors by six feet, winning the race from the sophs on their handicap allowance by fully forty seconds.   De Koven fainted, and Jack sat back very gritty and let his hand drop in the water. The crew were silent.   They felt that Bullock was a contemptible cur.   He came in fresh as a bird.   When they rowed up to the float Clark was there and half the freshman class.

"Rives," said the great captain, "you have one thing to learn. Never think you've got to pull the entire boat alone."

"By George!" laughed Gifford, highly pleased, "They all— all but—they all pulled like heroes."

THE RIDE HOME AFTER THE RACES.

"Get me some brandy, quick!" cried Jack, as they landed. "I'm dizzy, but don't mention it."

Harry had his flask ready, and Jack took a long swig.

He was himself again.   De Koven came to in a minute, and was soon all right.   In ten minutes the freshmen crew were all swimming about like corks in the water, conscious of all the glory of the afternoon.   They were the heroes of the day, and the ride home after the races, in the glowing mellow October light, was one long succession of shouts of triumph. How the girls smiled and applauded as they rowed past! As for Stamp—he barked himself hoarse. His cry sounded very much like "Humphty-four — Humphty-four—Whooper umph for Humphty-four!"

As they were coming home from the post office the next day, Jack's hand still being carried in a bandage, they happened to meet Captain Clark, who stopped and talked with them.

"You don't mean to say you rowed with a felon on your hand, Rives?"

Jack blushed a little.

"Why, man, you pulled harder than any man in your boat."

"So he did!" said Harry proudly.

The 'varsity captain whistled a lively air and turned on his heel. Then he called out: "See that you don't take cold in it, Rives. And by the way, come to my room in South Middle to-morrow night, will you? We are going to have a boating meeting."

"There," said Jack. "If I hadn't rowed, Harry, and nearly killed myself, I wouldn't have got that invitation."

He felt he was on the 'varsity crew from that hour, just as Harry believed he had a sure thing on the nine.

The first term of freshman year drew on to its end. Everyone in college but freshmen was busy getting ready for the Thanksgiving jubilee, which, though now obsolete, was at that time the successor of the Wooden Spoon Exhibition and a grand annual rumpus, tolerated by the faculty, at which all the jokes, the victories, defeats, and events of the college year were reviewed and caricatured on the stage. It began with minstrels and ended with a play.

But the poor freshmen had little heart, most of them, during those last weeks of their first term, for jubilees. They were glad enough for anything to enliven them. Jim Danforth went about with a long face, predicting that out of their class of 156 only a hundred would be left after the Christmas holidays. A freshman tutor by the name of Dilworthy had taken the entire charge of Danforth. Dilworthy was tutoring and at the same time attending the theological course with a view of ultimately becoming a clergyman in the up-country towns of Connecticut. He had one weakness—baseball. He couldn't play himself, but he loved to see the nine play; and he was tired of seeing them beaten by Harvard.

TUTOR DILWORTHY.

He watched Danforth, and made up his mind that he was one of the greatest baseball players that ever came to college. That settled it. He was his division officer, and although Jim flunked his Horace "dead," he kept getting the most amazing stand in Latin—a stand which brought him up in Greek and mathematics and carried him through the term. In fact Tutor Dilworthy had a soft heart for all disheartened freshmen. He was a queer, solitary, lonesome sort of man, and yet he was probably the most popular tutor in college, where tutors are usually so unpopular.

Twice a week he gave up an evening to about twenty low-stand freshmen. He called it his "fifth division." Those low-stand men! They studied very hard, too. But, as Tutor Dilworthy said, they were mostly "misfits." They had never begun right. The miserable "preparatory" system which they underwent—going from one boarding school to another, or getting private teaching from unworthy instructors, never getting the right kind of drill—brought them into college loathing all kinds of study.

It was less than a month now to the Christmas holidays, and the following night the Thanksgiving jubilee was to come off at Alumni Hall. There was but one recitation in review the next day, and it was a sort of "let up" night. Several freshmen dropped in, and they tossed up to see who should be sent out to work the "growler." The lot fell to Nevers, a jolly, good-natured little chap as ever drew breath. So good-natured that he was generally imposed upon.

"By Jove!" he said, "I hate to go out this cold, frosty night and leave that fire. Gad, fellows, *what a fire to roast a turkey!*"

"If we only had the turkey!" laughed Thornton from the lounge, where Stamp was lying, one eye open, his head on his master's lap.

"Turkey! I know a bank whereon wild turkeys grow—a turkey farm out by West Rock," said Jack quickly. "We used to run past it when Grannis took us on our four-mile trips in training. Gobble-obble-obble! They must be fat and tender now. Gobble-obble-obble!" He made their very mouths water.

"Ahem! Could you, me boy, could you lead me thither?" asked Coles facetiously.

"The owner is a crusty old farmer, and the farmer's big dog lay on the barn floor, and Bingo was his name, sir!" chimed in half a dozen others, admonishingly.

"Oh, Stamp here can chew the ears off any Bingo!" laughed Thornton.

It took only a little more talk to get Jack to say:

"If I could get three fellows—Bill Thornton, you, Harry—I want you, Coles—I'll get you two fat spring turkeys. Boys, we'll have a feast. Time! It's now nine o'clock. It's a two-mile run only to the turkey farm. Oh, if the old rascal makes any trouble, we'll buy them!   But, meanwhile, how would a lot of roast oysters go with turkey?

"You get the turkey, we'll provide the oysters!" volunteered Danforth.   "By Gad! I'll stop in and invite old Dilworthy. He'll come.   I'll make him bring his flute and he never need know where the turkeys came from."

"By all means !" laughed Jack, taking off his coat and vest for the long run out and back, and looking for his baseball shoes.

Harry went down to pacify Mrs. Gimly.

"Mrs. Gimly," he said, bowing to Samanthy, who was washing dishes at a sink in the next room ; "Mrs. Gimly, the fellows wanted me to give you this to buy yourself and Miss Samanthy a turkey Thanksgiving, and perhaps you won't mind our having a little supper to-night ?"

"Oh, no.   It's Thanksgiving time, an' of course——"

"We expect Tutor Dilworthy, and we may make a little noise, later on, ma'am."

"Oh, if the faculty is present, what is it to Samanthy an' me? We are not here to find fault with them.   An' if any tutor is with ye, I resign me charge."

Harry warned Mrs. Gimly that there might be a little extra ground and lofty tumbling too, and went back to the room and put on his running shoes, laughing heartily.

It was wicked, it was wrong—but it was Thanksgiving time. The butchers' shops had long since shut up, and turkeys could not be bought then.   Turkeys *must* be had to satisfy their sharp freshman appetites—and might not turkey be "crooked"?

CHAPTER XII

HARRY, Jack. Thornton, and Coles, four of the "cheekiest" toughest, smartest freshmen in Umpty-four, as Caswell said— Caswell was beginning to say very kind things of the freshmen—there were various vague rumors that the chief "sport" of Umpty-three was coming down in course of time—to mingle with them in the disagreeable curriculum of freshmen year) —out they trotted from Mrs. Gimly's freshman "Home" noiselessly, with that easy, loping gait that meant a long run. Along York Street to Elm, out Elm a long steady jog. The night was keen and cold and the moon seemed brighter than usual, making long clearly defined shadows beneath the leafless elms.

Thornton, tall and strong as an Indian, led them and they soon fell into line. People stopped and watched them. "Some crew a-training," they said. Harry ran next. He had an easy short stride which he could keep up, with short periods for meals, all day. Steady daily work in the old gym was doing our hero an immense amount of good. He had not an ounce too much. His skin was white and healthful, his eyes dancing with keen zest and excitement. Coles followed—puffing a little—he was not in as good condition as the others, but he had the heart and nerve of a veteran. He ran more carefully than the rest, saving himself as much as he could. Jack loafed along in the rear, enjoying the cool air and the charm of the *escapade.* How his heart beat! He knew that with Thornton along it meant, "Turkey or death!" Trot, trot, trot—on they go—I won't say *where* exactly (oh, present year freshmen, you may discover their route for yourselves!) past the little wooden houses of the outskirts of New Haven; past Hamden, a town of narrow size and at the time of most unsavory reputation—up a long, devious hill, where they pause and take breath; down again through a patch of woods, where the night owl screams to them as they silently run along the soft, sandy roadway.

" *You're* safe!" shouts exuberant Jack to them over his shoulder; "we're not out after owls!"

"Well—quit your *howls* then, and be quiet," cried Thornton, laughing, "for we'll be there in another mile!"

Trot—trot—again in silence, and Thornton stops a hundred yards this side of a farmhouse, near which stood a large barn, a long low whitewashed shed, and a number of outbuildings. The lights were not yet out in the farmhouse, and farmer Sniggins and his three tall sons were evidently sitting up late figuring out their profits for the approaching turkey season.

"Now," said Thornton, "there *was* a steal here last week"—and he looked at Coles, who leaned up against the fence to rest. "Yes—a steal—I don't mean to do that again, Coles."

Coles coughed dismally.

"I'm going to appropriate 'em this time."

"Exactly," said Jack, "they are contraband of war——"

"Well, I mean to leave a five-dollar bill pinned to the turkey-roost, for the first Sniggins who sees it. They can't lose anything then—and——"

"Why not try to buy them first, then?"

"Because I heard old Sniggins say himself that if he caught another o' them 'tarnation pesky students on his farm, he'd give him 'ticlar h—l, and fill his body with rock salt!'"

"Lord! do you suppose I'm going to run four miles for the fun of *buying* a turkey?" asked Jack. "Not much!"

"Well—I shall waste this fiver on them anyhow," and Thornton took out a greenback and rolled it up, as if ready for instant use.

"Now, boys; Harry and I'll do the appropriation act. Coles, you and Jack mount guard. They've got a couple of dogs, we'd all better get sticks. Bat the dogs over the head, if necessary. I don't want a dose of rock salt—but I don't believe they'll fire. If they do —rush in and grab the gun, boys, and then run in different directions—I'll manage one turkey sure—the farmers won't show fight; if they do, mind—rush in and upset them. It may be a sharp run; and we'll wait a few minutes, and get rested."

Just then they heard a loud "Bow—wow—wow—wow!" on the still night air.

"That's the Newfoundland, he won't bite," whispered Thornton, as they crept up near the house in the shadow of a picket fence. "He's only fooling!"

Then another dog began to bark.

"I guess they scent us," said Jack. "You will insist, Harry, on using such rank cologne! Tell me, will a dog's teeth go through corduroys?"

"You're scared already, Jack! I never heard anyone *pant* so in all my life!"

"Wait here," whispered Thornton cautiously. "I'll go in the yard and reconnoiter. Don't stir or make a sound, unless I whistle."

They saw Thornton advance across the moonlit yard and peer into the window. Then a black object came rushing around a corner, making a dead set for him, and on his way upsetting half a dozen milk pans which stood leaning against one another on the piazza. A terrible din followed. Thornton beat the dog off, and skipped around the corner just as the entire Sniggins family came out on the porch.

"Why, look at them pans!" cried a terrified female voice.

"It's thet new dog, mother; he's upsettin' everythin' lately!"

"Father—he's gone to git the gun!" said one of the Sniggins sons, a stalwart looking youth, as they could see, in the light of the doorway.

"Father, you put up that gun!" cried the female voice. "I aint goin' to hev no gun firin'—it's drefful dangerous, an' might go off an' kill us all."

An old man now appeared, holding a gun in his hand. "Ef it's anybody after them turkey critters," he said sadly, "I'm 'feared they'll git rocksalted—'cause this gun's loaded."

In the meantime it had occurred to Thornton, who had beaten off the dog, that by making a circuit of the house he could get into the turkey-roost under the shed before any active preparations were made to defend the objective point of their night visit. The same idea had occurred to Harry that no time should now be lost, as it was more than likely that the sons would, after their scare, go out and spend the night in the barn, in defense of turkey. He arranged with Coles and Jack to make a "diversion," as he called it, drawing off the attention of the Snigginses toward the road, while he skirted around and met Thornton at the further end of the shed where "King Gobble" was reposing.

"Oh, you want us to draw the rock salt our way, do you?" said Jack. "That's real kind of you!"

"Well, someone's got to suffer!" laughed Harry, "and we *must* have turkey, you know!"

Harry climbed the fence and ran like a deer in the shadows of some apple trees toward a carriage shed, into which, presently, they saw him disappear. The old man with the gun came out into the yard, apparently looking for game. Jack and Coles crouched close under some bushes which grew in a clump by the fence. "Sickem, Carlo—sickem!" he called to a dog. "Guess thaint no one around to-night!" yawned the old man, while his sons took seats on the steps as if waiting to see what "father was going to do about it."

Just then there rang out the most awful screeching and gobble-obble-obbling, on the night air; evidently King Gobble was making a desperate fight for life. The sons started for the barn, the old man after them with the gun.

"Now's the time for the 'diversion,'" cried Jack, rolling up his coat in imitation of a fat old cock, and imitating the turkey "gobble-obble-obble" capitally he started down the road in the same direction in which they had come. Coles chased after him, and the old farmer turned and let fly both barrels of rock salt in their direction. The sons came flying out at top speed, and Jack shouted to Coles to jump a low fence and hide at the first opportunity, as his blood was up and he intended to lead them a long chase around home to New Haven. It was well Coles followed this advice, as he felt that the hardy farmer's lads were gaining on him, every stride. Jack fresh from training was never in better trim for a long run, and he knew the roads which led back to town, which Coles did not. At a convenient ditch Coles ran wide, took a leap, and tumbled over a stone wall, down a bank into a pond of muddy water : there he crawled out on the bank, and waited as the farmer's lads ran by.

"Lord !" he cried, spitting the muddy water out of his mouth, " Wish we'd stood our ground and fought 'em." Coles, as a freshman, had more strength of arm than limb.

Somewhat less than an hour later, two turkey-laden freshmen emerged upon the road which led to West Rock, and so on into New Haven. Two fat king gobblers accompanied them.

" I say, Thorny, let's pick the confounded buzzard," said Harry. He was covered with mud and mire, and his face was flushed from the cold air and violent exercise. On his back he carried a fat bird weighing about fifteen pounds.

Thornton—Harry often remembered him afterward as he looked that night, so handsome in his bare head, his hair long and wavy, his face so boyishly brave and honest—Thornton said : " I'm glad I left that fiver. They'll get it in the morning—and I guess that's right for my bird and part of yours ! "

It was pure freshman honesty, reader—they *must* steal the turkeys, but yet the farmer should not suffer !

Getting near New Haven the boys took off their coats, and the King and his son the Prince were properly clad as they walked through Elm and York streets, even if their captors were not ! It was the work of a few moments, with kindly Samantha holding the lamp (it was now after ten o'clock), to scatter the black feathers all over Mrs. Gimly's yard ; and by the time the turkeys looked like fat babies ready for a bath, Coles showed up ; his face scratched, his clothes torn, and claiming he would not be obliged to use salt for a decade. Where was Jack?

"Why," said he, "I saw the last of the dear old boy as he started due west with two of those clodhoppers chasing after him down the road. He sang out to me to dive over a fence into a duck pond—and I did! Lord! how much of that salt mud did I swallow! You see, Chestnuts, we made a 'diversion' and you got the birds off safe, I see. Thunder! what big fellows!"

"And paid for too!" put in Samantha, holding the lamp.

"Cert!" said Harry.

"I hope Jack gave them a run for it—*we* had to gallop," said Thornton as he got rid of the last feather, "and it was no easy job to choke the birds—eh, Harry? How they did protest and object and ask for delay—they didn't die like true gentlemen at all!"

"The old man loaded and fired point-blank at us before we got into the woods," said Harry. "But I wish Jack was here—he may be in New York State by morning if he isn't careful."

"He was running away from them easily enough when I last saw him," said Coles. "And he knew the roads, so I'm not exactly worrying about him—still——"

"Who's here, upstairs?" they asked of Samanthy.

"Oh, Mr. Dilworthy has came," she said, "and there's lot's besides—and they do say that as for Mr. Caswell an' Mr. Holland, that they are dropped; yes, sir!"

"Dropped—into Umpty-four?"

"Yes, sir."

"Well, that's great! where did you get that news, Samanthy?"

"Why, ma she saw Professor Shepard in the street and he informed her—fer as she said as softmores they is unbearable, but as fresh gentlemen they aint so bad."

"Dropped—Cassy and Billy Holland! The faculty is getting awfully cheeky!" exclaimed Harry. "They're the big guns of Umpty-three."

"But they won't be in our class," said Thornton. "You'll see, they'll stay out. It's such an awful disgrace. I'd sooner be shot than drop out of Umpty-four. Think of dropping into space—for there isn't any Umpty-five, you know. Saving your presence, Samanthy—it isn't born, you know."

Samantha blushed.

"No, sir—it reely aint!" said Samantha. "Hee hee!"

The turkeys being now comfortably picked, and interestingly disemboweled, were ready, after a soaking in ice water, for their proper stuffing with sage dressing, preparatory to their roast before the fire upstairs when all was ready. The boys marched up bearing the turkeys aloft on platters and burst into a room full of freshmen—Tutor Dilworthy in their midst, and an atmosphere so dense with corncob pipe smoke that you could cut it with a hammer and chisel. Tutor Dilworthy had brought his flute, but he wasn't playing on it; no, that was reserved for after supper, when Jim Danforth intended to have "the greatest exhibition of musical and extemporaneous talent ever known in *Novo Portu,*" as he put it, "on any single occasion."

The turkeys were greeted with a great shout, and a "three times three." Danforth had got a big bushel basket of the finest oysters and no one but himself knew how many dozen of beer. "But—where—is—dear old—Jack?" cried Danforth, noticing that only three of the scouters had returned.

"On his way due west, will change keers at Albany," said Coles, laughing.

"Where did you see him last?" asked Jim anxiously.

"Why, as me an' de biler was a gwine up, I see him an' de smokestack a cumin' down," said Coles gravely. Whereupon Danforth pounced upon him, shook him, and they both rolled on the floor, Stamp snapping at Jim's ears in a highly amusing manner.

"O Jack—he'll turn up—this side up with care—he's safe—he's getting up his running, that's all—he'll lead 'em a dance!"

"Eh, what?" asked Tutor Dilworthy. "Is he in trouble?"

"Not the slightest, Tutor Dilworthy."

Although their beloved tutor was unlike any tutor ever at Yale before or since, and "unbended" among a few of his pupils whom he had begun to like, and really joined in their fun and became one of them, yet they under no circumstances were willing to let him know, of course, *in what manner exactly* they had purchased the King and the Prince of Turkeys.

"You see," said Harry, "Jack is anxious to get on the 'varsity crew next June, so he's begun training early—he runs every night—ten, twenty, sometimes thirty miles."

Tutor Dilworthy's eyes blinked. He couldn't believe it.

Little Nevers said, "Oh, I dare say Jack has slipped out to make a call on Prexy."

"I imagine he's putting on his dress suit ; he wants to appear in a costume befitting this august occasion," said another.

"Perhaps *he's* been dropped somewhere, like Billy Holland and Caswell."

"Are they dropped ? " Instantly there was a great hubbub.

"Their united stand only amounted to the sum total of 1.98," said Tutor Dilworthy with a grim smile.

"By Jove ! Let's welcome them into Umpty-four then—to-night ! " cried Danforth, as he ran a spit through King Gobble and hung him between two stools before the blazing fire.

"But poor Jack ! " said little Nevers, gazing out into the moonlit street, " where is he, *really ?* "

CHAPTER XIII.

THE TURKEY FEAST.

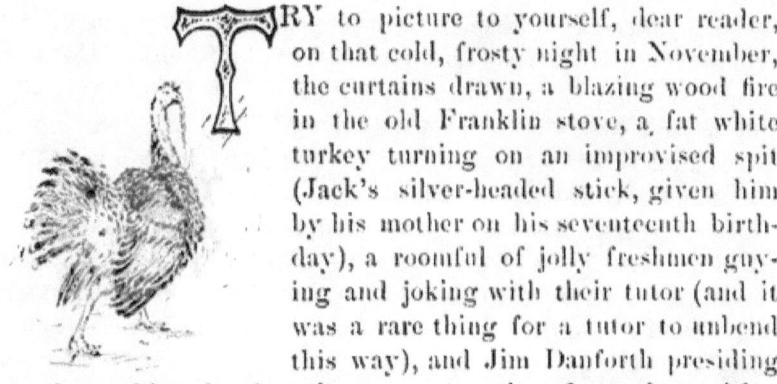

RY to picture to yourself, dear reader, on that cold, frosty night in November, the curtains drawn, a blazing wood fire in the old Franklin stove, a fat white turkey turning on an improvised spit (Jack's silver-headed stick, given him by his mother on his seventeenth birthday), a roomful of jolly freshmen guying and joking with their tutor (and it was a rare thing for a tutor to unbend this way), and Jim Danforth presiding over the cooking, basting the unctuous, crisp, fat turkey with a huge iron spoon borrowed from Samanthy (with many misgivings, doubtless, on her part); oysters roasting in the glowing coals; a dozen of beer on the table, and a box of cigars. Enter to these Caswell and Holland, bearing between them half a dozen magnums of Clicquot as a peace offering.

"Gentlemen," said Caswell, as he entered and the laughter subsided, "we meant to have taken you in to-night, but *diis aliter visum* (the only Latin I ever knew), you have taken us in. Holland and I are going to be with you next year. The faculty have dropped us!"

A subdued murmur followed, for to most present the announcement was no longer news. The faculty dared to drop the great Holland, the president of the D. K. campaign committee! How were the mighty fallen, indeed!

"Umpty-three is giving us her very tother best," said Danforth, "and we're proud to have you with us, though I must confess it won't—it won't seem at all natural not to have Mr. Caswell in the enemy's ranks."

"I shall wreak a full and hearty vengeance on Umpty-five," said Caswell earnestly, "for this wanton act of the faculty. However, let me say that you fellows are just my sort. It softens my fall to find myself landed with the 'Gimly gang.' "

"Hear! hear!" So loud and long that Mrs. Gimly's knock was heard. Harry hurried out and pacified her.

"Why," said Holland, as Harry returned, "your invitation to the turkey roast sort of gives me a turn, as the old lady said as she mounted her bicycle. It's mighty generous of you—particularly so, Mr. Thornton, as it came after you learned that we were dropped. By Jove! I was feeling blue, but this kind welcome of yours at this time comes home to me with a great deal of real, heartfelt—I don't know how to express myself."

There was a profound silence. Everyone felt very sorry for Holland, who had been so prominent and so popular in his class. Tutor Dilworthy said kindly: "There is one thing here at this pleasant affair, I think—we don't feel we belong to any particular class. I graduated some six years ago, but I feel like a freshman! I believe the true old Yale spirit of friendship is somewhere hiding about here. Um, um; I think I smell him!"

The fat turkey just then seemed to give out a specially delightful and delicious odor. "By the bye, how did you boys find such excellent turkeys? You are good judges, I dare say?" asked the tutor, innocently enough. No one gave the secret away, of course; but everyone knew he suspected. Presently Harry pronounced the turkey done. Thornton pronounced it done. Everyone gave his opinion, and it was pretty generally in the affirmative, for everyone was as hungry by this time as a Turk—for turkey.

"Now where is Jack?" roared Thornton, "I don't feel like eating without Jack!"

"Nor I," said little Nevers fearfully.

There came a thundering knock at the door. It was opened. Enter a really handsome girl, in blond wig, stylish hat, *gants de suède;* a roguish smile played on her pretty lips. She was dressed in the prevailing mode of the day, a high bustle which she wiggled coquetishly as she walked into the room, and smiled vivaciously on all assembled.

"Well, really, gentlemen," she said. "Aunt Gimly is letting her boarders do 'bout as they please—I *should think!* I've just come to town from Charmington, where I'm at school—ahem!— you know—to visit Cousin Samantha. I've only come down to spend a week. Miss Stout is *awfully* strict, you know—and I thought as you were all up here having a good time—don't you know—why—er—I'd just run up and join you!"

"That's right, Jack!" roared Harry.

"It's Jack in his jubilee suit he appears in to-morrow night!" laughed Nevers.

"Gentlemen! my name is not *Jack!* how *can* you? It's very mortifying to be called Jack among so many men! Oh, Mr. Caswell! I think you're so handsome! *All* the girls are crazy over you at Charmington; won't you just get fired (ahem!) and run up and see us again? And Mr. Holland? Well—really!"

"Oh, we're all Umpty-four men to-night!" laughed Holland.

"And—and Tutor Dilworthy! Oh! my long lost love!"

The girl tried to embrace him, then appeared about to faint. "Where am I?" she cried, falling into Coles' extended arms. "At a faculty meeting?"

At every one of Jack's sallies there were great roars of laughter and shouts of joy. Thornton helped the turkey, which was beautifully roasted, and Jack did the *cancan* on the table. What a dear girl he made! His features were very regular, and his eyes were large and handsome. Little Nevers fell in love with him forthwith, and declared that he should never be allowed to reassume his "original and only sex." He told them of his exciting adventures in his escape from the wrathful Snigginses, of daring leaps over ditches and stone walls, and how at last he doubled on them and got away. And what a feast they had! There were not enough plates to go around, but that did not matter. Some drank their champagne out of toothmugs, a few had glasses. Then came the roast oysters, and everyone talking at once, and two o'clock struck and no one knew it or cared; and Tutor Dilworthy sang a song, "Let every good fellow fill up his glass," and Caswell sang a song, and then everyone sang, but they voted the tutor's the best song of all.

At 3:30 A. M. they formed in a body, singing (oh, mortal insult to the juniors!) D. K. E. songs, and, pretending to be juniors, marched down on to the campus. Here Tutor Dilworthy, seized with a sudden spasm of conscience, disappeared utterly from their ken, and was seen to dart into the shadowy portals of Old South. So, with songs on the fence, ended at early cockcrow the famous Thanksgiving turkey feast of Umpty-four.

Oh, *stolen* joys of college life! How sweet they are *in esse* and in recollection! What jovial dreams come back to the old and enfeebled alumnus as he remembers the old times, the open Franklin stoves, the midnight feasts, the good fellowship, the dare-devil exploits, the rollicking fun, the jokes, and the perfect freedom from care, except as to that awful question which haunted like a "goblin grim" and made a hideous nightmare of freshman and sophomore years—"Am I below average?"

Ah, me! it is all very well for those who can sleep all day to keep up the racket all night, but to wake and hear the dreadful chapel bell ringing in one's ears, to hurry on one's clothes, to run for prayers at full speed for five minutes on an empty stomach—such was the cruel debt they had to pay to religion the next morning! If one cut, it was two marks ; if one was late, it was also two marks ; consequently no one was ever late at chapel. It amused Harry to see Tutor Dilworthy sitting grim and bolt upright in his seat as if he had not been eating turkey until two o'clock in the morning! But, oh, those long, dry, dismal morning prayers! The set phraseology, the quaint early English technique of theology, the dull appeals for grace in a shivering atmosphere, to a God who seemed for the moment extremely far away! The Bible reading of the prophets Isaiah, or Habakkuk, never listened to, never half heard by the five or six hundred students who are busy, heads down most of them, conning over their morning recitations. As between the question of losing his soul or his "stand" a college boy never hesitates. He is a worldling of worldlings, and to him there is no immediate hereafter. In the old days, in the old chapel, the seats were high-backed and favored casting hurried glances at text-books before recitation. We dare say all this is changed for the better now, and students really go to prayers to pray.

But why any chapel at all?

Perhaps in due time compulsory prayers will be relegated to the days of our Puritan ancestors when a man in New Haven never dared to kiss his wife of a Sunday! *Certes,* chapel prayers are no enjoyable affair to our freshmen with their swelled heads!

Of the absurdities of the Thanksgiving jubilee which took place in Alumni Hall the following night it will not be found advisable to speak until the later years of college life shall find our heroes upon the stage figuring in the grotesque melodramas which, interspersed with local hits, kept Yale students up laughing till all hours (in those days) prior to their departure for home. At this time it was the one annual outburst of wit and good fun—a good deal of it (it must be admitted) directed against the faculty and against unpopular professors and tutors. Thanksgiving jubilees at Yale are of the mighty past; they have followed the Wooden Spoon, the Burial of Euclid and Omega Lambda Chi into desuetude.

Then, next day after, came that pleasant four days of home. How delightful it was to swagger about in new clothes and (away from New Haven) sport a cane, and perhaps in stealth a beaver hat! Uncle Dick Lyman gave the boys a dinner at his club in New York and took them to see the beautiful Adelaide Neilson, then the reigning star in public favor. They returned to college and to study, with just a faint suspicion that there was a wider, greater life outside the university; but this suspicion hardly increased as time wore on.

The "little" life in college in the four years—how great and how large it seemed!

Of the hard month of study before the first-term examinations at

Christmas the less said the better. There was no desirable object in compelling the poor freshies to cram Euclid by heart, theorem, figures, and all. To Harry, who had a capital memory, it was perhaps an advantage, as he succeeded in memorizing his propositions so well that he obtained a very high mark on the examination.

CHAPTER XIV.

WHEN, after a jolly Christmas vacation in New York, they returned to college, Harry found that he had been elected to the honors of the second division. Jack was in the third, Danforth in the fourth, and Thornton, who took everything so easily, was in the first. The great event of Caswell's and Holland's fall from Umpty-three to Umpty-four had already become a nine-days' wonder, and the college had settled down into humdrum winter-term regularity, when a trifling little event happened which was to have a great effect upon our hero's after life in college.

Freshmen were at this time tabooed in New Haven. They were rarely invited out, being deemed in town as the college world deemed them—too raw for any social attention. De Garmo came up from New York and gave them dancing lessons once a week. They could dance with each other and whirl about, knocking knees, over the uneven floor of the dancing academy on Chapel Street, above a drug store, but further in social life they could not go. Harry and Jack knew a little about the art from their sisters. They despised dancing as "girly-girly" and silly. But one evening they found two invitations on their study table, one of which read as follows in printed writing :

"The company of Mr. Henry Chestleton, of Yale College, is hereby requested to attend the sixteenth annual cake walk of the Ebenezer Chapel Congregation of Free and Independent Colored Methodists, at the State House (basement), on Saturday, January 17, 18—, at 8 o'clock P. M."

Mrs. Gimly came up to say that a colored gentleman had called and left the "invites," and would call again later and collect twenty-five cents for each "invite."

MRS. MORIARTY.

"Shall we take in the cake walk?" said Jack, looking up rather blankly.

"Why not—by all means!" Harry laughed. "It's our first entrance into New Haven society. It may be the side door, but we must remember we are freshmen. Beggars must not be choosers!"

Thornton dropped in later in the evening and complained of an enormous and unsatisfied appetite, which one of Mrs. Moriarty's Welsh rarebits alone could vanquish. They put on their coats and sauntered down to the old-fashioned alehouse. About a table as they entered were seated half a dozen of their own class. It was quite true that Umpty-four had shown an immediate and apparently unquenchable fondness for Mrs. Moriarty's Bass and Burton. Mrs. Moriarty had been so far a mother to them, sympathizing and advising. She was always a kind mother to freshmen, often refusing a fourth mug of ale if she thought they had had enough. When the boys entered she was seated in her rocking chair behind the counter (wiped as clean as a plate), near the grate. She was in her clean calico frock and white apron, and looked tidy and neat as a Philadelphia Quakeress. Cook—pronounced Coook—a little dried-up Englishman, was seated at a table drinking, in a slow, leisurely way, a pint of 'alf and 'alf. Coook was a fixture at Mrs. Moriarty's, and there was a dim suspicion on the part of the students that he was "waitin' on" the genial widow, and was her "steady company."

"Are you going to take in the cake walk?" was the question on all sides. And every freshman present thought it would be a good joke to "black up" and attend in a body.

Presently in came Hetherington, "the Greek wonder," looking very feeble and old. He had hardly gotten over a week's spree. He sat down at the freshman table, bowing to everyone. He only seemed to be acquainted with freshmen. Hardly a man in the room but pitied him and looked down on him. Poor old Hetherington! His brain was still capable of great effort if well directed; but rum had so far "got him dead," as the freshmen whispered about one to the other, and his hand trembled as he raised his glass of Bass to his lips.

Here was a strong, able man, only thirty-three years old, going to the dogs—if he had not already gone. Harry looked at him pityingly. He and Hetherington had been good friends ever since that day at Brood's. He had been up twice in the boys' room in York Street and had told them long, interesting tales of Yale and her glories in the past. He had lasting reverences for the "great" and learned professors whose mortal frames rested in the old grave-yard near Center Congregational Church.

The freshmen sat about the round table—ten of them—and began with their "rabbits" and ale to get very noisy. Hodge, Dickson, and Brewer came in, seniors, with their awful glittering golden badges on their scarfs. Instantly there was a hush. The seniors were very great men. They seemed very important and old, older far than poor Hetherington, who sat silently leaning over his ale cup and looking solemnly down into the lees as if he saw there the dregs of his ill-spent life. His life was a lesson to those boys, but who received it ?

A night or two thereafter came the cake walk. Upper-class students might go out and dine with the New Haven nabobs on Temple and Elm streets ; yea, truly, and penetrate as far as the palaces of the rich and great on Hillhouse Avenue ; it was left for freshmen to shine at the great Ebenezer cake walk among the highest ornaments of colored society in the large empty hall beneath the old State House. Harry and Jack, well corked and wearing—as did many others—fantastic regalia hired for the occasion, presented their tickets in due form to a huge grinning darky in a dress suit, a sort of major domo, who stood at the door and bid each guest a hearty welcome. In the hall, when they arrived, there was already a crowd of fifty or sixty of "de bes' an' mos' refined cullud folk in de city," as a "cullud genman" informed them. A dozen dim lamps gave forth a dubious light, and in the semi-darkness the freshmen were not recognized. It was just a lark, and Thornton, who could do anything with his feet, executed a capital hornpipe for the delectation of the assembled guests before the walk began.

The spacious low-ceilinged hall was now getting to be crowded with colored brethren and sisters. A large barrel of cider at five cents a glass, with sandwiches for ten cents, stood on a counter on which was the enormous frosted raisin cake to be given to the winner of the cake walk. Jack and Harry walked about arm in arm, tried the cider, listened to the really good banjo music, and were attracted to one end of the hall near the darky band. Here, surrounded by a dense crowd, a showy, elegantly formed young negress was doing the sailor's hornpipe. Harry had never seen such dancing. It was a thing of art. He pressed through the crowd into the first rank, and the saucy *blue* eyes of the *danseuse* fastened upon him. She was very graceful, and Harry's admiration was clearly conveyed in the applause as she finished. She drew out a large yellow bandanna from her pocket and just touched her brow as she brushed by Harry, saying :

"Oh, go along ! Honey, you aint no nigger—sho ! "

"Nor are you ! " laughed Harry, "for I can see the white on your wrist."

The *danseuse* laughed very heartily. "We're just here for a lark. Three of us girls just blacked up and came along. Isn't it fun ! "

"You dance like a—fairy," said the lad, offering his arm.

"Oh, my sister is in the variety business. I may be, too, some day. She taught me. Come, there goes a waltz."

De Garmo had not yet perfected Harry in the waltz step, but he managed to do pretty well. It was not well enough for his "lady," however. She made him stop. "Oh, I'd rather walk ! " she said. Then, after a moment, she added : "Say, haven't I seen you up to the colleges ? I passed you one day. I don't forget faces. You were polite ; you took off your hat to me."

"Yes ; I remember now," said Harry.

"Oh, there's Mame and Minnie now," she laughed, pointing to two girls blacked as she was, who were talking to some students. Harry purposely led her away from her girl friends. He felt it was very wicked, but it seemed so pleasant to feel the girl's light, pretty hand resting on his arm. He felt a little thrill as she said :

"Say, I always liked you for taking off your hat that day. I've remembered it ever since."

" Have you ? "

" Yes ; and I've met you on Chapel Street four times, and you never looked at me ! "

Harry pretended not to hear this.

" Are you going to the Turn-verein next Thursday ? " she asked.

" The Turn-verein ?   What's that ? "

" The German ball."

" Well, I hadn't thought of it," said Harry, amused.

" Minnie and Mame are going and I guess I'll go if I can get my dress fixed.   I am going to have a new white muslin.   I've saved it out of my wages.   I only get five dollars a week, and I give mother three dollars, and that leaves two dollars, and oh, I have so many, many things I need.   I wish I had some new gloves for the ball.   I don't see how I can go."

" How much would they cost ? " asked Harry.

" Two dollars ; but I can get them at the store for $1.63."

Harry slipped a two-dollar bill into her hand.

" Oh, no, I can't accept it from a stranger."

" Why, *I'm* not a stranger, am I ? "

" Will you come to the ball ? "

" Yes."

" And dance with me ? "

" Yes."

" Say, what is your name ?   Oh, I think students are awful nice ! "

" My name is Wilkins.   I'm in Umpty-two—a junior, you know."

" Are you going to walk ? "

" No."

" Yes, do ; that's what we came for. Mame and Minnie are going to."

" Oh, well, I don't care, if you walk with me."

Blacked as she was he could see how graceful and pretty the girl was, and what beautiful hair she had.   He remembered the pretty shop girl now very well.   It was she who threw him a saucy kiss that first morning when he was out on the campus conning his Vergil. How long ago it seemed! And she had borne him in mind ever since! After all, what harm would ever come of a little fun with this pretty shop girl?

Before the evening was over he had promised absolutely to attend the German ball of the Turn-verein. He had done more; as he was evidently not a good dancer he had agreed to call at Ella's house, in the outskirts of New Haven, and she and Mame and Minnie would give him a few lessons.

That cake walk! He hardly cared what was going on. His head was in a whirl. He thought he wouldn't tell Jack, who kept hanging around and obtruding in the way, waiting for an introduction. He and the pretty Ella got some applause, but the cake went to two tall *bona-fide* darkies, a "Villikins and his Dinah"— "Villikins" was an influential deacon in the Ebenezer Church. Jack and his freshmen pals in some way got hold of Mame and Minnie, and before the evening was over Ella was introduced all around, and the Turn-verein was generally discussed. Harry was not the only freshman who agreed to be on hand at the German ball. Evidently Umpty-four was not destined to be entirely kept out of all "society" in freshman year!

The Turn-verein ball came off, and the boys had attended it in due form. They danced with Miss Frankenstein, Miss Himmeldeiner, Miss Rosenheimer, Miss Doppleschin and the Misses Gerhart, "Mame," Ella, and Minnie. "Mame" was Ella's sister. "Minnie" was a Miss Hansen. There had been plenty of beer downstairs, but everything had been very respectable and well conducted. There was no doubt at all in the minds of all the freshmen that Ella was the prettiest girl in the ballroom. In her white dress stylishly cut, her pretty ribbons, her long gloves with seven buttons, Harry had fairly lost his heart over her. He felt a strange amusement in the society of the pretty girl. She was very bright, rather gay, yet innocent. Harry amused Jack by his account of the Gerhart *ménage* in their little house in the suburbs.

"The night I went up there to call on Ella," he said, "she introduced me to her father, a horny-handed old inventor, with the head and brow of Jove. I take it the old man is a sort of an ex-machinist. You know those fellows are always inventing something. Mother Gerhart is a large, good-looking German woman, with fine eyes. Ella gets her eyes from her mother. They are very poor. But they go to one of the most 'stylish' churches in New Haven, they say, and the girls dress—don't they? —very nicely. When I called the old man had been working at his apparatus—something in electricity he told me. His hands were all greasy, but he didn't hesitate to shake. A funny thing was Ella saw it and blushed a bright red, while I coyly wiped my hand on my handkerchief. Ella seems so afraid that I will observe the evidences of their poverty. She's a great girl; she's got a good voice, and how fond they are of dancing! Even the old man, Jack; he is six feet high and a huge, kindly old fellow, well read in his native tongue, quotes Faust at you and Schiller; he plays the violin and mamma plays the old rattley piano. It is a family that has seen better days—in Berlin. Everything in the house is as neat as wax."

"Oh, by the way," interrupted Jack, "you were writing to your mother to-night. Did you—of course you told her all about the cake walk, the Turn-verein, and the pleasing Gerhart family?"

Harry looked up.

"I confess I have grave twinges of conscience, but yet Ella is a very nice, honest girl; and as long as I am not especially in love with her——"

"Oh, of course then I would not mention her!" laughed Jack.

"Did you write to General Rives about it all?"

"Why, no; the governor would probably imagine all sorts of things."

"Why, so would my mother."

"People at home are always so eager to jump to conclusions," laughed Jack. "Now, how it would sound if they heard all the facts!"

"Why, I consider it one of the reasons why a man ought never go to college in a place where his family lives. There are so many things——"

"Yes, so many things, ahem!"

"Things which are nothing in themselves but jokes, fun, part of the life here. You don't want our turkey episode blazoned out in print, eh?"

"No, nor our sign steals. By the way, that gold tooth hanging out of that dentist's shop on the corner of York and Elm—I will own that golden tooth some day, shan't I, Stamp, old man, eh?"

The dog looked up and winked knowingly.

"But about this girl. I've asked Ella to go to the 'theayter,' as she calls it, next Saturday night. Lydia Thompson, you know——"

"O Harry! don't. Everyone will be there and will see you!"

"By Jove, I'm not ashamed to be seen with Ella Gerhart!" Harry spoke with some heat. "Besides to her—I'm Wilkins!"

"Well, she is hardly in the set we will hope to be in eventually, is she?"

"I don't care," replied Harry doggedly. "I'm going to take her."

Jack was by this time undressed and in bed. He said nothing and went off gently to sleep, as Harry sat up in the glow of the fire and excused himself for his growing infatuation for the beautiful shop girl.

Winter term, with its Junior Promenade—the swellest ball of the year—passed so rapidly that Easter vacation came upon them with almost a sudden surprise. There was so much to do—the recitations, the lectures, the outside fun, the balls—they went to four—the "shows," the midnight escapades, the rows with the sophs, which gradually died out in fury as the year progressed. When they came back for the spring or summer term Harry was in the third division; he had dropped from his lofty perch in the second, and the two chums were together—he hadn't devoted much time to his studies.

"Ah," said Jack, "it is all that Ella Gerhart—give her up, Harry."

Harry drew himself up rather stiffly.

"She is one of the most innocent girls in the world," he said. "Besides, she will be a great help to me in my German."

Jack said nothing, but as he was going over to the "gym" for a row on the weights (he and Thornton were getting up a capital freshman crew to meet Harvard in July), he merely whistled incredulously and went out. After Jack had gone a buggy drove up to Mrs. Gimly's with a fast-looking nag. Harry muffled himself up in his great ulster, for the day was rather raw and "springy," and went down and got in. The livery-stable boy handed him a little bill. "Fifty-seven dollars!" Harry cried, amazed. "Why, this is an outrage!"

"Well, it's them 'acks fer them balls is included, sir, an' they's at least ten buggies, sir."

And the stable boy winked.

Harry drove off indignantly. He turned down Elm and out Whitney Avenue. Who is that tall, pretty young girl in red ribbons waiting on the path so expectantly? Ah, what a charming complexion! She is rather stylishly dressed, too. She has little feet and little white hands, ungloved. Our hero gets out and gallantly helps her in, and they drive away together into the sandy lanes toward Lake Whitney. She is very happy. She laughs and "giggles." She has implicit trust—and rightly, for is not Harry one of the finest fellows in all Yale College? A half hour later, if one could see them, along a side lane, the horse is walking and her pretty head has fallen upon his shoulder.

"And will you always—*always*—love me as you do now, Mr. Wilkins?" (Faintly.)

"Always; but of course you know——"

"Oh, crickets! Look at that cow! That's bad luck, sure!"

A cow crossed their track. Pretty Ella Gerhart sat up very straight and refused to be comforted. There were tears of anticipated calamity in her fine blue eyes.

"You're not afraid of a cow, Ella?"

"No, but it's a sign. Oh, Mr. Wilkins! you don't *really* care for me."

"I swear I——"

"No, I aint one of your kind. I know it. I ought never to have met you. I ought never to see you again. Never! never!" and she burst into tears.

He took her in his arms and kissed her, and the buggy drew out of the long winding lane into the highroad. They trotted home in time for his afternoon recitation, at which Harry made a dead flunk. He would do anything for that girl, he thought. Once or twice the crazy idea entered his boyish mind that he would leave college and marry her!

CHAPTER XV.

AS spring drew on Harry soon had his afternoons well taken up with his freshman nine. He practiced them every day at running, throwing, and batting. One day the "university" played them a practice game of five innings and had a remarkably difficult time hitting his pitching. Big Guthrie and huge Murdoch each fanned the air twice! It was in the early days, when an overhand throw was first allowed. Captain Harding, after fouling twice, hit a feeble grounder to short and was easily thrown out. The freshmen almost won the game, the score being 3–4.

An old ballplayer, who had played and pitched years ago on the Boston Excelsiors, taught Harry to pitch and to try some curves and "in-shoots" of his own device. When throwing came in Harry followed up his teaching and could curve a ball so that it was almost impossible to hit it. He could not explain it himself. He called it a "knack." Captain Harding had wanted at the first organization of the 'varsity nine to put Harry on with Jim Danforth, but upper-class politics at first prevailed.

One Saturday afternoon, fortunately, Curtis was ill and could not play. It was to be a practice game against the Amherst nine.

Danforth had been urging Harding to try Harry in the pitcher's box.

"Try him, Captain Harding," said Jim. "I tell you he can curve a ball so that no one can hit it. Give him a chance. The time has gone by when we can hope to beat Harvard by main strength and hard swearing."

"I'll think of it," replied Harding, and that afternoon he told Harry he could play in the Amherst game.

So it happened that Harry, who had played shortstop at Andover and had really pitched only one or two games before he came to college, thus became a college pitcher. The Amherst nine was a good one that year, but it could do nothing with him. Harry struck out thirteen men during the game and was allowed to pitch the entire nine innings. Yale won, 14–3. The college papers came out and praised him very highly after that day. He was getting his hand in and putting on new "twists," as they called them then. Danforth coached him.

"O Dan!" said Harry one day, "if we could put our freshman battery in the university nine!"

"Wait another year," said Danforth gloomily.

Meanwhile the days grew on into May and the summer term began in earnest. Somehow the various recitations seemed to grow easier, the whole college appeared to relax its tension, to grow more fond of amusement, to spend its time outdoors. The long looked for day arrived when freshmen were allowed to wear beavers, and there was in the Andover crowd a swell dinner in consequence at Gradley's. There were thirty fresh gentlemen present. The early part of the dinner was conducted with remarkable decorum; but the iced champagne was very seductive. Jack, really for the first time, quite lost his head. There were speeches commemorative of the occasion, and Jack could do nothing but sing and dance a ballet accompaniment. On the way home the freshmen marched up and "sung" before all the ladies' seminaries of the city and sang discordantly, too, all the old, old college songs. There were the usual signs of commotion at upper-window blinds. A candle was lit, a few flowers were dropped out of a window and eagerly seized by the uproarious students. Those midnight serenades at the seminaries, what terrible exhibitions of student singing they were! Yet how well rewarded! "Upidee," "When Freshmen First We Came to Yale," "Lauriger Horatius," "Nelly Was a Lady," all the time-honored songs howled with a champagny fervor, yelled at the top of their young vociferous lungs, always meeting with the never-failing appreciative response from the fair inmates! Perhaps they were well disposed in favor of the night howlers. The "fem sems," as they were called, evidently required a very moderate standard of musical ability in their student admirers.

Then came, too, in May the election into the sophomore societies. Harry and Jack were elected into Delta Beta Xi, while Thornton and Coles went to Phi Theta Psi. There was at this time about as much difference in relative rank of the two soph societies as there is between tweedle-dum and tweedle-dee. They have since met an untimely death by judicial decree. The tremendous secrets which were hidden beneath the Greek letters shall never be revealed by this pen! Nor shall the grip be divulged, nor the terrific initiation, nor the sacred penates be dragged forth into the light of common day.

Alas, these societies only exist now in their songs!

> " By fell decree
> Of Facultee,
> They are no more,
> Oh, Sophomore !"

The sensation of spring term in boating circles was the return of Ad or "Bob" Clark, as he was familiarly called, with the English stroke "in his pocket." He had spent three months in England, coached by boating celebrities of the London Rowing Club and by old 'varsity oars at Oxford. It was really to be an event in American rowing annals. The new stroke was said to be a novelty and to introduce a new principle. College boating affairs were at such a low ebb (even little Williams pushed the nose of her shell ahead of Yale the year previous at Springfield) that Clark was at once empowered to select his own crew and to test the new stroke for all it was worth. There were plenty of detractors and plenty of "kickers," but Clark fed and grew fat on adverse criticism. He got together a crew which would obey him absolutely. In fact he compelled them to obey him by first thrashing each member of the crew. Then he went to work teaching them the intricate English stroke. His perseverance was marvelous. The crew learned his stroke in less time than any crew had ever "got together" before. There were no coxswains in those days and the crews were composed of six, with the bow oar doing all the steering with his feet. Such was the general distrust in college, however, that the freshmen were put in the hands of Hamm, a professional trainer from Pittsburgh. Bob Clark said nothing, however, and even his enemies and detractors admired his quiet pluck.

The two crews, 'varsity and freshman, went to their training table about the middle of May. In those days—days so far back, oh, undergrad, that they date before the days of the new boathouse—the barnlike structure across the street fence, the steamboat wharf near the bridge, had only two lofts in use. In the upper loft were stored the antiquated boats of the old Yale navy. High on a beam was nailed the name of the first raceboat owned by Yale in 1843, called *Pioneer*, Yale, No. 1 ; near it was the outline of the old Yale boat *Excelsior*, which won many a race from the New Haven oystermen in the early fifties. In those days they rowed from Sachem's Head to the old wharf at New Haven. The shape of the old eight-oared *Shawmut* and a cut framed in oak hung near a dusty window. The *Shawmut* had stern-sheets for six passengers, and the captain's seat at the extreme stern of the boat was elevated above the gunwale, so that he could overlook the heads of his crew and spur them on to victory. There was a picture also of the *Osceola*, of eight oars and thirty-six feet long, which raced from the year 1847 to 1853. The picture of the *Augusta*, another eight-oared craft, contained beneath its frame a short and simple history.* The boat was clinker-built, of red cedar with boxwood ribs, copper fastened, and cost when new three hundred dollars, but was sold to '52 for a supper. She was wrecked one windy afternoon in 1853 off Crane's Bar while being towed with a load of straw toward the shore of Fort Hale, where the crew, dressed in white togas and with garlands of flowers on their heads, were intending to offer her as a burnt sacrifice to Neptune.

The old boathouse had no modern arrangements for "showers," and it was the custom of the crews (hardy young rascals) to jump

---

* For which we are indebted to Mr. Bagg's "Four Years at Yale."

into the salt, brackish water off the float after rowing, as early as March. It never seemed to hurt them. On clumsy racks were hung the 'varsity six-oared shells, of the "shell period" from 1864 to 1870, and the revered craft of '65 and '66, used by the famous "Wilbur Bacon" crews of those years, warped now and out of shape. At one side were some further old cuts and memorabilia on the walls. Among them an account of the "Prize Regatta of '56, the prize an elegant boat lantern." The distance was three miles, and the *Transit* covered it in 21m. 12s., with the *Nereid* second in 22m. 4s., the *Nautilus* and *Wa-Wa* third and fourth. The *Transit* was of the scientific school, with six oars only. There were several old regatta posters in frames of those old times "afo' de wah," when races of sharpies, rowboats, and all manner and kind of craft enlivened an afternoon on New Haven harbor. Near by hung a list of old raceboats, commencing with the *Atlanta*, 1850 ; the *Excelsior*, 1852 (six-oared) ; the *Shawmut*, the *Phantom* (five-oared),* the *Halcyon* (eight-oared), purchased from Harvard, and the *Undine*. In those pleasant old days (our grandmothers remember them) "the devotees of Mercury had boats consisting of forty feet of quarter-inch plank, brought together at each end, carrying nothing but the crew and two boat hooks, gliding swiftly past with their ambitious load. The claims of Venus are not to be despised, however, and the broad, velvet-cushioned, prettily painted barges of the earlier day go struggling after, laden down to the water's edge with their fair burden of New Haven's fairest."

This marked a vast change in the sport of College boat racing, *i.e.*, when ladies ceased to be admitted to the race barge !—and the race became not a thing of pleasure but a stern struggle for glory and *prestige*.

By the middle of May boating life was well started. Clark went ding-dong at his 'varsity crew, introducing several new little points of coaching they had taught him at Oxford. He took them far up the Quinnipiac, "far from the madding" crowd of student

* From a list in the *Yale Literary Magazine* of June, 1857. The writer adds: "That larboard bowsman must have been a Hercules !"

and town onlookers, who used to congregate on the old bridge and criticise the crew as Clark stroked them out around the oyster stakes and so on up the river. The crew did not look promising, and the rowing wiseacres shook their heads.

"We're trusting a good deal to Clark and his new-fangled ideas," they said. The fact that Yale was a "tail ender" the year previous was one reason why Clark was allowed more freedom of action than he otherwise would have had.

CHAPTER XVI.

 SUMMER days were drawing on apace. Harry was very busy with his freshman nine and Jack with his crew. Harry pitched several games on the 'varsity nine, but so far wicked upper-class favoritism prevented his becoming the regular college pitcher. Danforth kept gaining steadily in favor, as the fine plays he made at second base were often what the reporters called phenomenal.

The event of importance about this time was the giving out sopho. society elections. Freshmen were expected to set up a spread to their upper-class friends in their rooms. The Gimly gang combined together to make a bowl of very deadly punch for the sophs, and as well to set up cigars and ice cream. The ingredients were suggested by Nevers, whose mild and benevolent purpose was to repay the sophs fort heir trouble by enabling them to get very drunk on mighty little liquid.

He meditated a punch consisting of a bottle of brandy, a bottle of whisky, a bottle of gin, and a bottle of champagne, no water, one lemon, and a cake of ice!

"See here," protested Jack, who was now in strict training, "we don't want all of Delta Beta Xi and Theta Psi roosting with us all night! Why, they'll never be able to get out in the street alive, man!"

Jack was pledged to Phi Theta Psi, owing to an "accident," as he called it. The chums could have gone either way they chose. But Bixby had got him to pledge his way. "It wasn't a pledge exactly," said Jack, "but I'm not going to ask him to let me back out. I'm awfully sorry. Harry, we'll still stick together sophomore year."

Harry, who was feeding Stamp dog biscuit, looked at his chum a moment.

"No, I want to room across the way with David Alum and 'Aunt Sarah.'"

"You know Davy and she are now already well on in senior year studies and contemplate entering the theological school and taking up Hebrew next year. Why, the young dig is all brains and horn buttons. He'll be a somebody some day, when you and I, Harry, are merely trying to live within our income."

"Oh, I know better! Valedictorians always use themselves up in college and are good for nothing else afterward. I am very thankful that I'm not one of them."

"No—ahem! There would be no more strolls with pretty Ella Gerhart, eh?"

"Ella is a good girl."

"I saw her at the ball game last Saturday with Brown; she watched you pitch as a cat does a mouse. She seemed so proud of you, Harry. Has she forgiven you for parading under the name of Wilkins, yet?" Harry reddened.

"She comes out there very often—with her sisters, sometimes."

"I know. Going in, Granniss and I were together. We met Ella. I introduced him. He was awfully taken with her. She's a great coquette. She saw he was mashed on her, and she used her fine eyes with great effect. Look out, Harry, he'll cut you out!"

"Granniss is such a great, good fellow I should be sorry; he's so in earnest."

Jack went to the window.

"Then, even if I am Theta Psi and you Beta Xi, we'll stick together, eh?"

"Yes, Jack."

"And you still—you still love me?"

"Yes, Jack. I love you *still*," replied Harry earnestly.

Out of the purest fondness for each other, the liking the one had learned to have for the other's good qualities, they put on the gloves and sparred a couple of rounds. They were pretty evenly matched and were quick on their feet, dodging, feinting, striking, and retreating. When they got well warmed up they didn't seem to notice how much noise they were making. Chairs went over, the lamp fell with a crash—it was nothing. At it they went, hammer and tongs, in friendly desire to make the other "quit" first. There came a knock at the door, but they paid no attention to that. The knock came louder, but Jack merely called "Come in, if you dare," and sailed in with his left, catching Harry under the chin, when——

Holy Moses!

The door opened, and Professor Shepard, *in persona non gratissima*, stood there, umbrella in hand, thunderstruck.

It was never the way of the faculty in those days to pass over anything lightly, to be amused at the dazed attitudes of the two boys, to pretend that it was all proper enough. No, indeed! It was *de rigueur* to show rigor. Professor Shepard secretly was enjoying the spectacle immensely, but his outward manner was all censorious in a high degree. He frowned, and turned to Mrs. Gimly, who was standing behind him.

"She's been to see him at last!" said Jack, and he hurriedly slipped off his boxing gloves.

"This is study hour," observed Professor Shepard grimly, in the doorway. "I was passing and I thought I heard a noise; it sounded like a thrashing machine—like two thrashing machines. Rives and your roommate, Chestleton, must report to me at my study—you know where my house is—next Thursday, at 6 P. M. I will see what can be done—er—come prepared to take tea and spend the evening—er—er."

With that Professor Shepard hastily departed. They thought they heard him chuckling as he went downstairs.

Jack sank back on a chair. "Well, you may knock me down with a feather!" he laughed.

Mrs. Gimly came running up again as soon as the kindly old

professor had gone. "Now don't go for to lay no blame on *me*," she said anxiously. "I didn't fetch him in, though the good Lord knows I has occasions. No, I don't mind your thumpin' now. The long vacatin's soon a-comin' an' I won't hear no sound then —and it'll be lonely for the poor widder and her orphing child. An' if he expels you both you can't say as I done it, Mr. Rives or

THE DOOR OPENED, AND PROFESSOR SHEPARD STOOD THERE.

Mr. Chestleton, for, as Samanthy says, you've acted as gentlemen should, payin' your way like honest young gentlemen, an' I haint had no reason to find fault with you ever."

This was a long speech for Mrs. Gimly, and Harry, knowing she feared exposure as to her methods of extorting money from her lodgers, immediately put on a long face.

"We are summoned to Professor Shepard's study next Thursday," he said, "and he'll ask us, and we'll have to tell everything."

"Oh, don't be the ruin of a poor widder and a fatherless orphing! Don't tell Professor Shepard!"

"What do you think, about what do you judge, we ought to be paid for our silence; eh, Harry?"

Jack put his boxing gloves on the nail over the mantel where they belonged, and turned to conceal his laughter.

"I should judge it was worth about ten dollars," said Harry soberly.

"Oh, gentlemen, gentlemen, I haven't the money! I'm a poor lone widder as keeps boarders, though it's a hard life an' full of thumpin's overhead and noise, except when ye are at recitation or asleep mostly."

"In consideration, Mrs. Gimly, of your being a ' widder,' and in consideration of Samanthy, we will remit the ten dollars on your agreement, no matter *what* we do, *never* to go and tell Professor Shepard."

"Indeed I will not. Indeed, sir——" Mrs. Gimly rose. They each shook her hand by way of league and covenant, and she went downstairs a sadder if not a wiser woman.

So it was with feelings somewhat relieved that the "Gimly gang" prepared to receive their sophomore friends on "election night," the day following. Mrs. Gimly did not come up to ask for even a reasonable degree of quiet. She it was who now feared Professor Shepard's awful discipline! The tables were turned, and Nevers proceeded to compound his fearful "combination" punch to bring confusion upon the hated sophomores, without a qualm. It was the custom at that time for Beta Xi and Theta Psi, with their soph thirty, headed by a big headlight lantern (Diogenes searching for an honest man !) to search out the freshmen, as it were, and finding them (with all preparations and a bowl of punch, cigars, or a basket of champagne in readiness) "at their studies," to confer upon them the glorious election to the soph societies.

As the classes averaged then about 125, and not more than 40 were elected in each society—about the same number that entered Phi U and D. K. E. in junior year—it was not considered in college a very great privilege to get in, but an outrage to be kept *out* of a sophomore or junior society.

Almost all the freshmen congregated in Harry's large room, awaiting the onset. Nevers had had some assistance in concocting his punch, and one or two freshmen were already very talkative. A large china bowl, with a cake of ice in it, occupied the table in the center of the room. On closer observation the cake of ice was seen to be floating in a dark amber colored liquid. As the punch gave out Nevers and Steele stood ready to replenish it out of a tin canister. It meant very little to Harry and Jack, who were in training. Each tasted a little of the stuff, and Jack suggested an addition of a bottle of Jamaica ginger.

Then, as always with the modern student of an American college, where two or three are gathered, the talk fell upon the prospects in baseball and boating. Everyone in the room said it was a shame that Harry was not allowed to pitch on the 'varsity as a regular thing. Jim Danforth, who, amid all the crowd and the smoke, was poring (poor fellow, he worked hard enough to stay in) over a Jevons "Logic" in one corner, called out :

"If he pitches I'm going to catch, and where would Harvard be ?"

"Seven runs ahead on the last half of the ninth !" laughed Jack.

Dan returned to his "Logic."

Presently they heard in the distance—it was now about ten o'clock :

Phi Theta Psi ! Caw ! Caw !
And oh! Phi Theta Psi !
    Most glorious band
    In all our land
Is, oh ! Phi Theta Psi !

How the fine song reverberated up the empty street under the elms ! What a thrill it brought to our freshmen, waiting behind their redoubts of punch and cigars !

Then up the street in the opposite direction came another chorus :

> And Theta Psi had better hence,
>   Do da, do da ;
> For Beta Xi has got the fence,
>   Do da, do da day !
> Oh, we're bound to sing all night,
>   We're bound to sing all day,
> The glories of our Beta Xi.
>   Forever and for aye !

Then the tramp, tramp of many heavy feet. Thornton and Jack looked out, and then everyone was pell-mell at the windows. They saw two great locomotive lamps approaching.

"Here they come, boys !" cried Thornton, "both singing—and there ought to be a fight, but there won't, because rows are only between classes."

They heard cries of " Put out that light, freshie !" and presently both societies were gathered on the sidewalk before the Gimly house.

The leaders and some of the others were in fantastic outlandish costumes, high-pointed white hats and masquerading in long coats and knee-breeches. The red-haired Theta Psi leader was in a long duster, and seemed to tower high above all the rest. Each society was singing its song at the top of its lungs and trying to smother the other. There was, however, no scuffling among them, and only a friendly rivalry. But night was made hideous enough with the combined efforts and stentorian lungs of the valiant sophomores.

Presently the committees of each society ran up, singled out their freshmen, gave them their election in as formal a manner as possible and a hearty grasp of the hand. Then the fun began. The doors were opened and about sixty men came tumbling upstairs. They had already visited several freshmen dens and were in a pretty fairly " happy " condition.

Coles and Nevers ladled out the punch in tin cups and goblets, and the innocent "sophies," and not a few juniors, began to feel very happy. They hugged each other, hugged freshmen, and swarmed all over the house. When Thornton went up to bed that night he found Simpkins, a junior, asleep on his bed. When awakened he begged that Thornton would not write a letter home about it, and Thornton made him very unhappy by telling him that the faculty had concluded to expel him instanter. The effect of the punch was to first render them foolish and then completely idiotic. There ceased to be any class distinctions—freshmen hugged and danced with juniors and shouted for Beta Xi and Theta Psi with the utmost desire to do the square thing by each. When things were very mellow with Beta Xi and the first supply of the Gimly punch was getting in its deadly work, D. K. E.'s crowd came booming and singing up the street. Nevers renewed his punch bowl and made ready for D. K. E.'s attack on it. On they came, their leader dressed up in a high white hat, a long veil, and linen duster. They had captured a bass drum somewhere and had no hesitation in beating the terrible thing right into the house and up the stairs. Mrs. Gimly's feeble protest could be heard above the din, "Gentlemen—please less noise!" Such *was* student life, dear mothers and sisters, and we would draw a veil over the jovial scene in Harry's room, and shed a gentle tear!

When Jack thought they had had enough of it he started the cry of "Faculty! faculty!" but not with the result that he expected, for the sophs, and juniors who were old hands at the game, dove, most of them, into the bedrooms and under the bed. Jack's little 6x10 room must have held fully twenty fellows, packed sideways, lengthwise, under the bed and on it. Harry's room was made a retreat for as many more. A few jumped out of the second story windows upon the soft flower beds of Samanthy's geraniums. Gradually order was restored out of chaos, and the two rival societies—half the members were already *hors de combat*—proceeded in some sort of array to give out further elections down the street.

High up in her window, looking out upon the noise and confusion, sat "Aunt Sarah" with her nephew, David Alum. The two societies passed their house without a recognition. There may have been a secret longing on the part of Miss Alum to join in the fray and be "one of the boys," but David looked down upon it all with supreme contempt. "I cannot understand their paucity of intellect. They have so little brains that they are willing to let them be 'stolen' away without a protest. Oh, why will students forget their privileges in this great institution and devote their valuable time to these tomfooleries?"

"I suppose it's a part of college life, and always has been."

"Then in the New Yale, that is to be, I hope the custom of these annual sprees will be abolished."

"I fear the new Yale will be different," sighed Aunt Sarah, "but boys will always be boys. David, I—I wish you were given an election. I—I think it's a perfect shame. David, I could cry."

"I am supremely indifferent. But I will let them hear from me yet. I intend to take every first-class honor at Yale from this time forth!"

"Davy, Davy, don't be too sure! Sometimes I wish that you would smoke."

"Smoke? Waste my time over tobacco and cigars? My, aunt! what can you be thinking of? I have a future and a name to make. You know we are poor. Would you have me like these fellows howling like dogs along the street?"

"Well, I wish you had more knowledge of the world."

"I live in the ancient world."

"But we are with the present."

"I'm not. I glory in the fact that I am a contemporary of Plato. That is the era when I *would* have lived! Ah, those glorious days!"

"Yes. They drank in those days, too."

David moved away a little.

"Those feasts of Venus, David!"

David colored. "Very natural times of festivity. Times of mirth. They were not gross. Look out and hear them sing! Beta Xi and Theta Psi, foolish societies for foolish boys to waste their foolish time. The faculty ought to abolish all this sort of thing. It's absurd, it's costly, it's—it's——"

A knock at the door. Enter a sophomore, not intoxicated, who with a businesslike dispatch says :

"Mr. Alum, I offer you an election to Delta Beta Xi. Do you accept ? "

Aunt Sarah jumped to her feet. "Yes!" she cried, delighted, before David could get the words out of his mouth. "Certainly he will."

"I'm sorry an election cannot be offered to you, Miss Alum," said the sophomore dryly. "Then I understand your nephew accepts? Beta Xi always has the valedictorian."

"Well," said David, flattered by the election. "I—I think it's very foolish, but I accept gladly ! "

TEA at Professor Shepard's! An honor indeed! Long before six o'clock arrived that day Harry stood before his glass tying and retying his scarf, and troubled with the problem whether he should wear a high collar or a turn down. Jack, on the other hand, was off with his crew on the harbor and ought to have been back by this. Here it was a quarter of six, and Professor Shepard, like all the old professors who felt their daily life to be an exemplar for student imitation, was most exceeding "prompt" always. On the stroke of six Harry well knew that Professor Shepard would be seated at his supper table, surrounded by his numerous boys, asking the blessing. He was all ready now, brushed and feeling very fine in his new light gray summer suit. He leaned out of the window. The beautiful elms of York Street drooped gracefully over an approaching horse car, out of which Jack leaped, clad in his boating blazer, cap, and blue shirt.

"Hurry up, Jack! I've got your togs all ready."

Jack looked up, smiled, and dove into Mrs. Gimly's front door and almost knocked that good lady flat against the wall.

"Oh, Mr. Rives, you aint a-goin' to tell Professor Shepard about them presents to me?"

Poor woman! She had hardly slept all night by reason of her fears. She actually trembled before him.

"No," said Jack. "But it's understood that you won't say anything about us in future, eh?"

"A quieter set of young fresh gentlemen never had rooms in my house, Mr. Rives. Oh, you never make no noise that me and Samanthy ever notices, and aint a circumstance to Mr. Caswell an' Mr. Holland a year ago. No, sir, Mr. Rives."

Jack sent Harry on ahead to "hold the supper for him," as he expressed it, and followed ten minutes later, apologizing to Professor Shepard and his wife for his tardiness. The old white house with its tall Grecian portico and its mathematically arranged flower beds bordered with box in front—can any old Yale man forget the quaint old New England home, with the great drooping elms on either side of the brick walk? The family of ruddy sons, half of whom were at the time progressing in the various classes through the academic department, was enlivened by the presence of a Miss Walker, of whom the boys had often heard vaguely as being considered a great flirt, and as being very beautiful. Indeed, Uncle Dick Lyman had spoken of her as being a great flirt in his day, and wondering if she was married yet.

Miss Walker was a capital talker, and she seemed to know better than anyone everything that went on in college affairs.

"You remember, Miss Walker, Dingley of '63?" asked the professor, stirring his tea and taking a bite of the thin, the very thin, bread and butter.

"Dingley? Oh, yes, indeed."

Miss Walker had been engaged to Dingley, though doubtless Professor Shepard had forgotten it, and no one else at the table was familiar with the circumstance.

"Do you know what Dingley is doing now?" asked the professor.

Miss Walker pretended to think the remark was not addressed to her.

"Do you know Dingley is going to be the next United States Senator from Colorado?" continued the professor.

Visions, swift as light, entered her brain. She thought once she had really loved Dingley of '63. But then came Blanchard of '67, and Thomaston of '68, and she thought she loved them, too, at the time.

But now strangely there came over her the thought of what her career might have been with Dingley. It would have been fine to shine in Washington society as "Mrs. Senator Dingley." Swift visions (poor soul!) came to her before she spoke of the way she parted from Dingley. He had gone to the war, and before he returned she was engaged to Frank Blanchard of '67. Dingley, broken hearted, went West, in order to grow up with the country. He had never married. The professor, with the forgetfulness of the niceties common to elderly men, went on harping about Dingley and praising him to the skies, as college professors always do when an alumnus succeeds in life and they wish to show their fatherly interest in him.

"Why, Dingley was a sort of numskull in college," he said, "and we never thought he would ever amount to anything. It makes me feel unsafe in predicting much about college boys. There hasn't been a valedictorian who has done very much; but there have been many surprises among the low-stand men. They seem to wake up later in life. Their brains are not developed in college. There's Dr. Blaisted—a perfect little fool in college, getting into scrapes all the while and being dropped once for low stand—he is to-day at the head of his profession in New York; think of it, a perfect little fool!"

"Would you advise a man in college to be rather foolish in order to amount to something afterward?" asked Harry, with a jocular intention.

"No! You boys never need try to make fools of yourselves!" At which all at the table laughed.

"In your experience of students, Miss Walker—[how she hated him for that word!]—don't you think that nature does that for them?"

"I'm sure I don't know. Men in college seem very much alike to me. I don't think I distinguish the wise from the foolish very much—and if I do I prefer the fools."

"And so that's the reason for your telling me you like fresh men," laughed Jack.

She gave him a quick, motherly little glance. Jack was handsomely tanned, and his eyes were as clear and bright as months of training could make them. He had felt the charm of Miss Walker's manner at once (she knew what the college genus liked, and it had been her life study), and his admiration betrayed itself in his glance. "I must say I dislike the solemn, intense young man," she continued—"the young man with what are called 'high hopes and high ambitions.' He is to me very much of a bore. He gets these 'high ambitions' off at you as if they were something new and original. Ten to one, if he aspires very much in college, he ends by the flattest kind of a failure in life. I believe things go by opposites. The men who are always attitudinizing in college and talking about their future 'careers,' and who are solemn and struggle and all that, are very apt to get too greatly discouraged later on. I would tell a college man to enjoy the college life to its utmost, in spite of all the faculty can do to prevent him!"

This was a dig at the professor, and he replied, with a laugh: "Miss Walker! You're a pessimist, a cynic, and an enemy of good conduct!"

"I am not!" she replied. "But if I went through college to-day I would have a good time and make warm friends, and I would snap my fingers at the faculty!"

"Hear! hear!" cried the professor's sons, laughing also.

The professor said: "Why all this cry against the faculty? Sometimes I pick up the *Yale Lit.* and read the dreadfully 'wise' fulminations and critiques directed against the faculty by students who imagine they know better than we do how to run the old college. It makes me positively amused. They accuse us of every known crime, but particularly of being behind the age and of having backwoods, up-country Congregational clergymen as our trustees. One would think that old Yale wasn't good enough for the present generation—of vipers," he added laughingly. "Do we want to become a mere business institution without a moral character, without a soul, without a high purpose to develop character as well as intelligence?"

"Oh, I think it's your duty to let character alone," said the eldest son. "The German universities do."

"Well, thank God, we are not going to pattern after Göttingen and Berlin! Just see the freedom we give to you students. You can go and come as you please, provided you go to chapel and attend recitations; we give you absolute freedom, and how do you behave? You build bonfires on the stone porch of the chapel, you tear up the fence, whole sections at a time, you break into tutors' rooms and daub them all over with red paint! A nice set of young scoundrels you students are and always have been!" he laughed. "And what could we do with you, if it were not for our summary discipline once in a while? It's all very well to talk about not having anything to do with character or conduct and devoting our time to your boy brains, as the Germans do. But what would become of us if we did? In three weeks there would not be a brick left in the chapel. You'd raze it to the ground. Long experience has taught me to distrust you. At this very moment Jack Rives here is planning to steal the college Bible out of the pulpit, just as his father did before him!"

"Did he? Oh, tell us about it!" cried Jack eagerly. He was only too glad to have what he called a "pointer" on his dad.

"We were classmates back in '41," said Professor Shepard, helping himself to a third cup of tea, which his beaming but silent wife in her pretty lace cap had handed him from behind her rampart of tea things, "and for out-and-out rascals Tom Rives was—well, he was almost as bad as I myself!"

"Oh, professor!" protested his wife, who was always horrified at these college reminiscences, which were the delight of her husband to tell.

"At that time we had chapel twice a day, and prayers were four times as long as they are now. Then we had two sessions of church on Sunday, besides chapel, all of which were compulsory, in addition to a prayer meeting in the evening, which, while not exactly compulsory, was understood to be incumbent on all to attend. Ambitious young seniors used sometimes to make use of these prayer meetings to cultivate extemporaneous oratory, I regret to say, and they used to introduce all sorts of topics, I remember —even politics and international questions.

"Well, Tom Rives got it into his head one Sunday that there was too much church going in the college. He thought that the faculty ought to be contented with one prayer and one church on Sunday, just as you young men think now there ought to be no prayers and no church on Sunday. You see we have had 'Young Yale' in the past to contend with, just as we have them now; if you give them an inch they will take an ell. Your father got it into his head that if he could give the faculty a hint—a strong hint—about the matter it might have some effect. So he set his wits to work. Now, at that time good old President Day used to preach about an hour and a half in the morning and an hour in the afternoon. A great many people attended service in the morning, and it was at that time that the choir did their best, and made the old chapel ring with their hallelujah anthems.

"Those who remember President Day's sermons—and those of us are getting few who do—remember very well how fond he was of bringing in the Angel Gabriel and the last trump toward the end of his sermon. He worked in Gabriel and his trump as a climax, and pictured to our terrified ears the awful day—"*dies iræ, dies illa, solvet sæclum in favilla.*" Few of his great efforts but contained a description of Gabriel. Tom Rives knew very well that he could count on the good old man's bringing it in somewhere in his sermon, and especially the sermon just before closing college for the then three or four weeks' vacation, when the occasion was very solemnly taken advantage of to warn departing students of the perils of the outside world.

"I well remember that Sunday. It was one of those mild, warm December days when the fires in the great stoves which used to stand at either end of the chapel made the interior so warm that they opened several windows to the south to let in the air. Now, as you well know, North Middle stands in the old brick row just south of the chapel. Tom Rives was then in the choir. The pulpit was very high in the old chapel and came nearly up to the choir loft at the other end of the church. Well, the sermon neared its end, and we were all expecting the Angel Gabriel to appear as usual with his trump, when, just as President Day—he had a terrible voice, it rings in my ears to this day—reached his climax and shouted out, 'Suppose the Angel Gabriel should appear *now*. *Now* would he sound his last trump to a dozing, sleeping audience!' Well, just at that point, by all that is true, the angel *did* appear! Yes, I remember rubbing my eyes, it was so sudden, and then an involuntary laugh went through the five hundred students and everyone in church. About midway between pulpit and choir hung a full-blown angel marked 'Gabriel' holding a card which said on one side, 'This is my last trump,' and on the other, 'There will be no more chapel now!'

"Tom had given the signal to his confederate from inside and the effigy of Gabriel had been swiftly pulled in through the open window on a fish line which ran over a pulley fastened in the opposite pillar of the gallery. The effect was very startling. A lady—the mother of a boy in college, who had come on to visit him —shrieked out, 'Save me, save me!' and fainted dead away. They couldn't reach the line to cut the thing down and there it swung, facing President Day—a great red face, goggle eyes, and a yellow wig—the worst-looking angel you ever conceived of. Your father sat up there in the gallery as innocent as any lamb. You see, his confederate—a fellow who pretended to be sick that Sunday— worked the line from outside when he gave the signal. The faculty were terribly indignant. They examined every man in the two lower classes, but Tom was never found out. Ah, your father, Mr. Rives, was a very great rascal, sir, in college—as he was a great fighter afterward in the war. I shall never forget that Angel Gabriel and his last trump card. The whole thing came in so pat. The idea was that there would be at least one pleasant feature connected with Gabriel's coming—*no more chapel!* "

The professor laughed heartily over this reminiscence, and all rose and went out on the portico beneath the high white pillars.

"Miss Walker, you must remember a great many of those old-time jokes?"

But Miss Walker, on Jack's arm, had swept with a graceful motion toward the farther end of the piazza and was out of hearing.

CHAPTER XVIII

THE BASEBALL MATCH.

I DON'T see how you dared sit off there so long alone with Miss Walker," said Harry, as they walked home from Professor Shepard's around by the fence and the colleges half an hour or so later.

"Why, how old do you suppose she is?"

"About twenty-nine."

"No; only twenty-five, that's not very old. Harry, I never knew any girl seem to understand a fellow as she does. I think she's one of the finest women I ever met."

Jack spoke with a serious air, and Harry concurred with him also seriously.

"Of course I haven't met many yet," pursued Jack. "But Miss Walker, I wish I knew what her first name was. She said that there was something about me so—so different from other college men."

"It must have been your *sang-froid*, commonly known as cheek," said Harry. "Few men have it in such quantity."

"Oh, but father must have been a very devil!" and Jack whistled and laughed, then whistled again. "I asked Miss Walker if she knew him in college!"

"What a break! you put your foot in it!"

"She rides horseback. I wish our confounded crew was not in training. She is coming out to see us row."

Harry laughed a little.

"She knew Hetherington. She said he was one of the most famous men of his day. He had taken the *Lit.* medal and the Deforest medal, and was, while in college, famous for his Greek

157

recitations. She gave a little sigh as she spoke of Hetherington." Jack found out long afterward that the "Greek wonder" was on her numerous list of rejected suitors.

Not having as yet any fence on which to roost, the freshmen were in the habit of gathering in front of the gymnasium on Library Street. Here, on their way home, the boys found a number of their classmates gathered about Jim Danforth, who, as soon as he saw Harry coming, gave a great shout: "Hi—hi—hi—the 'varsity pitcher!" and ran forward and grasped his hand.

"We've got it! You're to pitch in Saturday's game!" he cried. "It's all fixed; Harding has just been here looking for you, old man."

"Is that so? Is it so—honest?"

"Yes."

Harding sent for Harry next day after morning recitation, around to his room in the top story, north entry, of Farnam Hall. Harry ran up the circular wooden stairway two steps at a time. Harding's room was on the south side of the entry, facing the campus. As he knocked and entered the 'varsity captain was leaning out of his window, talking to someone on the ground below. Harry stood a moment, waiting for him to turn around. The four walls of the room were covered with oars, flags, pictures of famous boxers, and old baseballs, gilded and hung up on strings, with the names of the various nines from which they were won painted on them in black letters.

Harry gave a slight cough, as he found that he himself was the topic of conversation. Harding turned around.

"Oh, Chestleton, it's you. Sit down. I've decided to let you try your funny business on Harvard. They think someone else is going to pitch, and I want it kept quiet that there are any serious thoughts of putting you in the box."

"Everyone seems to know it."

"Surprising how things of that sort go all through college in half an hour. I've wanted you all along; there was tremendous opposition. But I've settled it, and the nine themselves favor you. They'll support you well. Don't feel you're not among friends.

That's what I've tried to encourage in the nine—a friendly feeling and no class distinction ; and I don't know how well I've succeeded. Nothing breaks a man up so in a close game as to feel he's being severely criticised all the while by the infield. It spoils his play."

At this period in Yale's history only one annual game of baseball took place. The success of an entire year might turn on a throw-out at first. It made the game doubly exciting, but it made the nervous tension of the players almost too great to bear. In those days it was common enough for either nine to get badly " rattled " three or four times a game.

Presently it was proposed to go out into the gymnasium lot and practice.

"Curved" pitching had been spoken of in the newspapers several times, but was not attempted by the professional baseball pitchers. In fact, professionals have never invented any especial feature of baseball play.

They kept the plan of Harry's being sent into the box on the "dead quiet," as the slang had it, and Harding prepared the dismal forebodings of defeat with which the *Record* and *Courant* both teemed. This man's finger was broken ; that man was lame ; the whole nine was crippled. Harvard would win " hands down." Probably Yale's succeeding athletic policy of decrying her teams was first instituted by Harding with a view of making Harvard over-confident, and of getting on the right side of Dame Fortune, who is said to be easily fooled by an obsequious humbleness. However this may be, it succeeded in making every Yale man very discouraged.

Harvard stood with an unbroken record for five years. Archie Bush, famous still in the memory of old college baseball men, was their captain. Their infield was a veritable stone wall. They had won victories from several professional teams. No wonder that, if Yale was to stake everything on the abilities of a new and almost untried pitcher, the chances of war were desperate indeed !

Friday came. Friday night.

Fretful, and feeling rather " dragged," Harry went down to the post office after supper, hoping for a letter from home containing some cheerful, helpful words from his mother or sister. They were just as excited over the game at home as he was, but he found no letter at the office and felt a little angry about it. He started to walk back to the colleges.

"Hello, Harry!"

It was Ella Gerhart's sweet, vibrant voice that called to him on the sidewalk.

"So you're going to pitch, Harry! Isn't it grand!"

Somehow these words were just exactly what he wanted—what he needed just then. "I've got to do one or two errands for pa," she said. "He wants me to carry him home a great bottle of acid—he's experimenting all the time over his electrical machines."

"I'll help you carry it," said Harry. He wanted to hear her talk more about his pitching to-morrow.

They walked along together down the busy, crowded street, meeting many students on their way to and from the post office. Harry noticed many inquiring and some indignant glances. He suddenly realized that he now was a "notable" in college, and that everyone knew him.

"Let's go down a side street," he said.

"Why?" she asked innocently. He looked at her a moment, hesitating. She had never looked so pretty to him. Her eyes seemed to have a peculiar sweetness and a love light in the dusk of evening.

"Because," he replied desperately, "I've got something I want to say."

"I'd rather not," she said.

But they kept on Church Street past the City Hall, walking slowly side by side. "I thought everything had ended between us, Harry?" she said.

"Just because I hadn't been to see you for two weeks?"

"Yes."

"Oh, you silly! I've been too busy over baseball!"

"Someone else has been to see me!"

"Who—not Jack?"

"Oh, no. Guess! The queerest man I ever knew—one of your class. He's dreadfully in earnest, too."

Harry thought for a moment. "It can't be old Grannis, can it?"

"Yes!"

Harry whistled. "So he's my rival?"

Ella gave a pretty little conscious laugh, and the dark fringe of her eyelids fell upon her cheek.

"He's very queer, but he's good, Harry; he's so truthful. I shouldn't like ever to tell him an untruth."

"Oh, so, you—so you are beginning to fall in love with the lone fisherman!"

They were in the shadow of a huge old elm. Ella swiftly threw her arms around the lad's neck and kissed him passionately. She made no other response. She told her secret.

Then they walked along together by the green in the sweet twilight in silence, hand in hand. Suddenly she said. "Good-by, Harry. Good luck, *auf wie der schein*—I'll be there to-morrow!" and she flew off in the dusk.

Harry stood looking after her in silence.

"Poor Ella!" he muttered. "By Jove, I wish old Grannis *would* marry her!"

The great day came, freighted with the hopes and fears of a college year. Would Harvard be vanquished at last? No one knows how much the happiness of college life depends upon these annual contests. No event in after years stands out so decisively. Everything—studies, recitations, stand, college politics—is forgotten, but never the game. At this time, too, but *one* game.

Harry jumped out of bed and, for luck, blew thrice and cut his Bible to the following verse at the right-hand upper column: "*Now the height thereof was eight cubits, and the width thereof ten cubits.*"

He closed the Bible and stood meditating a moment. Could the dim meaning of the verse portend the size of the great Archie Bush as he would walk off the field after victory? Finding it was only six o'clock he got back to bed again for another nap. Presently Ella Gerhart was acting as umpire, and pitch and twirl as he would the balls flew anywhere but over the home-plate. The Harvard nine came on the field clad in complete armor. They had large scoop nets, with which they caught the balls of iron, with which they insisted on playing, and instead of a pitcher they shot these balls out of a cannon. It was impossible to hit them. Poor Yale protested, but protested in vain. Ella, as umpire, absolutely refused to listen to reason. The score ran up to 2801 to nothing, and every Yale man on the ground was in tears. He tried to pitch, but his arm was powerless and hung by his side like a pump handle. From this maddening dream he awoke to see Jack and Thornton standing over him at his bedside.

"'Awake, awake, the lark at heaven's high gate sings!'" laughed the pleasant-natured Thornton.

"Thank Heaven—it's not true—is it?" asked Harry drowsily. "The game hasn't been played yet—has it? and Harvard won by 2801 to 0?"

"Yes—you were hit by a ball off Archie Bush's bat in the eighth inning," laughed Jack, "and you've been out of your head for a week."

Thornton kept close to Harry all that morning. Made him lie down for an hour, and kept out the freshmen.

"You coddle me like a young infant," said Harry.

"I don't want you to listen to all the rumors and get nervous, my boy. You'll have strain enough. I want you to go on the field fresh."

"Don't fear—he'll be fresh and green enough," laughed Jack from the corner where he was feeding Stamp. "How is your voice to-day, Stampy? All right?"

He held up some of the biscuit out of the dog's reach, and he began to bark: "Umpty-umph! umpty-umph!"

"That's all right, old man. You want to save your voice for the ninth inning. So don't overbark *now*. Don't you think you'd better lie down now, and soak your head, Stampy? I want you to be perfectly *fresh* when you go on the field."

"See here, freshman, you're letting yourself in for a big lick-ing," growled Thornton facetiously. Jack intimated that it would be dangerous for the weak little stroke to tackle the bow that morning, and in a few moments they were amiably pulling and hauling each other over the floor. Thornton, strong as he was, had a gentle way with him and never exerted his full strength in these bouts. There was something very kindly in the nature of this strong, handsome lad. He was so true-hearted, so modest, so gentle. "They never told their love"—but Jack and Harry had for him an affection which his early death the succeeding vacation, while rescuing two women in the surf, turned into a holy memory of their first year at Yale.

This is what college life gives most of all—friendship—the most enduring and lasting of a man's life. The Latin and the Greek depart, but the ties of kindly feeling are never quite shaken off. No, not even when we grow somewhat tired of alumni dinners and "beloved classmates," and the familiar, "one tie shall bind us ever —we were classmates at old Yale"!

The great Harvard nine arrived, bronzed and burly, about noon, and put up at the Tontine Hotel, below the beautiful green. Their presence was signified by an army of small boys and curiosity seekers, who hung about before the hotel doors.

Accompanying the team were fifty to a hundred Harvard students, done up in red ribbons like bandboxes, mostly of the very "swell" type—patronizing the college teams was not so universal as it is now. They came down to New Haven perfectly confident of victory. They affected to look down on Yale as foemen hardly worthy of Harvard's steel.

Most of the Harvard sympathizers besides their ribbons wore gentlemanly little rosettes of red, while the Yale men swathed themselves in blue ribbons. Yale hated Harvard and its toplofty airs, but feared it. The unmistakable air of "Bostonese" gentility pervaded the whole delegation. The very appearance of the nine on the field was in keeping with the well-bred air of the little knot of swells who came down from Cambridge to back their nine. There was not that terrible over-earnestness of the Yale nine. They played easily and smoothly, while the Yale team, in clumsy uniforms and caps with queer long peaks, made twice the honest effort to play well, but seemed to meet with astonishing ill-success.

Long before the game began Hamilton Park was crowded with carriages, and the field was lined with spectators from the little grand-stand behind the catcher to either side of first and third base. The student crowds were not organized as they now are to give concerted cheers, with a view to disconcerting the enemy's pitcher. The rival 'rah, 'rahs rang out, however, and the excitement and nervous tension was as great then as now. The rivalry of the two great universities seems to be bred in the bone—inherited from our fathers who fought on the lakes of New Hampshire and Massachusetts for aquatic supremacy. Old rows never forgiven, old sores never healed, bled afresh on these occasions.

This bitterness gave additional point to victory and intensified defeat.

The umpire was at last chosen, and in the toss-up Harding lost and Yale went in to bat. The Harvard team sauntered out into the field as if conscious of victory. Their crimson uniforms were neat and "becoming," as Miss Hastings observed from her aunt Miss Mulford's carriage, which had drawn up in a capital position behind first base. Miss Hastings signified her loyalty to Yale, as did her companion, by wearing blue ribbons galore in her hat and around her parasol. Her companion to-day was *not* Miss Mulford— the elderly spinster had no head for baseball, she said, and ever since the overturning of her landau on the way to Lake Saltonstall, had kept out of the way of "student performances." The young lady at Miss Hastings' side was another Charmingtonian, and it was her first visit to New Haven and her first game of baseball. She was of a lively disposition, and at the moments of the most intense excitement in the game kept up a rattling fire of questions at a tall senior who stood on the steps of their carriage.

"Does he try to hit the batsman?" she asked. "He doesn't succeed very well. What is a foul? I should be ashamed to make a foul play. Is the ball made of rubber? How white it is—oh, what makes that man throw his bat at the catcher so and run this way?"

Harry was seated on the players' bench watching Harding, who was first at bat, "slide" to second, when someone tapped him on the shoulder. There were in those days none of the present formalities of ropes and policemen to keep back the crowd, and a majority of the students squatted on the green turf, while three or four Harvard men swaggered about offering odds of two to one on their team and finding few takers.

Harry looked up. "Why, hello, Uncle Dick! I didn't know you were coming up."

"I thought I'd run up and encourage you a little, my boy. I think you're going to win. Don't get down on your luck. I think you've got 'em. They are so cocksure, and when a man is cocksure of anything he is pretty sure to lose. How they strut about! Perhaps they'll go home and feel sick to-night. I'm so glad you're going to pitch, my boy. Your mother wants me to telegraph her as soon as the game is over. Hello! Harding gets third, and only one out. I always think the first inning is the most exciting in a ball game—geewhitaker, what a catch! but Harding gets home, one run, and the inning is half over."

Then came the change of sides, and Harry rose, threw off his blazer, and strolled out to the box. No one of that vast throng imagined his heart was throbbing wildly and that he was clench-ing his fists to hold himself down. The Yale crowd, led by Thorn-ton, gave him an inspiring volley of cheers. Harry overheard some one of the Harvard nine remark laughingly, "Oh, I guess we're going to have a picnic; I'm sorry for the poor freshman's family—I suppose they're all here to see the kid distinguish him-self." He had pitched in games before, but never surrounded by such a turbulent crowd. It seemed as he stood there, ball in hand, waiting for Captain Harding to set his men, as if he could see every face fastened on him inquiringly and doubtingly. He even saw Miss Hastings, in her carriage, who was examining him critically through an opera glass. In the third row—with Grannis —sat Ella Gerhart in a bewitching hat and ribbons (of all crea-tures!) smiling down at him. Behind third were about a hundred freshmen, with Thornton standing up waving a cane and leading the cheers. Over by first was the little knot of Harvard men, waving red flags and openly guying him. How he hated and feared Harvard that day! The Cambridge men had never yet been beaten by Yale.

If he failed, he failed so openly, so pointedly, that he felt he would rather die than face the college again. He seemed to be alone. He turned around and looked at Jim Danforth, who was leaning his hands on his knees off second.

"*I'm here, old man!*" were Jim's words, half whispered, half sung to him. Instantly he felt himself. He knew Jim was ready there, whatever happened. He delivered the ball, and then there was a mighty crash, as if every throat had opened and bellowed out of pure nervousness and excitement. It appeared that the great Archie Bush had struck at, but had not touched the first pitched ball.

Now, instantly, Harry felt every face to be kindly and in sympathy. The next ball was a foul. The next a "ball," the next a feeble grounder, Bush did not hit squarely, and Jim Danforth, apparently not noticing particularly, and as if it was of marvelously small importance, picked the ball up and carelessly tossed to first. One out.

Henceforth Harry knew that the crowd was with him. They were friends now—they had always been so, of course, but *he* did not *feel* it. He recovered himself, and the next man went out on three strikes. Then a close observance of his pitching on part of the Harvard nine, and a hurried consultation. Gad! the kid *could* pitch, after all. The next man encouraged the enemy a little; he hit a long fly—but Harding pulled it down after a long run. Score 1–0. Even innings.

Then the game settled down to one of those long, hard, slow fights common enough in the long list of games since. Not one of those eighteen players but was in dead, solemn earnest—except perhaps "Dan," whose nervous tension seemed only to betray itself in a ridiculous *over*-coolness which amounted at times almost to indifference. He played a brilliant, errorless game, having that perfect intuitive knowledge of what he was to do which marks the best professionals. If he caught a hot fly, unlike most amateurs, he wasn't satisfied with *that*, he sent the ball instantly where it ought to go. He was a rock at second, and came in for the greatest applause. Tutor Dilworthy looked at Dan only all through that game. He had eyes for no one else.

In those days scores usually got up into the twenties, and by the eighth inning the score was 19 to 17 in Yale's favor. Once Harvard got into a streak of batting and led by 5 runs; then Yale pulled up and passed her. Harry looked up and saw Miss Hastings' face when Yale was behind. She seemed unable to control her tears. But she smiled again when Yale led. And so it came to the eventful ninth inning. No one sat on the ground now. Every play was followed with the most intense excitement. Was Yale destined to win, after the long years of fruitless effort? It seemed so.

Harry nerved himself to do his best, but he was really very tired. It wasn't the mere pitching, it was the strain that told on his inexperience. Yale made no runs during her half of the inning, and the last half came on with Harvard two runs behind.

If Harry was able to hold them down the game was won. Through the entire game our freshman had sent in the ball with a precision and force that astonished even Yale's reliable back-stop. Two runs in one inning was pretty hard to make up, and it would take three to win. Harvard men looked very glum and hardly gave a cheer when Harry failed to strike out their first man, who reached first on a fumble by Yale's third baseman. The Harvard player started for second the third pitch, and Crosby was a little too slow in getting the ball into Danforth's hands. It was a close decision, but the umpire called it safe. Then the Harvard crowd yelled itself hoarse, but quieted down as their next man retired on a fly to right. The Harvard man on second stole third. Then a man hit the ball hard to short, who threw home to head off the Harvard man on third base and prevent his scoring, but the batter reached first safely and on the next pitch stole second. It was now a toss-up who would win and Harding, to steady Harry, walked 'way in from center and whispered, "Take it very slow, and worry the batsman."

The wait had a good effect on Harry, who afterward confessed to Jack that he was nearly in a bad state of "rattles." He struck out the next man, and the crowd breathed freely. But it gave a great sigh of uneasiness as Archie Bush was seen selecting a long willow bat from a bundle the Harvard nine had brought with them from Cambridge. Bush was tall and handsome, with a long, wavy mustache. He was tanned very dark, and as he stood there perfectly cool, waiting for a ball "where he wanted it," he was a perfect specimen of an American college player. Probably Harvard has never seen his like since. It seemed to several as if Harry weakened before him, and sent in balls without much swiftness. He let one or two go past, then swinging his bat with a tremendous effort, hit the ball fair and lifted it in the air. Devin, Yale's crack left-fielder, ran back to the rail which separated the race track from the field. Even then the ball was ten feet over his head. No such bat had ever been seen on the field. Bush trotted around the bases, following the other two men home, and Harvard had won the day, but won it by the narrowest margin. The Yale crowd went home in gloomy silence. It was like a funeral. They thought they had the game. Miss Hastings, driven rapidly home, passed the team as the players were slowly riding back to college. She did not recognize Harry, and did not bow. The whole world seemed at a standstill to him. The weight of defeat was almost more than he could bear.

"Boys," said Bush, as the Harvard contingent gathered round him and raised him on their shoulders, "that freshman will beat Harvard the next three years—you take my word—another year will make that young rascal invincible."

CHAPTER XIX.

THE great races at Springfield, to be held the first week in July, now took up a great deal of time and attention. Jack went up with his crew a week before the "annuals" began, and Harry a day or two before the races, partly because New Haven began to fill up with strangers for commencement week, and he felt that a freshman was out of place, and partly because he wished to avoid the assiduous attentions of the Gerhart family. It got so that Father Gerhart began to regard him in the light of a future probable son-in-law. It was getting to be a nuisance to have him come to the room, and sit and smoke and talk about his new patent electrical lamps, and the millions he had "in sight." Grannis met him once or twice, and when he found he was Ella's father, struck up a warm friendship with him. Grannis, with his rough red beard shaved off, and a mustache only, was not a half bad-looking fellow. In spite of his roughness he was very much of a gentleman, and always in dead earnest in everything he did.

He had tasted almost every kind of border life, and he longed he said "to get acquainted" with refined, educated women. He appeared to be surprised that he wasn't "invited around more." To him the Gerharts were the only exception, but even the Gerhart girls made a great deal of fun of the strong, gritty, honest red-headed fellow. He was very kind to them. The fact was he was secretly in love with the pretty Ella. But of this fact he never spoke to anyone; he merely said she reminded him of a girl he had known in Keokuk, who had died.

It was the thing in those days, and perhaps it is a custom still honored, to cram for "annuals" while sailing among the pretty Thimble Islands or cruising off New Haven Point. After Thornton, Grannis, Jack, and the rest of them went with their crews to finish training at Springfield, Harry and half a dozen of the Gimly gang hired the catboat *Fannie* and spent all their time on the water, except when in bed or in Alumni Hall. The "Annuals were a bore-ore-ore," as the song went—a decided bore! It was only by interlarding these disagreeable torture-chamber ordeals with a day of calm, beautiful sailing on the harbor and Sound that they were able to be satisfactorily endured. The *Fannie* always carried a good lunch, and it must be admitted that the text-books generally lay unheeded in the cabin—not neglected, of course, but unheeded! Why read in Horace of the "rare violet sea" when it lay all about them? Why enthuse with the soldiers of Xenophon over "Thalassa! Thalassa!" when the blue waves lapped the sides of the *Fannie* so musically and lulled them to repose as sweet as that of Odysseus upon the Island of Cyprus?

On one of these delightful days of *dolce far niente*, they had sailed far out into the Sound and were lying becalmed. Far to the north and east rose the white column of the light-house, like a finger of alabaster in the shining June sun; to the south lay the wooded shores of Long Island, and in the offing a hundred white sails caught the soft glow of the sun and made as beautiful a marine picture as one would care to see. It was high noon, and Best, Coles, Nevers, Steele, De Koven, known as the "Immaculate," Ritch and Harry, comprising the *Fannie's* crew of that day, were all stretched out on the deck and on the long side seats asleep, when suddenly, loud and clear, not very far away, came the sharp pop of a champagne cork.

De Koven and Harry were on their feet in an instant to repel boarders!

A large schooner yacht was idly flapping her great sails not sixty feet away from them.

" *Hello there—Umpty-four!* " shouted a young man, holding a bottle and glass in his hand, beneath the awning at the stern.

"Why—it's Caswell!" exclaimed De Koven. "Where on earth has *he* dropped down from?"

As the boats drifted together an old gentleman came out on deck and called to the boys pleasantly, "Come aboard, youngsters— we're just going to have lunch!"

"Come aboard!" shouted Caswell. "We want to hear the latest news about the race!" Harry turned red and then pale— there was—yes—it was Miss Hastings, in a pretty white yachting suit, standing at Caswell's elbow!

"We shall be most delighted!" shouted De Koven with a polite bow. The "Immaculate" was never at fault, either in knowing what to say or in appearance. Caswell, who had just returned with Holland from abroad in time for the 'varsity races, was over-joyed to get the latest college news. "Who's gone to the senior societies?" was the first question to be asked. "And so you made that little, smart Dave Johnson chairman of your Delta Kap Campaign Committee, did you?" Meanwhile he introduced them all to "father" Caswell, a portly old banker who said he had gradu-ated at Yale way back somewhere in the previous century, and one by one they met the ladies of the yacht, which flew the pennant of the N. Y. Y. C. at the foretop.

At last he was formally introduced to Miss Hastings by Mrs. Caswell.

"Clara, let me present Mr. Hazleton—Miss Hastings," she said.

"Chestleton," corrected Harry, blushing and laughing at the same time.

"Oh, we have met before—often, haven't we, Mr. Chestleton?" said Miss Hastings.

"Yes; I feel we are old friends," said Harry. "Do you remem-ber the first time we met?"

"Yes; in the drawing-room car."

"Yes." He looked at her surprised. Had *she* remembered it?

The feeling that he was now no longer a very fresh freshman gave him courage. Indeed, he wore on his white scarf the square society pin of Delta Beta Xi. Yes, Miss Hastings accepted him as a sophomore. His bosom swelled with pride. She was not ashamed she knew him.

"I hope you have fully recovered from the upset you got on the Saltonstall road?" he said, by way of beginning conversation.

"Oh, yes; but we have met since then—on the ball field—poor old Yale!"

Miss Hastings pretended to wipe away a casual tear.

"Oh, wait till next year!" laughed Harry. "Archie Bush leaves college this year. Now it will be *our* turn."

"Oh, I shall never, *never* get over that horrid ninth inning!" exclaimed Miss Hastings. "You don't know how I felt. I went home and cried. I couldn't take any tea; indeed, I could not!"

Harry looked at her admiringly. In the first place she had never looked prettier in her life; in the second, she was a true blue Yale girl, and he felt they had a common cause. How different she was from Ella Gerhart! He stood in great awe of her, however, as yet, and there was one thing that worried him : how came *she* to be on the *Caswells'* yacht?

"Do *all* the students at Yale now pass their days on the water?" asked the old commodore. "In my day we had, now and then, a recitation—just by way of variety, you know."

"Oh, this is 'annual week,' sir," said Harry. "We are cramming for examinations, you see. We have a day in between each exam. It's quieter out on the water, sir, and we are not interrupted in our work."

"Very sorry *we* interrupted your studies," laughed the old gentleman. "But can't you bring your books aboard? Miss Hastings and the other young ladies, who are just from Charmington, can assist you."

"I suppose you were worn out with studying all the forenoon, and so fell asleep out of sheer brain fatigue?" laughed one of the young ladies.

"I believe the faculty recommend sailing during annuals," said Caswell, Jr. "Oh, you girls at Charmington never know what real study means. It means wet towels and cold tea all night, and a swelled head next day."

"We study very hard at Charmington," said Clara Hastings, her head very erect. "We don't *graduate*. I despise a girl who does anything so like—*men*. But we have to work very, very hard. And Miss Stout's class in 'the Law of Love and Love as a Law' is famous!"

There was a general laugh. "Ah," said the old gentleman, "I suppose they even *teach* the law of love nowadays. Has love-making become a lost art, then?"

"You don't quite understand," said Clara Hastings coldly, and the old gentleman winked facetiously at Harry. Luncheon was announced presently in the spacious cabin, and a delicious one it was. The yacht *Tarquin*, it seemed, was out for a few days' cruise only, and was, if the wind sprang up, to put into New Haven harbor at sundown. It had picked up the Charmington party at Bridgeport. One of the four Charmington girls was a relative of the Caswells, and the whole party, chaperoned by Mrs. C., was now on its way to the races at Springfield.

After lunch Caswell glanced at his father admiringly, and holding up a glass of champagne proposed a toast to the class of '43.

"Rum boys in those days!" said his father, "a tough, fighting, roaring, devil-may-care lot of dogs. A great many fire-eating Southerners—why, we had a duel once a week. What do your little rows between classes amount to nowadays—*pish!*—we always killed half a dozen at least in our fights! I *had to* fight in college. We fought the townies and the firemen then. I carry a scar on my neck still where I was cut with a saber by a fireman. Did you ever hear of the fireman who was shot? Well, I know who shot the fellow, but it's a secret, and I'm not going to let out his name now, because he is living."

Of course the ladies looked horrified.

"Father, tell us about one of those old banger rushes, won't you, and about the herd of cattle you turned loose in the chapel?"

"Why, in *our* day," laughed the genial old gentleman, "we had the faculty all at our feet. They never dared say a word. They were the *under* dogs then, and we students were on top. Why, when a professor walked across the campus and met an upper-class man, he always touched his hat."

Harry held his breath.

"And when any tutor became unpopular, we just gave him a coat of tar and feathers in the good old Southern style, and rode him on a rail clear out of town and dumped him in the Quinnipiac. Oh, *we* never stood any nonsense from the faculty! We had it all our own way. My son tells me it's the other way now, and the faculty is not behaving as it should. To me it seems that old Yale must be going to the dogs!"

Was he not laughing at them?

"Here is Teddy—'*dropped*.' My son, if you had been in '43 you never would have been dropped. No, indeed! you would have made the faculty conform to *your* standard, and I doubt not but that we would all have had an easier time of it. I tell you, students were scarcer in those days, and the faculty used to encourage every one of us to stay on and graduate. They needed our term fees. They never dreamed of such a thing as dropping us. About those cows we got into the chapel—well, we just did that to show the faculty we had our own ideas of propriety, and weren't to be tampered with."

After lunch, when Harry and Miss Hastings were seated on deck a little apart from the others, she said: "Of course you didn't take for earnest all that Mr. Caswell said. He's the greatest tease and the greatest joker in the world. He is always quietly 'grinding' Ted Caswell. By the way, they say he's going to give Yale a new dormitory."

"Is he?"

"Yes; he's very rich. To *my* mind it was awfully brave in the faculty to drop his son. I think that's the reason he's more inclined to give them the dormitory——"

"I'm glad they did it!" exclaimed Harry, "because he's now in Umpty-four."

"I know a lot of professors' families. A braver, more self-deny-ing, hardworked set of men never lived!", said Miss Hastings, her

"WHAT A—YALE GIRL YOU ARE!"

eyes fairly glowing with feeling. "You students never give the faculty their due!"

"Why, I never looked at them as particularly *brave*," laughed Harry.

"But they *are*. Look at their salaries! What men of their ability would not prefer to go out in the world and earn a fortune? Money-getting would be easy enough for some of them. Professor Maynard is very rich now. What with his arithmetics, Aunt Mulford says he is worth half a million. Yet every day he teaches and gives his salary to the college. Oh, I think it is grand!"

"What a—Yale girl you are!" exclaimed Harry with enthusiasm. "You even admire the faculty!"

"Well, I ought to be; I had an older brother who left Yale in his sophomore year and went to the war with fifty others. He was killed. I was a little girl then, but I remember his funeral; all his classmates gathered around his grave and they sang their old time-worn college songs. I cried my eyes out, because the songs weren't solemn—just the songs he used to sing, that was all." Miss Hastings looked away a moment. "Oh, Yale is one of my traditions. My aunt, Miss Mulford—you saw her that day—*she* has a history. I'd like to tell you if there was time. It was a love affair, and she was a very beautiful girl in those days, just before the war, and the college was full of Southerners. She was wildly in love with a young Virginian, and nearly eloped with him; but they stopped them, and afterward the Southerner was killed in a duel at Richmond. New Haven was very gay in those days, not so frightfully dull as nowadays! I imagine people entertained a great deal more. Southern families came North and spent the summer there. Oh, I have heard such *romantic* tales from Aunt Mulford!"

"Are *you* romantic?" asked Harry.

"*Can* one be romantic in these dull times?" asked the beautiful girl, looking about the yacht and not realizing the charming romance of the hour.

"Of course, we are more practical," said Harry. "Yale is more of a grind now, I fancy. From what I can gather, in those *old* days it was one grand holiday ! ”

“ Why *can't* we bring those days back again ! ” she sighed.

“ Are you fond of holidays ? ”

“ Not always. I love work. I've read all of Emerson's essays, and one of Macaulay, in one term, outside of my regular studies too, at Charmington.”

“ That's great ! Was Caswell rusticated there then ? ”

He watched her narrowly. Was Caswell to be his deadly rival with this girl ?

“ N—no—I think it wasn't *then*. It was before—I knew— (she was going to say “ you”—but said) ‘ Emerson.’ ”

“ He's very ‘ popular ’ ”—a frequently used term at Yale. “ He's a swell too,” said Harry solemnly.

“ Yes—and he deserves it—he's got the best heart of any man I know. I like a man of heart——”

There was a little pause.

“ He's to be in Umpty-four next year. That will be nice for us.”

“ I—I hope he will behave.”

“ Are you so much interested ? ”

“ For his family's sake.”

Harry looked around the yacht. “ His father is a dear old boy,” he laughed. “ I wonder *when* Yale men grow old ? ”

“ *Never !* ” exclaimed Clara Hastings. “ I never knew an *old* Yale man. When you speak of the old college, do you know it's sort of like oats to horses ? They prick up their ears, and get real jolly and young again—just as Colonel Caswell does. Why, I've known old grads to actually come up to call, and try to *kiss* my aunt for the sake of old times ! ”

“ Oh, dreadful ! *Horrible !* ” groaned Harry. “ I hope I should never get to be such an intense Yale man as to want to *kiss* anyone ! Even for *auld lang syne !* ”

He looked into her lovely gray eyes, and she concluded to look down.

She had a sweet, meek little air, as if she was almost afraid to listen to him; yet he felt she was ready at a moment's notice to riddle him with some amusing sarcasm all her own. In her yachting suit and charming tan Clara was bewitching, that day, on the beautiful yacht, on the blue water. There was a seriousness too of which he had not believed her capable; a pathetic note in what she said, which was very captivating.

"I've only one more year at Charmington," she said. "Then I expect to come 'out.'"

"Then I'll be a junior—I want to speak now—in good season for every waltz at our Junior Prom."

"Granted!" she laughed. "Now, don't you forget me!"

"*Forget you?*" Harry's fine eyes fairly blazed with light.

Miss Hastings laughed a little. "Oh, you must write your name on my fan, Mr Chestleton," she said, "and add 'pitcher.'"

"Oh, I shall be delighted! Do you know, I've heard so much about you? I've heard you're a wonderful pianist. I've heard you sing too. I've heard you know Greek and Latin—better than—a—a—theologue or a freshman tutor. I've heard that you're a wonderful skater."

He leaned forward in his seat, while she looked down so demurely. "I want you to write your name on my fan," she said, "and for a motto you might add, 'Little pitchers have big ears!'"

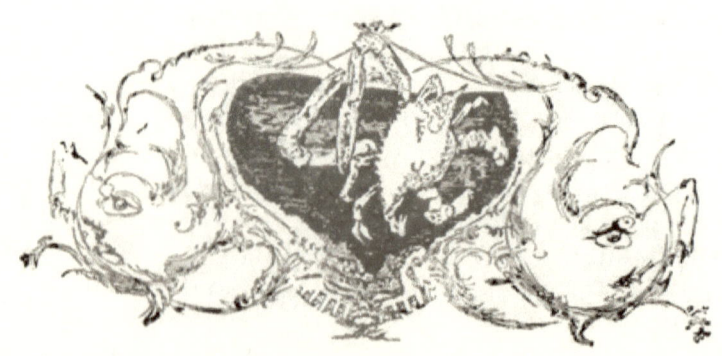

CHAPTER XX.

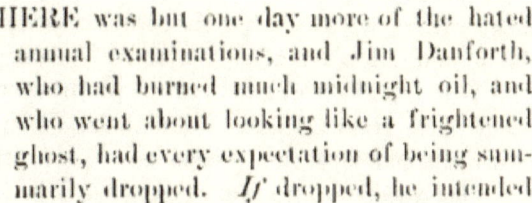

HERE was but one day more of the hated annual examinations, and Jim Danforth, who had burned much midnight oil, and who went about looking like a frightened ghost, had every expectation of being summarily dropped. If dropped, he intended to punish the faculty, he said, by going to Harvard and beating Yale for the next twenty years at baseball! Luckily for Yale, Danforth managed to slip past freshman year with only four conditions! He went up, with a broad grin on his face, with Harry to Springfield to shout and hurrah over the winners of the great races of the college year, the never-absent Mascotte "Stamp" shambling at their heels to add his trained voice to the din.

The newspapers had already made a great deal of the races, and several New York papers had given columns each day to the solution of the great question—who will win? There was Amherst, which had won the year before. There were Williams and Dartmouth and Brown, each with good, stocky crews. There was Harvard with "Dicky" Strainer, a plucky and good second-rate stroke, with the great Goodwin at No. 3; and, last of all, there was Bob Clark, with his "dark horse" Yale crew, whose English stroke, the reporter said, was the combined result of profanity and the hip-joint disease. Who would win? Would Clark force the nose of Yale's shell first over the line? He had some splendid "beef" on his crew. Yale "beef" was always a drug in the market. But beef alone is of no earthly use in a shell except as drilled and regulated by the most patient coaching. The more beef the more coaching, is the rule. Hamm, the fat Pittsburgian who had put the freshman crew into the "prettiest" shape ever seen on the river, openly sneered at Clark and his English notions. The boat "dragged," he said; "the stroke was too slow;" "there would be no more of Clark after the race." As a proof of what he said, the Yale freshmen did actually pull in very fast time, and won easily over Harvard and Columbia freshmen crews. They swept down the course with a precision and "prettiness" which would have been worthy of a 'varsity crew. Umpty-four shouted itself hoarse. They carried Jack on their shoulders about the streets of Springfield and into all the hotel bar-rooms. Thornton, who stroked the crew, said that it was the easiest race of the year.

"By Jove!" said a classmate, "I wish our freshman crew was our university——"

"You do, do you?" said Thornton. "Well, it's a fact that night before last, in the dusk, the 'varsity beat us two lengths in a two-mile sprint," at which everyone opened their eyes.

Pretty soon the cries about the hotel lobbies—it was the night before the race—were: "Even money, Yale against the field!" Thornton had let the cat out of the bag.

The eventful afternoon of the race arrived. A dusky haze lay over the broad river, and a smoke from the busy manufacturing town hung above the high railroad bridge.

All the morning what a noisy, shouting concourse of students it was! There was a band of Williams men, with a purple banner, headed by a big bass drum, visiting hotel after hotel and bar-room after bar-room. Here, at the Blaight House, were the Harvard supporters gathered *en masse*—a noisy, bumptious crowd in those days, accustomed to victory and feeling they belonged to the "biggest university in the United States, and owned the world." They despised the little fresh-water colleges. They wore very stylish clothes and displayed any quantity of crimson ribbon. At the Massasoit House Yale hung out her blue banners. The hotel was crowded from cellar to garret. Men slept sixteen in a room. All colleges were packed in together there. It was a good thing to get the different colleges acquainted with one another— to rub elbows, as it were—the fine, free-hearted, splendid American college boy—none pluckier, squarer, quicker witted than he in all the world ! Cornell men were somewhat oddly dressed in those days, many of them in black doe-cloth, looking like incipient ministers, with flaring red neckties and an inclination to blow horns—but they were plucky and jolly too, as the rest.

Among the fresh water colleges little Williams has always been considered the swellest, it being the alma mater of many rich men's sons, who are sent up into the Berkshire Hills to pass a healthy, if not an especially studious, four years. Williams men always " showed up well," it was said. They appeared to be men of the world. Their clothes fitted ; they went to a good tailor. Not so Amherst or Dartmouth. At Amherst the corrugated brow, the pall of "earnestness," of desperate efforts after the unattainable, were the characteristic signs. Their faces were set ; they rarely smiled ; they abhorred betting ; they avoided the bar-rooms. The Dartmouth boys, on the contrary, were a jolly set of country farmers' sons—hearty, healthy, rough, and noisy—always, if possible, introducing in conversation the subject of the great Daniel Webster, who, they modestly intimated, graduated and afterward wept over their alma mater. Honest New Hampshire boys these, the pith and marrow of subsequent famous lawyers .and statesmen. Brown Baptists from Providence were fonder of their cups, it appeared, than the Wesleyan Methodists. The Brown crew was in very good order, and by many believed to stand a show with Harvard, to whom many of the small colleges conceded the great race.

So came on the great eventful afternoon regatta. Masses of people, pushed and pushing, walking and riding, made their way to the grand stand at the end of the course. Pretty girls—such pretty, enthusiastic girls! in all hues of ribbons. Yale girls among Harvard girls, Amherst girls among Brown girls—cheering, "wah—who—wahing," after the manner of Dartmouth, or rah—rahing, after the manner of Yale and Harvard, or siss—boom—ahing after the manner of Princeton. There were agitated young men in college colors and enormous badges, who were supposed to be the regatta committee, running about here and there among the carriages and the crowd. There were policemen trying to keep some semblance of order, and there were very crimson students shouting, "Harvard even against the field!" Such a crowd and such a scene met the eyes of Caswell, Harry, and their party as they drove down from Idlewild, where the young ladies had been stopping—the pretty country villa of Miss Garland on the heights above the river to the north.

When the coach took its stand Harry amused himself by calling out to his classmates who passed by mingled in the crowd, and pointing out to Clara Hastings some of the "great men" of the senior class. "There's Edmund, the man who never smiles," he said, pointing to a handsome melancholy young man with an intellectual air about him. "There's Pitkins—that short man with him.'

"What has the great Pitkins done?" asked Clara amusedly.

"He simply *is* Pitkins," said Harry; "the most popular man in his class. And there's Franklin, chairman of the *Lit.* Board—the greatest literary light that ever came to Yale. See what a fine mustache he has! And there is Murray—in red——"

"A Harvard man?"

"No; oh, no! He can't help his hair. Don't you see the blue ribbon in his buttonhole? He's the most pious class deacon, they say, in college; and there is little Starkas, the poet."

"Hello, Harry!" called out a cheery voice just below them.

"Hello, Uncle Dick!" and Harry was off the coach in an instant, being hugged and shaken hands with by Mr. Lyman, who, with a lot of old Yale men living in New York, had come up to see the race.

"This is my nephew," said Uncle Dick proudly, as he introduced the tall handsome lad to his various friends. "He pitched on the nine—and we came nearer beating Harvard than we ever did in ten years. Well, Harry, my boy, so you're a sophomore! How time flies!"

"Yes. I feel as if I had been in college a lifetime."

"How comes it you are in the Garland coach?"

Here Uncle Dick bowed to several ladies on the coach he knew.

"Oh! I'm one of the party," said Harry. Then one of Lyman's New York friends said in a whisper: "There's that beautiful Miss Hastings—the belle of Charmington—she's Collins' niece. Say, Dick, get Collins to introduce us old fellows! She's a Yale girl, and we want to know her!"

Presently the whole party was introduced all around, and Clara Hastings, swathed in blue ribbons, found herself the center of the admiring Yale delegation.

The scene was a charming one. The coach, together with several hundred other carriages, occupied a grassy bluff above the river, opposite the finish-line. Below and at one side was the grand stand, now closely packed with students and ladies wearing every shade of color. Blue prevailed; but blue is not a striking color, and in masses has an unpleasant way of appearing black. The river was smooth, with scarcely a ripple. The western banks were lined with people as far north as the eye could see. It was very hot, and a mass of thunder-claps foreboded, in the west, the usual summer afternoon's storm of the Connecticut River Valley.

The Garlands had put up some hampers, and the coachman was getting out their magnums of champagne for a bumper to "dear old Yale," when the cry came, "They're off! They're off!" But this proved to be a false alarm, and the solemn coachman proceeded with his duty without looking round. "Here's to dear old Charmington," said Uncle Dick, raising his glass to Miss Hastings, who sat above him as he stood by the side of the coach, holding a glass in her hand.

"And here's to the belle of Charmington," laughed one of Lyman's New York friends, "who's just graduated!"

Miss Hastings frowned. "We do not have 'belles'—nor do we 'graduate' at Charmington," she said icily. "It isn't considered ladylike."

The other Charmington girls gave her glances of high approval. "No!" cried Uncle Dick, who was engaged in shaking hands with Mr. and Mrs. Caswell, who came up in another carriage. "Nothing so absurd and *low* is ever done at Miss Stout's."

"No one can—it is impossible to pass her rigid examinations," laughed old Mr. Caswell. "No young lady was ever yet able to take a degree at Charmington."

All laughed, and there was another cry, which made everyone leap to his feet and frantically wave handkerchiefs—" *They're off—and Yale's leading!* "

"Oh, glory!" cried Harry, mounting to the highest seat on the coach, where he stood, one foot on Uncle Dick's shoulder, waving a flag.

" *Rah—rah—rah—Yale!* " roared up and echoed from across the river.

On came the slender, narrow racing shells—Amherst and Cornell and Brown, over in the center ; Harvard close to the east shore ; Yale to the west, hardly visible in the dusk ; Harvard just beneath them, tugging and straining in beautiful form. It was a grand race between these two great rivals—leaving the others far behind. On sped Harvard just beneath the bank. They were going very fast, and Uncle Dick shouted up to the coach :

"Yes ; it's Harvard's race !"

"Heavens and earth! why don't they break an oar!" cried Harry.

"Dicky Strainer—Dicky Strainer! rah—rah—rah !" jauntily shouted the Harvard "willies" near them, " we've got it all right !"

But see Yale! It is something new those six men are doing out there now in the middle of the river. The great English stroke is beginning to tell in the last half-mile. The crew is not pumped—is not pulling as if they were at all excited. It's a slow movement of the back, but lightning with the arms ! But see the boat *jump!—jump!—jump!* It is a revelation. It is science. It is what forty years of rowing in England is teaching America. Harvard pulls and pulls with desperation. The men are pumped with that quick, " snappy " stroke which looks so pretty and is so heart-breaking to pull. The cannon booms. All is over—except the little colleges coming tagging in one after another in hopeless confusion. The cannon booms again, and rowing in America from that moment starts on a new basis. Yale has won the day, and Bob Clark is the greatest man in the universe !

At the grand regatta ball that night, Jack, Thornton, and Clark of the crews were the heroes of the hour, and Harry yielded to Thornton two one-halves of his dances with Miss Hastings. How glad he was he did this afterward when that flower of his class, that handsome lad, met his death in saving the lives of two women at Watch Hill during the ensuing summer vacation. The last time Harry ever saw Thornton was when he, in his immaculate dress suit, smiling with victory and handsome as an Apollo, was dancing with the beautiful girl so elegantly that others stopped and admired. The lights, the music of the ball, the dancing—ah! the "Beautiful Blue Danube" waltz never sounded to Harry's ears again without his remembering the picture of that fine young friend of his who, when the moment came, quietly and without a word gave up his life to save the lives of strangers. Thornton, Vale! Mayst thou rest in peace!

Long vacation found Harry home after another day at Springfield—a day devoted to a picnic, a garden party, and a dance at Miss Garland's. He went home very much disturbed in mind. He was beginning to be in love with Clara Hastings, and he believed that Caswell was by long odds the favorite in the beautiful girl's good graces.

His mother had taken a pretty cottage for the summer on the south shore of Long Island. Mrs. Chestleton was a tall, pale, rather nervous lady, who had as yet rather crude ideas of college life. From Harry's yarns, with which he regaled her and his sister, she made up her mind that Yale College was a very "rough" sort of place. Uncle Dick spent his summer with them at Seaside Beach, going up to business every day but Saturday and Sunday. The cottage was large and roomy, and there were always some people visiting them. Kitty Chestleton had, it seemed, innumerable friends. She had grown to be a charmingly healthy, red-cheeked, jolly young girl, who could ride as well as her brother, and who seemed to have as decided taste for outdoor sports as he. She was just at that age when college students were beginning to be, as she said, "glorious fun." Harry had not been home a day before she was wearing, in her innocence, his Delta Kap pin. When Jim

Danforth arrived he gave her his Beta Xi badge. She thought Jim Danforth one of the "nicest" men she ever knew.

To their mother, who had been brought up delicately in the old-fashioned method of keeping the girls of the family housed up within doors, all this outdoor life was very queer; it seemed wrong to her—she could not understand it.

Of course Uncle Dick Lyman, her brother, explained to her the great change that had come over things since the war. Harry's father had not been a college man. As a well to do business man, he had been fond of horses and billiards. These were *his* relaxations. He had been very brave in the war, too, being an old Seventh Regiment veteran, and rising to a position on General Rives' staff in the Army of the Shenandoah. He had been twice shot and the second wound, through the lungs, had been the indirect cause of his death a few years after the war and two years before our story opens. The friendship of Jack's and Harry's fathers had dated from the battle of Antietam. Harry never forgot the sight of General Rives—the one-armed veteran, pale and stern with his sorrow over his old comrade's death, marshaling some of the old Seventh veterans at his father's funeral. From that day—and even before it—General Rives had been a second father to him. Bessie, Jack Rives' sister, had been at school with Kitty. It was a natural thing that Jack and Harry should be chums at college.

"You boys," said General Rives one day, as they all sat out on the sands, watching the surf—the general and Jack were spending a week with them—"shall go through college together, and then, when you graduate and come down to New York, you shall go through your five years in the dear old Seventh together. I know of no finer experiences in all our splendid American life for young men than Yale *and* the Seventh! If you are not gentlemen *then*, God help you—I know of nothing that *can* help you—I wash my hands of you both!"

"I never had any militia valor!" said Jack, laughing.

"Militia valor!" burst out the old gentleman. "What is peace given us for except to prepare for war? Peace means preparation, drill, learning to be soldiers. I marched down Broadway with the Seventh in '61—captain of my company. Harry Chestleton was in the front rank—though he'd only been married then a year. I didn't know him then. The Seventh was at once dissipated into officers. I got a regiment. Harry was made captain in it. By George! our 'militia valor,' as you call it, my boy, served us in good stead."

"Oh! but there'll never be another war——"

"Don't be too sure! War is not an unmitigated evil—and there will be wars to come, and you may be in them. I fully believe inside of fifty years there'll be a war between labor and the state. I want you to be ready. By ——! I want you to understand that a country like ours, worth living in, is worth fighting for and dying for, too. The war changed many things. It changed college life at Yale in one way—it made it much more cosmopolitan. The West sent very few of its sons to college before the war. The South sent only the scions of wealthy families. But since the war, which brought the States together shoulder to shoulder, and nationalized our country as no other event could do, the great universities of New England became the centers of national university life as never before. Take the catalogues of Harvard and Yale in 1860, and compare them with the catalogues of 1870. Harvard is no longer Boston, and Yale is no longer New York and Connecticut. The West is sending her sons East to be educated. And the Western money-making, pushing man of practical ideas admits that the old colleges of New England are after all the best educators of youth."

"The West is getting some splendid institutions, too, of her own," said Uncle Dick. "Even California is crowning her career as a State by an institution the like of which is hard to seek in the Eastern States, and drawing some of its professors from Yale."

"But I hope they won't adopt the class-room system of Yale in their new Western institutions," said Harry. "It's the worst way to 'instruct' a man I can conceive of. No tutor, except perhaps dear old Dilworthy, ever gave us one word of real teaching. They merely listen to what you've got to say—and mark what you *don't* say. *They* are dumb as oysters, merely blink at you if you go wrong or 'flunk'—never think they are put there to inform you of anything. 'Chestleton!'—I rise. 'Proceed!'—and I proceed. Not a word do they say except to ask a few questions about grammar, or some rot about the times of the author, and then, 'sufficient'—and then they call up the next man. I say it's all so absurd. The English system of private tutors, with lectures and exams, is ever so much better."

"Oh yes!" cried Jack, digging up handfuls of sand. "I wish we had the Oxford system. Even I could hope to learn something then!"

"STAMP."

CHAPTER XXI.

MRS. CHESTLETON ADMONISHES.

A WEEK later, while they were enjoying their pleasant sea-side home, came the dreadful news of Thornton's terribly sudden death in the surf at Watch Hill. Harry and Jack were summoned by telegraph and went on at once to the funeral, at Southdown, Conn., where the Thorntons had their country seat.

It was a sad day for "Yale, Umpty-four." Thornton was by right the king of the class. Brave, strong, good, and a gentleman. The women were saved; two ladies who had foolishly ventured too far out. Thornton had spent his last ounce of splendid young strength in holding them up until the boat came. Then he sank out of sight in the merciless seas and they found him that night far down the shore—drowned.

When Harry returned home, after the funeral, he was melancholy and silent for days. He had loved Thornton—had worshiped him. He could not realize he was really gone forever.

"Half of our class attended," he told his mother. "The funeral was the saddest you can imagine. Dear, dear old Thorny! —oh—it was terrible." The tears sprang again into his eyes. "Thorny looked so natural—he'd never had a sick day in his life —and his face didn't look as if he were dead. There was a smile on his lips, and they filled his coffin with not white roses only but red and pink—and our class glee club did all the singing. President Stout came up from New Haven. Thornton's father looked like a dead man—his heart was bound up in his son. Oh, why was that strong, beautiful, dear fellow taken? The two ladies he saved are very rich and they were there, dressed in deep black. They have requested Mr. Thornton to be allowed to erect a white marble Greek tomb."

His mother was all sympathy. "Oh, if it had been you, Harry!" she kept saying to herself. "If God had taken *you!*"

"We stood about his grave—fifty of us—and every fellow's eyes were full of tears. He was so popular. He was like a brother to everyone. He was a Christian—but liberal; full of fun too—a splendid oarsman."

His uncle and sister came out on the piazza where they were sitting, and Kitty went up and kissed him in sympathy. The dear girl had cried many tears over Thornton.

Presently Uncle Dick and Kitty strolled off on the sands, and Harry continued: "I could tell just what a boy he had always been from the poor farmer folk who came to the funeral. They'd let Thorny shoot, ride, fish—anywhere in the whole township. They worshiped him, and when his crew beat the Harvard freshmen at Springfield they turned out and burned blue fire at Southdown, and Thorny made 'em a speech. Why, it was just as if a calamity had broken out in the town. There's a girl they told me about who had loved him—they were engaged—and she's ill in bed and won't recover."

"O Harry! she *will*," said his mother. "Time heals these terrible things. We forget them. I wish you would not go out so far when you go in bathing."

"Oh! *I'm* not good like Thornton, my dear mother."

"I want you to be, Harry," sighed the good woman. "I want you to be like your father."

"I wonder if he went about falling in love with every pretty face he saw," said Harry, gloomily and self-recriminatingly.

His mother looked away. Harry came and sat down near her, and his head fell on her lap. She caressed his head a few moments, and then said slowly: "Harry, dear, there is one episode of your dear father's life I have never told a soul. I think the time opportune to tell it to you. You know that he was a very handsome man—a splendid soldier—brave. We had not been long married when he went to the war. It broke my heart. You were a little boy then. I was so nervous and afraid the news would come any moment that he was wounded, that I kept a trunk packed in readiness to set out for Washington. Those were trying times. Now, in one of his marches your father had occasion to stay a month on an old plantation in Culpepper County, Virginia. There was a family of women gathered on the old plantation. Two or three families of the higher class country folk were gathered together there, and of course they made no pretense of opposing the Union forces. General Rives made it his headquarters, and your father was with him, and several other young officers, who had little or nothing to do.

"There was there a daughter of a rebel general—a very beautiful girl, Marion White. She was tall, had dark hair and dark eyes, a laughing, sweet mouth, and eyebrows penciled in the most beautiful arches. She was a great rider and loved outdoor life. She was a great flirt, too. She set out to flirt with your father. To do her justice, she did not know he was married.

"All those weeks of September, I remember, when your poor father *I* supposed and imagined being riddled with shot or lying dead on some battlefield—for he wrote then very seldom—he never was a very good correspondent—not as good as you, Harry—all those dreadful weeks he was sunning and basking in the light of Marion White's beautiful eyes. I forgave him when he confessed afterward, but it was only after a long while."

"I can't think of father, whose books and sword I revere—the idea of *his* flirting with a pretty girl!"

"Well, men are all alike, my dear boy, and when you get older I doubt not but that the day will come when you will flirt too."

Harry writhed in his chair, but said nothing. Hitherto the boy had never had anything he was ashamed to confess. He had told his mother of his many boyish *affairs*. It seemed to him that he had almost always been secretly in love with someone very much older than himself. He remembered as a boy in church secretly worshiping the back-hair of a young lady who afterward became the wife of their clergyman. "He never told his love, but let concealment, like the worm i' the bud, feed on his damask cheek!" He cogitated as to whether he would speak of Ella Gerhart to his mother, while she continued:

"Your father, I am sure, did not discourage Marion, neither did he particularly encourage her. She was beautiful, and she possessed a daring soul.

"It shows how a man can't have any intimate relations with a woman unless one or the other sooner or later really falls in love. This Platonic love they talk about exists only for old, steady-going, tea-drinking people, who are more or less *passé*.

"It must have been very pleasant in the old Culpepper Virginian country house during that month. I never blamed your father very much. After a week or so of protestation and love-making, to his horror he discovered that Marion White was wildly in love with him in earnest!

"She had started out with the idea of winding him round her finger, but she ended, as he expressed it, in following him wherever he went, like a pet spaniel.

"He, of course, felt like a villain. It got so that he *dared* not tell her he was a married man. She was so horribly tragic that he feared she would commit suicide. The agony *he* underwent was of course very severe. It had been agreed that no one should let out his secret. Indeed, each one of the officers went in to have a good time and tell no tales."

"Oh, father! father!" laughed Harry, "I'm afraid you were not *all* that we could wish in your young days!"

"Your father was the soul of honor. He felt it his duty to confess to the beautiful Southern girl that he was married, but exactly *how* he could not determine. He was afraid to shock her. Her high Southern pride was so great that she would as lief kill herself as not. He grew cold and distant, and did everything to send her to the right-about—but it was of no use.

"She wished to go North, although she had three brothers at the front fighting under Stonewall Jackson—just out of love for him!"

"Poor father! what did he do?" asked Harry.

"I tell this story to you, Harry, because it will be a lesson to you—a warning," said his mother solemnly.

"The time came when the army moved on toward Richmond,

and General Rives changed his headquarters. Your father wel-
comed the day when he could depart and leave his inamorata at
Culpepper. What was his chagrin to learn that Marion White
proposed to accompany him! At his wits' end, he went and told
General Rives. The general gave your father a severe lecture,
then told him to leave matters with him.

"Marion followed after the army with a faithful colored servant
woman. Your father says it wrung his heart to see the girl, so
wistful, so lovely, following on in all the ragtag and bobtail, 'so as
to be near him.' On the second day she was suddenly arrested as a
spy, and she and the servant were sent to Washington and put on
parole. They were treated with especial favor and were soon
allowed to go home. Then a report was sent to her that your father
was killed. Marion White survived that wretched announcement,
and afterward married a rebel colonel, who is now in the Senate.
She is Mrs. Senator Collingsby; and her hatred for the North,
and Northern men, is still proverbial. It was not till afterward
that your father found out that she was really a spy all the time
and conveyed news to the Confederates extorted from him. It did
not help matters much, for your father said that he had had suffer-
ing and remorse enough from that affair to cure him of flirtation
forever. How is it with his boy?"

"A chip of the old block, I guess!" laughed Harry.

"I hope there is no girl in New Haven whom I don't know
about, Harry?"

"Freshmen are not supposed to have love affairs——"

His mother playfully boxed his ears.

"Tell me, Harry."

"Tell you—what?"

"Who is it?"

"Mother, I—I——"

"I don't intend to scold. A mother makes a great mistake in
not entering into a son's real feelings, and trying to sympa-
thize——"

"You would not think it was right in me, mother. You would
tell me never to see her again. She's a shop girl——"

"I would want my boy to be honorable and high just as his, father——"

"*Wasn't!*" laughed Harry. "Ah! yes; I know he *was*," he added, as his mother's face fell. "But, mother, college is queer. There are lots of thing one doesn't speak about at home, you know. You wouldn't understand——"

"Ah, Harry! you will make me suspect dreadful things——"

He threw his arms around her and kissed her. "Poor little mother," he said coaxingly, "don't ask me and I'll tell no tales. Don't suspect dreadful things—please don't!"

"Then tell me all about her." There was a silence of a few moments; the sea moaning and rolling along the shore.

"There were two," said Harry, and his mother, like Rory O'Moore, took comfort in numbers and gave a sigh of relief.

"One was a shop girl—far below; the other was a Charmington girl—far above." He laughed, while his mother said not a word.

"You see freshmen are not tolerated," he went on, "and—at a cake-walk——"

"A cake-walk?"

"A darky affair—lots of fun, all the fellows go—I met Ella Gerhart, a nice, honest shop girl—pretty as a fawn—nothing bad about her—full of fun. Her father's a mechanic, an inventor. Oh! I—I took her riding a few times, and—oh! it's nothing——"

Still his mother said nothing, and Harry, feeling rather encouraged, went on. "Oh! I'm rather drawing *off* now. She was always so jolly! There's a fellow named Grannis in our class, a rough, good, honest fellow, who *now* is more devoted than I am. But she seems to care for me a good deal. She has written me three times, and she is going to join her sister in a variety troupe this Fall!"

"Oh, my boy!" she exclaimed in anger.

"Why, mother! what's the matter?"

"You've made her care for you, poor girl! and now you mean to coolly throw her overboard!"

"No," said Harry, with affected earnestness. "I mean to leave college and marry her. The old inventor and I get along very well," and he laughed. "He'll make an excellent pater."

His mother didn't seem to like this side of the case any better, so she murmured, with a sigh, "Well, tell me about the other one —the one you look up to."

"Her name is Miss Hastings. She's the niece of Miss Mulford of New Haven. She was on the train when I went up with Uncle Dick to college. Oh! she will never look at me—*that way*. Then, her carriage tipped over once and I helped her up. She's perfectly beautiful, and she can say *awfully* sharp things right to a fellow's face and never let on. I'm hoping *next year* to have a better show—but, mother—after all—don't worry over me. It's nothing. I care more for winning the Harvard game next year than for any girl that ever lived. Girls don't seem to be a part of college life very much in the early years. Now, don't lie awake nights and fret. I have been perfectly frank and told you every-thing."

"Harry, my boy, I had no idea——"

"I never told you about the fem. sems. at Andover, did I?" laughed the young lad. "Well, there were two *there*—but now, see—I've almost forgotten their names!"

"But I am so sorry for the pretty young shop girl. I dare say she is perfectly innocent. She probably thinks a student is next to a young god. Ah, my boy! your duty is to be chivalrous, to protect the innocent, to be strong where they are weak; but I'm afraid you have the ignoble idea of girls—they are lawful prey. *That* is the old-fashioned notion."

"I mean no harm."

"But suppose someone should treat Kitty—should make love to her and not mean it?"

"Oh! that's a different matter."

"But is it?"

"If any man treated Kitty unkindly, I—I would thrash him within an inch of his life!"

His mother rose and went to the cottage door. "Think of these things a little, Harry. That pretty young shop girl touches me.

Oh! it is so sad for a girl to have to be sent out to work to earn her own living. She needs so much *more* respect and more kindness. Her life is so dreary. She is apt to be easily influenced. She has so many trials, so many temptations. If she is pretty, it's so much the more dangerous for her. And you say she is going on the stage?"

"Yes; so she writes."

There was a short silence.

"Oh! I'll give her up," he said.

"Harry, I don't want you to. I want you to use your influence over that poor girl *for her good.*"

Then his mother went into the house, and probably, poor woman, up to her room, to weep and pray for her darling boy.

Harry walked out on the sands in the moonlight alone. "*For her good*," he muttered over and over to himself. It was a new idea to him. The remembrance of Ella flooded him with a mild kind of remorse. She had been so confiding. He was filled with a boyish anguish of soul. He feverishly hurried into the house and wrote her a long letter full of *brotherly* kindness and advice. Henceforth he *would* be a brother to her.

The next day they set out for the mountains, and left Uncle Dick alone in New York. At lunch, after Harry had gone out, Mrs. Chestleton said, the day they left, "I'm afraid Harry is very wild."

"I hope so," said the old fellow.

"Hope so?"

"A man *has* to sow his wild oats sooner or later. Sometimes he doesn't sow them in college. They grow up later and are far worse. Let him have plenty of rope *now*. Depend on it, his athletics will keep him from going very far. What has he done?"

"Nothing."

"Well, don't nag him, sister—that's all."

CHAPTER XXII

THE SOPH YEAR BEGINS.

HARRY went back to New Haven with his mother and sister a few days before the Fall term opened. The boys had selected a room in South Middle, "in the thick of it," as it was said.

It was great fun meeting the fellows again and hearing what they had done during the long vacation, but Thornton's sad, heroic death threw a strange gloom over the old campus now. Things hardly seemed the same. It was not like "old times."

Umpty-four had apparently sent her 130 young men into every State of the Union. Some had joined an expedition of Professor Marsh across the plains and into the Rocky Mountains. Some had been at the seashore—Mount Desert claimed five. Others had been in the White Mountains, or in Canada fishing; but a majority had gone quietly to their rural homes and led quiet lives of study (!). All had proceeded to fall in love as frequently and as regardlessly as possible. Jack Rives had been most of the time with his father, mother, and sister at the camp in the Adirondacks. He had great stories to tell of enormous trout he had caught and the deer he had shot. He was tanned like an Indian. He said he had put on a good deal of tan paddling a canoe, in which there happened always to be some girl. "I thought I was hard hit one time," he said, as the chums went to work with a will to furnish their room in red chintz and get it ready for occupancy by the opening day of the term. "She was a Miss Susie Fairweather—a regular daisy! oh, such eyes! and she was only eighteen, and yet she pretended for a long while she was twenty-two—just to lord it over me and put me down, you know. There were lots of girls up at camp, but she was the prettiest!"

"Well," said Harry, holding a few nails in his mouth, "do you know I've got so—so——"

"*Blasé*," interposed Jack, laughing.

"Well, a girl is insipid—she is stupid, if she's too good; isn't that so?"

"That's bosh!" laughed Jack. "I know lots of girls you could never kiss, even with parents' permission and a letter of indul- gence and authority from her resident pastor, yet they are bright, jolly, well-behaved, nice girls, too."

"Now, there is my sister," laughed Harry. "I suppose you'll try and kiss *her*—won't you, Jack?"

"Only in a brotherly way."

"Try it—Kit's awfully strong. She'd box your ears well for you. She's strong enough to do you up!"

Seeing their room lit up that evening, a number of their friends, of the old famous Gimly gang and others, dropped in while Mrs. Chestleton and Kitty were there. De Koven (who had spent his summer at Newport) was one of them. He had developed a great deal. He was much more "stocky" than when he rattled the sophomore crew at Lake Saltonstall. When he went out, Harry's mother said, "What charming manners that boy has!"

"Boy!" laughed Jack. "For the life of you, only speak of us as 'men' now! We are sophomores!"

"Well—*man*, then. I should know he was a New York boy— *man*, I mean! Well, *he's* a good pattern for you."

Presently Steele, Nevers, Coles, Ritch, and one or two others came in in a body, and then, when they saw ladies, tried to bolt out again in a body; but Harry detained them and presented them.

To Kitty they were "men" indeed! She sat on a cushioned window-ledge, with Stamp seated admiringly beside her. The dog liked people who weren't afraid of his ugly mug, and Kitty had treated him from the first with the utmost frankness and fearless- ness.

"Did I tell you Stamp saved my life in the woods last summer?" said Jack. "I fell asleep on the grass deer-stalking one night, and a rattler—a rattlesnake, you know—began to coil itself close to my foot. If I had moved he would have bitten me. The first thing I knew, Stamp had fastened his cast-iron jaws on the reptile's neck, just behind his head. I awoke and killed it—but it was a long time before Stamp would let go. When he did I took him down to the lake and washed out his dear old mouth. Father scolded me for a whole day after that. But do you see Stamp's new silver collar, with *Fides* on it? Father got it for him and fitted it himself. I think the general likes Stamp now just as much as I do."

Little Nevers and Kitty fell into a highly literary conversation. They spoke of several American novels, and of the last one of Howells.

"The men are all so priggish!" said Nevers. "In novels men are apparently changed into refined women—the American novel is written for old maids, and the characters are always at work dissecting their own motives. But Howells is a great moralist, and that is why he *is* great. I don't mind telling you that I'm going to write a *Lit.* essay on him, so don't think what I say is the work of the moment. I've sized that delightful author up. He's a great moralist—it's my own idea."

"He isn't generally so considered," said Kitty. "I've heard people speak of him as a photographer, he is so accurate."

"Oh, just wait until you read my *Lit.* article! Between us, Miss Chestleton, I have my eye on the *Lit.* board—it's a great honor to get on, but somebody's got to get there out of our class next year, and why not I?"

"I believe in being ambitious," said Kitty, "even if things *are* beyond one."

"Oh, Mrs. Chestleton! Do you know what your daughter is saying to me?" laughed Nevers, who was the frankest, most good-natured little fellow in the world. "She says the *Lit.* board is beyond me!"

"I didn't mean——" said Kitty, blushing; "Mr. Nevers, really——"

"She only meant that you were beyond *it*," laughed Jack. "But go in, little lad; who knows but what you are a nice little literary genius?"

Then all the "men" in the room began to chaff young Nevers unmercifully, to take the conceit out of him. When they were through, Mrs. Chestleton said:

"Why not have a good, high ambition? You Yale boys are very fond of dragging everyone down. You are great democrats. You are levelers. No one must declare for anything. You say it's bad 'form.' You are dead set against all youthful enthusiasm. Now, I like it. It accomplishes great things sometimes, unless it is killed too soon."

"No!" said Harry. "We are right, mother, dear; we believe in letting what we *do* speak for us, don't you know!"

"Oh! that's ridiculous—it's unnatural in young people. You teach yourselves to be too greatly self-contained. I believe in expansion. It's the only way to tell what you're good for."

"It *is* the trouble with Yale," said Nevers thoughtfully. "It is too terribly afraid of being 'young.' My brother, who was at Oxford a year, said that English students are a thousand times less dignified and have a better time."

"I'm sure we were young enough last year, what with hat-stealing, class-rushes, and all that," laughed Coles.

"Oh! but freshmen don't set the true Yale tone," said Harry. "Mere boys!"

"The true Yale spirit sits on novelty and orginality—I shall make *that* another topic for a *Lit.* article," laughed Nevers.

"It's too conservative. We are old before our time," insisted Ritch.

"That's what Uncle Dick says," said Kitty. "He was oldest at graduation. Then he began to grow young again. To-day he's quite frisky."

Presently Coles was persuaded to open the piano and sing some of his comic songs. He had finished one amid great laughter, and was beginning another, when an ominous knock was heard on the door. They opened it. There, with kindly smiles, stood the lank, lone, and lorn Tutor Dilworthy with a book in hand.

"Oh!" he cried aghast, "pardon me; I had no idea—ladies——"

But they seized him and carried him pell-mell into the room and presented him. He was greatly embarrassed.

"I came in to hear—some music," he said timidly, and sat down in a corner.

So Coles sang some more, and attracted by the music, half a dozen other fresh-faced, nice-looking lads entered the room. Mrs. Chestleton looked about from face to face in the light of the lamps and gas. There was a hearty, whole-souled, manly look about them. She was instinctively aware that these athletic young men—the representatives of so many well-bred American families—were, after all their fun and chaffing, pervaded by a nice sentiment of honesty and manliness. They would not go far wrong, any of them. They might drink a little and on occasion—but they would not "go to pieces." But their lack of boyishness she thought distressing.

As they walked back to the New Haven House, across the moon-lit campus, Kitty said sorrowfully, with a pathetic little sigh, "I can never be a man—I can never be a student at Yale!"

"Oh, wait until our Annex is started!" said Nevers at her elbow. "Or why not try the Art School?"

Just then a great cry of "Fresh!—Fre—e—esh!" resounded under the elms.

"Think how we'd haze you girls!" laughed Jack, "and how we'd snatch your bonnets—you'd wish you were a girl again pretty quick!"

A week later it came time for Mrs. Chestleton and Kitty to return home. Harry and Jack were now comfortably housed in their sophomore den in South Middle, and the mother and daughter had spent many pleasant hours arranging and "tidying" up their quarters. Pictures were purchased, knickknacks bought. Tutor Dilworthy was consulted as to the best general reading for their new library.

"*After* the Latin authors," he hesitated, "I should choose—Thackeray."

So a set of Thackeray was purchased, and then, of course, Dickens and Scott had to follow. Jack got his victorious Springfield oar and hung it above the door. Harry hung up a trophy of his baseball victories. Stamp, in his new silver collar, felt that his new home was not unworthy of him.

The night before they went away Harry and his mother sat alone in the latter's room. Kitty was—somewhere—with the irrepressible Nevers, presumably discussing literature.

"Harry," she said, "I have been to-day—while you were at recitation—to see that Gerhart girl."

Harry stood up, amazed.

"Why?" he gasped.

"Because, somehow, I felt sorry for her. I'm glad I did so. Kitty doesn't know it."

"Was that the reason why you were dressed up so when I came to supper—your very best? Oh, mother——"

"Yes, I did wear my best, Harry; I wanted to honor her. I found out where she lived and drove there while you were in recitation. I saw Mrs. Gerhart. I saw the Jovelike old inventor. I saw Ella alone; she's prettier than you told me, Harry——"

The lad said nothing.

"She looked quite pale. She had been home, she said, from the store, sick. She was very busy at work, sewing on some tinsel costumes—she's going on the stage."

"So I am told."

"Harry, for a long time I just sat looking at her, and hearing her prattle about you and about her sister on the stage. It was neat as wax about the house. They are evidently a good middle-class German family. They are very poor—but they have, what I like, a pride of poverty. When I went in, the good 'mutter' was reading aloud and crying over a beautiful copy of Faust. I saw they were frightened at my advent at first, especially as I said at once that I was your mother. Mrs. Gerhart said, 'you were a nice, good boy.' Ella behaved like a shy kitten, until I stroked her and petted her a little; then she lost her shyness. *That* pretty

creature forced to earn her own living! It was pathetic—the way
she talked about the store, and the hard work it was, and how tired
she was. They are not low class; they are very much better than
I expected. Ella was a picture. She was so pretty! I dare say
it was her illness——"

"Ella would make me a capital wife?" Harry glanced at his
mother quizzingly.

"If you have led her to think so, then I think if your father was
alive he would say it was a scoundrelly performance—making her
love you——"

Harry flushed angrily, but his mother was very cool and did not
apparently notice him.

"It was peculiarly so because of her dependence. Some girls
are, I suppose, naturally wild. They are hard and coarse. What
I dislike in this affair is that you have never seen—or realized
what is so apparent—her unusual delicacy. Of course, no one ex-
pects you are going to marry for years yet—and, of course, you
must marry in your own class—so we won't talk of marriage.
But you've done this girl a great wrong. You have, Harry. It
is written in her pale face. She loves you."

"By God! I've never injured a hair of her head," cried the
lad, excitedly.

"I don't mean that you are guilty of anything as bad as *that*.
But she loves you, and you made her love you, this is your sin——"

Harry sat down on a chair and his head fell on his hands. "I
couldn't help it," he said huskily. "I thought I loved *her*. She
was always so full of fun, until the last. We used to laugh and
joke one another. I hardly believed she was in earnest."

There was a short pause.

"If you could see her now, to-day! the dull, vacant look in her
eyes. Before I left I wormed her secret out of her—poor child!
Poor child! These Germans are so full of emotion, and of sentiment. She sat quietly telling me how good you had been to her
—how kind—as if you were dead and gone. Well—I cried, and I
took her in my arms. She poured her heart out on my shoulder.
And I told her that she must not grieve so. O Harry! the poor

girl—you have broken her heart. She stopped crying in a little while, and said that she was afraid ever to see you again. She had made up her mind, and she was going to be with her sister, so as to get away from New Haven—and you!"

"Mother! mother! you will drive me crazy. If you say much more I will jump into a hack, go get her, and hale her before a clergyman and marry her. Do you wish that? I tell you it won't take much to drive me into it! I'll throw up my life at Yale; I'll go and heal her broken heart, if you tell me so. *I* feel her sorrow as much as you do. It is with me night and day. If she was stronger, harder, less dependent, it would not be so hard on me. Do you think I am so selfish? I'll give up my life and make her happy. We can go abroad. I'm willing. Come, decide!"

He stood up, very pale, and confronted his mother with folded arms. She admired her son as he stood there before her, so manly and so heroically willing to repair what wrong he had foolishly done the (not entirely) innocent girl. He had spent many bad half-hours over the remembrance of Ella Gerhart that vacation, for he began to realize how very lovely she was, and, if yielding, how her yielding came from love of him.

"I have done wrong," he insisted. "It was worse because she was poor, because she was more at my mercy. Ah, mother, she was very sweet! But if you think——"

"No! But I want you to see this thing clearly in its right light and the harm it brings. She never did you wrong. Why did you go out of your way to persuade her to love you so—she, a poor working girl? I spoke of it to your Uncle Dick. He said it was what all students did; it was 'puppy love.' He made light of it. I wish he could have seen poor Ella this afternoon, her face like that of Beatrice Cenci. The life had gone out of it. Do all students enjoy spoiling the innocent lives of these poor girls? I say it's outrageous! a sin and a shame! Dick Lyman laughs and pretends it's the everyday thing with students. I don't say these are the days of chivalry, but yet I do say that, as regards all that class of poor girls who are forced out into the world to earn their living, a greater duty falls on all honest, right-minded men to protect and befriend them. Oh, my dear boy! perhaps I feel too deeply and say too much, but I have just come from her. I can't bear to think that you have taken advantage of her helplessness——"

"Of course I never have," he replied indignantly. "Oh! I know I've done wrong—I deserve it all. But I will say this for myself —that I did believe I was in love. I couldn't resist her. I've acted as squarely as I knew how. I never promised to marry her."

"No—I presume not!"

"We just drifted together and then apart. I wouldn't harm her for the world. You know I wouldn't!"

Mrs. Chestleton, as the reader may have surmised, was a woman of high sense of her duty, and she felt deeply the affair of Ella Gerhart—perhaps too deeply. She made too little allowance for "the time of golden youth," when love springs up every hour and day, and students, with their freedom from care and their peculiar monastic life, are especially susceptible to female charms. She was a woman who, once having said her "say," was apt to turn about and be very kind and lenient. She now made Harry sit by her, and she kissed him and petted him and told him how much he was to her and how she saw, as he grew older, that he was just exactly like his father. "It may be that Ella Gerhart will, after a time, marry too, and forget you, and I don't think you were to blame—only you were thoughtless. Let it be a lesson. Every woman, Harry, young or old, *is* more or less weak and defenseless. I would like you and your fellows to take a new view of our sex— a more chivalrous view. I—I keep thinking of Kitty alone—out in the world!"

"Mother, don't!" groaned Harry.

"*I must* speak," she went on. "A new era is dawning for women. They will have more and more opportunities for earning a living. They need more and more the highest, finest, most chivalrous protection, since the protecting influences of home are taken from them. The old idea that they are 'lawful prey' is hideously barbarous. It is cruel, wicked—don't deny it! It's brutal—I want my boy to see that it is—it is cruel to make love and not mean it. It's simply contemptible!"

"I don't think it's the college view at all."

"No, perhaps not among all the swell sets. But there must be a great number of good boys, too, who are not so worldly-minded.

I would like to get up into that chapel pulpit and preach a sermon or two. You can depend upon it, *I* wouldn't waste two hours over a minute question about the origin of the Pentateuch!"

When the chums, accompanied by Jim Danforth, saw the mother and daughter off at the station, Mrs. Chestleton cried a little at parting, and told Harry that she had not meant to be too severe. "But you are present with me day and night, Harry; I am thinking about you all the time. Oh, a *girl!* She grows up of her own self. She never seems to want to go wrong —but a *boy!* Mercy! they seem to be forever trembling on the brink of a precipice."

THAT NIGHT, IN HIS MAIL, HARRY FOUND A LITTLE ENVELOPE.

Harry smiled and kissed her. Danforth, who had brought a pretty parting gift of a bouquet for Kitty, said afterward, "By Jove, I wish I had such a mother! Why, Harry, your parting from her seemed to me like—lovers!"

"She is my good angel," said Harry, with a sigh—"only I wish she wasn't *quite* so good!"

The next day but one Harry, full of pity and goodness of heart, went up to call on Ella Gerhart. She had left that very day to join her sister's company. They had gone to play in a "burlesque" at Pittsburg. That night, in his mail, Harry found a little envelope directed in Ella's well-known cramped little hand. It contained some rather melancholy printed verses she had cut out from some periodical; that was all:

" How badly is the course of life adjusted,
    That where sweet roses bloom sharp thorns abound ;
    What though the heart has dearly, fondly trusted,
    The hour of parting will at last come round.
    Of thy fond glances once I read the meaning ;
    They spoke of joy and happiness for me.
    God bless thee, love ! it was but idle dreaming ;
    God bless thee, love ! it was not so to be.

I dreamt of peace and hours of tranquil pleasure,
    When unto thee my pathway led me nigh ;
    Then through my soul a flash of joy went gleaming,
    Fain would I pledge my youthful life to thee.
    God bless thee, love ! it was but idle dreaming ;
    God bless thee, love ! it was not so to be."

CHAPTER XXIII.

BOGEY IS HAZED.

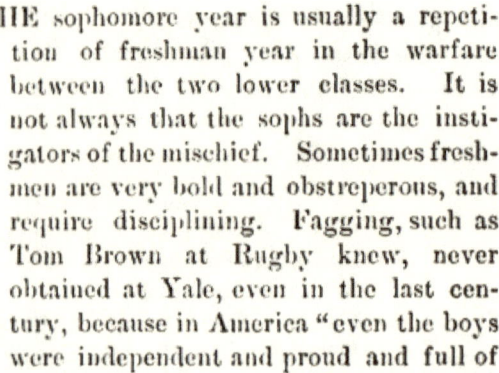

THE sophomore year is usually a repetition of freshman year in the warfare between the two lower classes. It is not always that the sophs are the instigators of the mischief. Sometimes freshmen are very bold and obstreperous, and require disciplining. Fagging, such as Tom Brown at Rugby knew, never obtained at Yale, even in the last century, because in America "even the boys were independent and proud and full of personal pride and manfulness." * They were more obsequious than at the present day to upper-class men, touched their caps (all wore caps in college, except seniors, in those early days) and probably ran on a few errands, but no one had his especial fag, or servant, among the freshmen. The institution of hazing dates from time immemorial. Doubtless freshmen always have been very green, and always fell a prey to fun-loving students. It is often the young lad's first venture from "home and mother." Nowadays the lad so often goes away to a preparatory school, where he learns a great deal about college life, that he never comes to pass his entrance examination for college quite an ignoramus.

There came to college in the class of Umpty-five a young chap by the name of Bogey, whom our sophomore crowd claimed to be greener and more ridiculous than even Lambda Chi Briggs ever thought of being. Barney said himself that that "red-haired

* See Letters of Lafayette, 1804.

yowling terror of a freshman, Bogey, orter be took down an' a reef took in his sails."

He lived (as all freshmen were compelled to do, owing to lack of dormitories) in a boarding-house on Elm Street. There were several other freshmen in the house, and the plan was adopted one night, to quietly get into Bogey's room, then lock everyone else out, and fumigate the freshman to their hearts' content.

About 9:30 o'clock one night in November half a dozen sophs stole out of old South Middle. Each had a clay pipe and plenty of tobacco. Arrived on the street, near Bogey's boarding-house, they put on black masks.

Harry was expecting to go on this expedition to Bogey's room, but Harding sent for him, as there was to be a baseball consultation in the captain's room, in South, over a proposition from Harvard to play three games next year instead of one only. Steele was in the crowd—quite changed from freshman year, too, for he had succeeded in growing a formidable mustache.

They strolled along the brick sidewalks two by two. Presently Ritch struck up

> Room, boys, room !
> By the light of the moon !
> Isn't this a jolly night to find your way home !

and they all joined. As they passed a freshman's window they sang out: "Put out that light, freshy!"

And generally a window flew up, a freshman's head flew out, and a taunting reply was flung after them.

"It's a red-hot, cheeky class," said Steele, "and it needs to be 'tuk down,' as Barney says."

"But if you think we're going to have a picnic or an easy time with Bogey, you're mistaken," spoke up Jack hotly. "There'll be two freshmen to every one of us. It's a fight from the word 'go.' It's no soft snap. Bogey knows we're after him. Depend upon it, it will be a tough old 'hit-from-the-shoulder' row. I'm glad we've all got on our 'mud' clothes. All the night-rushes put together this year won't equal to-night—mark my word! There's

Stillman, who Bob Clark says shall go straight onto the 'varsity crew—he's a young ox—the strongest man at Andover last year —he rooms in the same house."

"Yes, and there is McCullogh, the freshman single sculler, who is captain of their crew; he lives there, too," said Ritch, "and

they say he swears he'll get even for the rough initiation we gave him into Delta Kap. So get ready, boys! It's to be a scrimmage — and we may get left."

They heard footsteps, of some one on the run, behind them.

"Stop him if he's 'fresh'!" whispered Jack. It was Caswell.

"Why didn't you tell me of this?" he sang out, out of breath. "I went up to your room, Jack, and no one was there but little Nevers, crouching

"NO ONE WAS THERE BUT LITTLE NEVERS."

down before the fire with Stamp's head in his lap. He said you were all out after Bogey, and were bound to get into trouble— well, I thought I'd like to be in it, too."

"We thought you were off doing the society racket on Temple Street," said Jack, alluding to a dance that was to take place at the residence of a well-known resident of New Haven that night, to which *he* was not invited.

"Well, I'll take that in later," said Caswell laughingly.

Neither he nor Holland quite occupied the place in Umpty-four they had filled in Umpty-three a year ago. Men who drop back into a lower class are seldom quite as popular as they were in their own. He was not the unmitigated "terror" he had been, however. At first, like Paul before conversion, he had gone about breathing threatenings and slaughter. Then he had openly asserted that this rowing between classes was "brutal" and ought to be abolished. It really astonished Jack and his friends to see him so ready to mingle in the fray once more. October had been a "rough-and-tumble" month. There was a rush of some sort nearly every night. Everyone had ready his "mud" clothes, adapted to wrestling 'neath the dim light of some glimmering street lamp. The days of "glorious barbarities" were not then over. The modern sophomore probably looks upon such long-continued animosity as "ungentlemanly" and absurd. The days whereof we write are perhaps passed forever, gentle reader, but, while they existed, developed a certain hardy manhood, and kindled a certain sense of respect for personal courage and "sand." There were real *heroes* in those days, and "Chestnuts," as Harry was called, was one of them.

Presently the gallant little band of sophs—setting out on the laudable errand of smoking out the freshman Bogey—arrived within close proximity to the latter's boarding-house. The night was not very dark, and they drew closely together in the friendly obscurity of an alley to consult as to the best method of approach. Should they boldly go up in a body or one at a time?

It was decided to steal up softly, and yet in a body, in Indian file. So, Jack leading, up they went—seven maskers—bent on their fell design. At the top of the stairs, as luck would have it, two freshmen happened to be coming down. They immediately ran back upstairs, shouting "Lambda Chi!" at the top of their lungs. Of course, Jack and the sophs hurried up, and bursting into Bogey's room, hastily slammed the door to. Bogey looked up from where he sat. When he realized what was going on, he hurled text-book, lexicon, and patent framework at the heads of the sophs and made a break for a window. He was quick as a cat and strong as a colt, but he wasn't too quick for

Jack to nab him and trip him up. He began to shout like a shrill newsboy: "Umpty-five! Umpty-five! Look alive!"

"See here, freshman, shut up!" said Caswell sternly. "Your doom is sealed, and you had better make your peace with Heaven, and die in quiet."

Bogey at once kicked the harder and yelled the louder. As the freshmen were by this time trying to break in the heavy door of the room, Jack left Caswell to hold Bogey, and joined the others in sustaining the barricade. Very heavy pressure was being brought to bear outside.

Meanwhile Caswell was having all he could do to hold Bogey. Jack pounced on Bogey and tied his hands behind him with a strap he had brought for the purpose—and he was harmless.

Bang—thump—bang! It shook the whole house! Would the door resist that attack?

"A nice brave lot you are—seven on to one!" laughed Bogey. "Oh, I know you, and we fellows in Umpty-five will make *your* life miserable, Mr. Caswell!"

"Shut up, freshman!"—in sepulchral tones.

All proceeded to light their pipes, taking care to blow their clouds of smoke always in Bogey's direction. Presently the room was dense and thick with smoke, so that you could cut it with a knife. The banging at the door ceased, and Jack correctly surmised that the freshmen had gone in search of some heavy article which they could use as a battering-ram.

"Say, see here," coughed poor Bogey in the dense smoke of seven puffing pipes, "you'd better get out of here. My class will be back here a hundred strong in five minutes——"

"Freshman, sing a song!" called out a mask, solemnly.

Bogey, coughing and swearing, sang:

> "When freshman—first I came—to Yale——
> ALL. Fol—de rol—de roll—rol rol!"

When Bogey got through sputtering and stammering out his song, they called on him for a speech; this is what they had to endure:

ALL PROCEEDED TO LIGHT THEIR PIPES.

"Gentlemen of the great class of Umpty-four:

"At this entirely unexpected and, I assure you, gentlemen, entirely unsolicited honor, my feelings nearly overcome me. That *I*, a humble freshman, only lately from the 'wild and woolly,' should be singled out to be offered incense to as a god, completely unmans me. I am too well aware that Umpty-four is low down enough to worship almost anything in the firmament [murmurs of rage], but that they should select poor unpretending me passes the wonders of the times."

"See here, freshman, don't think too small pumpkins of yourself—it isn't like you," growled Coles. Meanwhile the smoke grew thicker and thicker, so that poor Bogey was all but invisible in the cloud.

"Go on! Go on!" they shouted.

"Well, gentlemen, I will go on. I'm no hog on smoke, though, nor ham either, and if you prefer smoked herring you can get it cheap down at the corner grocery. Perhaps you take me for a Yarmouth bloater—but I can tell you right here and now, I don't intend to bloat worth a cent. Why, I'm used to smoke—lived in a ham-curing establishment in Cincinnati three years."

Jim Danforth, who ordinarily was rather a quiet performer at these hazing performances, at this speech gave the table a kick, and down came Bogey in a heap. Jack caught him in his arms. He was pale and sick and dizzy.

"I'm knocked out," he gasped. Jack carried him to a window, and opening it, placed Bogey's limp form across the sill.

Meanwhile the sophs were made painfully aware that the freshmen had returned with re-enforcements. They had procured a heavy beam as a battering-ram, by means of which the door began to give signs of falling inward. Caswell danced up and down at every thump now. He fairly ached in his excitement for the row that was to come.

Ritch was for jumping out of the window into the soft flower-beds below, but Caswell would not hear of it. "Let them be twenty—thirty to one!" he shouted—for the noise was now very great—what do we care?—we're going out of that door and down the stairs and out like gentlemen!" At the instant the hinges flew off the door, and it fell inward over the furniture they had piled up against it with a mighty crash. Stilwell was the first freshman to leap over the débris. Jack and Danforth caught him, whirled him to a window, and threw him out. It was now hit from the shoulder, hot and heavy. Jack and his friends got their backs up to the wall and knocked down freshmen as they came up, as if they were nine-pins. The freshmen were tough and strong, but had little science. They surged about the sophs, yelling and swearing to kill them. But the sophs slowly beat a retreat, not without many a blow. Down the stairs they went fighting and shouting, and out into the street. Here a great crowd of "townies" had gathered, and two policemen came running up, waving their clubs, and threatening to arrest every mother's son. Instantly fresh and soph turned on the "peelers." The "townies" joined in the cause of the latter, and it was now " Yale against the town."

A huge "towny," well known as an ex-prizefighter, a boxing teacher, and a man who hung about Gradley's bar-room waiting for odd jobs, came running up, and taking in the situation, fought on the students' side. He didn't care very much *whom* he hit, provided he hit something, and he bowled over one or two students by accident. It was now a great fight all along the line. Caswell was knocked senseless and his head cut open by a heavy stone, and then came the well-known cry of "*Faculty!*" "*Faculty!*"

Ritch came running up. "They've arrested Coles!" he cried. "Shall it be a rescue? Four peelers are walking him down across the green to the City Hall!"

Others came up. Jack and Jim Danforth and Ritch started on a run between the chapel and North Middle, across College Street cross lots to where poor unfortunate Coles was dragged. On the edge of the crowd was a stocky, well-built young man who seemed to be prowling about as with an object—a serious object—in view.

"By gad, Harry! it's you, is it?" cried Ritch as they came up. "Oh! we've had a time!"

"Hush! I know," said Harry; "I just came out of Harding's room and heard the racket. They've got Coles—and there will be the divil's own time if they lock him up. The faculty will visit on *him* the whole affair—especially if it leaks out he was in your hazing crowd. They will expel him."

Harry had taken in the situation quickly. Coles was watching. When they dropped his arms to pass the gate, he dropped on his hands, and the peeler in the rear received a stinging blow behind the ear from Harry's right. It stunned him, and Coles got away like a deer. Harry walked leisurely away as if nothing had happened.

"It's him that struck yes!" pointed out a small "towny."

Harry quietly took off his coat. The peelers started for him, but he spurted off in the direction of old Trinity Church and was soon out of harm's way. Coles made a wide circuit, and in ten minutes was in his room and in bed, and then up and out again half an hour later. One by one all the sophs dropped back very quietly to South Middle. The great row was so far over, and—best of all—no one appeared to be caught.

As if there had not been noise and confusion enough already for one night, a great crowd had gathered at the fence, principally to guy and chaff a lot of townies who were standing opposite the fence over in front of what was then known as Toadley's. Every old Yale man will remember the way Toadley used to bawl down the dumb-waiter, "Two eggs on toast!" and then sneak downstairs and cook them, as he was his own cook and bottle-washer! Toadley lived principally on cold hard-boiled eggs, in the rear end of his little store. He was terribly dyspeptic in consequence, and the disturbance in front of his place caused him to be mortally fearful lest one of his front store windows should be broken in. He was tall, lean, and lank. He came out and expostulated with the crowd, and advised and prayed them to go home "for the love of God!"

Presently it seemed as if everyone in college had come out on the campus at the fence. Classes intermingled. It was now "Yale against the town." All the good singers of every class gathered in the fence corner, where the soph fence joined the junior, and the good old songs echoed high beneath the elms. Such grand music from a thousand throats! "Lauriger Horatius, Upidee, Cocahelunk, Bingo," etc. But singing was not enough. Presently from out of the darkness came barrels, boxes, sticks of timber, bundles of hay and straw, and dumped themselves together beneath the high-drooping elms. Fifty bright, intelligent young men were carefully searching the backyards of the peaceful citizens of New Haven for fuel.

A number of sophs poured a tin can of kerosene on the pile of débris and touched it off. The flames caught the light tinder and the oil, and rose high in the air. A splendid blaze soon lit up Chapel Street as far as Temple, and flickered against the white façade of the old State House.*

Sophs and fresh joined hands and danced madly round and round the flames. Does not every alumnus recall such jolly scenes? Every now and then parties would come triumphantly in bearing some empty barrels and bundles of odd pieces of timber, which they would throw on the flames. Presently a keg of beer protruded itself through the fence. Whence it came, who brought it, no one knew. But it was there all the same.

Just when the fun, which had sprung out of nothing—for things often go that way in college—was fast and furious, came the ominous cry, "*Faculty! Faculty!*"

Professor Timster, with a notebook in hand, came stalking across the campus from Elm Street. Professor Maynard, enveloped in a long black cloak, came prowling around the corner of South College. Tutor Dilworthy, looking very sleepy and never known to report a student for any sort of misdemeanor, came out of his entry, and Tutor Smile (whom the students hated) out of *his*. There was a grand scattering of all but a few juniors and seniors, who bravely sat on their fence, each one having, of course, a *mens conscia recti*. Professor Timster stalked straight up to the beer keg and turned the spigot, so that it should empty itself to no good

---

* The bonfire would have done some damage to-day if lit in the same place in Osborne Hall.

A FORAGE FOR FUEL.

purpose on the ground. A groan went up from the juniors.
Other members of the faculty appeared, and everything became
quiet as death.

The moon, which was struggling through a bunch of clouds,

threw down a pale, flickering light. The campus was nearly deserted now. Tutor Smile approached his entry in Old South.

Suddenly someone darted past him and seized his notebook. He grabbed the fellow, and the next instant found himself whirling in the air, and then dumped on the ground "in a very undignified and unwarranted position," as he related in faculty meeting next day.

Unluckily Jack's cap fell off in the scuffle. Inside were his initials, "J. C. R. Umpty-four." Tutor Smile picked it up dazedly, and went up to his room.

Jack ran around the old Lyceum and into north entry, South Middle, before he became aware of his loss. He went back, but no one was to be seen.

"If Tutor Smile has got that cap, I'm done," he said to himself, with a sinking heart. He looked at the torn notebook in his hand, then went back meditatively to his room. Harry and Stamp were sitting up eating crackers, and Harry was drinking beer.

"A big night, Jack!" said he; "a great night for old Yale!"

"Yes, and a sorry one for me——"

"How so—you weren't spotted for hazing Bogey, or the street fight afterward?"

"No, but Smile has just spotted me. I snatched his notebook. Here it is—lots of fellows will get off with a warning; but he grabbed me and I threw him—and my cap fell off, as luck would have it—he's got it!"

"By Jove!" Harry whistled.

"I went back, and the cap was gone. He's picked it up, and my initials are in it. You remember Kitty sewed them in on a blue ribbon last summer—on Long Island."

Jack sank down on the sofa, and Stamp jumped up and licked his face affectionately.

"Dear old dog!" said Jack, "I guess we'll have a chance to see a bit of rural Connecticut shortly, for I shall be rusticated sure!"

CHAPTER XXIV.

TUTOR SMILE.

TUTOR ALPHONZO SMILE was an ungracious, hairy, red-bearded little man, possessed of no tact whatever, and who curried favor with the faculty by spying out and reporting delinquencies which were of no consequence whatever. Doubtless he meant to do what was right—but he had a "durned queer way of showing it" as old Grannis frequently observed. He had come down from a small mean little up-country Connecticut village—and he was a small mean little man. In college he had been a pious "dig," rarely mingling with his classmates, and in his two later years assuming the position of monitor, a position which to his spying mean little eyes was exactly what he was fitted to. His own class raked him mercilessly on class day, for being the means of getting one of their most popular men suspended.

As tutor of Umpty-four, he soon made himself as unpopular as it was possible to be. His windows in old South were often most mysteriously broken, and in celebrating the great victory over Harvard the summer previous, at Springfield, a sky rocket entirely by accident flew straight through his window curtains, into his room—he was absent fortunately—and burst in a blaze of glory against his mantelpiece.

Such little attentions on part of his friends, the students, made Tutor Smile like Evalena when she caught a porgie as the old song says, "infernally mad," and the madder he became the more silly and ridiculous jokes were played on him. They nailed up his recitation room door; they dropped red pepper on his stove; they tarred his chair and desks; they wore crape on their arms at his recitations; they had telegrams marked "Rush" and "Urgent" delivered to him by messenger boys during recitation hour, announcing his election to a professorship of Bricklaying in Kamschatka University: they sent him anonymous notes warning him that he would be buried alive some night, up to his chin, on the campus, and left there to greet early morning chapel goers next day!—if he did not turn over a new leaf—so that, full of "threatenings and slaughter," Tutor Smile went prowling about under the elms, "spotting" men's names in his notebook. The "divil" or some evil "diabolological" fiend inspired Jack to run up behind him suddenly and snatch his book out of his hand. He fancied, guilelessly, that it would be just the "boss" thing to do to wind up that glorious old "Yale Night," and then go to bed and sleep the sleep of the pious and honest "soph" till the chapel bell rang him up in the morning. Alas, poor Jack!

When next morning came Tutor Alphonzo Smile awoke with aching bones.

> Oh, Tutor Smile is full of guile!
> But he gets come up with once in a while!

These wicked words of the doggerel chorus rang in his ears too—he'd heard them sung outside his windows quite too often of late. *Now* he'd have his revenge. He laid Jack's natty little cap with the letters "*J. C. R., Umpty-four*," so tastefully sewed in the lining, before him on the table. "John C. Rives—I know the rascal! I'm not sure but he wrote the verses about me which they are always singing. Threw me down, did he? Well the faculty will surely expel him—it's a terrible misdemeanor—the whole faculty will certainly resent an insult of this gross nature to one of their own body"—

> And the Tutor's Smile
> *Was* full of guile!

He walked over to his breakfast and thence to morning prayers full of his terrible secret. Yes, Rives of Umpty-four should be expelled!

But the day passed without a word from the faculty. Old Grannis was very much disturbed. "It's all because I was off singing bass up there in Linonia Hall and the glee club," he said regretfully, "or I'd been with you, Jack, and taken care of you. It made me so tired singing all the evening that I came home with Nevers and we went down to Mory's, had a rarebit, and a mug of Bass, and came home to bed. We heard a lot of noise, but we didn't think it was a town and gown row—our room looking out on the west, we didn't know anything about the bonfire. But Tutor Smile is a cad. He'll be sure and report you, and I don't see but what they'll *have* to do something to you. You laid hands on him and 'dumped' him!"

"I had that satisfaction," laughed Jack ruefully. "It wasn't *much*, but it was something—and I got his book. He had Guthrie and Murdock down—juniors, think of it! and Bixby, a senior —gad! think of that heavy swell being 'up for it'! He had Bob Clark's name down too, though Bob was only walking across the campus to his room. Bellamy Storrs' name was down, too, and poor Baby Finck of our class, who hasn't got over his rush in freshman year yet, and was only out to see the fun. Lambda Chi Briggs was down, and rightly, because he stole Prexy Stout's front gate, they say, for the bonfire. Stranahan too—lots of juniors who were singing harmlessly at the fence. Bullock was down, too. Strange how you never hear of Bullock *now*, and first term freshman year he was the 'coming' boating man—but they are safe now, unless Tutor Smile thinks fit to remember them. But I think he'll only bend all his energies to bouncing me. He hates me anyway—and now he's got his inning."

So all that day they heard nothing, and the next day came. It was a Wednesday, and on Wednesday afternoons took place those solemn conclaves so pregnant with fate to students—the weekly faculty meetings.

Hetherington dropped in their room that morning, and they told him of Jack's scrape, and asked his advice. He was looking cleaner and better. He said that he had sworn off from all "hard" drinks for three months, and had hopes of sticking to it. Some of his classmates were interesting themselves in getting him a Greek professorship in a new Western University in California. "Oh, they've tried to do this before," he said sadly. "But as soon as any inquiry is made here, in New Haven, they give me away. They say I'm an 'habitual drunkard'—and so I am. Yet I think if I could only get away from New Haven, and go West, I might do better."

Harry and Jack expressed their commiseration. It was really very sad. "Dear old Professor Shepard, one of the noblest men that ever lived, has always been my friend," said Hetherington. "But others on the faculty naturally distrust me."

They told him that he ought to go away, change his name, and begin life over again somewhere. "How should I live?" he asked. "Professor Black helps me a good deal. He gives me a lot of Greek work on his new grammar to do. I make ten dollars a week out of it. Oh, Black's very kind to me. Students he hates—they bore him dreadfully. He ought never to try to teach; he doesn't know how. It's a great knack, teaching; few possess it. They don't know what it means at Yale—this class-room business is of little use to a student. They pump out all the time, when it strikes *me* they ought to pump *in*."

They asked Hetherington what Jack had better do.

"Do nothing," he said. "If they *send* for you to-day it means bad business. It means they will vote on your expulsion. The reason they send for you is that they want to give you a fair hearing—a sort of inquisition. It is the French inquisitorial process; utterly opposed to our common law practice. In all our courts a criminal is not to be deemed guilty until so proven, nor is he without counsel. To-day they'll hold a meeting, and as I say, if your case comes up, and they think it an expellable offense, they will send for you. If it's merely to give you a few marks or suspension from college—they'll not send. If they do send for you, Rives, I advise you to be humble, and try and explain your wrestling match with the tutor, if you can. The best explanation would be that you thought it was a classmate and you merely threw him in sport."

"No," said Jack. "I can't say that. I knew it was Smile. I won't lie about it."

"Then,". said Hetherington, smiting his fist on the table, "they'll expel you. They are very technical, and if they have no excuse to hang a little mercy on, they'll logically be obliged to punish you very severely, for no student may lay a hand on a member of the faculty—and live!"

"At least you can apologize," said Harry, "and say you're sorry for dumping him."

"No, I'll not!" said Jack dismally.

"Well, your previous good character will help you, perhaps," said Hetherington; "you've done pretty well. If you can explain that it was a sudden overwhelming frenzy to steal that notebook——"

"That's what it *was!* " Jack laughed.

"Well, explain it that way then—say you were out of your head. The excitement had crazed you. Insanity is a good defense," laughed Hetherington.

Harry had secretly been to Tutor Dilworthy and Professor Shepard and confided in them, and had telegraphed Uncle Dick Lyman to come up from New York. Before Hetherington left that noon Mr. Lyman put in an appearance.

"Upsetting a tutor! That's punishable by death—eh, Mr. Hetherington?" he said. Uncle Dick set his bag down on the boy's table, lit a cigar, and proceeded to get out all the facts. He had met Professor Walker on the way up Chapel Street from the depot and had had a talk with him. Professor Walker liked Jack and promised to do all he could to save him, but he had told him that it was a grave offense—as grave as any that had come before the faculty of late years. "As *he* put it, it does sound rather bad," said Lyman, puffing out a cloud of smoke, "and it was wise—your sending for me, Harry. As soon as I can get all the facts I'm going to see everyone I know. It would break your father's heart, Jack, if they expelled you. But they won't, if I can help it —and I think I can. Now tell me, Jack, why, *why* didn't you just snatch that notebook and skip?"

"He grabbed me, and to get rid of him I threw him over my hip," said Jack, "and then my cap fell off—and he picked it up, I suppose, and so got my name, inside."

"They will say you were in the *act* of stealing, or rather it was highway robbery. O Jack! Jack! But be calm when they send for you. Just say it was a spontaneous insane impulse which led you to do it."

"That's what we all agree—to plead insanity!" laughed Harry. Uncle Dick left after talking a little while. He took a grim lawyer's view of the situation and saw plainly its weak side. He was industrious however, and saw as many of his old friends and cronies in the Faculty as he could. There was dear Dr. Wister his classmate, now in the med. fac., who was an old chum. Dr. Wister went without his dinner for Lyman's sake, and had an interview with President Stout himself. The faculty met at two o'clock, but by that time Lyman had seen five, and Dr. Wister seven of the faculty, and had gotten them "well disposed," at least. They would concede nothing, and promised nothing, but Lyman felt pretty certain that they would not vote to expel.

He went without his own lunch, and saw the last professor file into the meeting room in the little "cabinet" building, in the rear of the chapel. If it had been his own son, or himself, he couldn't have felt more disturbed over Jack's possible fate, for he was very fond of the dear boy.

He went back to the boy's room in South Middle, and found Caswell there, lying on the lounge with bandaged eyes. He was rapidly recovering from the bruise in the head he had received. Coles was there also. Caswell said:

"Oh, pshaw—they won't expel anyone! Why, I've been before the faculty more than once. Your character's good, Jack; mine never was."

"I ought to have got Jack to come in," said Harry ruefully. "But Tom Coles' bacon was all I could save that night."

"Yes, it's owing to you, Harry, that I'm not up before the faculty," said Coles, and he went on and told Uncle Dick about Harry's rescue.

Lyman laughed heartily. "You boys in Umpty-four are a tough lot," he said. "In after years they won't believe such rows were possible. The New Yale that is to be will be much tamer—but I like you hearty fellows well enough as you are."

As they were sitting there in came Grannis and little Nevers, who was very sympathetic with Jack, and presently a number more of his friends entered. Jack was popular, and the deep concern in their frank honest faces was unmistakable. What if he were expelled!

Poor Jack was in a bad scrape! Presently there came a knock. It was a knell to that little assembly of friends. Even Stamp was quick to recognize a difference in the quality of the sound. His hair bristled up, and he uttered a low growl.

Instinctively *he* recognized the hand of the faculty!

The door opened. There stood Professor Walker, looking rather pale, anxious, and worried. He called Jack out, and told him he was summoned before the faculty meeting, at once. Lyman went out and talked with Professor Walker, while Jack went back to brush his hair and "fix up" a little. As he stood there brushing his coat, everyone was silent, but when he went out they crowded around him and shook his hand. It was dreadful, his being summoned! It meant that they were actually contemplating his expulsion. Poor Jack!

Lyman walked with Jack and the professor as they went back of the colleges toward the cabinet building. He simply told Professor Walker that it would kill General Rives if—if Jack was expelled, and that he would give a personal guarantee that, if they would pass this thing over, Jack would never give any further trouble. "It was a sudden, boyish, insane impulse," he urged, and "he was crazy when he did it."

"I will do what I can," said Professor Walker kindly. "But the feeling seems to be very strong that young Rives has committed the most severely reprehensible act possible—he has laid violent hands on a member of the faculty who was acting only in the line of his duty."

"Yes, yes—I know, professor. But after all it doesn't argue moral turpitude, but merely a sudden act of frenzy."

He kept reiterating this idea, and had been pressing it upon other members of the faculty until some of them who did not know Jack believed that the lad really must be a fit candidate for the lunatic asylum!

Jack followed the professor up the stairs. He looked "nervy" and determined. At the landing Uncle Dick grasped his hand warmly. "God bless you, my boy," he said; "stick to the insanity dodge, they won't expel a lunatic! it wouldn't be legal!"

Dare we, in the interests of this our tale of Yale, lift the veil which hung over that solemn tribunal, which was sometimes inexorable, sometimes merciful, but never quite forgiving? Many of those quaint scholastic minds which passed upon Jack's case have since passed away. Not one of them but aimed to do the right —splendid intellects doubtless in their own departments of art or letters or science—but moving little in the world, and sometimes governed by motives and by a scholastic reasoning which would not obtain in a coarser atmosphere. May one dare, also, to venture upon any mild criticism of so august a body? Are these gentlemen of the faculty, then, to be convicted of any unfairness in their dealing with student delinquencies? Did they ever err on the side of mercy?

Every old Yale grad. who reads these lines will answer this last question warmly in the affirmative.

CHAPTER XXV.

THE FACULTY MEETING.

S Jack entered the room, he saw the members of the faculty, in solemn conclave, seated to the number of thirty in chairs arranged in the form of a semicircle, with good old President Stout in the center of the horse-shoe. The room was hung with portraits of grim straitlaced old Puritans, who had formerly occupied either the presidential chair or that of some important professorship. The tutors sat together at one side and in bunches of two, since by the existing rule of the faculty two tutors were necessary to constitute one vote, and it was easier thus to count them.

It was a solemn, august body of men, where highest intelligence predominated over every emotion. Professor Black bent on the young lad his keen, searching, almost malignant glance. Tutor Smile sat sulkily looking over some loose leaves which, as he was rather near-sighted, he held close to his eyes, and turned his head continually from left to right as he read. Professor Maynard blinked behind a large and momentous pair of gold spectacles, Professor Shepard looked rather sad and vexed, close by the president, but as Jack entered he smiled and nodded to him kindly. How his heart thrilled at that one kindly recognition in all that cold assembly! He loved the professor from that hour. He was appalled by the coldness of the glances cast at him. Even Tutor Dilworthy looked down on the floor, and dared not give him the satisfaction of a friendly nod. He was a culprit already condemned, already sentenced! Thoughts of his mother and his father, and of their consternation at his expulsion, came over him with a terrible rush of despair. He made up his mind then that he would not go home again—he could endure the stern glances of these men who, he was led to believe through college traditions, were his natural enemies, but he could *not* endure the silent misery of his mother, or the hard bitterness of his father, the general.

He would go away somewhere West. He was only eighteen, and there were plenty of ways for him to earn a living. Good old Grannis would help him perhaps into something out in Keokuk. There was little regret present in his mind for what he had done. Pah! upset a tutor—what was that! A sneak of a tutor who had to go and tittle-tattle! He was perfectly assured inwardly that he would have done the same thing over again! He stood up straight, and manly, and handsome as a picture. There was no shame at all in his face or in his attitude. He didn't cringe and fawn and beg for his life! Not he—poor Jack!

Possibly, had old General Rives been present, he would have secretly admired his son as he stood there before the faculty. In the student code of ethics it was no sin to steal a tutor's "spotting" book out of his hands, or no crime to trip him up. It was considered a daring act—a brave deed!

The faculty through the mouth of President Stout gravely gave him *their* diametrically opposite view of what he had done:

"Mr. Rives, you are charged with a—and what it appears to me to be—a very wanton and offensive act of insubordination. Never since I have been an incumbent of the office of president of the university have I met with such an exact state of facts. As I understand from what has been said, you, without provocation, last Wednesday night or Thursday morning, at about the hour of 1 A. M., attempted to steal and did take away property belonging to a tutor of this college. In the encounter you wantonly threw the tutor upon the ground and kicked him, and then ran off. Mr. Rives, this constitutes a very grave offense. But before we, as members of the faculty, proceed to pass upon your case, and mete out the punishment due you, I will add that it appears that you have previously borne, as far as we know, a good character; that is to say, you have hitherto done or performed no overt act which would warrant the faculty in concluding that you were a hardened wrongdoer. Mr. Rives, you come to us from Christian parents, and from a Christian home. Perhaps the action of the faculty, whatever it will be, may be salutary in affording you, perhaps, an opportunity to—to return to its benign influence. Mr. Rives, will you come forward a little? You do not seem to be one who is especially hardened, or who is incapable of improvement."

Jack wondered whether he was expected to reply to this, and Professor Shepard spoke up slowly:

"What have you to say, Mr. Rives? Won't you please tell the faculty exactly what happened that evening?"

"All the evening?" asked Jack.

"Only in connection with this affair with Tutor Smile."

Jack coughed, then after a moment said, "I was on my way to my room, after seeing the bonfire, and was greatly heated and felt very thirsty. I saw Mr. Smile coming along putting down names in his notebook. A sudden fancy struck me that it would be a good joke to snatch that notebook out of his hands and run with it. I don't know *why*, but it was a sudden overwhelming insane idea. When I did so he grabbed at me, and then I accidentally upset him in tearing myself loose. I did not kick him. The notebook I threw into the fire. It contained two or three dozen names of men who were not out that night at the bonfire—to my certain knowledge. There is one thing I wish to add, sir, emphatically: I did *not* kick Mr. Smile when he was down."

Professor Walker had told him that that would be the charge. "Ah, yes, but did you kick him at any *other* time?" asked Professor Black with a keen glance, "and if so, when?"

"No, sir, I never kicked or touched him before."

"We think differently," said Professor Maynard, who, after he had spoken, seemed to retire again behind his spectacles and blink profoundly again.

"I state the fact, sir," said Jack simply. "That is all I can say."

"But he *says* you kicked him," said another professor. "He states you kicked him twice as he lay upon the ground."

"That's untrue, sir," insisted Jack. "How could I? I was trying to get away as fast as I could." And he smiled.

Tutor Smile shook his head. Very likely he really believed that Jack *had* kicked him as he lay stunned and astonished on the ground. He was greatly shocked, no doubt, and believed that his treatment had been far worse than it really had been.

"He kicked me twice," said he. "They were sharp hard kicks. I feel certain they were produced by blows from the foot. There was no one else present at the time of the assault, and I conclude the kicks proceeded from, and were produced by the shoes and feet of, Mr. Rives of the sophomore class."

"That is false!" cried Jack hotly. "I wouldn't kick anyone—especially a man who was down. I deny utterly that I did anything more than upset Mr. Smile—and if he received bruises they were caused by his fall only. I don't care what happens—those are the honest facts. Ask anyone in my class if I would do such a thing! If I did I ought to be expelled at once. It's untrue! It's false! I was merely after the notebook in which he had written name after name of men who were not out there that night. I seized that and was off."

No one who saw him could have helped being impressed with his honesty. But if the faculty were moved, no one gave expression to it. They all sat sterner, harder, and silenter than before. "You admit all the facts except the two kicks?" asked the president.

"It happened as I said—and *just* as I said," said Jack. "I was crazy, I suppose."

"State exactly what you did during the entire evening, beginning at six o'clock," said the president.

"That I prefer not to do," said Jack. It occurred to him now that his "jig was up" anyway, and there was no use in relating all the particulars of hazing Bogey, and so "peaching" on his friends, and getting into worse difficulties. This was the most heinous sin in the college student catalogue—to "peach."

"You must answer," said the president more sternly. "It's the rule of the faculty."

"I would rather not," said Jack firmly.

"You *must* answer," said Professor Black with anger, "at once."

"It will be better for you," said Professor Shepard kindly.

"Why," said Tutor Dilworthy, rising, "I don't know about that. In a court of law a prisoner is not permitted to inculpate himself. I can't see why we need go into extraneous matters. Perhaps Mr. Rives was calling on someone earlier in the evening whose name he doesn't wish brought into the affair. Suppose it was some refined young miss—would anyone wish her name brought in in this connection? Or he may have spent his evening in some other way which, while proper in itself, he is unwilling to put before the faculty."

"And *were* you calling on someone, Mr. Rives?" asked Professor Black, with a great show of sternness, under the circumstances.

"Ye—yes, sir." Jack felt this was only a fair answer, although the freshman Bogey was hardly a refined young "miss."

"But we stand to you in the relation of parent and child," said Professor Sinister, who hitherto had not said a word, but who fidgeted nervously in his chair as if he would very likely fall off in another moment; "in *loco parentis*. Would you not tell your father where you had been?"

"Yes, sir—I would tell my father—and he could tell you if he saw fit—as he's a lawyer and I'm not."

Everyone looked at the other as if this speech was particularly "wanton," and at least ill-mannered.

"You will not answer?" asked the president again, in the manner of an auctioneer giving his last call.

"I'd rather not," said Jack.

"*Then you may go!*"

As luck would have it, too, as Jack went out the door caught a gust of wind as he made his exit, and banged to with a terribly insubordinate and loud "wanton" sounding bang. "*Oh, I'm done for!*" he muttered to himself, and ran over to South Middle, feeling that he had made a bad mess of it before the faculty. There was a great crowd in his room as he entered, and you could cut the smoke with a knife. Uncle Dick had just been telling them his great, if apochryphal, story of Sedgwick, the lithe Southron who captured the valedictory by a neat murder of his rival in old South. All were waiting for Jack to come in.

"Boys!" he cried excitedly, bursting in at the door. "I'm a goner!" Then he told them everything that had transpired, down to the slamming of the door as he went out.

Uncle Dick Lyman dove his hands deep in his pockets. "Gad!" he said, "it looks like expulsion—but Professor Shepard will do all *he* can. And so will Tutor Dilworthy, and all those friends of Dr. Wister's."

"We'll get up a monster petition," said Coles. "If Jack goes, I go too. By all the gods, boys, let's even go as far as to say we'll light out and go to Harvard!"

A universal groan indicated that this was a step which hardly anyone in the room was quite desperate enough as yet to contemplate.

A knock was heard. Bob Clark entered with one or two juniors. He shook hands with Uncle Dick and Jack. "We can't let the faculty expel *you*, Rives, for you're going to row on the 'varsity next summer if I have my say. I told Professor Walker to-day. He understands it. He intimated that his daughter had said a good word for you also."

Harry smiled and said nothing, but what a sensation! to have Bob Clark go out of his way to make a point of coming up to their room! Everyone was silent as death. It was a historic scene. Jack felt dizzy. Oh, if he had to leave college *now*, how terrible it would be! *On the 'varsity!* He? Jack? Oh, they could not be so cruel as to send him home when Bob Clark had interceded in his behalf!

"Oh, yes," said Harry. "As good luck would have it Miss Walker was at a tea at Professor Shepard's which we were at, and Jack put in one half hour with her on the piazza."

Jack blushed. "She's awfully good to speak a good word for me," he said. "I—I shall never forget it."

"Why, I used to know Miss Walker myself," said Uncle Dick—

"Adele Walker. Her full name is Adelaide. She used to be quite pretty—she was a belle long before my day. Why, she must be thirty-five if she's a day."

"Thirty-five! She looks twenty-one," said Harry. "How girls do deceive a fellow!"

"Pshaw! if Adele Walker has got her father on the right side of the question," said Uncle Dick, "I don't think we need fear anything so bad as an expulsion. Oh, no, Jack! They'll do something certainly. They'll suspend you, but they won't expel. Cheer up, my boy!"

"But even that will break the governor all up!" said Jack ruefully.

"We'll take care of that. We'll keep it all from him. It's easy enough."

After they had sat a little while longer all hands went out across the campus to the soph fence, which faced College Street. Here were already gathered, in the growing dusk of the late afternoon, a number of their classmates. The sun shone through beneath the elms against the old brick row, and lit up the long homely facade with a peculiar glory.

"And I will have to leave it all!" said poor Jack sorrowfully. "Just when it's beginning to be so pleasant—and college life only really *begins* when you get into the dormitories."

They all perched on the fence with Uncle Dick seated in the midst of them and Stamp at his feet. "Come," said the old boy, "let's cheer our hearts with that song of songs, 'Gaudeamus igitur.'"

Uncle Dick repeated each verse with solemn emphasis, and they sang it after him. In the light of Jack's going away, perhaps his expulsion from college, the song made a deep, never to be forgotten impression.

> Gaudeamus igitur
> Juvenes dum sumus.
> Post jucundum juventutem,
> Post molestam senectutem,
>   Nos habebit humus.

After that followed

Ah me, conditione
Quid meus pater dicet me
Si redeam Conditione.

and Nevers gave them the warble, "Oh, where, oh, Where has Mine Leetle Dog Gone?" and they sang, "When the Matin Bells are Ringing," "Those Evening Bells, and "Stars of the Summer Night"—all gathering there; dear, beloved Jack in the midst of them. What rows, initiations, escapades, had not the "Gimly gang" already participated in together? While they were all talking and laughing and encouraging Jack, Harry slipped away and hung about the door of the cabinet building, where the faculty were still in session. He strode back and forth nervously, along the path in the rear of the chapel. Presently he saw one or two professors making their exit. His heart was in his boots. What was the verdict?

"I wish it was I," he kept saying to himself. "I wish it was I—I don't see how General Rives will ever forgive Jack." He thought he saw Tutor Dilworthy striding over toward old South. He ran after him, and caught him. His face was pale, and he fairly trembled as the kind-hearted tutor said, "It was a hard fight, and very close—but it was decided finally to suspend Rives for eight weeks and give him twenty-five marks."

Harry threw his cap up in the air. He didn't shout, for he saw Professor Shepard just behind. He impulsively went up to the dear old professor, and grasped his hand. Tears stood in his eyes. He said nothing—he couldn't. He ran down between the Lyceum and South and across to where Jack was on the fence.

"Rusticated—only eight weeks!" he shouted, and immediately everyone tumbled over one another to get a shake of Jack's hand.

Uncle Dick Lyman stood on top of the fence where the crowd held him in an upright position, waving his cane.

"*Gaudeamus igitur*," he sang at the top of his voice.

Gaudeamus igitur
Juvenes dum sumus !

How they sang the brave old Horatian ode that second time!

The old boy was the most excited among them. "Nothing will do but a dinner at Gradley's," he insisted. "O Jack! we will prevent your father's knowing this—not a line shall reach him. I'll fix *that* with Mrs. Rives. Thank the Lord it's no worse than it is! Why, it's really nothing at all!" And he slapped Jack heartily on the back.

The dinner at Gradley's—which was sufficiently lively and uproarious to have completely satisfied the conscience of even Uncle Dick himself—for the many toasts to dear old Professor Shepard, and "noble" old Dilworthy, and even Professor Sinister and the unworldly, high-minded old President Stout, and others among the faculty who, they believed, had been friendly to Jack—and the deep damnation and death to Tutor Smile and Professor Black—all the toasts and the wine, and the dog fight afterward in Gradley's pit, at two o'clock in the morning, between one *Stamp* (by King of Terrors out of Lady Macbeth; owner, J. C. Rives, Esq.) and Fighting Tim (by Dan out of Nell; owner, George Gradley, Esq.)—being the result of a lot of loud talk in Gradley's bar-room after dinner, and which fight was won in a "jiffy" by Stamp, who killed Fighting Tim in nine minutes, and sent Uncle Dick back to New York next day very sleepy, but with fifty dollars in his pocket after paying for the dinner, the wine, and everything else the boys had at Gradley's that night—the dinner at Gradley's, we say, left the "Gimly gang" in very poor condition for recitation the next morning, but in the highest spirits.

Faithful old Alston, their sweep, nearly pulled Harry out of bed as the chapel bell was ringing.

Jack called out sleepily from his bedroom, "As long as I am to be sent off anyway in a day or two, I suppose, I guess I won't be particular about the 'literary or religious exercises' any further!"

So he turned over to blissful repose once again, and went fast asleep.

In the course of the day it came out that Caswell also was suspended—his connection with the street row becoming known through the physician, who was also a member of the faculty—Another man, a member of the freshman class, was also suspended—the row and the bonfire had been considered a very grave breach of discipline by the faculty.

Very often suspension, or rustication as it was called, punished only the poor innocent parents. But in this instance Uncle Dick went immediately to work to prevent General Rives getting any letter from the faculty whatever. He went to the general's law office in lower Broadway, and after explaining the situation to his law partner, an old Harvard man, he arranged to inclose any letter from New Haven which had in the left-hand upper corner, "If not called for within ten days return to Box 443, New Haven, Ct.," to him, Lyman, as soon as convenient. He also went to Yonkers, where the general lived, and saw Mrs. Rives. He made light of the rustication, and persuaded her to think it a *bagatelle*. "My dear Mrs. Rives," the good fellow insisted, "there is no use in punishing your innocent husband—he will only suffer terribly when Jack has really done nothing out of the way. Why punish *him?*"

"But if it is nothing——"

"Yes, but *he* is of the old school, he won't understand; times have changed since your husband was in college. His being in the army has also made him very fond of strict discipline. He will be very angry with Jack—who is the bravest, dearest fellow in the world."

"Oh, he will be *so* much *more* angry when he finds it out!" she laughed.

"But he never *will* find it out, not till long after Jack is out of college."

The good woman, who (as was the case with all who knew the kind-hearted, unselfish fellow) yielded to Lyman's persuasion, the next day received the faculty's letter, and inclosed it unopened to Lyman. He put it away in his safe. "Some day Jack and his father will read that letter, and there'll be a great laugh over it," he said to himself. He felt he had been very kind to General Rives—kinder indeed than to Jack himself.

The day following Jack was duly notified that "on and after twelve o'clock, on the Saturday following, you will be required to take up your residence at a distance at least ten statute miles from the State House in the city of New Haven. Nor will you be permitted to return to New Haven for a period of eight weeks from that date."

He was permitted to go north, south, east, or west, but must go away at least ten statute miles. "Banished!—from all I hold dear!" He cried—"from you, Harry [mock tears] f—from the d—dear o—old college! from Tutor Smile! Oh I c—cannot I ca—ca—cannot endure the disgrace!"

"And—I—" groaned Caswell. "They've sent me up too! When I got my head broken by that towny, I think I had punishment enough! They spotted me because my character was N. G. They made no charge against me!"

"Rather a discharge!" laughed Jack.

"And now I feel obliged to spend a part of my rustication in Charmington. Jack, that's the place for us. Besides, I'm more than half in love—I can't help it—with the Hastings."

Harry looked up from his book quickly. Caswell pretended not to notice it.

"Oh, it's time I left fooling away my time here at college—and married and settled down. I'm twenty years old. Father says college life will be the death of me and him and all the rest of the family. I had better quit after this year. Then there's Emily Garland at Charmington now, too—the Garland is a whole bunch of flowers."

"I think Charmington would be the last place to go to," said Harry. "A dull place with nothing to do—of course they'll warn off all the girls at Miss Stout's school. You mustn't hope to be received *there.*"

"Well, but I do," Caswell laughed, lighting a cigarette. "Why not? I know Clara Hastings *very well indeed.* Then I know Emily Garland—and I may have other cousins up there later on. There's a deuced pretty Miss Carringford there from New York.

I met her once at a dance. Jack! shall it be Charmington for us
—after a few days in the metrolopus?"

"Oh, I don't care where I go," said Jack. "I'm going to have
some shooting and fishing; that's one thing. I'd like to run down
to Long Island a week. If father doesn't know it, I'm not so
terribly anxious to stay in New Haven. I'd just as lieve have a
little change as not. Or I'll go down to New Orleans with you
and take in the Mardi Gras."

"No, that's in March," said Caswell. "This year."

"Well, I'll—go anywhere——"

"Very accommodating, I must say!" laughed Caswell, whose
head was still in a bandage. "I think we'll do New York—on the
strictly *incog.*, you know; then a week's shooting on Long Island,
at father's gun club, which includes 'sons of members'—you know
the famous '*Sons of Guns Club.*' Let me see, it's the 1st of
December now—that will bring us to, er—a week before Christmas, and we'll go up then to Charmington and get a little acquainted
before the Christmas holidays. There will be—two weeks out for
vacation—eight weeks will be up about February 15th, I take it.
Why, we can manage, by running down to New York every week
or so, to have quite a jolly time. That Carringford is a daisy.
She's tall, has a small waist, dark hair, brilliant complexion, and is
almost as beautiful as Hastings—but Hastings is more intellectual,
see? She can talk like a book. She can dazzle a feller once in a
while. Do you remember, Harry, how she sat on that old grad
from New York who thought they were so low and unrefined as to
graduate at Charmington? How her eyes snapped!"

"I remember she got into you, Caswell, pretty often."

"Indeed she did. She's been down on me ever since I upset her
and her aunt going to Saltonstall. Heigho, how tempus fugits!
It was only yesterday that that happened, yet it was a year ago.
You fellows have grown a dozen years older. I *feel* like Methuse-
lah. Egad! I ought to be a junior now with my class. And
here I am only a soph and rusticated at that! [Without a change
in his voice] I say, when shall we start for New York, Jack? I
hear there's to be a big send-off."

"Of course," said Harry. "We've got a brass band and tin horns; we're going to do the thing up proud at the depot."

"I suppose you'll expect speeches," said Jack, who was binding a patch over Stamp's left eye, a sole reminder of the fight with Gradley's Tim. Stamp he intended to take with him wherever he went. The fight with Gradley's dog had ended a great deal of bickering which had been going on for a year. Stamp was now a hero. The dog seemed to appreciate and feel the new honors achieved by him. You may say what ugly things you will of a bulldog, it is the most human and most faithful creature in the whole world.

Before Jack had destroyed Tutor Smile's notebook, he and Harry and Coles had copied off a list of the names which the tutor had "spotted." Many of them were not out the night of the bonfire, and had their names come before the faculty would probably have been warned or punished by marks, or in some cases even suspended, on the strength of the tutor's statement. There had been so much rowing the last two years, the faculty were making every effort to suppress it. Many a man came up and thanked Jack for what he had done, and when he and Caswell, in the carriage driven by the smiling Barney, moved in procession headed down Chapel Street on the Saturday morning following, I doubt if there was a more pleased, contented, and delighted, and *un*punished under-class man in all Yale College.

"What are eight weeks anyway?" said Caswell. "It's a vacation from all the everlasting 'literary and religious' exercises. We will manage to have a pretty good time. We can do what we please. New Haven is only a small part of the world, anyway."

"I suppose it doesn't seem so to the faculty, or they wouldn't think it such a terrible punishment to send us ten miles away from the city environs," said Jack, as they rode along listening to the singing and the music of the brass band.

"They judge us by themselves," laughed Caswell. "Think how queer it would be to rusticate a tutor—cut him off from his salary —or suppose they compelled Professor Black to live away from New Haven—what a small potato he'd be in New York, eh?"

First at Brood's and then at the depot (then the old underground affair on Chapel Street) there were parting speeches, bottles of champagne, and much hand-shaking. If Tutor Smile had happened down there at the time he would have met with a somewhat overpowering reception. The college world, dear reader, is not the "parental" world—it is a world by itself—and Jack in college parlance had been very plucky and "square," and his hard luck was not "deserved."

As Harry grasped his hand and their eyes met for the last leave-taking, a pleasant smile came to both.

"I haven't thought much about you, Chestnuts, the last day or two," said Jack; "you'll be lonely—but you'll come up and see us when we get fixed in Charmington—or wherever we go. Good-by, old sporty. Thank the Lord it's no worse than it is!"

> " Good-by, Jack,
>   Don't stay long;
> Come back soon to your own Chickabiddies!
>   Oh, good-by, Jack,
>   Don't stay long!
> For we all love you, Jack, like a broth —er!"

So sang his classmates, and the whistle blew, the bell rang, and Jack Rives waved his hat, and he and Caswell were off together for New York, on their enforced vacation. In the eyes of most of the faculty they were indeed *Arcades ambo*—blackguards both!

CHAPTER XXVI.

THE VISIT TO CHARMINGTON.

"WELL, what's happened?"
    "Give us the news!"
    "Who has taken the *Lit.* medal?"

These were Harry's first greetings a few weeks later, when he met Jack and Caswell walking in the road as he drew near Charmington on top of the old stagecoach, then driven by the famous "Ammi." Old Charmington girls all remember "Ammi."

Caswell and Jack had concluded to rusticate in the pleasant little Connecticut village, after ten days of New York.

Harry proceeded to give them all the college news. Everyone was grinding for the examinations and thinking about the Christmas holidays. The Thanksgiving jubilee had guyed Tutor Smile terribly. The faculty were going to suppress the jubilee. There were hints, too, that they were going to suppress all the freshman societies except Gamma Nu, which, remarked Caswell, was already turned into a sort of prayer-meeting.

"Well, how is Charmington?" said Harry. "How is Miss Stout? How are all the girls? Do they know I'm coming? what a treat is before them?"

"No; we haven't said a word," laughed Jack. "We're going to let your presence burst upon them like a box of Rising Sun stove polish!"

"I suppose Miss Stout has got up a little dance, or some entertainment for to-night?" he laughed lightly.

"No; but we've got up a skating party for you this afternoon, about a mile to the north'ard, on the river down by the 'old red bridge.' The skating is fine—and Carrie Hastings skates like a swan."

"That's a libel!" laughed Harry.

As the stage slowly toiled up a hill beneath some fine elms, they passed several grand old colonial houses standing a little back from the street. The whole aspect of the peaceful village, strung out, New England fashion, along the one wide street, was charming and delightful, but a deathlike stillness prevailed. It seemed, as Harry observed, that no one quite dared to speak above a whisper.

Springing down from the coach, as it stopped before a little white hotel, the genial landlady came out to greet them. Caswell and Jack were already prime favorites with Mrs. Watt, and she took pains to make their stay as pleasant as possible. No one whose lot it was to visit Charmington at this period can help recalling her jolly face, her kind ways, and her motherly kindness to young people coming to and going from school, and she was one of the best cooks in all the little Nutmeg State.

It was just the dinner hour, midday, when they arrived. And how they sailed into Mrs. Watt's chickens *à la Maryland*, and her lamb pot-pie with its delicious gravy! And how good the new cider was—and the fresh celery—and the pickled butternuts —and the hot mincepie—and the cream, rich, thick, and delicious!

"Charmington is not so bad. I think a man might well stay here *two* days!" laughed Harry, as they rose from the table and lit their cigars. They were the only guests.

Harry, being remarkably good-natured, could be teased and persuaded into doing almost anything. They started out for a walk and soon approached Miss Stout's, where they intended persuading him to make a call. At a turn in the road on the way, clad in a long dark cloak with a gray fur collar, a neat, trim little knit Tam o'Shanter cap surmounting her dark hair—her whole aspect so demure, so scholastic, yet so *comme il faut*—walked the beautiful Miss Hastings herself.

Dare he approach? What was the thing to do? Harry stood there spellbound, unable to decide. He did not know the etiquette of Charmington.

"Bow coldly and pass her like a stranger," whispered Caswell, who knew what was what. But Harry couldn't do that. He went forward and extended his hand.

"Mr. Chestleton! How very sorry I am!" she cried.

"I'm not!" he laughed as he grasped her gloveless hand.

"That you're in such bad company, I mean"— with an amused smile in Jack's direction.

"Oh, those fellows have no power to harm *me!*" he laughed. "I'm not rusticated, you know. Do you think me capable of such a thing?"

"He deserved a worse fate," said Caswell, "than to be *banished* into the presence of Miss Hastings."

"Yes, the faculty are keeping his nose on the grindstone!" laughed Jack. "He is not to be allowed the inestimable privileges of Charmington except for over Sunday."

"Over Sunday! Then I shall see you at church?"

"Yes—and—aren't you going to skate this afternoon?"

Clara Hastings glanced furtively down the broad street to see if there was any teacher in sight. Some elderly ladies were coming out of the school-gate, and she said hastily, "Yes, at four o'clock at the old red bridge."

Then she quickly walked on.

It is not to be supposed that the boys were unmindful of their appointment.

At four o'clock, while Jack and Caswell chattered and bustled about and put on the girls' skates for them by the old red bridge, Harry stood back awkwardly, unable to say a word. Clara Hastings overwhelmed him with her beauty to-day. His usual presence of mind was all gone. He looked "all broken up," Jack said afterward. Visions of pretty Ella Gerhart came to him then, but he knew that Ella's was an affair of the "past." He was now, he felt it, *really* in love. It was no matter for amusement. He was flustered, excited—didn't know exactly what he was saying. "May I have the first dance?" he asked Miss Carringford before she had risen from the turf bank where she was sitting. Oh, what a break!

Miss Carringford, a charming young blonde from Baltimore,

looked up, saw his seriousness, and laughed in his very face. Both girls were capital skaters, and were up and off in a fine "outer edge" together before the young men could get on their skates.

The ice on the old mill-pond was good and free from snow. It was a pretty place, surrounded on three sides by fine old timber. The old mill, which was a picturesque wooden affair with a large wheel, afforded an excellent retreat in case of cold. Not far off the old red bridge gleamed in the sun through the trees. As they all skated slowly around to the bridge, they met two more scholastic Charmingtonians, and there was an introduction all around.

The new girls seemed to have the air of feeling it was all very wicked, but jolly—as if it were all a sort of lark.

"Mr. Chestleton and I are old friends," said Clara Hastings, who seemed to have no embarrassments.

"Yes, old chums," blurted out Harry. It was not at all what he wanted to say. He couldn't control his tongue.

"Oh, pray tell us what awful thing *you* did to be sent up!" asked one of the girls, while Clara, turning down the corners of her mouth, skated off with Jack.

"I—I—killed a tutor—not entirely by accident, I assure you," said Harry, with his eyes fixed on the graceful retreating pair, "and afterward, to conceal the crime, I burned his body in my stove—my coal gave out."

"So the faculty went and rusticated you for only that? How cruel!" laughed one of the girls.

If Clara Hastings kept far away, he found he could talk glibly enough with the other girls. How jolly it was skating about with these pretty young *scolastiques* and no chaperone in sight! His eyes, however, kept wandering off after Clara Hastings. She had thrown off her cloak now and was skating in a sealskin sack, her Tam o'Shanter, with its red tassel, danced in the wind as she flew by like some skimming bird over the ice.

How divinely she skated! *He loved her;* but he would never dare confess it, because she must think him so clumsy and stupid. He could skate very fast, but he could not do the "outer roll" at all. By George! he would try it, though. He did—and over he went, his feet up in the air, at Clara Hastings' very feet! Everyone laughed. It was the first fall of the afternoon. Miss Hastings laughed, too, and gracefully stooping, gave him her hand.

"Come, I will teach you," she said rather patronizingly. When a girl can excel a man in any outdoor sport how *very* condescending she always is!

The mental picture he conceived of himself was really quite distressing. To her he was a manly, handsome fellow, and plucky, too, for she remembered the brave fight he had made against Harvard last June. She rather liked his honest awkwardness, in her secret heart, under her tuition. He tried to catch her light, *spirituelle* grace, and endeavored to become at once easy and graceful himself.

"Eyes—up—up—up!" she laughed as they swung under the old red bridge with a grand sweep.

He stopped suddenly.

"I—I—please don't look at me so!"

"Not look at you, Mr. Chestleton?"

"I can't stand it. You think me a clumsy idiot—you're the only girl I care to—to—not have—I'm going back on Monday."

She did not smile. Her heart was beating strangely, too.

"Sometimes I have wished it was you and not Mr. Caswell who had been suspended. I don't like him."

Could he believe his ears?

He fairly trembled as he said eagerly, "If I thought you cared to have me here I'd go back to college and steal the clapper out of the chapel bell—and get caught by Smile—anything to be here near you——"

"*No*," she cried firmly; "if you want *me* to care a pin for you, go back and beat Harvard next July!"

Then she skated swiftly away, and he thought he heard her merry laughter ring out, though she turned her face away from him. Evidently the idea of his being rusticated on *her* account began to strike her as immensely funny. It was an offer of an act of devotion which confirmed her quick feminine instinct as to the real situation after their meeting on the Caswell yacht in mid-sound the previous summer. Harry then imagined himself in love!

He did not see very much more of her that day. Clara cleverly avoided any more little *tête-à-têts* on the ice. The girls took their leave of them at the old bridge, after skating until they were tired, and after a promise to take a stolen walk the next day (Sunday) in the later afternoon.

As Harry, Jack, and Caswell lit their cigarettes and watched the laughing knot of sweet, lovable girls disappear in the growing dusk up the roadway, and the stars began one by one to creep out and shine like lamps above the horizon, Ted Caswell—the worldly —the "wicked," as he was denominated at college—Caswell himself gave vent to their common thought, in the delicate poetic outburst:

> Rah—rah—rah—
> Rah—rah—rah—
> Rah—rah—rah—
>   *Charmington!*

In the long brisk walk they took, two by two, on the Sunday afternoon following, Harry could not, for the life of him, bring their conversation to personal matters. Clara Hastings was a laughing, charming, whole-souled sort of girl, who apparently had not the least desire to flirt. Of rich parentage—her family now lived in Cleveland, O., and owned a beautiful house on Euclid Avenue—she had the rare good sense to enjoy what came along, and yet to avoid the pitfalls of flirtation into which so beautiful a girl is often tempted.

Presently Harry and Clara became separated from the others, and found themselves walking along the hard smooth road through a piece of woods. Their talk had been very sedate and serious. Harry had told her a great deal about himself and his life at Yale —his hopes and fears for senior year societies. He told her, too, about his mother and what a noble woman she was, and of his sister, who, he expected, would enter Charmington in another year.

"I should like to meet her—it's such a pity! I shall leave Charmington next year—perhaps go abroad with the family. My

HARRY AND CLARA BECAME SEPARATED FROM THE OTHERS.

father's health is not good, and he and my mother and elder sister
are in London. I wish you could see Jessie," she cried with
enthusiasm; "she's a real beauty—and she's made a tremendous
hit in London society."

"I can't bear to think of your going over there—and being
'noticed' by the Prince and all that."

"Oh, *me!* No one will ever notice me," she laughed.

" *By Jove!*" cried Harry energetically, then subsided.

"My aunt wants me to spend next winter with her in New
Haven," pursued Clara—"especially if the house is closed and all
are abroad, as they expect to be."

"Oh, do!" he cried, delighted. "It will be our junior year,
and we'll try and make you have a jolly good time." Then he
added, "Do—on my account."

"You—what would you care?"

"I—I—" again he paused.

"I know students pretty well!" she laughed gayly. "They are
all the same. They say the same things to each girl they're with,
and the girls always relate to each other what's said—and there
you are!"

"Oh, yes! I suppose you girls tell each other everything.
That's where *men* are different. *We* are always silent as a tomb.
For instance——"

" Well?"

"Do you think I ever let Jack know how much I care for you?"

It was a puzzling question to answer.

"I don't think you *ought* to care for anyone now, Mr. Chestleton. I think you ought to think of your studies first." She gave
a pretty toss of her head.

"I do—but second——"

"Thanks, I don't care to be second to anything"—and she
walked on very briskly.

"Miss Hastings, you know how to be aggravating. Of all
girls in the world——"

"Well, I like *that*." (Heightened color.) "Aggravating!
Well, Mr. Chestleton, do you think I'm going to all this trouble

for you and risking Miss Stout's displeasure, though I know she wouldn't mind as long as we had met before—to hear that I am aggravating?"

There was a dangerous, mischievous flash in her pretty eyes, and Harry hastened to say:

"I know I am awfully stupid not to see you don't care for me one bit, and that you like—I know whom you like."

"Well, who is it?" She paused, and her chin went up in the air.

"It's Ted. Yes, and I shouldn't be a bit surprised to hear the next thing you're engaged."

He said this defiantly, and though very angry, she said, "It's a case of little pitchers again! I'm *not* engaged, and don't intend to be. Oh, do let's hasten on and catch up with the rest! Here we are quarreling already. I'm sure that I meant to be amiable, but *you've* been perfectly horrid."

"I didn't mean to be," he said meekly.

"Well—you've been very 'young,' at all events—dreadfully 'young,'" she said as they parted.

He recognized this as being one of the most crushing things a Charmington girl could say.

Slipping on his ulster after supper, Harry strolled out and down the street. The bell was ringing for evening service at the meetin' house opposite the school, and as he approached the white simple edifice, he knocked the ashes out of his pipe, feeling half inclined to enter. This affair with Clara was a deeply serious thing with him. He felt that if he couldn't win the love of the beautiful girl he would leave college and go into business out West somewhere. The Ella Gerhart affair had been a useful episode. He discovered how sweet a thing a girl's love is, and it taught him to value Clara's affection only the higher.

He entered the church and took a seat way back in the rear. The schoolgirls came trooping in two by two. It was not to be a regular service—it was to be a "service of praise." A lady whose face was unknown to him presided. The girls seemed to have somewhat less constraint than in the morning. The atmosphere of the plain white meeting house was much less chill; but he felt lonely, he being the only male being in church, and as Clara did not come in, he looked furtively around with a view of making an early escape. He realized that he had only entered for the purpose of staring at the back of Miss Hastings' head and of observing the abundant coils of her dark luxuriant hair.

What young man is there who has ever loved who has not dreamed away hours in the sanctuary over the distant view of the bonneted and beribboned fair one? The purity and sanctity of her surroundings make a heaven for her lover out of the cold, gray church walls. His love is pure and beautiful at such times. He worships—her!

He was alone. He felt timid, weak, discouraged, hopeless—when Clara Hastings herself, accompanied by a slender little girl of thirteen or so, entered hastily his very pew and knelt by his side, fairly crowding him along further in the pew. The little girl eyes him admiringly, and Clara rose and gave him a sweet, forgiving—dared he say *loving* glance? No; it wasn't that; it was pitying, rather.

It was a brave thing she was doing, there before Miss Stout and so many girls, but, after all, it was the act of a lady. She knew he had no hymn-book; she knew that he was alone; she knew he was unhappy, so she felt drawn to him (!).

She was wholly and overwhelmingly lovely to him. Her hair, slightly disarranged, hung low on her white neck. She had a slightly wearied air, too. Her pretty hands, with their rings, held the hymn-book open on her lap. He did not mind the stares of the girls—even the giggles. What a strange, impulsive, beautiful girl she was! His heart beat fast as they rose to sing, and his hand just touched hers. His soul soared high into realms of peace and purity and love. He never forgot that sweet little white church afterward during his life—the trembling organ, the choir of sweet girl voices, the smoking lamps suspended from the ceiling—ah! it was heaven to him that night.

As they went out Clara presented him to Miss Stout—not with a coy shamefacedness, but with a calm, high-bred demeanor which disarmed her preceptress.

When Harry slowly walked back to the "colony" with Clara Hastings, both were rather quiet. At the gate, as they parted, he asked a question, "May I write?" The moon covered her fair white face as she answered, shaking her head, "I don't think——"

"Then I *shall!*"

CHAPTER XXVII

VACATION AT HOME.

ULE-TIDE saw our hero at home in the comfortable New York house in West Thirty-sixth Street. Clara Hastings was at New Haven with her aunt, and perhaps would find time to answer the letter he had written during Christmas vacation. How anxiously he inquired every day at home if a letter had come for him!

At last one day his mother asked:

"Do you expect a letter from Ella Gerhart?"

"No."

"What has become of her?"

"She's out West somewhere in a theatrical *troupe* with her sister."

"She has never written you?"

"No; but she has sent me half a dozen programmes at different opera houses and theaters, with her name in the cast."

"Who do you expect is going to write you, Harry?"

"Oh, I don't know."

"Tell me——"

"I wrote to her first, at Charmington."

"Tell me her name. Of course, Miss Stout doesn't want her girls corresponding with everyone."

"Mother, am I—*everyone!*—Clara Hastings said once she didn't dislike me. I told her I was bound to write. I didn't care *what* she did about it. I wrote her after I visited Jack at Charmington. That was over three weeks ago. She hasn't answered it."

"Of course she won't."

"But my letter was very formal. I just told her that I hoped

I would see her in New York this vacation. She's in New Haven now, you know."

"Where did you first meet her, Harry?"

"On the Caswells' yacht. Mrs. Caswell introduced us."

Mrs. Chestleton appeared mollified. "Of course it's *some* one you young fellows are eternally after," she laughed; "and I'm glad it's a lady this time, and not a shop girl—is she pretty, Harry?"

"She's the prettiest girl at Charmington!"

His mother kissed him.

"She is Miss Stout's especial favorite."

"So was *I* in my day."

His sister Kitty, coming in at the moment, the conversation changed to other matters.

Kitty Chestleton had shot up into a tall, healthy young girl, without the slightest touch of sentiment and with the greatest desire to tease anyone who could be convicted of having any. She held a square envelope in her hand provokingly. Harry could see it had a monogram on the back. The handwriting was large and very straight, up and down. His heart stood still as Kitty laughingly held the letter high in her hand, then thrust it behind her.

."It's from a girl—I'm sure it is," she cried; "and I think mamma and I ought to read it first. Don't you, mamma?"

Harry tried to appear indifferent. "Mother, don't you think Kitty is getting too old for this sort of thing?" he said, getting a little angry. "Let me have it," he added; "it's probably a notice about something or other. Is it from New Haven?"

"You shan't know!" and Kitty, to tease him beyond endurance, lit a match as if to burn his letter to ashes. He sprang up and made a dash for her, but Kitty was too quick for him. She ran laughing out of the room. It was a long stern chase, but he got it at last.

Having captured the letter Harry retired into his room and locked the door in order to devour its contents in peace and quietude.

Very little comfort the letter gave him! It was couched in that cold, formal, stilted style a young lady can reduce herself to when desiring to be particularly impressive. "She had not written in reply to his very kind letter in Charmington, because she had been so very busy with her music. It had been very gay in New Haven during the holidays. The De Lanceys had given a grand ball, and two hundred people were there. She had met a 'Mr. Davis,' of Umpty-four, and liked him very much. She had danced with him three times." This piece of startling information was underscored, as if to impress Harry, but it only made him full of wrath.

"She's always throwing some other fellow at me!" he cried, "when she *must* know a man can't stand it. What does she think a man is made of?"

When he got back to college for winter term he waited exactly four weeks before replying to her letter. His letter gave Clara Hastings a graphic account of the gayeties. It brought a long reply inside of a week, couched in most motherly terms, and urging him to study harder and give up "foolish amusements" and "trifling nonsense," etc. Harry flattered himself he was beginning to understand girls pretty well. The French say that when two people are in love one is always the victim. Harry was obliged now and for some time during the rest of his sophomore and junior years to feel the pangs of unrequited love, but he managed to keep his passion boiling and bubbling well within himself. He began to go out in New Haven society a good deal, and to "ease his heart" he devoted himself to several pretty girls at once. When the Junior Prom arrived in February he managed to flirt and make love in the old time-honored sophomore style as if there was no lovely Clara Hastings at Charmington, holding his heart by a chain of steel. He used to sit and talk to Nevers and Coles and Ritch and old 'Gran' at Mrs. Moriarty's, and eat rarebits and drink ale and lay down the law about love and woman till the small hours. What a knowing set those sophs were, to be sure! with old Gran, who had been brought up on a Western farm—and who had less of an idea of what a woman was made, as Jack said, than a donkey!

"Boys," Grannis often said, when they were all through talking, "boys—there's one thing—women want to be treated *honest.*"

There was a world of philosophy for you! Old Gran treated everyone "honest," except, of course, the faculty. The letters *he* wrote for his poor old mother to copy and send to his division officer (and which had once brought tears to dear old Tutor Dilworthy's eyes)—never brought a blush of shame to *his* cheek. But with women and common men he was—honest!

Grannis returned from the West, after a three weeks' absence, at Christmas in a very cheery frame of mind. His business affairs were prospering to a very great degree. But better than all he had seen Ella Gerhart, now known as "Eline St. Pierre" in Cincinnati, and she had yielded to his persuasions sufficiently to promise to leave the stage when her engagement was up. He told Harry that she was more beautiful than ever; that she sang and danced so that men were bewitched who saw her.

He never confided in Harry to the extent of telling him whether he and Ella had come to any definite understanding. Harry inferred that she had been unwilling to say anything very definite. Grannis told him something about the Gerhart Electric Light Company, however, which surprised him. "A capitalist in Cleveland has put in twenty thousand dollars," he said, "and the Gerharts move there next week. If Papa Gerhart succeeds, he'll be ten times a millionaire. Sure!"

"Then Ella won't be such a bad match, after all!" said Harry.

"Do you think I care for her money?" growled Grannis. "I'd marry her and leave college to-morrow if she came to me penniless!"

Harry looked at him admiringly a moment. They were in Harry's room just after noon recitation, and were meditating a stroll over to the fence. Grannis was seated on the window-cushions, and as the day was warm in the sun the window was open. Everything pointed to spring. The grass below them was endeavoring to paint itself in a living green, and the seniors in front of old South were at their senile games of top-spinning and marbles—in college the surest signs of the coming summer known.

Our hero had seen a little of society and of many girls during the term, and Ella Gerhart, and those jolly Bohemian hours of freshman year passed with her, now seemed very far away. He wondered now why he had looked at her twice. Visions of another face, a finer mind, a deeper nature, came to him as he thought of the beautiful Clara. He even pitied Grannis for caring so much for that pretty, light, *tête de linotte* Ella. "But," he reflected, "Grannis is *Western*." And there was no accounting for tastes.

At the post office that night Harry found a long letter from Jack Rives, postmarked not Charmington but Mitford. As Jack's letter was characteristic of the boy we give it entire, with the mild request that our feminine readers will skip the following three pages, as matter of no interest to them.

MITFORD, CONN., March 2.

MY DEAR OLD CHESTNUTS:

Here we are—not tired exactly from Charmington—oh, no—but mildly requested to seek more congenial quarters, that's all. You see Cassy got too demonstrative, and sent too many bouquets to Miss Carringford, or Hargreaves—I've forgotten whom it was; and then Miss Stout heard something about the way we took the girls out walking of a Sunday afternoon—poor girls! They never have any relaxation from the steady, hard grind at Charmington; and the first thing we knew, up came a letter from the faculty requesting us to select some other less interesting village in which to rusticate. Someone told us of Mitford, and we're glad we're here—the loveliest town in Connecticut—and too, for its size, the liveliest. Well, we hadn't got to town from dear old quiet Charmington five minutes, before we recognized the fact that it was a "horse of a different color." No girls here, Harry—but a lot of village sports instead—good fellows, who are fond of horses and dogs. As soon as Stamp began to get acquainted a little, a half dozen "gents," who congregated in the hotel of an evening, got to talking about a dog in town "what could bite the head off that there pup"—and at first we paid no attention to them. But as time went on, they got to bragging so about their dogs and about a Bridgeport dog that, by George, Cassy and I couldn't stand it. Were we going to lie down and admit Stamp was only a ladies' pet? Not much—and Stamp himself began to get provoked. Now Stamp, in Charmington, had just followed along like any amiable lapdog, and he let the girls pet him as much as they liked. But in Mitford—well, he wouldn't hardly let me handle him—he knew what sort of a town it is, and he had gone in privately to train for a fight—he knew what was coming.

Well, things worked along sort of so-so the next day, and Mr. Steems, our landlord, came to me and offered his big barn, if we'd consent to try conclusions with some Mitford fighters. I talked it over with Caswell, and he advised a fight—London rules. So we put up a challenge in the bar-room as follows :

" *To all whom it may concern :*

" The subscribers will back their bulldog, *Stamp*, against any three dogs (one at a time) owned in Mitford, for one hundred dollars. London rules. Each owner to handle dog.

" J. RIVERSON.
" T. CASSY."

You see we didn't want our names to appear, it might get up to the ears of the faculty. Well, it wasn't long before our challenge was accepted, and the date of the fight set for last Saturday night. For three days before the fight we took Stamp on long ten-mile walks, and fed him on raw beef, and he was fit to fight for his life (and he had to) when Saturday came. There was a crowd of townies and sports from Bridgeport, and half a dozen juniors down with their big dog Dan—how they got wind of it I don't know, unless Cassy wired them—though he promised to keep it a dead secret. Well, we took every bet offered, and Cassy's old classmates covered a lot of side bets also. I wish you'd been there, old boy ! There were fifty people round the pit in the barn, and everyone there was certain that the " Yale doggy " would have no show. You see they played sharp on us, and wouldn't let us see their dogs until they brought them in for the fight. We had a wrangle over the referee, and were getting into a snarl, when who should walk in but Charley Gradley, and we agreed on him at once. How he ever heard of the fight and came down from New Haven I never shall know, I expect. Well, let me get to the fight.

The first bout was between Stamp and a black cur about twice his size. As ugly a looking brute as I ever saw—a regular half mastiff. Well, Stamp said nothing, but went in and got a grip on his right foreleg and crushed it, while the brute chawed Stamp's auricle. The leg was broken in four minutes, dog whined, stopped fighting, and owner removed dog for repairs. We made fifty on this fight.

Second bout, a bull half-breed—Brindle. Stamp vicious—no more legs for him. He grabbed opponent by the throat, hung on, and finally opponent keeled over dead ; time, 11 minutes, 33 seconds. Rough and tumble while it lasted. We coopered thirty dollars. I examined Stamp, and found he was all right except his ear, which was well chawed. We bathed him in alcohol and water, and soaped his neck well, for his third fight was with a thoroughbred bull smuggled in (Mr. Steems knew all about him, too) from Bridgeport. It was a rotten shame, but Stamp seemed anxious to take down the Bridgeport pride, and after consultation and announcing the fact of the owner's residence, we made the bet one hundred to seventy-five, and the dogs went at it. It was a hard fight. They weighed even. Bridgeport was fresh, but Stamp was waiting for him. I never saw such a fight. Nip and tuck all the way through. The pit and the barn floor was covered with blood. At the end of the first round we threw ice water on them to separate them. Honors even.

Round 2.—Poor Stampy was groggy, but was all there and fought gamely. He lost blood from his ear. It was a —— shame to ring in a thoroughbred fighter from Bridgeport on us at that stage of the game.

Round 3.—We washed our dog, and they went at it again, hammer and tongs. Everyone was silent as death. Bridgeport's handler yelled out "a hundred even," and I took it. That money's in my pocket now, but I'm afraid Stamp, dear, faithful old Stamp is done for, but hope for the best.

After some rough and tumble "in" fighting (very bloody) Stamp got a grip on Bridgeport's foreleg—his old trick. We could hear the bones snap between his old iron jaws, but the other dog had got on to Stamp's neck and gouged a piece out, and hung on with a grip like "death to a dead nigger" until, by great good luck, Stamp made a splendid "roll over"—a neat wrestling trick (I wonder where the old chap learned it ?)—and shook himself free. Bridgeport's day was over, he fell over on his broken leg, and Stamp grabbed him by the throat and killed him. Time, 39 minutes, 40 seconds. But Stamp is a mighty sick dog to-day. We've got a veterinary surgeon and a Bridgeport dog fancier at work over him. Dear old dog! He lies by the stove in a box of rags and cotton, and can only wag his tail a little, feebly. We give him milk and seltzer every half hour. The men say he'll never be fit to make a big fight again, but we think differently. Steems lost a hundred and fifty dollars on the fight. I'm glad of it. He's down on Stamp. Ted and I spend all our time nursing the dog. Dear old Stamp! *He's* a fighter!—regular Yale sand in him! Please send my collars, etc.

About four or five days later Jack wrote again :

The faculty must have got wind of the dog fight in some way. We have received notice that our hotel is *twenty yards* within the limit of ten miles of the New Haven State House. It means we've got to get out,* and go further west, east, north, or south! We've heard of a jolly place down on the Housatonic River, about two miles west of here, down on the Sound, Mrs. Mead's,

---

* This is based on actual fact. Professor Maynard had figured out the exact distance by trigonometry, and it was this reason the faculty gave in a similar case in real life.

where there are several pretty girls in the family. We're going to hunt it up.

Stamp is getting better. He'll be all right in a week more. We are taking the best sort of care of the dear old fellow, etc.

This letter of Jack's spoke for itself. Sometimes Harry wished he had been suspended along with his chum, he felt so lonely in his absence, and Jack and Caswell seemed to be having such a lively time of it wherever they went.

He tried knocking about in other fellows' rooms and visiting his classmates—a dreary sort of thing when one only does it for the sake of companionship. He hunted up all sorts and conditions in his class—from Miss Alum and her nephew David, who was easily the first in the class with a stand of 3.92—a phenomenal stand and fully equal to perfect. The queer old-fashioned back country couple still had rooms on York Street, and David complained a good deal of the "overbearingness" of the set of Andover freshmen who now inhabited Mrs. Gimly's lodging house. Harry called one night on Mrs. Gimly herself and Samanthy, but Mrs. Gimly sternly barred him out, he being confessedly a sophomore, and he could only parley a moment with her in the crack of the door.

By pushing out in this way, by reason of his loneliness, Harry first became acquainted with old "Penelope" Jones—a shrewd old Connecticut Yankee, who got his name one of the first days in freshman year, by not sounding the last "e" of this name in Greek recitation. He met the "godlike" Jasper, a tall, big, overgrown light-haired fellow, whose baby face and kind heart endeared him to his classmates in after college years. Then there was the sphinxlike George Pistol, who lived all alone in a loft over the gymnasium, and got his schooling for his services; a strong, athletic fellow, who was afterward to become well known in college as an oarsman. He admitted that, in the lonely vigils of the night, when he could not sleep, he would rise, and going down into the ghostly creaking gymnasium pull a thousand strokes on the weights to harden his back muscles! He it was who confided to Harry that he had fasted a full month for poor Thornton, who was his special friend. Every grade of society seemed to be represented in Umpty-four—it even contained a negro, who recited very well, kept his own counsel, and was respected and liked in consequence. Harry visited about in every set and every clique in his class. He spent an evening with Weedy Pink, whom he had known at Andover, and whose kindly if watery eyes gave him a friendly greeting when he hunted him up in North Middle. Then there was dear old Jed Gilson, who had such a dreadful time with his conic sections and his Demosthenes, and whose bibulous nature led him to always keep in readiness for instant use a pair of what he called his "Drunk pants." There was "Dooney" Paris, a wit of a high order, an intellect remarkable for its marked power—he found "Dooney" rooming with a hirsute dry old stager by the name of Whipple Whayles. Paris was of delicate, consumptive tendency, and usually pursued his evening studies with his long legs curled about their tall coal stove. Whipple never failed to loudly object to this arrangement, but being a heavy, great good-natured up-country fellow, yielded to the witty persiflage of his more intellectual chum, and submitted to his fate. In the closet of this remarkable pair always stood a barrel of apples and a barrel of cider, fresh from some Connecticut up-country farm. Opposite them roomed cheery Fred Closter of Missouri, a 'varsity ball man, and his chum Matthews. Matthews was a remarkable ball player also and a remarkable "bummer." At the time he was chiefly noted in Umpty-four for smoking cigarettes and inhaling the smoke while he drank a glass of beer and then let the smoke percolate through his nostrils. He had also a strange hollow place where his heart ought to be, and it was rumored in the class that he would throw up his hands and die some day, while making a home run!

Even at that comparatively early day—winter term of soph year—speculation was rife as to who were going to senior societies in the class. The honor of belonging to one or the other (there were only two senior secret societies at the time we speak of) was considered the chief reason for remaining in college. Distinction of any kind was eagerly sought for, even in Delta Beta Xi, and Phi Theta Psi, the soph societies. Tremendous wire-pulling was done to get on the society campaign committees, or to make a hit in the theatrical exhibitions which the two societies gave regularly once a month. The question was always being asked —will So-and-so go to Spade and Grave? Where will So-and-so fetch up? To hear a knot of men talking on the sophomore fence one would have imagined that the elections into the senior societies were just then about to be given out. Then as now the senior societies were considered as more or less of a reward of social standing, or merit in the class. There were certain men whose honors always entitled them to membership, such as Yale *Lit.* men, prominent boating and baseball men, popular men, committee men or high-stand men. In the soph societies, which did not even try to keep up the debates and speaking of the freshmen secret societies, the regular recurring "bums" gave opportunities for scoring as actors; a man who made a good hit would be talked about even by juniors and seniors and would become known. Umpty-four contained in two or three men the best actors in college: Jack was a very successful end man afterward in the Jubilees, and Tom Patch really developed marked ability as an actor—so successful was he that he was offered a large salary on his graduation by one of the best stock companies in New York. Already the two "crowds" were becoming sifted out for senior year. Harry by virtue of his repute as a ball player was generally named as good for Spade and Grave. He had terrible misgivings himself however, and wondered whether, if his arm should give out or become injured, they would continue to have any respect for him? His plucky fight against Harvard had made him a well marked man even as far as within the remote regions of the Sheffield Scientific school. It was and is a great thing to be a 'varsity pitcher. There is never more than *one* who really fills this position in the entire University Catalogue. Even in soph year things are decided, the "leading" crowd knows its men. They are called the most "popular"; in reality they may be greatly disliked by a majority of the class. There may be men in the *select crowd* who are actually hated and feared by their classmates.

This does not matter if they are "in the crowd." Upper-class men reason largely by observing who runs with whom. Harry was already becoming aware that men in the class—Davis, for instance, a small, neat man with a trace of a mustache, and one who usually wore a high hat to make up for his size—were getting very "chummy" with him. They considered him a good man to be seen with. Two or three rich New Haven men began inviting him a good deal to their houses, and he began to see more or less of society in consequence. He wondered if it really could mean that these fellows considered that he had a "dead thing" on a senior society? It got to be so, before Jack came back to college, that he was donning his dress suit nearly every other night of the week. He began to have a delicious sense that he was a "prominent man" in his class. He wanted to be really liked too, and he wanted to do good work on the nine. Ah, it was delightful though, hearing the dear Yale girls flatter him and praise his powers of putting a twist on a ball!

If only *one* true Yale girl, now temporarily resident in Charmington, would write him a word of encouragement! But no, her letter never came!

CHAPTER XXVIII.

THE GENERAL VISITS JACK.

 SOPHOMORE year was lonely in college in spite of his "society" duties in New Haven. He missed Jack. He missed Stamp—and the dog's prowess at Mitford only emphasized to him his many good qualities. How he longed for the term of Jack's rustication to be over! Jack was always so jolly, so good-natured, so amusing. It was quieter now, and there was more time for study, but—"oh, for the bang of a vanished fist— and the sound of a bark that was still!"

He was sitting one night at his working table, digging out his Theocritus with the aid of "Liddell and Scott" beneath the light of his student lamp. Every one in old South was quiet, cramming hard on the difficult conic sections or trying to get up a "stand" in "Iphigenia."

> In sophomore years we have our task ;
> 'Tis best performed by torch and mask

was hardly true, Harry thought, of Umpty-four! He began list-lessly poring over his conic sections, when he heard someone at the door, and without a knock two elderly gentlemen hurriedly entered the room. They wore long beards, spectacles, and carried heavy canes. He was quite startled and rose to demand who they were, when, with a laugh, they locked the door, and threw their false beards, spectacles, and moustachios on the table. It was Caswell and Jack on a "sneak" from the Housatonic. "You wouldn't come down and see us," said Jack, grasping Harry's hand with a hearty laugh, "so we made up our minds to run up and see how things were getting on."

"If the faculty catches you——"

"Bosh! The faculty won't catch us. We're going to spend two or three days with you, Harry. In the first place the governor has written saying he is coming up to see me Wednesday —that is, to-morrow, and I've written a nice letter to Prexy, asking permission to be with my father in New Haven to-morrow. It will be too late for him to reply, saying I *can't* come, d'ye see? and so it will be all right. Father will be here on the eleven o'clock express and I'll meet him, and then we've got to take him in hand and keep him away from any of the faculty."

Harry laughed. "By Jove! I'm glad to see you," he cried. "*Awfully* glad!"

"I guess I'll slip over to see Holland," said Caswell, rearranging his beard, and wishing to leave the chums together.

"I'll walk over with you," said Harry, rising.

"No, better not. They might suspect. I'll just run down and up around where they are building the new chapel."

Caswell went out, arranging with Jack to be at his room in Farnam about two o'clock the next day. Holland and he had one of the show rooms in college, fitted up at great expense, and Jack wanted his father to see it. He knew that General Rives would insist on going about in the colleges and buildings to a certain extent, and he was going to depend upon Tutor Dilworthy and Dr. Lyman to give him the faculty's view of his son's standing and career. The rest he and "Barney" would manage very well, in a long drive, and a broken neck-yoke—anything to keep the general from calling on his old chum Professor Shepard, which they feared he would be bound to do. They let a few friends know of Jack's arrival and went down to see old man Brood, and see if his Catawba cobblers were as rich and rare as Jack's fancy still painted them. They took in Gradleys' also, Jack keeping on his disguise and mystifying Charlie Gradley not a little. At Mrs. Moriarty's at the "Quiet House," a number of their class joined them and they sat up to a late hour over rounds of Welsh rarebits and that rare delicious Burton ale, which they drank then out of their pewter cups, and were never to meet with, alas, afterward in the cold unsympathizing postgraduate world! After Mrs. Moriarty's, Jack wanted to serenade the fem. sems., and even try for the famous golden tooth which hung at the corner of York and Elm Streets. But Harry persuaded him to go quietly back to the room and to bed, where next morning Jack awoke and threw a shoe at Alston the sweep, in the same old, friendly, sophomoric way!

Wednesday arrived. Harry had Alston smuggle in a capital breakfast for himself and Jack from the New Haven House. The kind-hearted old darky entered into the affair with great zest after Harry gave him a dollar "extry." The breakfast was served after recitation, Jack enjoying the luxury of sleeping till half after nine, and Harry attending recitation and chapel, as he had often done before, on an empty stomach. A lot of the Gimly gang silently made their appearance—and Jim Danforth skipped out and bought a couple of magnums of champagne. They pulled down the curtains and sat around the room smoking, while Jack gave them a graphic description of Stamp's great dog fight in the Mitford Tavern barn, and proceeded to make them envious of the delightful life he was having on the Housatonic.

"Imagine," said Jack, stuffing his mouth with the broiled lobster Alston served him, "a large country house with a lawn sloping down to the river. In the house three girls, more or less young and more or less pretty. The best cooking in the world. A good piano in the parlor—we're teaching the girls how to play a banjo. And as if that were not enough, opposite, behind high gates, the country place of the Dolphins of New York. There are two Dolphin girls—full of the mischief—spending the winter there, and a stable full of riding horses. Then there is Stratford a mile one way and Mitford two miles the other. Fun! We have the greatest fun you ever saw—beats Charmington out of sight—much more freedom, you know. We skate, ride horseback, take all the girls to New York for a matinée—Lord! what fun we have! Fill up the glasses, Alston! and go out and fetch another bottle. I wouldn't miss my rustication for the world. Lord! how I pity you poor devils, made to go to recitation three times a day, while we sit about, make love, and go on a twenty-mile canter with the girls! Here's a photograph we had taken in Bridgeport. This one is Annie Mead, that's Marie Dolphin. This is Louise Dolphin, isn't she a beauty?"

"How's Stamp?" someone asked.

"Stamp's getting out again. He's a little lame yet—and he's cross as two sticks. But he's enjoying the country mighty well, as Ted and I are. Talk about training for the crew, I was never more fit in my life. Cassy and I box four rounds every day while Louise Dolphin holds the watch. I boxed the best man Stratford could set up last Saturday. He wasn't in it. Caswell is for getting a Bridgeport bruiser down and having it out with him for a championship badge, but I say No. Stamp says so, too. He and I are only going to spar with gentlemen 'amatures' after this!" and Jack laughed heartily.

It was wonderful to see the effect of his presence on Harry. Life brightened up again for our hero. The end of the world did *not* seem so near at hand while Jack was about. Things put on a cheery, hopeful aspect. Perhaps Ella Gerhart would *not* go to the bad, and Clara Hastings would show a little concern for him yet.

General Rives shook hands with the boys at the depot, and preferred to walk rather than enter Barney's inviting hack at the top of the stairs. He wanted to stretch his legs, he said, and look about a little. He hadn't been in New Haven for many years. He wondered when it would be the best time to go and call on Professor Shepard.

Barney, who had the wink from Harry, followed along slowly as they walked up Chapel Street, ready at the slightest nod to pull up, and take them off for a drive. *He knew his business.*

But the general didn't want to ride. They were in great dread lest, as they passed old Trinity and drew near the colleges, they would meet Professor Shepard, or some one among the older professors, whom the general would insist upon stopping and talking with. It was really a great risk, not letting him know of Jack's suspension. They felt certain he would be terribly angry about it, if he knew. Uncle Dick had gone so far as to volunteer going to New Haven to "steer" him away from all dangerous shoals and reefs of the faculty, but Harry thought this was not necessary.

The walk up to the New Haven House was fortunately quite enough for him. He did not care to ride, however, even then, and so they walked him rapidly over to their room in South Middle.

"Ah, the old brick row," exclaimed the old grad, "just the same as ever—not a brick changed—looks just as when I was in college. All the new buildings seem to be up about the north end of the campus. Suppose we go up there and walk about; we may run across President Stout."

"Oh, see the room first!" exclaimed Harry and Jack together.

Rather objecting to their odd insistence the general went up with them, and had a glass of sherry and a cigar. They seated him as far away from the window as possible, and listened to his reminiscences of the old college life of long ago.

"Why, this very room," he said, "used to be occupied by two classmates of mine, brothers—from up in the center of York State—Utica, I think. They were tremendous big strong fellows, and they had a standing offer of ten dollars to any two men they couldn't put out into the hall. I remember once they broke the door clean off its hinges. The only fire that ever occurred when I was in college came from their upsetting their stove. Their name was Wright, and Ben Wright was our class "bully"—always carried the banger in our class rushes. I guess you chaps don't know what a real hard banger rush means. They called me a fighter in the war. Well, all the fighting I ever learned, I learned in those banger rushes."

Then after a pause, and a puff on his cigar, with a drawl:

"I rather like a college man beside me in a fight. Oh, but nowadays I imagine college life is very tame. You are good hardworking schoolboys now. Well, perhaps it is better so!"

"We are more studious, we have to study so hard," ventured Harry, with a wink at Jack.

"Our parents sent us to college for a purpose," added Jack, "and we must not waste our time in rowing and fighting"—he added in a whisper, "What a joke on the governor!"

The general looked a little annoyed. "Oh, you'll waste time enough in one way or another," he said. "Boys at college always did, always *will* waste time. But a real hard fight now and then —yes, it's good for you."

"I wish you'd tell us how you lost your arm," said Harry.

"Why, it was a saber cut down to the bone, before Richmond. A squad of cavalry were in full retreat, and I saw the danger of their going back on a gallop and spreading consternation among the troops in the rear. So I seized a fresh horse and rushed out and stopped them. The officer said that they could do little with the men, and begged me to lead them back for at least one charge. Well, I did so. The enemy met us with a counter-charge. I was unhorsed, and the next thing I knew, I felt my arm drop powerless at my side; then I fainted from loss of blood. That was all there was to it; they had to amputate my arm at the shoulder. But now I think I'll go over and see Professor Shepard."

Both lads jumped to their feet at once. "It's dinner time; he'll think he *must* invite you to dine," cried Jack. "Better wait till afternoon."

"Oh, no; I don't think I need to dine with him, but we will see him and arrange for a drive later—we'll take out Mrs. Shepard also."

"Was Miss Walker in your day, sir?" asked Harry, thinking of the pretty college "widow" as a last resort topic.

"There were several of that name I think, but they are married, and grandmothers probably by this time."

As they were going out of the room Jim Danforth entered, having run up the short wooden stairs two steps at a time.

"We are just going over to see Professor Shepard," said Jack, with a horrified stare. Dan quickly took in the situation and acted accordingly.

"Why, he has just gone down Chapel Street, I think," he said.

"Had we not better go in and have dinner now, then?" urged Harry, looking at his watch. "It's one o'clock."

Dan walked with them over to the hotel. The general acqui-
esced without a murmur.

At the dinner table, he was full of reminiscence of college life
of forty years ago, the town and gown fights, the firemen's fights,
and the exciting rows of other days long forgotten. He remembered Danforth's father in '44 very well. "A little red-cheeked
little rascal," he laughed. He ordered a bottle of Pommery Sec,
and set up around of *pousse cafés* after dessert. They got him talking, and prolonged the dinner as late as they could. When they
came out on the street and walked to the fence, smoking the best
regalias, he said bluntly, "I'd like to go over to Spade and Grave
while I'm here." To Yale sophomores a senior society is the "be
all and end all" of existence. They fairly trembled with agitation
to hear him mention it in such an off-hand way. Perhaps the next
thing he'd do in his "old graduate" innocence would be to offer to
take them into the sacred building!

Here was a new source of danger. If the general insisted upon
visiting his old society hall, how could they manage to prevent his
finding out, from some joking allusion or other from some senior,
the fact of Jack's suspension?

There was Barney standing there by the door and winking at
them, and there, coming round a corner, was Professor Shepard
himself! The general did not perceive his old friend, nor he him.

"Come!" cried Harry quickly, "jump in this carriage, general,
and we'll drive right around to Professor Shepard's, and then we
can take a ride out to Hamilton Park and around."

They did so. Barney whipped up, drove down Chapel Street so
that they need not pass the professor, and then up George Street to
the old white house where he lived.

Of course the professor was out, and it was uncertain when he'd
be back. Harry climbed up on the driver's seat with Barney, and
looked at his watch. "He's got to take the five o'clock train, and
it's just half-past two now.".

Barney winked again. "We'll go out to West Rock first," said
Barney, "and that there off hosse's collar aint goin' to last more'n
halfway out!"

Barney was as good as his word. He drove rapidly about the city, up Hillhouse Avenue and out Prospect Street, and so on over toward Hamilton Park. The afternoon was mild and pleasant. When they were about entering the Park, the hack came to a stand.

"Only a part of the harness broke, that's all," called down Harry from the driver's seat.

"Well, well!" said the general, "I'm afraid I shan't get to see Professor Shepard after all!"

And he began to look rather glum and gazed at his watch.

"You can run down some other time," said Jack. "It only takes two hours from New York."

"Two hours! It takes a whole day, and do you think a whole day is nothing to me?"

"I didn't mean it that way, father. But you know this is your first visit, and I *enjoy* having you come so much."

The general looked mollified. "It takes me back to my early manhood," he said. "But I—I must say, Jack, I—I'd much rather spend my time on the campus than out here in this forlorn place. What's the matter with the harness?"

"Oh, it's only a strap thet's bruk," said honest Barney. "But it tak's toime to mend it, sor."

The general was out of the carriage in a moment, giving orders to Barney how to repair the harness. It may be confessed that Barney played his part very well, and it took him a mortal half hour before he was willing to proceed. The general fidgeted and swore once or twice at the faithful hackman's stupidity. Each time he swore he apologized. "Jack, Harry, forgive me. I didn't mean it—army habits, boys; that's all. Don't mind me, and *don't pattern after me!* Swearing is not only unnecessary—it's ungentlemanly—[to Barney] you damn fool! don't you see the strap will not work if you twist it that way? It reminds me of our mule trains on the Shenandoah."

When they got back to town Harry bade the old gentleman good-by at the fence, and Jack remained with him in the carriage.

"I think we could just drive over to Professor Shepard's door?"
he suggested.

"Just toime fer to git to the train," sung out the smiling
Barney, and he hurriedly drove them off down Chapel Street.

"Jack," said his father solemnly, as they paused behind a street
car.

"Yes, father?"

"You must be in debt? *I* was always in debt in college."

"No, father."

"Eh? not in debt? eh, my son?"

"No, sir; but it's only by the strictest economy, father." Jack
looked very pious.

"Your mother is very anxious about you, Jack, my boy. She
doesn't want you to row any more."

"Neither does Bob Clark," laughed Jack carelessly.

"Let me see—are you in Brothers or Linonia, my boy?"

"Neither."

"You *must* join one or the other."

"They are both deader than door nails!"

"Eh? I'm sorry for that. Your ridiculous baseball and football and boating have killed those best debating clubs in America!
It's a shame, Jack."

"They tried to revive them, but it's no go."

A long silence.

"Jack!"

"Yes, sir."

"You must be sure and go to Spade and Grave. It would break
my heart, Jack, if you didn't. *That's* partly what I came up here
for, Jack—you and Harry."

"Well, senior year is 'way off."

"Not at all. Are you aware that you will be elected to a senior
society in just about a year from now?"

"Why, that's so!"

"Now, if I'd only seen Professor Shepard——"

But they arrived now, opportunely, at the depot. Jack stood
in great awe of his father, who was usually rather stern with him,

but he was very proud of him and his armless sleeve. It was a pity he was obliged to deceive him! Unsympathetic, relentless, hard-hearted parents; to what lengths you drive your children when you make too much of their little shortcomings!

Jack bade his father an affectionate farewell at the depot, and saw him into a seat in the smoking car. As the train started he jumped on the last car of the train himself. At the Housatonic bridge all trains stopped, and the lad slipped off in the darkness and ran half a mile by the road to where he and Caswell were stopping at Mrs. Mead's. It was a large old-fashioned country house, with a lawn sloping down to the river. As he entered the door, Stamp, who had now nearly recovered from his fight at Mitford, and who was on the watch, ran out and gave a joyous, if husky bark. Jack took his head in his hand, tenderly.

"No, Stamp, I don't deserve any of your honest old affection," he exclaimed rather dismally. "It's the first time in my life I ever, in any way, even acted a lie to the dear old governor!"

But Stamp was glad to see him all the same, and was apparently of the opinion that the deception they practiced on the old general was done with a motive for his best good. For in what way do these college rustications punish anyone but the innocent parents?

CHAPTER XXIX.

NCLE DICK was very kind to Jack at this time, and carefully kept all intelligence of his rustication from his father. He had been a college boy himself only half a dozen years or so before, and *he'd* been rusticated from college himself. His poor mother had been driven nearly distracted by the terribly gloomy missives of the faculty, couched in the judicial terms of a criminal court. Of course discipline must be maintained at college, but Lyman believed that sorrow for nervous mothers and stern fathers was not the faculty's province.

The days of Easter vacation brought Jack's days of suspension to an end. Caswell and he came back for their examinations in the best spirits and health. Stamp was as glad to get back as they were, and what a triumph the dog had among his friends in South Middle! He enjoyed college life at its best—there were no religious or literary exercises for *him!* He could lie in the sunny window ledge of their South Middle room and sleep the hours away, with a clear conscience.

When they left college for home Harry said, as they stepped off the train at the Grand Central Depot:

" By Jove! almost half our college life is over, and yet it seems as if we had just entered. Thunder! how Tempus does fugit!"

" Mr. Chestleton! Mr. Chestleton!"

Harry and Jack, dressed in the very "latest," were sauntering down Fifth Avenue, laughing and talking in the easy manner of

274

college lads off on a holiday, a few days later, when they heard this name called.

A stylish brougham drove up to the sidewalk, drawn by a pair of neat little gray cobs with jingling harness. Clara Hastings' beautiful face was at the window.

A richly dressed lady sat by Clara's side, who was presented as "Mrs. Hargreave."

"I'm spending Easter with Bessie Hargreave, one of 'our set' at Charmington," said Clara to Harry. "I saw you go past. Oh, Mr. Rives, you look so swell I really shouldn't have known you!"

"Even *you* are not wearing a red Tam o'Shanter on Fifth Avenue!" laughed Jack, admiring her great and truly magnificent spring hat. "Tell me," he added with deliberate intention, "are you going to the theater to-night? if so, which one; I want to avoid it."

"What I wished to stop and say was," and Clara glanced at a number of people passing, "that I am at No. 1111 Fiftieth Street, West. Will you not call?"

Harry, who had hardly spoken a word, blurted out, "Can't I take you to church next Sunday, Easter, you know—anywhere you say?"

Clara looked down. "Come up to-morrow night," she whispered; "we'll talk it over." Then she bowed; Mrs. Hargreave laughed and bowed, and the brougham rapidly started off up Fifth Avenue.

He called, and he persuaded Clara that Easter morning in old Trinity would be simply "glorious." Easter would have been glorious anywhere with the idol of his choice.

Easter morning turned out bright, warm, and fair, as it usually is in the "gayest city of the western hemisphere," and since Clara Hastings had promised him to go down to old Trinity for morning service, could anything be more delightful? Harry's good mother was a little disappointed that he was not going to church with her and Kitty.

Clara was waiting for him, ready for church, in the reception

room of the richly decorated Hargreave mansion. She was a
vision of light, pretty spring colors, her hat something very large
and bewildering. Beneath it her lovely dark eyes looked up
demurely with the saintlike air of a young *religieuse*. She was
putting on her gloves, and her ivory-covered, dainty little prayer-
book, with its gold clasps and gold cross, lay in her lap.

He had the suspicion, without knowing it, that Bessie Hargreave
had just left the room as he entered. He thought he heard a faint
rustling of her dress on the stairs.

"Bessie thinks it's *perfectly* dreadful for me to go off to church
alone with a young man," said Clara; "but I promised you, Mr.
Chestleton, and whenever I make a promise——"

"I knew you'd do it for *me*," he said.

And instantly she rose, and they went out down the high stoop
to the street.

Out of the house, the fresh coolness of the morning air, the
sight of several sweet young girls going with their fathers and
mothers to church, restored Clara Hastings' mental balance. They
had to walk a block or two to Fiftieth Street, and they followed
behind three pretty young girls and their mamma.

"Poor girls!" laughed Harry.

"Why?"

"Oh, see the queer hats and queer gowns they have to wear to
be in the fashion! The hats—the slightest wind will carry them
off to the top of yonder building! and—well, I pity you girls—
but——"

"But, you are going to say it is all very becoming?"

"Yes; you are made into pretty flowers—as if we could not love
and admire you enough as you are!"

She gave him a bright glance. Many turned and looked at the
charming girl. She had never seemed so lovely to Harry.

The day was so bright and fair, the street so full of gayly dressed
churchgoers, that even the somber, stately, brown-stone palaces
on either side seemed to smile. Flowers tinted every window.

Swell little coupés passed them, the coachman and footman
wearing little rosettes of violets. The grand gloomy avenue could

not help assuming a gayer, more good-natured aspect for the nonce.

They turned down Fiftieth Street and presently his mother, in her quiet black, and Kitty, decked out in all the soft, pretty, spring Easter colors, passed on the other side. His mother bowed and put up her lorgnette.

"Mercy, how that lady stares!" was Clara's comment.

Harry turned red, and stammered:

"That is my mother and sister."

"Oh, I—of course she stared, to see her son being carried off by a strange female!" and Clara laughed.

"Yes, completely carried away by the stranger!" he laughed.

"Well, she's very handsome. I like her face. She is so *good-looking*——"

"I want you to meet her."

Clara walked a little more rapidly. The ground was getting a little "slippery," and so she turned the subject.

Going up the elevated stairs she said, "I once said that you and I—could be friends if you beat Harvard next June."

"And enemies if we don't?"

"There are several very nice Harvard men in Cleveland."

"Ah, yes! but you're a Yale girl—double-dyed. You had a brother at Yale, and I know you never could bring yourself to look at a Harvard man twice!"

Harry felt less tongue-tied with her to-day for some reason. All the way down to Rector Street they talked and laughed, forgetful that anyone was overhearing them. Very young people only become absorbed in this way. When they grow older they become aware that people are within hearing. It is true they felt an exhilaration in each other's presence. How does love begin? Is it not when thought matches thought, and ideas spring into existence, never dreamed of before, under the magic of pretty eyes? They were a little early, and so obtained very good seats far up before the beautiful altar. In the great church a reverent feeling took possession of them. The solemn air of the old vergers dressed in English fashion, the simple poor folk filing into the side aisles, the grandees invading the pews on the sides of the middle aisle, the splendid roll of the great organ as it began the preliminary music, then the masses of pure white lilies piled high over the choir, made them forget each other in the reverent, thrilling sense that they were in God's Holy temple upon one of the most glorious festal days of the Church. Clara knelt at his side, and he felt that as she prayed he was in her thoughts. The subtle perfume which came from her mingled with the scent of the church flowers, and his heart thrilled with feeling as they stood up at the entrance of the clergy and choristers. After the splendid full cathedral choir service they went slowly out, and wandered in the quaint old burying-ground which points its quiet lesson opposite Wall Street and the great stock-gambling centers of America. Jotted down between high buildings, the old graves reared their headstones in simple rows, many of them fast falling into decay and becoming indecipherable.

"I have always wanted to see Charlotte Temple's grave," said Clara, her eyes filled with a sweet enthusiasm, the result of the music and the service. Harry followed her about in silence until she paused before a simple flat stone containing the name and date of death of the famous love-stricken girl. What the tomb of Abelard and Heloise is to Paris, Charlotte Temple's grave is to New York—the Mecca of lovers. Harry had never heard of it, and on their way home Clara told him the sad story as she had read of it.

"A man who would make a poor, defenseless girl love him and then desert her deserves——"

He stopped short. A cloud came over his face. Had *he* behaved so very honorably with Ella Gerhart? Was it for *him*, of all men, to judge harshly the whole race?

"Some girls are not so defenseless," sighed Clara. "Men may be ever so manly, but a girl may flirt and lead them on. It is all in the way one is brought up. Oh, dear! [she turned suddenly to Harry as they sat in the elevated car] I hope I never said anything to you—to—lead *you* on."

"No!" he laughed; "I just follow along at my own gait!" and he laughed.

When Harry returned home his mother greeted him with a kiss. "She's a raving beauty," she said; "I'll say *that* for her, Harry."

"Well, she's just as good as beautiful," he replied rather sadly. "But she don't care a rap for me, nor for anyone. Mother," he added after a pause, "I wouldn't want *her* to know about Ella Gerhart. She would think me an awful wretch."

"Is she then such a terrible little puritan?" mused his mother. "She has such charming color—such eyes! Kitty is in raptures over her. My boy, I hope she's good; remember beauty is but skin-deep!"

"Well, she's too good for the likes of me!" and the dear fellow laughed dismally.

So Easter vacation passed and left a cloud on our hero's mental vision. Clara had not been quite the same girl to him he felt she was as they stood by the "colony" gate in Charmington. Would she ever come to care for him? His vacation had been an odd mixture of love and practice at pitching under the instruction of Mr. Mike O'Toole, a professional who was supposed at the time to be the greatest ball tosser in the country. O'Toole knew how to put a "valuable twist" on the ball, as he said, and Harry profited greatly by his instruction.

The theater engrossed his evenings, and he managed to have a busy time of it, although he did feel a little discouraged over the "distance" Clara managed to keep between them. His sister Kitty forbore to tease him, and his mother asked no questions, Uncle Dick got up theater parties, and had the Rives family, with their pretty young daughter Bessie Rives, down to a dinner and opera party afterward. Bessie and Kitty struck up a warm friendship, as devoted in later years as that of Harry and Jack. It was their sole ambition at the time to go to Charmington to school, and to be as ardent Yale girls as their devotion to their two brothers should naturally demand.

At the dinner table the two old grads, Lyman and General Rives, told many yarns of college life. The general laughed as he told the story how, after posting a notice all over the campus that there would be no chapel next morning, they succeeded in turning the chapel bell upside down and filling it with water so that it froze stiff by morning, and half the college, not hearing any bell, slept in peace until recitation time! Uncle Dick told them all about the famous Wooden Spoon, a feature of college life which had risen and fallen since General Rives' time. The "Society of the Cochle-aureati," he said, "started in 1844. It was more or less intended as a burlesque on junior exhibition at first. I remember one of the early old-time jokes was a colloquy called 'Influence of humbug on large assemblies,' and it was stated that the five juniors who were to take part in it would commence speaking in the order of their names. Well, the audience waited and waited until the idea began to dawn on them that the colloquy was a practical joke on themselves.* Another joke was a 'March' by the band, in which the band marched down the aisle and back again with their in-struments slung over their shoulders. In 1857 'Music by Dod-worth's band' was in a footnote 'excused on account of absence from the city!' Sometimes the programmes were shot out of a cannon into the audience, sometimes ladled out of a big bowl with the Wooden Spoon. *E novem unus* was the name of the 'Coch,' Eno in '67, the 'Innate Gentleman' stepping out of a figure 8 in '68. The 'Inbred Gentleman' stepped out of a huge loaf of bread in '63. 'The Perfect Brick' is the best one of many, and incloses the 'Coch' of the year '62. Other 'opening loads,' as they were called, were the 'Bursting Shell,' 'Rise in Flour,' and the 'Bird of Paradise;' in which case the programme casually stated that, 'owing to the difficulty of obtaining the *animals* of Paradise the committee decided to leave out the opening load.' *

"Those old college shows," went on Uncle Dick, "were ten times as funny as any 'theatricals' students get up nowadays. Students become imitators of well-known comic actors and tragedians when they attempt to act plays. It's a pity, a great pity, the Wooden Spoon exhibition is given up, because it was always *original*, and people went to it from far and near because it was so ridiculous. It was unique. It began as a take off on the regular exhibition, in which the high-stand men alone were permitted by the faculty to

* See Mr. Bagg's "Four years at Yale."

take part; so on the programmes there used to be at first the oration, high oration, dissertation, dispute, colloquy, philosophical oration, etc. The subjects of these orations were sometimes ridiculous burlesques of the queer subjects given out for the real exhibition by the faculty, viz., 'The indeorepulsiveness of capillaceous substances if electrolysized by catenarial and grindstonical agencies,' 'The phosphorescence of putrescent fire, sublimated in the correlation and conservation of invisible luminosity.' 'The political influence of peanuts as applied to elephants.' 'Elephants as orators,' 'Hairrangue on whiskers by a man named Beard.' I was 'Coch' of my class," said Lyman proudly, "and I regret that the Wooden Spoon isn't still an institution. People will go far to see an exhibition of real student life as it is—they don't care a son to see students act society dramas or well-known plays. A Greek play is different, but it is not funny. I wish you boys would revive the Wooden Spoon. The take off on the ridiculously solemn commencement exercises always brought down the house. The night before we used to have a ball, which became the Junior Promenade as it is now held at the present time. A funny bit of college life can always be turned into a play by some clever student, and it is the life on the fence and in the yard, and the pleasant rooms that people want to see on the stage."

"It seems to me," said General Rives, "that a great deal more goes on now in college than ever did in my day. You are always having these tremendous athletic events, and you must spend a great deal of money over them. In my day we used to have more debating for prizes, more public oratory. I'm sorry it seems to have fallen into disfavor. Where now are Brothers and Linonia?"

"Yes, Brothers and Linonia, two societies which flourished up to my day," said Uncle Dick, "are now dead and forgotten. These should be resurrected at the same time with the witty Wooden Spoon exhibition—you boys run too much to athletics. Only a few can be on your nines and crews after all. There should be exhibitions of wit and brains as well as of muscle."

When the boys went back to college they did try to talk up the Wooden Spoon among their classmates, but it was "no go." "An institution once dead at Yale never revives;" such indeed has always been the fact in the history of Yale organizations.

Late one night, soon after Harry's return to college, Grannis came and sat in his window in the moonlight. "I stopped at the post office," he said—"I have a private box—as I came past, although it was after twelve. I found a letter from old Father Gerhart at Cleveland. The business promises great things, Harry. I'm glad I lent him the money, but——"

"What's the matter?"

He knew instinctively that there was something wrong about Ella.

"Well, Gerhart writes they haven't heard a word from Ella for ten days, and she always wrote her mother every two or three days. She isn't with her sister, but is in a 'comedy company,' and was playing in Chicago. Harry, I am afraid something has happened to that girl. Her father said her letters were very melancholy of late—and as if some dreadful thing had happened to her."

Harry moved uneasily where he sat. Grannis—great, strong man that he was, and in perfect training on the 'varsity for the great races at Saratoga—began to walk to and fro in the college room in a state of deep anxiety.

"*Good God!*" he cried; "if she's gone wrong it's *your* fault!" The moon poured in its white beams across the window-sill, where Harry sat in silence, holding Stamp's ugly mug in his hands. Grannis was in his 'varsity cap and blazer, and under his white flannel sweater, with its huge blue "Y," his heart bounded as it never did in a great race. His "strength was as the strength of ten;" his honest face was knit as with an awful strain. Harry heard his words—and wondered. It was the first time Grannis had accused him of any wrong to Ella. Why did the keen Westerner jump to such a conclusion now? His face was full of intense feeling as Harry, rising, retorted:

"My fault? I treated her always as a gentleman should, and while I was crazy over her for a while, yet I always respected her

—you must know that, Gran, if you know me. And now, it is all over."

Grannis looked deep into his eyes, and shook his hand silently. There was a short pause.

"Harry, I was once engaged to a girl who died. I thought I loved *her*, but I never knew what love was until I saw Ella. It is a fierce passion which burns within me. It crazes me. I am not fit to row on the 'varsity. I can't study. I am of a thousand minds each day. You know I'm twenty-eight years old—I've been in the world making my own way since I was fourteen—this quiet college life seems small to me. I would have left college at Christmas and gone out into the electric light business with old Gerhart. He wants me to come now to Cleveland. To-morrow, if I find by telegram there is any trouble about Ella, I shall leave for the West. I don't care what Bob Clark says. Jack Rives is a good bow, and they can readjust the crew easily without me, and the dear boy can get his heart's desire. I am going where she is —to find her, if I have to go to Alaska. I shall bring her back safe—and—and if she is not married I shall kill—the man— who has——"

He spoke slowly, solemnly.

"But why do you assume such a dreadful thing?"

Grannis shuddered. "I don't know. Oh, I can't tell!" he groaned.

Harry then proceeded to confide his own woes, and Grannis, as he heard Harry's confession of his love for Clara, assumed a more and more cheerful aspect. He brightened up at last, and said:

"Then Ella is no longer——"

"My dear fellow, *that's over!*"

"I thought she wrote you."

"No."

"Sends you play-bills?"

"Oh, well—not often."

"You don't care for her?"

"Yes—I want to look out for her—for *her own good!*"

Grannis seized his hand and wrung it nearly off.

"Take care! I want to pitch another Harvard game," laughed Harry. Grannis went out softly, looked back, said, "Good-night—see you before I go—if I go—to-morrow, old boy."

The honest Westerner went up stairs to his old South Middle room with a lighter heart. Both these young off-shoots of the East and the West thought a great deal more of each other, after that midnight conversation, than ever before.

But the next morning Grannis came in hurriedly with a tele-gram in his hand. He packed his valise and left on the noon train for New York. Ella Gerhart had not been heard from, and Grannis de-termined to start in search of her. And so Jack Rives obtained his heart's desire. He pulled on the 'varsity that year in Gran-nis' place.

To Umpty-four general-ly, and to all his friends in college, it seemed at first a terrible thing for Old Gran to do at this juncture, because he was an im-portant man on the 'var-

BOB CLARK CRUMPLED UP HIS MORNING PAPER.

sity crew and Bob Clark depended on him for a seat in the waist. But yet Harry knew that Grannis was right. Ella Gerhart must be saved! Her life was more important to Grannis, who was infatuated with her, than a dozen boat races. He kept the true cause for

Grannis' sudden departure a secret, and attributed it among his classmates as due to a business opening. It created a great stir in college, and the New Haven papers actually hinted that Harvard had bought the Yale giant off! His leaving college was first announced in the *Palladium of Liberty*, there was no college daily then,

A TROPHY.

and Bob Clark crumpled up his morning paper and swore direful oaths when he heard of Grannis' "defalcation." The latter wrote him a letter from Cleveland, and said briefly that, owing to business, he was obliged to leave college, perhaps for good.

Grannis also wrote out a letter on a typewriter for his mother to sign at Keokuk, and send to President Stout in New Haven, explanatory of his sudden departure to the faculty. His mother, who for many years had been supported and kept in comparative luxury by her son, always obeyed him implicitly. She believed "her boy" was the salt of the earth—everything he did was simply perfect.

She usually inclosed the faculty's letters concerning Gran back to him, unopened; and he sent out letters for her to send in reply —pious letters they were, too, full of praise for her "hard-working, studious son." He took great delight in these facetious replies to the faculty, and got Nevers to help him with Scripture phrases and Latin quotations. It amused Grannis most of all to hear his division officer, Tutor Blakely, say: "Mr. Grannis, you have a noble mother, sir, a noble mother!" and then read him passages from the letter *he* had himself written!

The next day, after the honest Westerner left town, Jack was recuperating from his Theta Psi "bum" of the night before. Out in the sunny harbor he went with the crew that day, and a more pitiful sight of cruelty to animals than poor Jack, after that eight-mile row in the broiling sun, could not be seen on any canal tow-path! Bob Clark cursed him for an awkward clown, and he got the boat once nearly upset against an oyster stake by his wild steering. It was quite possible that the astute Bob was aware of the condition of the bow-oar the night before, and so resolved to "take it out of him." Jack went to bed early that night, sore as an old stage-horse, but happy as a clam at high tide. Bob had told him he could row until Grannis got back, and Grannis never came back. So Jack rowed on the 'varsity crew at the end of his sophomore year.

CHAPTER XXX.

"SKINNING" METHODS.

RANTING that the numerous athletic and social events of college life absorb a large portion of the students' time, the reader must not imagine that our sophomore friends did not have to apply themselves pretty closely to their books.

The second term, soph year, was always the "toughest" of the four. In freshman year Umpty-four had dropped twenty-seven men. At the end of the first term, soph year, six more had to depart for 'pastures new.' Others came in and filled their places, so that the size of the class was still about the same. Many were the methods adopted by the low standers to scrape along and pass the term examinations. No one can appreciate the misery of their existence. It takes a peculiar gift (rather common perhaps among all Americans) to stand and deliver suddenly all one knows of a subject. Some men are thrown into a state of hopeless mental confusion. This helplessness, combined with a lack of good preparatory drill, has made, to some, the four years at Yale a period of mental disquiet and despair. They resort to every sort of trick to get a good mark. Caswell was an adept at "skinning." By this word is meant any scheme by which a high mark is obtained by what the faculty would term to be "wanton and corrupt" means. Every known device for escaping that awful announcement, "Mr. Blank, you are below average," was tried and often found wanting by Caswell, Holland, and their "set." More time and ingenuity were wasted in concocting schemes to outwit their examining tutor or professor than it would have taken to learn their subject ten times over. Shiny boots could be written upon with a soft lead pencil; finger nails could be covered with fine diagrams in ink; shirt cuffs could be written upon inside and out and covered with the "interesting" formulæ—anything to make a "rush," as the successful recitation was called.

Caswell had the greatest number of "devices." Tutor Blakely, in his tremendous enthusiasm for Demosthenes, made the class commit to memory an analysis of each oration; and the phrase "a digression to establish two points" became a sort of slang in the class ever afterward. To Caswell and Rives, who were out the first half of the winter term, the committing to memory of these long analyses was as bad as Professor Walker's Euclid "exams." Caswell gave it up in despair. Then he conceived the scheme of having the analysis, which had been given out by the tutor in printed form, photographed minutely, so as to be held easily in the palm of the hand. He had a number of these little photograph books made, and the fourth division of low standers had little difficulty in making the most brilliant rushes on this part of the examination. Caswell carried a "pony" of the text boldly in an improvised inside pocket. Tutor Blakely was near-sighted, and he made a dead rush on the translation also. He missed fire on a number of questions as to the use of the second aorist and the pluperfect subjunctive, but he caught the whisper sung up to him from a back seat as to several of these, and succeeded in fetching himself through. Neither he nor Jack had studied more than an hour a day during their suspension. There were too many horseback rides, too many pretty girls, too much shooting along the Sound marshes for study!

The recitation room for conic sections was on the second story of the Athenæum, and it was a very easy matter for the "glorious fourth" as it was called, to engage a confederate to show up on a blackboard in South Middle the diagram, theorem, and proof, as soon as he knew what the man sent up to the board wanted. The distance between the buildings was not more than ten feet and Tutor Beck, the mathematical instructor, sat at the opposite corner of the room. The first thing Caswell did, when he was given his problem on the board, was to write out in large letters exactly what was wanted of him. This telegraphed to the confederate in the bedroom in South Middle exactly what he wanted to know. It also gave Holland and others an idea of what "Cassy" was struggling over, and whatever skinning paper or information of any kind that any of the honest fellows had was at once at Caswell's service. But his confederate outside got to work at once, and Caswell copied down the figure in fine shape from his blackboard held to the window. They had arranged a signal to be given by Caswell of A.A., in case the tutor took it in his head to walk across the room and play the detective. Tutor Beck, rather wondering at Caswell's accurate figure, lettered exactly as it was in the text-book, thought he would watch him from a nearer standpoint. Caswell at once put up his signal A. A. at top of the board, and the confederate and blackboard dropped out of sight. Presently the tutor went back to his seat without having discovered anything wrong, but Caswell in his trepidation forgot to take down his signal. Of course his friend outside did not put up his blackboard again. Caswell was in despair. He stood feebly making letters, which he would rub out with the same care with which he wrote them down.

"Don't you think you had better take your seat, Mr. Caswell?" said Tutor Beck. "You don't seem to be getting on——"

"Oh, it will come to me in a moment, sir," said Caswell hopefully.

Tutor Beck, who was good-natured enough to want Caswell to succeed, smiled and went on with another man.

Meanwhile Caswell by accident rubbed out his signal. Instantly up went his long desired blackboard at the South Middle window again. Caswell, who was an impulsive sort of fellow gave an exclamation of delight. The tutor noticed it and looked around.

"I've got it," cried Caswell, while all the division smiled; "I knew it would come to me at last!"

Caswell gave a dinner at Gradley's to a number of his low-stand friends afterward, and they organized themselves into a regular "ring" or club for the purpose of, as they expressed it, "staying in college to spite the faculty."

Harry and Jack were safely ensconced in the second division. They used to laugh at Caswell and Holland, and inquire why they expended their energies upon these nefarious skinning schemes.

"I don't know," laughed Holland, "I suppose it's love of excitement. I wouldn't be safe in the first or second or even third division for a thousand dollars. There is no interest in a recitation, if you don't know that a flunk will possibly send you below average. I tell you, Harry, I have moments of the highest, most tense nervous excitement in recitation, which you fellows never can experience. It's a sort of gambler's life. In our low-stand set—the best fellows in the class, you must admit—we regularly form a pool before each recitation; we each chip in a dollar, and pick out what problem we think is absolutely unrecitable. If any of us get yanked up on that problem he gets the pot, or if two or three are called to do it the pot is divided between them."

"A new way to make recitations interesting," Harry laughed.

"Well, it consoles a man who makes a flunk," replied Holland.

They were sitting in Harry's room before the fire one morning shortly after summer term opened. The weather was raw and damp "regular New Haven weather," and a number of fellows had gathered to discuss reorganizing the Umpty-four baseball nine. Holland was there in a reminiscent mood. "Did you ever hear how it was Cassy and I were dropped?" he asked. "We've kept it a profound secret, but I don't mind telling you fellows."

"Go on; we won't pipe it," said half a dozen at once.

"It was at Thanksgiving time a year ago, and Cassy and I knew mighty well that we both stood way down on the subcellar floor, not 'one-ninth of one hundredth of a degree,' as Professor Maynard says, above average, either of us. We hit upon the scheme of 'making up' recitations in chemistry. Professor Wells we found marked a fellow very much higher if he made up a recitation in good shape. We cut half a dozen chemistry recitations, taking care to see that our excuses were accepted, and Professor Wells arranged a certain Saturday morning to hear us make them up. We knew that if we passed well above average it would bring us up in trigonometry and in Latin, in which we were lowest of all, but if we fizzled it meant 'drop.'

"The first thing we did was to buy a box of chalk crayons similar to those used at the board. We hardened these by soaking them in alum water, and covered them with diagrams, and everything in the lesson we knew would prove 'interesting.' We had thus five chalk pencils arranged in each of our five pockets, and of course if Cassy needed one of mine, or I one of his, we very easily exchanged our chalk. He would lay his piece which I wanted down in the rack, and I would absent-mindedly pick it up and use it, or we'd reverse the operation. We worked away right merrily, and Professor Wells had no reason to suspect anything. When he approached near where we were at work, we'd slip the chalk into a pocket. We wore our patent examination coats, you know, full of inside pockets. Well, we'd nearly got the work done, and done in best first division style too, I can tell you, when Caswell by accident dropped his piece of chalk, and it rolled across the floor to where Professor Wells was standing. Caswell made a d've for it, but old Wells picked it up, apparently didn't notice it very especially, and handed it back to him. At the close of the examination he coolly complimented us very highly on our work, and then asked to see the piece of chalk that had dropped. Ted promptly gave him a new clean piece. But you ought to have seen his 'childlike and bland' smile. 'I mean the piece of chalk with the formulæ on it,' he said quietly. Of course the jig was up. Caswell shook hands with the professor and asked him to be as lenient as possible. He smiled again, and—well, we were quietly dropped."

Presently they all went out and strolled over to the fence. What a pleasant rendezvous on a May morning! It was the center of college life. To an old graduate the dear place does not look the same, with that gorgeous "efflorescence in brown stone"—the Osborne Hall entrance. Much of the democratic, popular student life passed away with the removal of the fence.

On this especial warm May day, the sophs were regaled by a

strolling Italian "harpist" and a squeaking fiddler, who gave "Il Trovatore" in grand style. Then presently there was a tremendous Halloa! and Hannibal, a dapper young darky, comes along, selling his "natty, unique Turkish caramels" at ten cents a paper. On other days it is Candy Sam "who gropes his sightless way along" and sells his "choice 'lasses candy," or perhaps it is a day when Daniel Pratt, the great American traveler, has happened in town. If so, the students mass about him, stand him on the roots of an elm, and before he has got well started on his oration rush him bodily down the street, where some generous soph treats him to a glass of beer.*

Soon it became one o'clock, and the soph eating club to which Harry and Jack belonged strolled over in a body to their quarters on Elm Street. Jack announced at dinner in as pleasant a tone of voice as he could command that the 'varsity crew had at last been definitely made up without him. Bob Clark had come to him and with real regret told him that he was just a little too light. There was no question about his pluck or his nerve. It was a keen and bitter disappointment to Jack, who pretended he didn't care a rap, and who said that he had made up his mind not to act as first substitute, but to go out of training altogether. After dinner, and before going out to Hamilton Park to practice, Harry ran over to Clark's room. The famous stroke was lying on a sofa, his feet against the mantel shelf, talking to three or four members of the crew.

"*I* don't know as I've done the wisest thing," he was saying. "Young Rives is very plucky, but Crossman is stronger, if a little bit clumsy, but a bow oar must keep his nerve——"

Harry overheard this as he entered.

The men shook hands with him, and there was an awkward silence. "I suppose you've come around to d—n me for crowding off your chum," said Clark with that easy indifference for which he was celebrated.

*Pratt was a most curious, half crazy traveler from college to college in those days. He used to turn up at every New England college at least once a year. Whether he went on foot or not was never known. His "orations" were always upon the Degeneracy of Modern Politics.

"I wanted to ask why you suddenly made up your mind to do it —it's broken him up—as he's been rowing with the crew all the week."

"He isn't the right weight to balance the boat."

"He weighs too little?"

"There are more reasons than one. I want to favor Jack Rives —he's plucky and a good oar—but it's strength I want. I've thought the thing over carefully. I don't say he won't row Harvard. But I want to have the best—that is in *my* opinion the best—material used. Now I'll say this: I may put Rives back on the crew within three weeks of the race. Tell him I want to see him, and don't let him break training."

"I'll tell him—he's going to row!" And Harry left the room with a light heart.

CHAPTER XXXI

COLLEGE FLIRTS.

NOW again rolled round those pleasant spring days 'neath the elms, when every night at the fence many songs were heard, and fun went on and jollity. There was always the Italian "band"—a violin, a harp, and a flute—who played for coppers after supper in the long evenings. Nevers and Harry often sat late together chatting, reading, fixing up some trifle or some trophy, or smoking and talking of Grannis and his search for the lost Ella Gerhart. Now and then letters came from him in some queer, out-of-the-way place in Omaha or Idaho, where he had had traces of her. All this was a secret. Harry did not even confide in the garrulous, good-hearted Jack. Nevers alone knew.

The warm baking Saturday in June came for the first Harvard "roasting," and Harry covered himself with glory by striking out fourteen men. He no longer felt stage-fright, surrounded by the "'rah-'rahing mob." Jim Danforth and he, the great "battery," played with the coolness of professionals. A great crowd of graduates from New York and Hartford and from everywhere were out at Hamilton Park to see Harvard "waxed" for the first time in the history of baseball contests. They felt sure of the game from the start. It was a sort of walk-over. The Harvard nine were now on the anxious seat, as Yale was the year before. When Harry walked out into the field there were tremendous 'rah-'rah-'rahs for the crack college pitcher of the year. The game all through was very one-sided. It was evidently, to all beholders,

Harvard's off year in baseball. The score was 6 to 2, and if the Yale team had been pressed it could easily have doubled the score. That is to say, it *looked* so, though baseball is "mighty unsartin," and there is no telling how a game *might* have been played. The great American outdoor game, as played by the college teams, is never ended till the last man is out. That day in the box Harry sported a diamond-shaped pin for the first time on his jersey, bearing the mystic Greek letters B. K. E. The initiation into the junior society took place the night before, and Harry was excused early on account of the game. Professor Walker and Miss Walker, with Miss Daisy Stevenson and a tremendous number of girls whose faces seemed familiar, but whose names were forgotten, beamed with sisterly affection from the grand stand. There was no question to-day of their support—and of everyone's support and sympathy. If he did make some little error it was quickly forgiven, quickly condoned. Dan might throw ten feet over second—the crowd laughed and enjoyed it—they felt so sure of him—and of the game. Men of all ages enjoy a college game, first because it is played for "blood," as the sporting phrase is, and, secondly, it is the one game every boy plays from his infancy. *They understand* it. It is inborn in them, as cricket is inborn in an Englishman. The defect of the game, as compared with cricket, is that it requires training to play it. Not everyone can catch a swift-thrown ball, and not every old player is in a condition to catch one, or to throw one accurately, while cricket—anyone can play it after a fashion without any extra preparation. It is strange that neither game makes much headway in an adopted country. Baseball is such a pretty game—and so neat and so decisive when rapidly and scientifically played!

Harry and Jack went around to tea at Professor Walker's after the game, and Clara Hastings was there in a soft, white mull gown with a bunch of roses at her slim, pretty waist. She went at Harry with airy persiflage, taxing him with avoiding her glance at the game, and with a desire to avoid her generally! There were several upper-class men present—but Harry was the lion of the evening. It seemed to him that it was only because he had won a

Harvard game that day, that the beautiful girl noticed him at all.
She had no regard for *him*, but she liked to monopolize so distinguished a young man, for the nonce, and have him at her feet.

The Walkers had a pretty garden behind the old-fashioned house,
divided by the professor into mathematical figures by box borders.
After tea on the veranda, Clara and Harry walked in the garden.
She had a beauty of the aggressive kind—it drove men wild and
forbade any rational conversation. He could only compare the
roses to her and quote poetry, and swear that she made his life
wretched for him and that she knew it, and that she was heartless
and cruel to him.

"Love—there is no such thing," she laughed, pulling the petals
from a pink rose which she held in her jeweled fingers. "It's so
silly! You college men are all the same. You don't know what
love is—it doesn't interfere with *your* sleep or digestion! To test
you, which will you have—me or the next Harvard game?"

"You—every time, my darl——"

"Mr. Chestleton!"

She gave him a glance of the most righteous indignation, and
hurried into the house. Harry dallied in the garden a few minutes,
hoping she would come out again, but she did not. He went in
and found her laughing and chatting with Stevenson of Umpty-
two, who spoke to him patronizingly, while she avoided his glance.
She seemed just as nice to Stevenson as to him. He went over and
sat down near Daisy Stevenson, who said: "We are going to read
Vergil every morning at half-past ten. Want to join our class?"

"Who's in it?"

"Well, Clara *isn't*"—and she gave him a pert glance. "At
Charmington, I believe, the classic authors are not thought to be
ladylike!"

If it had not been for Clara he would have liked Daisy Stevenson very well. He might have made love to her. He knew he
liked her very much. She was amiable and bright. Men liked
her, not because she was beautiful—though, like every young girl,
she had her moments of looking very pretty—but because she
was essentially *charming* and clever.

Daisy Stevenson was an accredited college flirt; indeed she admitted the soft impeachment without the slightest hesitation. "What else is there to do for us poor girls in a college town?" she asked, "and as for the students—hasn't someone said that to love a clever woman is an education in itself? Well, they say (I don't) I'm clever. So you see I'm really teaching these bright young men. By rights I ought to be one of the faculty, and receive a salary!"

Latterly she had begun to study art in the art school. Her brother being a prominent man in Umpty-two, she naturally saw a great many of his senior classmates. But she confessed she liked the sophs or even the freshmen best. "Seniors are apt to be pompous and stuffed full of wind," she sighed. "They are too knowing, without knowing anything. I despise most of the conceited solemn-pated 'about to be's.' Here and there there is a nice jolly senior, not having mental cramps over his 'ologies, but he's a rare bird. Most of them turn atheists, to be led tamely back to church later on by their wives. As for me, give me the ridiculous, boyish jolly soph. I love him always!"

Harry sat and talked and laughed with her a long time; at last she cried, "Mercy! What eyes Clara Hastings is making at me!" (pretending to be frightened.) "She needn't be afraid of poor me! Tell Clara I shall never marry, Mr. Chestleton. I have wedded Art—with a big 'A.' Art is *my* master. I'm going to Rome next year with my brother. I expect to live abroad four or five years."

"What? you won't be at our Junior Prom?"

"No; my college days are over, I fear. There, Clara is eying you. She wants you and [rising] they want me to play." And she left the room.

"You've been flirting!" said Clara, as Harry approached her.

"I admire Miss Stevenson so much that I don't think it possible for her to flirt," he protested meekly.

"Oh, *don't you!*" And Clara fanned herself with a bewitching, knowing air.

The girl set his heart on fire. He was idiot enough to say, "I wish she would paint your portrait."

"Thanks, I'd rather not! She'd make me out a hideous nightmare! Wild horses couldn't *drag* me to have my portrait done by *her!*"

She rose indignantly and flung out of the room, leaving Harry to wonder what he had said to make her so angry—and so provokingly handsome!

A week later and Bob Clark had reinstated Jack on the 'Varsity, and he was obliged, in consequence, to go up with the crew the week before Commencement to Saratoga Lake. The second game with Harvard was to be played at Saratoga the day before the race. Yale had one game to play with Princeton on the latter's home grounds, having beaten her in a close match at Hamilton Park. The nine went down to Princeton flushed with their victory over Harvard, prepared to show the Presbyterians a few tricks.

Princeton had not at this time grown to the size and importance it has to-day. It was trying its level best to grow, however, and had sent up crews to the great intercollegiate contest at Saratoga, which it had trained in the muddy waters of a canal not far from the college campus. Princeton has always shown pluck, however, and it was she who, after Yale, taught in its perfection the present game of football.

The American college student is pretty much the same all round. He is brainy and full of high courage. He wants to win, and win he will; but the practice and code of sporting ethics differ. At Yale a player must fairly be in college, a regular student, to be in her nines or crews. No one has ever—to her glory be it said—accused *her* of importing a professional football-player, or oarsman, or ball-player, for the sake of a "win." When the nine arrived at Princeton they found they were to meet a new "battery" —the pitcher, hitherto unknown, by the name of "Brown," of "Umpty-three." When they came to look at "Brown" he was a tall, strapping Irishman, with an unmistakable Corkonian jaw.

Harding laughed in his face. "Bring me any Latin text-book you've been over," he said, "and we'll see if 'Brown' can translate it."

"Oh, but he has just recently joined the class," said the captain of the Princeton team, Blake, a handsome fellow and first-class ball-player.

Sure enough, they produced a regular certificate that "Brown" was in college, O. K., and signed by a professor in due form.

"How can he have entered college since our last game?" asked Harding indignantly.

"By special permit of the faculty."

There was no convention rule on the subject, and Yale had to submit. Thomas, the regular Princeton pitcher, played in right field. All Princeton was out on the ball-ground, certain of victory.

"By Jupiter!" cried Harry angrily, "let's go in and do these Princeton fellows up. Don't let's protest—it isn't Yale's way." He felt in good condition, and was confident that all the professional pitchers from New York to Chicago could not prevent Yale's winning the day.

Princeton village is "nothing much," but the college grounds are very beautiful, and Nassau Hall never looked better than that sweet June day, when parties of pretty girls, escorted by students, trooped over to the ball-grounds to see the pride of Yale taken down. Yellow and black are capital colors for decorative purposes, and although a few Yalensians had come up from Philadelphia and down from New York, their blue was literally "out of sight." The game began with Princeton at the bat. For some reason they struck out in one-two-three order.

It made Jim Danforth smile. Caswell, who had run down with the nine, was forced, after the first inning, to give long odds. The new pitcher was very swift, but he was not at all accurate. Dan guyed him from the first, so that he lost his nerve.

Murdock hit a three-baser, and the Yale delegation began to laugh and howl with glee.

"Now, Pat, what do they pay fer the like 'ave yes fer the

game?" called out Dan.   Even the Princeton crowd—a finer lot
of young Americans never was seen—who wanted to see fair
play, joined in the laugh.   In the fourth inning, with Yale 5 and
Princeton 0, Captain Blake put in his regular pitcher, Thomas,
and Harry let Stickney, a freshman, try his hand.

But the Yale team were now romping toward victory, and they
hit the ball hard all over the field.   The final score was 11 to 3.

At the close of the game the Irish "imported" pitcher tried to
"lick" Danforth for "insultin' of him."   He struck at him once
and cut his ear.   Captain Blake promptly interfered.   Danforth
turned very pale with anger, and his eyes had that tigerlike look
Harry had seen in them on occasions when Dan had proved himself
most dangerous.   Harry tried to stop him, but Dan was too quick.
Dan struck out viciously and knocked the Irishman clean off his
pins.   For a moment it looked like a general scrimmage.   But
Harding and Blake cried "Shame!" and there was no further
trouble except a shower of stones as the team boarded the train.
It was evident, however, that the stones were thrown by townies.
The stories in the New York papers of the morning following were
promptly denied by a letter from Harding to the *Herald*, who
insisted that the majority of Princeton students "did not approve
of employing the professional McSwyny to pitch, or have anything
to do with the firing upon the Yale team."   McSwyny was, it
turned out, a rank professional from Philadelphia.

In the *Courant* of the following week Harding wrote: "This
will always be the difficulty Yale and Harvard will have with the
smaller colleges.   In order to win, it will be easy for them to put
in batteries or oarsmen who are really professionals.   The true
competition is and always will be between colleges of equal
degrees and numbers. . . Another thing—large crowds, shouting,
yelling, and such nonsense do not benefit college sport, but injure it.
In years to come the authorities of all the chief colleges will tend
to make laws which will make these great crowds and gatherings
at games and races impossible, and Yale and Harvard will doubtless have their contests eventually on their own grounds.   This is
what ought to happen."

This letter made a great sensation among the colleges where "intercollegiate" competition was now the proper thing. Subsequent years, however, are proving the general truth of his words. As a rule Harvard and Yale are tending year by year to a dual competition in athletics. Princeton, however, has proved such a doughty antagonist, and such a plucky one at that, that her followers need never fear that she will be left out of the fight as far as Yale is concerned.

CHAPTER XXXII.

SAILING parties in the soft, warm moon-lit nights of June, after the heat of the day, to the lighthouse point, where oyster roasts on the rocks kept them idling till a late hour, were now the regular thing every second or third evening. How the poor *chaperons* begged and entreated to go home! and how the girls entreated to stay! and how oftener wind and tide kept the sailboat lagging till an early hour in the morning! But what care youth and health for sleep—while the moon shines and the banjo strings are not snapped?

Now, at the close of sophomore year, was beginning the period of early, strange, "puppy" love. Generally with the famous class of Umpty-four, many now became closely attentive to the mails who cared not for mails before. Others found in New Haven certain charming creatures who seemed not averse or unsusceptible to the slowly developing whiskers of this redoubtable class. Very few indeed who did not find *some* sympathetic heart either in a native-born beauty, or some friend or classmate's sister who had perchance come on for the "exercises" of Commencement, or in some sweet schoolgirl graduate of the many boarding schools. Some there were, but few. Look back now, dear alumnus, and recall the time, if you can, after freshman year when you were not fancying yourself in love with some pretty face? You, fortunate Episcopalian,* who gazed down from the gallery in Trinity (on the

* Episcopalians were excused from attending regular chapel exercises, and were permitted to sit (sleep) in the gallery of old Trinity.

green) upon the fashionable beauties of the period—you had a large variety of loveliness (whether you were acquainted or not) upon whose pretty bonnets and back hair you could, with bowed head, bestow an admiring gaze. Attendance at church of a bright June morning was a worldly display for you. You dressed with greatest care, and on your way purchased a rose or a bunch of violets for your buttonhole. And for you—oh, ye of Presbyterian and Congregational descent! the opportunity was small, 'tis true, but the "snab" in the chapel gallery—the pretty, curious, interested girl who peered over the railing and down at you below—you all remember *her*—and loved her! Such was puppy love!

But some there were who loved not. Love never entered the mind of David Alum, for example. His loves were books. His classmates respected his acumen immensely, for brains are admired in college, where they are apt to be a scarcity, as much as skill in the ball-field. His aunt sat up in the gallery of the chapel and looked down at him—yet it is doubtful whether *she* inspired any sudden passion in anyone! A queer, unlovely, up-country, quaint old maid she was—taking care of David a great deal of the time and nursing him; for the raucous New Haven climate disagreed with the delicate young man, who was somewhat inclined to consumption. Nor did honest Thomas J. Anderson permit himself to yield to the tender passion. "Old Andy" was one of Umpty-four's four monitors. He was popular because he sometimes forgot to report a man who was just on the "edge" for being absent. It was honest Andy's delight to sing old-fashioned tunes out of his hymn-book, every night after coming back to his dormitory room after dinner, in South Middle or the first story of North Middle, where he lived until graduation, having given up his "choice" of room junior year for a modest sum. "Old Andy" had no mind for the fair sex. *He* riveted his gaze on the pulpit, on the curriculum—and on the faculty. *He* knew the College Laws. They were engraved on his memory in never-fading tablets. He used to quote III, chap. I, with unction: "The professors and tutors, severally, shall have power to govern the students, and to punish them for any offense, except in cases referred by law to the Faculty: *Pro-*

vided that they may not, in any case, proceed contrary to the advice and direction of the President;" and again: "VI. Persons examined as above and approved shall be admitted to College on signing the following statement: '*I hereby acknowledge the obligation on my part while I remain connected with Yale College—of which by this act I become a member—to submit to the authority of the Corporation and the Faculty.*'" The matriculation oath, now long since abolished, and of monitors: "Monitors appointed by the Faculty shall designate, on bills provided for the purpose, those who are tardy, or who egress, or absent themselves from prayers or other appointed exercises, which bills they shall return, as directed, to the Division officer in charge."

Those faithful, simple-minded old monitors of Yale! Doubtless they had all their youth dried out of them in those long years of painstaking subserviency—and so often became tutors in self-defense!

Many thoughts used to enter Harry's mind as he sat listening to the long, dull sermons of a Sunday—sermons chiefly upon some theological, hair-splitting point of no general interest—as to who, of all his friends, was like him, "hopelessly loving and helplessly left." Clara Hastings attended service with her aunt at Trinity, and he saw little of her, except on a sailing party, or a dance, or a ride, now and then, over to Saltonstall, and a picnic and a row on the lake.

At times she made his heart beat with joyous hope. Then, again, she told him plainly that she was never going "to care particularly for anyone—that a girl always had the wrong end of the love bargain—and that she never intended to marry anyone." To a young lad, unreasonably and idiotically in love, what can cold reason do to dissuade? Finally, whenever they were alone together, she complained to him that his sighs and protestations were positively becoming unendurable, and that, in all decency, he must *not* make a public spectacle of himself and her!

So the summer term ended, and Jack went up with the 'varsity to Saratoga. Harry remained in New Haven over Commencement, as the nine played Princeton and Columbia during Commencement week. His curiosity was aroused over the "exercises" of that most "glorious" week of all the college year. But he was not in a very happy mood. He was rather silent, and secretly wretched. He got some satisfaction out of striking out batsmen—*that* was something—but Columbia, who is nothing if not on the water, and, Princeton, who was only capable that year of a very tame, weak sort of game, were an easy mark. All over the country Harry's name and fame had spread abroad; yet what did he care? Clara looked away from him! Love is such an absurd, incomprehensible, foolish nightmare! Clara certainly seemed to think so! *Crudelis semper femina!*

Commencement day! He observed Professor Sharp, full of vain-glory and importance, arrayed in Oxford cap and gown and waving a baton, at prompt 9 A. M. leading on the hosts, headed by a brass band—a long line, with its right resting on Chapel Street in front of South, and its left draggling along endlessly away over by Darfee. *Imprimis,* the faculty, headed by pale, anxious President Stout. This is their great day of days. The great men of brains marched two by two—sincere, pure-minded, scholastic, solemn, reverencing Yale, working with poor apparatus and on small, inadequate salaries for her glory and renown. Then followed the oldest alumni, also two by two, some leaning on staves, some obscure clergymen, some great in the eyes of the whole country—judges, lawyers, ministers—who were all to be present at the alumni dinner later, and there would be wit and lemonade *ad libitum* in Alumni Hall.

Harry saw the alumni go by, and finally the seniors in caps and gowns,* looking like scared nuns going to a martyr's stake.

A little later he strolled with Coles down to Center Church on

---

*Caps and gowns worn permanently would, on the whole, be a desirable uniform for students here, as at Oxford. It would aid the faculty in assisting decorum, and in discipline ; it would put students more on an equality as to dress, and it would save the student some expense. At Yale the scholastic uniform is worn only by seniors on class day or Commencement, and only then by special vote of the class.

the green. The day was hot, and as he gazed in at an open window it seemed that there were no men present except on the stage, and that the long, double file of men, led by the brass band, had utterly disppeared. He saw bonnets, hats, light dresses, fans innumerable. The delight of the average young female in squeezing herself into these hot, dreary, long exhibitions of oratory struck him then, and for many Commencements afterward, as something remarkable. He observed Miss Stevenson walking along the elm-roofed Temple Street with her brother. She nodded, and he and Coles approached.

"Did you ever *see* such a jam?" she asked in her rapid, interested way. "I could not wedge myself in—the church will not hold another fan! and the salutatory is over, and now it is just the dull monotony of the 'philosophicals,' with now and then a 'dissertation' sprinkled in by way of excitement; though, for the life of me, I can't see why a 'colloquy' or a 'dissertation' differs a mite from a plain ordinary oration. Can you?"

Harry looked around at the crowd of students, old alumni and recent, who stood beneath the high white pillars of the church portico, or who loitered about beneath the trees, on the brick walk.

"It's all about the same thing—in fact everything is the same!" he said. "And the world is hollow. Everything is monotonous. Victory gets to be so. But there is Harvard yet to beat once more, at Saratoga."

"Did you know we were going to Mount Desert—did you know *she* was going there? [in a little whisper]. So we shall see *you* at Bar Harbor?"

"I had better go to Kamschatka and hang myself!" he laughed dismally.

" 'Hang the pitcher on the pump!' song and dance"—she laughed. "Well, if you can persuade yourself to spend July and August at Mount Desert you'll have an awfully good time, and see so many pretty girls that *one* hereafter will not suffice thee!"

Daisy Stevenson twirled her large, lace-trimmed sun umbrella while she talked. She was in becoming white, and pink ribbons.

"All ready for my graduation!" she laughed gayly, but her face in repose was sad.

After a little he left her, and went up the steps and tried to get into the church. He did succeed in getting in a little way in the crowded aisle. The band played an interlude, and a senior in a dress suit, white tie, and patent leather shoes, looking pale as grim Death at noonday, stood up. He was nervous, and began, after bowing first to the Prex. and then to the faculty and audience:

"When Thackeray died in 1863, Charles Dickens, in memoriam, said of him——"

But he couldn't remember what the Dickens he said! A voice prompted him from up in the gallery:

"Another good man gone wrong!" said the voice. At which a sensation ran through the church, and each member of the faculty craned their necks to see who the daring reprobate could be. Harry thought he knew. Best, who came near being fired in freshman year for stealing caps from the sophs' recitation room, possessed, as he knew, the gift of ventriloquism. He looked around for Best, and saw him seated near a window under the gallery, with a pretty girl. He sat up stiff and solemn, and Harry knew he was up to some deviltry or other by the way he behaved.

"Go on, my good fellow!" called out the voice again, from another part of the church. 'Don't let us embarrass you! We are mostly girls in the audience, and we don't pretend to understand——"

A titter ran through the church, and the speaker having been prompted, went on with his oration. He had regained his nerves and was hastening on to his peroration, when the voice, this time from over where Professor Shepard sat, called out distinctly:

"*Stopping there!*"

A roar went through the house. The poor student orator paused when the voice, still from the faculty, called out:

"Proceed! proceed! You may now translate into Latin—come now—don't be an idiot!"

The student bowed and was off, and two constables, with tipstaffs, looked fiercely about, moved vigorously up and down the aisles, and tried to find out who it was who dared to invade the dignity of the occasion. Harry remained for a little time, but Best kept quiet. Harry remembered that the senior whom he had interrupted was the man who had quarreled with Best for some reason and who had succeeded in keeping the young soph out of Phi U. Best had had his revenge. The tall senior was so discomfited that for years it is said he never showed his face again in New Haven.

CHAPTER XXXIII.

THE next day the nine went to Saratoga and put up at the United States Hotel. Harry and Danforth, as soon as they had removed the dust of travel, sauntered out to see the town. The great University Race, in which thirteen colleges had entered, was to take place, wind and weather permitting, on Thursday, the Harvard and Yale game on Wednesday, and it was now Tuesday. Before they went out of the hotel Harding cautioned his men:

"Strict training till after the game, boys—and especially no spring water!"

They walked about the streets, followed by a number of small boys who recognized them.

"Dere's Chesllton, de great pitcher o' de Yales!" shouted one of the boys.

"Dere's Danferth, de back stop!" shouted another. "He's a stayer!"

Already the street gamins were familiar with the players of both crack college teams. It was arranged to play the game in the morning so that President Breen of Harvard, and Wayten Crebb of Yale, the originators of intercollegiate athletics, could get in their games for the afternoon, at the race course. The town was not yet crowded with students, but they were beginning to drop in, in squads, from all the colleges of the country. Thirteen were to compete in the race—even obscure little Hamilton, situated upon a hill, a dozen miles from any water, and many miles from a lemon, had caught the aquatic enthusiasm, and had sent a crew, which, had it received proper coaching, might have come near winning the day. Trinity at Hartford, Princeton, Wesleyan, Brown, Cornell, Columbia—what college had *not* availed itself of the privilege of entering the great race? Such a universal gathering of the clans had never been seen before or since. The newspapers had not columns but pages and double pages on the great event. All the country seemed to stand still and await for the cannon to boom over the victory of the first crew to cross the line. Clark was now the chief authority at Saratoga Lake, and it may fairly be said that the Yale crew was not matched even by Harvard. Grannis departing when he did, for the West, on his quest for Ella Gerhart, did not hurt the crew, for Bob Clark ordered Jack Rives into the bow and shoved the men down one seat. On the whole Clark was satisfied that the speed of the boat was helped, for Grannis, with all his magnificent strength, was just a little slow in recovering.

Harry, with some of the nine, hired a hack and drove out to the lake, to Yale's quarters, that afternoon. When they arrived the crew was out for a spin, coached by Gifford, who coxswained Umpty-four's first freshman crew to victory at Saltonstall. Gifford had caught Clark's "ideas" and he was a natural waterman. They had no steam launch for coaching purposes in those days, and they rowed around Gifford, who sat in a wherry, and pulled along with them. It was a fine crew, as fine as Yale ever has had, and it was entirely confident of victory.

Can any college man forget the thrill of excitement he feels as he sees his crew stripped, in the boat, and their bronzed backs shining in the sun? One feels no such sense of delight over a race horse, or a crack ball team, or a great student sprinter. Ah! the boat race is *the* thing, after all!

"How prettily dear old Jack handles his oar!" exclaimed Danforth. "Oh, fellows, we've got that race in our pocket. It's glorious to see that boat move!"

They stood on the improvised float and watched the crew as Gifford practiced them on starts. The beautiful lake was as smooth as glass. On all sides, as far as the eye could see, to Snake

Hill, where Cornell had her quarters, were crews of all the colleges being coached by their professional trainers. Only a keen and knowing eye could pick out the different crews. But, there! Over by the shore came a crew as different from the rest as a city-trained horse differs in gait from its country cousin.

"'Vast! there!" they heard Bob sing out from the stroke, "There's Harvard." His keen, sharp eyes had seen their rivals. When Harvard saw she was noticed she stopped rowing like a sulky, pert schoolgirl caught in a piece of mischief.

Columbia, which has always been very friendly with Yale, came up nearly alongside the wharf. No one thought especially of Columbia's winning in contrast with the Yale and Harvard crews. Columbia had a poor sort of Harlem River-waterman stroke, which, while it gave her a fast sprinting speed of two miles, was thought good for nothing in a three mile race. She had a handsome crew, however—and Harry thought it an unusual crew. The papers had cried them up a good deal, but the betting men and the oarsmen who *knew* did not class them with Yale. In personal appearance they were very handsome, dashing, swell looking men in the Columbia crew, and the Yale crew was sturdy and ugly. As a rule, sporting men never favor beauty, except in horses and women.

The best opinion two days before the race favored either of the greater New England universities.

As they stood watching, Clark turned and headed his craft down the lake, and they set out at a slow, steady swing past the Harvards, who lay on their oars and watched them, hoping to catch their time. Little Hamilton pulled up rapidly, and passed them easily, gaining vast credit to itself from a party of ladies who were seated over upon the new grand stand, near Moon's Hotel. Further down the lake and out of Harvard's sight, Clark put on a little steam, pulled up to, and passed Hamilton, as if the latter was anchored. Yet Hamilton was pulling "their darndest," as they said afterward.

When Clark came in he secretly gave out that he feared Cornell the most, Harvard next, and Columbia third.

Jack clasped Harry's hand. "You *have* conquered, Chestnuts; and with us it's all a lottery."

"We may lose to-morrow's game," said Harry, with a smile, as if to say, "Rats—I'm sure of it!"

Then Jack whispered in his chum's ear the "time" on practice of the crew, 16. 10. "We know it's the best on the lake," said Jack, plunging into the water off the float. As he came up, and his head appeared above the water, he spluttered and sung out, "Keep it dark, old chap!"

They admired the muscles of the great crew as they stripped for their well-earned bath: Bob, with his clear eyes, and his back of iron, and his tongue of brass, as Jack said; Collins, a white untannable giant, fair as a woman, strong, and in perfect wind; Jack, himself, agile and clean cut. It was an unusual crew even for Yale, and they were bound to win. The big man of the crew, Muchison, had once thrown Clark over his shoulder—a feat which, in the captain's estimation, entitled him at once to a seat in the waist. He was from the West, and had in his father's large iron rolling mills worked as a common puddler for the sake of the experience. He pulled a good oar, and had won the Southworth cup for single sculls, at New Haven.

In and around the quarters everything, including Stamp (who reigned there supreme, and had killed one large yellow dog for loafing too near, in order to overhear what went on at the dinner table), betokened a suppressed mysterious excitement. Stamp wagged his stumpy tail at Harry, and yet it was evident that he didn't admire men not in the boating line. The baseball men were all very well in the college yard, but at Saratoga they and their little game, it was evident, to Stamp's discriminating mind played second fiddle.

At ease in their blazers and sweaters before dinner, the crew talked of the coming event and "Yale's chances." It was astonishing how moderate very strong men are—how modest. Harvard had a good crew, Columbia really surprised them, Wesleyan had a strong crew, Williams had a crew which was made up of men who would go to make up a good class crew at Yale. Trinity rowed for "glory." Presently, the freshmen crew trotted in. They had been out for a four-mile run—great lubberly fellows—Clark took no stock in them. "*Row!*" he said sneeringly. "They can't pull a boat as fast as a mule can trot backward!" They were a good-natured, jolly lot of freshmen, and it was hard to keep them under control. "Oh," said Bob, with a sigh, "it isn't our freshman crew of Springfield a year ago—you wouldn't say they came from the same college! Why—even Princeton will beat them hands down!"

Presently dinner was called, and the ball men stayed and ate with them. Everyone was full of suppressed excitement. The race! the race is the thing, after all—and such a grand affair as this!

The next day was sultry, and both the Yale and Harvard teams played the last championship game rather listlessly. Yale won by a low score of 4 to 2, and the nine broke training. Any old oar or old ball man may recall the delight of that first smoke or first glass of fizz after the toil is over; it is worth all the self-denial to enjoy that perfect bliss. Think of what these young men undergo, and how much self-denial they exercise, ye parents and guardians who are so afraid of your sons and wards going into athletics! Many a boy has been saved from ruin and reckless habits by training; many a weak character made firm and strong and manly by that period of discipline. Many a lad has, in training, formed habits of self-control which have lasted through his life. And we have yet to learn of the first student who has been physically injured thereby.* The athletic men are generally the leaders in college, and their influence is very great upon all their classmates. They are always a conservative element; never drinking, never smoking, keeping early hours, and preserving always a certain dignity of carriage. Training and discipline teach them courage, perseverance, self-reliance, pluck, hardihood, and *nearly* all the Christian virtues. At least, they teach all the Spartan virtues. Think of rowing in the sharp, icy spring winds, and then in the

---

* At the present day all the college nines and crews are under the care of competent physicians, who carefully watch for any injurious effects of training or "overtraining."

broiling sun, sometimes sixteen or eighteen miles a day! For such was the stern discipline of those days—a discipline which trained up a crew really to row a race of eight miles instead of three, and, unless the crew was naturally a very strong one, often worked the men stale before the day of the race.

Crews are apt to do too much work. Fast crews are crews with plenty of life and enthusiasm and freshness for their work. They are not muscle-bound with over-training—ten-mile runs and twenty-mile rows. Every now and then a crew gets a stern, uncompromising captain, who works his men to death. Bob Clark had learned from his experience that too much work would kill the prospects of the best crew that ever sat in a boat.

Oxford will pull four miles and perhaps a quarter of a mile further, in $19\frac{1}{2}$ minutes, while Yale will pull four measured miles in 20.10. The Oxford crew has been together perhaps not a month, while the Yale crew has been rowing ten, twelve miles a day all the spring. The reason is the Oxford 'Varsity is a crew of selected and *tried* men, whereas the Yale men— some of them may never have previously sat in a boat. The whole systems of the two countries are different. The better opinion is in favor of that of Oxford. They get very fast "springy" crews together in what we should consider no time at all. Probably those same Oxford and Cambridge crews would row in worse time if they were worked to death like canal horses as we energetic Americans work our crews, months before the race.

In the days of college life of which we are writing athletics were to a certain extent "just beginning." Geo. Walker Breen, the famous pedestrian and all round athlete of Harvard, and Wayten Crebb of Yale had gotten up during the year an intercollegiate athletic association including all the colleges. Their first meet at Saratoga, the afternoon before the great races, was naturally overshadowed by the greater event. But they were the first successful college games, which, afterward, were destined, as years went on, to be one of the great annual college "events," viz.: the baseball championship, the football championship, field games, and the race.

In those days field sports or games were in a very crude condition. Harry saw men contesting in the walking match in ordinary clothes—the Amherst man who won, beating Geo. Breen, the modest Harvard athlete, by nearly a mile, having merely thrown aside his hat, coat and vest, collar and suspenders! The runners sprinted in ordinary canvas baseball shoes. The great event was the tug of war, in which Lehigh proved superior. The 100-yard dash was made in 15 seconds. Other times were in proportion.

The race course, on which that first intercollegiate meet was held, was dusty, uneven, and ill adapted to sprinters. At that time there was, outside of New York, hardly a single sprinting track in the country. Jack and Harry often sigh when they see the beautiful track of the present Yale Field, and tell the young undergrads what time they made in the old days! At Saratoga Harry "just for fun" entered in the mile run—and was a good second to a Princetonian. How different are these days of well-trained and disciplined athletes. That meet at Saratoga would by them doubtless be thought a meet of duffers! In baseball and in boating, however, the "form" of the contestants does not appear to have greatly improved in twenty years. Probably no better college four ever sat in a boat than that which *almost* beat the crack London Rowing Club four at Philadelphia in 1876. Its form was perfect, and the London crew acknowledged that if Yale had known how to steer as well as to row, they would have won. As it was, the London crew were so done up that the next day they were beaten in slow time by an obscure Albany crew. So, in baseball, the game is no better played now than then. Errorless games were common in those days. The game was understood. In matters of training for the nine, of course, improvements have been made. Sliding to bases, stopping balls, throwing with a straight shoulder throw, catching the ball with the hands in a certain position—these matters are now the A B C of baseball, and were not *taught* but acquired by instinct in the days of Harry Chestleton.

The great day of the race came—and it rained, blew, and stormed. "The entire American people," as a New York paper sarcastically put it, "would be obliged to undergo another weary day of suspense, owing to the insalubrity of Saratoga Lake." The great hotels were crowded with noisy students, who rushed about in gangs of thirty or forty, waving flags of all colors—the purple of Williams, red of Hamilton, cornelian of Cornell, or yellow-and-black of Princeton. Then it was the famous "Siss—boom—ah," the sky-rocket war cry of Nassau Hall, was first heard in the land. Harvard and Yale men met, bragged, lorded it over the small colleges, swaggered, and betted their last cent. The thirteen colleges made that day and night a grand pandemonium, which all the Congress water they could pour down would not allay. Extras came out every hour with the latest details of the crews. "What Bob Clark said," "What Dicky Strainer said," "What Ostrom thought," "What Goodwin predicted"—the whole town was in a tremendous fever of excitement. Springfield the year before was nothing to it. No New London race has ever come anywhere near those great contests at Saratoga for general interest and crowds and excitement. The New London race to-day is a tame affair in comparison. Betting men, gamblers, sports, racing men, dropped their game and came and bet on the college crews. It was amusing and instructive to hear in the barroom of Congress Hall at 1 A. M. "gamey" looking sports bandying about the names of our various seats of learning, as if they were race horses! "Twenty to one agin Trinity," shouted a fierce looking dyed-mustached "gent" in a check suit, and could find no takers; "Three to one agin Yale," and the "gent" was promptly accommodated. "Hayverd, one to five," found plenty of takers; "Karnell, one to six," and so on. As Dan and Harry, with their crowd, shouted about, drank whisky and "champ," with hosts of old Yale grads, who were rejoicing over the baseball championship over Harvard—they thought what a jolly idea these great intercollegiate contests were, but afterward, on wise reflection, all Yale men certainly agreed that they were too crowded and noisy for any real enjoyment. Certainly these great affairs were detrimental to the best interests of college life. Drinking was much too common. In later years it dawned upon the larger universities that they were simply advertising the fresh-water colleges by participating in these cumbrous affairs. When

Yale and Harvard drew out, the "Intercollegiate" became a thing of the past.

Not, dear alumnus of Columbia or Cornell or Wesleyan, that you cannot send up crews worthy to compete, but you cannot be depended on year after year. Your conditions are not the same. Is it not better that you have a race among *yourselves?*

There was a dance at the Grand Union the night before the races at Saratoga, and Harry strolled over with Danforth and looked in at the open windows. There were plenty of pretty girls wearing ribbons and sashes of the various college colors. Harvard and Yale did not seem to be half as popular as Columbia, and her blue and white colors predominated.

They saw De Koven dancing with a pretty, spirited girl near the open window. Presently he stopped, and they came out on the wide piazza. She recognized Harry's bronzed, handsome face instantly, giving him her gloved hand. She was all college enthusiasm and excitement. "Oh, Mr. Chestleton," she said, "how proud you must be! And *poor* Harvard beaten three straight games!"

"They expect to win to-morrow and make up for it."

"Oh, but they *won't!* Do you see this? [indicating some blue and white ribbons tied above her pretty round shoulder.] Columbia is going to win. I had a dream saying it wouldn't—and dreams go by contraries."

Harry laughed good-naturedly. "Are you Columbia's mascotte?" he asked.

"No, but I feel *certain* about it," she insisted. "Whenever I have such a distinct dream about anything, I feel sure I'm right. Now, I dreamed about Clara Hastings——"

Harry glanced quickly into her face. "What?"

"Didn't you hear? She's engaged to a Mr. Saxton, a great swell, a Yale man, class of '68, who lives in New York. It's a fact—she wrote me——"

It seemed for a moment to Harry as if everything swung about him in a circle. He murmured a few commonplaces, bowed, and seeking out Danforth, walked hurriedly toward their hotel.

"What's the matter, old man?" asked Danforth, who was engaged in smoking a huge cigar.

"Dan, don't ask me. I've heard bad news. I'm going home to New York to-night—I'm——"

"No one sick?"

"Oh, no. Don't ask me, Dan. Will you see Jack, if you can, before the race? Cheer him up. Don't say I'm not here. Don't let any of the fellows know. O Dan! Dan!"

He covered his face with his hands and reeled against a tree. "What is it?" asked Danforth, getting alarmed. "Let's go get some brandy for you."

Harry suffered himself to be led into the café of one of the great hotels. But he would drink nothing. He went over into a corner of the barroom, and his head fell on his arm on a table near at hand.

"Dan," he said, "just go away and leave me. I am all right. I'm not sick. I've heard bad news—it's a girl——"

"Oh!" said Danforth, much relieved.

"Just leave me, Dan. Go and have all the fun you can with the fellows. If her dream comes true as her other one, bet on Columbia."

Danforth looked perplexed. "Egad, Harry! I believe you're wandering in your mind."

Harry pulled himself together.

"Dan, don't think I've gone crazy, but I've been a fool. I set my heart on a girl—and she's going to marry another, and I've naturally—I just heard it, and I've made up my mind that I won't go back to college next year."

"Not pitch another year?"

"No; now, I'm just going home to-night to get away. I don't want any brandy; I don't want anyone to stop me. If anyone tries any funny business on me he'll get hit—that's all."

Harry looked at his watch calmly. "The New York train goes at 11.30," he said. "I've got half an hour to pack my bag—I'm going. The race—I saw the last one with *her*, Dan!"

When he saw that Harry was obdurate, Jim Danforth quietly followed him upstairs to their room on the fourth story and

went to work and helped him pack, and at the same time packed
his own traps. Harry was too full of his grief to notice what he
did. He walked to the depot like a man in a dream. He was a
little surprised, however, when the train reached Albany, to have
Dan walk into the car where he sat. They had bidden each other
good-by at Saratoga.

"I kind of thought I'd run down to New York with you," said
the good fellow. "I confess I don't care much about seeing the
boat-race——"

"O Dan! That's a flat-footed whopper. You get out of this
train and go back——"

"No—too bad we can't get a sleeper, isn't it? Lots of people
who don't care a rap about the in-ter-co-le-giate races left Saratoga to spend to-morrow in New York, they say, and the berths
are full—political sort of people, they say, who don't know that
Yale College exists!"

"Dan, I insist on your going back. You know you wouldn't
miss the race for a thousand dollars. I shall never forgive myself
if you miss it. Go back, Dan, for my sake!"

"I'd rather read about it in the New York papers. It's the only
way I ever enjoy a ball game—I'm so—excitable!"

"Dan—*Dan!* don't be an ass!"

"I'm in good company," he laughed, and the train rolled out
and away from the depot. Presently Danforth, after cracking a
few dismal jokes, made himself comfortable in a seat and went to
sleep. Harry sat up until the gray dawn appeared and they rolled
into the Grand Central depot. Would *he* have done this for Jim
Danforth?

There is a period in the lives of all young men when any such
catastrophe to their hopes seems very final. A disastrous love
affair, or a worrying gambling debt, or a serious family quarrel
may kill between the ages of nineteen and twenty-two. The
young man believes there is nothing beyond!

At thirty-five these trifles never make him desperate. He begins
to see that half the fun of life is its disappointments.

But at nineteen his outlook seems, as in Harry's case, to be finally closed, because of the simple fact that he suddenly finds a girl he has set his heart upon does not love *him*. All the currents of his young being have set to her. He would rather die than not possess her. Her touch is magnetic. The crisp sound of her dress is music. When she speaks her words enter his soul. Never again is love so engrossing, so all-powerful. It is then keyed exactly to a woman's love; it is as unselfish as hers, as pure and sweet as hers.

He stealthily took out a Russia leather wallet, and from one of the compartments removed three photographs of Clara—one taken on horseback after one of their rides in New Haven; one in a street dress and hat, taken at Charmington, and one, just her head alone —the one he liked best. He sat for ten or fifteen minutes gazing at them, his knees up against Dan's seat in the car. So, she was lost to him! going to marry that graduate Saxton of '68, with his long mustache. Her beauty, her exquisite hair, her lovely eyes, her high soul, which he exalted now the higher and worshiped the more devoutly since she was lost to him—how he realized the hopelessness of it all now! He felt sick and faint. He thought he would go to the door and get a breath of fresh air. Instantly Dan was on his feet following him.

"I wouldn't go out there," said Dan. "The cars twitch so around these curves you might accidentally get thrown into the Hudson River!"

Harry suffered himself to be led back to the seat. "I feel half sick," he said. "The windows don't seem to be able to let in any air."

"Oh, we'll go get our breakfast and then go get a Turkish bath in New York," said Dan. "Then we'll get your mother and Kitty, and we'll run off down to Long Branch and put ourselves in connection with the telegraph office. Now, I predict Yale first, Cornell second, Harvard third, Columbia fourth—and I saw Brown rowing in good form, and so I'll put them fifth and Ann Arbor sixth, and Oshkosh seventh, and—and—the University of South Dakota eighth, and—and—Bowdoin——"

But here he fell asleep again.

Harry must have dozed himself, for the next thing he knew they were going through the dark tunnel toward Forty-second Street.

His first two years of college life were over. He was home once more; the wicked soph year was a thing of the past.

He was sad and disconsolate over Clara's engagement, and the news of Columbia's win and Harvard's fouling the Yale boat did not add to his comfort. The world was all awry.

CHAPTER XXXIV.

AT MOUNT DESERT.

BY degrees Harry got over the first shock of the news of Clara Hastings' engagement. By the end of August he had written her a passionate letter of farewell and received a cold, formal reply. It was all over. His heart was crushed. Girls were no longer attractive. He wished there was a first-class war going on somewhere in the world where he could go, and leading a charge against great odds, be handsomely killed!

His mother had sympathized with him, and with the greatest tact, never ceased to praise the beautiful girl, of whom she had had but a glimpse that Easter Sunday on Fiftieth Street. Gradually his heart had healed a little. It was about this time he received a letter from Grannis, dated Denver, Col., and saying he had found some traces of Ella, and expected shortly to start for California. The disappointment seemed to bring him and his mother closer together than ever before. He did not want to be long out of her sight. He refused half a dozen offers of local New York nines to pitch games for them. He refused everything and stayed quietly at home, smoking a long brierwood pipe, heaving desperate sighs, and reading Heine's poetry, until it came time for him to take them up to Mount Desert.

The summer vacation at Bar Harbor, passed in the then simplicity and jollity of Rodick's Hotel, was a pleasanter one than Harry would naturally have anticipated. Mrs. Chestleton wisely preferred the hotel to taking a cottage—she wanted Harry to be alone, in his then unhappy frame of mind, as little as possible. Bar Harbor was not fashionable, but comfortable, in those days. Social requirements were relaxed. Chaperons were not deemed necessary. The young people lived in a beautiful Arcadia, in which good behavior was a matter of course.

In those days, gentle reader, it was possible, probable—nay, polite—to call for one's summer girl (hailing, too, from blue-blooded Boston, smart Murray Hill, or Walnut Street—or the city that lies near Druid Park), at say, 9, A. M., with self, horse, and buckboard, to load upon said buckboard said girl, to drive around the island (twenty-four miles), dining at a hotel at the opposite point, near Southwest Harbor, and returning in the moonlight along about 9 or 10 o'clock P. M. ! *Honi soit qui mal y pense.*

When Daisy Stevenson came to Bar Harbor she readily fell into its accepted customs with spirit. Harry found himself thrown with her in sailing parties, buckboard parties, and climbing parties a great deal. He liked her because she let him talk about Clara by the hour and never forbade him. Doubtless it bored her, for she never esteemed Clara's mental gifts very highly, and she only cared for people of brains. She and her brother had a fine Indian canoe, which, after a while, she taught Harry to paddle with her among the porcupine islands.

Yes, and what a different girl she was, too, after a few weeks of sun and sea air and exercise! She became positively pretty! It was odd what comfort the lad took in being with this art-prize girl!

With Clara it had always been: "Do the correct thing," "What does society expect?" "So and so is not good form," etc.

With Daisy it was always some topic outside themselves. She had read and devoured all the novels that were ever written, apparently. George Eliot's "Mill on the Floss" was her favorite. She set Harry to thinking and reading. She lent him "Middlemarch." Unconsciously she became a summer school of philosophy to him.

One day Harry experienced a slight sensation. It was the last week in August. He had resolutely frowned on any girl and all girls except Daisy, so far. His heart was crushed and dead, etc. He preferred foggy, rainy days; then he retired to his little room *au quatrième*, stretched himself on his corn-cob bed, and read about sweet Dorothea and Casaubon and the disillusionment of love.

Those days of the first disappointments in love how a lad takes to heart! And what a dear old ass he makes of himself!

One day he came downstairs, his finger in a book which he was reading. He looked about for Miss Stevenson, expecting her to appear pleased at his coming, and willing to go canoeing in her canoe with him, as usual.

But, lo and behold! she had gone down to the wharf with *another* man—and a Harvard man at that! a man whom she had hitherto shunned and avoided with a marked disdain! Did Daisy Stevenson actually mean to take this man canoeing? Heaven forfend! There were plenty of other pretty girls sitting about in their cool, white dresses eying him respectfully (the distinguished Yale pitcher was considered a great swell), and eying him even wistfully. At Rodick's, that season, there were exactly four girls to one man.

He threw his book on a table and walked away gloomily up the path leading toward Bald Mountain, and threw himself under a tree on the grass. He could not understand *why* Daisy's action affected him so. Somehow her flat defiance, as he pretended to think it, had driven Clara's image entirely out of his mind for the time being. Could it be possible that, had he not met Clara, he would have fallen in love with Daisy? She had charm. Her artistic ambition—now that she was the prize pupil of the year she was deemed well advanced on her career—lent her an added grace. He discovered that she had the most vivacious and brightest hazel eyes, that her light blond hair was beautiful in the wind, that she had a most lovely tanned complexion! As he lay on the grass looking off to sea he saw a commotion on the water. Had a boat or canoe capsized? Had the clumsy Harvard man upset her? He seized his hat and ran down to the wharf. Miss Stevenson and the Harvard man, safe on dry land, passed him on the way. She was in no danger—she gave him a bow, which seemed to mean "See—I am fond of a little diversity." Not cold, not distant, but—not her usual smile and *intimate* glance. He returned to Rodick's more surprised than ever. He suddenly discovered that everything was at an end between them, if everything ever had a beginning.

Could he have seen her that night in her room, crying as if her heart would break!

Daisy Stevenson, with her keen insight and bright mind, saw too clearly that he never would really come to love her; that it was rather her mental endowment he respected, not *herself* he loved. Gently, nobly, and with consummate tact, the girl, in their daily intercourse, repressed her own feelings. She fought down her own wishes, her own love, in those pleasant August days. How willingly, if she had allowed herself to go, she would have given up all her high hopes and ambitions for marriage and quiet life with this kind, sweet-natured lad! It was her crown of martyrdom, and she concealed it from everyone. She even led Harry to believe that she did not care for him in the least—in *that* way. She showed him, too, that in his heart, deep down, there still lay the image of his goddess Clara. One day she jestingly said: "Do you think, indeed, that I, with my pride, will ever consent to play second fiddle?"

"If you allude to a certain Miss Hastings, her image has gone out of my sight forever!" he said calmly.

"Nonsense! How you would start up, flush, and grow pale again, as people are said to do in novels but never do in real life, if Clara should suddenly appear over that ledge of rocks! *You love her!*"

And the next day Daisy and her brother left for a trip through Canada, and he saw her no more that summer.

After the *Olivette* carried Daisy away—fated steamboat, how many lovers hast thou separated in thy day!—he seemed to return more to his old cheerful self. He began to amuse himself—to even permit himself to indulge in a mild flirtation with a pretty Philadelphia girl, a Miss Fleeting. Miss Fleeting was the belle at Bar Harbor that summer—she was a pretty, laughing, jolly round-eyed creature, and it gave him a little amusement to cut out two Princeton grads, who were supposed to be of the bluest Philadelphia blood. There were plenty of Harvard men at Rodick's, and to his surprise he found most of them amazingly good fellows in spite of the foul at Saratoga. They got up a nine, and he pitched for them. He delighted in the success his pretty sister Kitty had become. She took very well among the young fellows at Mount

"IF YOU ALLUDE TO A CERTAIN MISS HASTINGS, HER IMAGE HAS GONE OUT OF MY SIGHT FOREVER," HE SAID CALMLY.

Desert. She was always ready for any sort of a long walk, a hard row, or a climb up Newport or Green Mountain. By the time vacation was over Harry was in a comparatively cheerful frame of mind. He had become reconciled to Clara's engagement. He determined the rest of his college course to work hard, study, and give up girls forever. "Jack, old man," he said, a day or two after they were established in their pleasant rooms for junior year in ivy-clad Durfee, "Jack, women only bring sorrow and disappointment—take all I have known."

"Oh, the devil they do!" laughed Jack, who was engaged in putting on a sweater and preparing to go out to the football field, "Women are God's best, last gift to man! you just bet your life!"

"I'm going to leave them all severely alone after this—they've brought it on themselves!" and Harry laughed.

"That's right, of course; and, old fellow, I understand of course what a time you've had all summer. Oh, I've been there myself! *Often!* But I find that every new girl I meet has some new additional charm. I love not one, but many! I have serious intentions of becoming a Mormon when I graduate—and marrying, say a dozen dear girls I have met, and loved!"

"O Jack—what an incorrigible flirt you are!" And he laughed. "You're as bad as Solomon!"

"No worse than you—you old girl-crusher! you always pretend to be so serious, but you get there all the same! Foxy!"

They were juniors now, and scuffling was beneath their dignity, otherwise Harry was minded to give his chum a lesson in respectfulness. Jack swung out of the room whistling a popular tune and hied him over to the "gym" lot, where the football team was to meet for the first time that season. Football had at the time hardly the importance it now has, but science had already begun to be displayed on the game, especially at Princeton. Yale had beaten Harvard the year before, and this year the plan was to train an eleven "from the word go" and beat both Harvard and Princeton. Yale had some great players, notably Godolphin, a "scientif," and Dobson, center rush. Cushing, too, had shown great ability the year previous. They called him facetiously "Old Cushion, the Man Mountain." Little Bailey, the quarter-back, could writhe and twist himself through a knothole. Jack found quite a crowd gathered at the gym, and presently was mustered in on the 'Varsity side. He was bold and strong, and a week later was asked by the Yale captain to join the regular training table. He wrote home to his father at Yonkers about it, and received a reply positively forbidding him to go on the eleven. He continued all through October to play with the team, however, taking care not to give out his true name to the reporters. Football was Jack's natural game. He was quick, active, strong, alert, and plucky, and presently it was found that the Yale team *could* not get along without him. Again Jack, the rascal, planned to deceive the "old boy" as he did in his rustication.

As for Harry, he began to take long walks to East and West Rocks, and to the famous old "brewery" with Nevers, who was busy over his *Lit.* essay, and to "sport the oak" and to do no end of general reading. He got Tutor Dilworthy to write him out a long and varied scheme for English history. In his secret heart he had some vague and indefinite plan of going in for a Townsend and taking the DeForest medal in the coming senior year. He thought he'd begin early and read up! How Clara's eyes would open when she beheld the college pitcher, not content with athletic honors, sweep in the greatest literary prize in college! In everything he did he could not help having the *fiancée* of one hated Saxton of '68, ever before his eyes. Ah, me! dear elderly alumnus, we have all been there, "many a time"; we have all worked for the one girl— and perhaps lost her, but she was still the girl of girls to us. Harry sported the oak theatrically; made no calls on his New Haven girl friends—he did this with theatrical intent. He wished to pose. Clara, who was in town for the winter, flirted, rode horseback, and went about in society that fall, apparently indifferent not only to Harry but to Saxton of '68 as well. Jack was devoted to her. The handsome fellow was so "profoundly insincere," as she said, that she almost loved him. She drove out to all his football matches, where he usually played under an assumed name, and applauded his dashing plays until her *gants de suède* were burst, and she made him buy her others.

So with Harry at work and Jack at play, the Thanksgiving game with Harvard at New York approached—but that, as Mr. Kipling observes, is "another story."

CHAPTER XXXV.

ALE men for many years have been well acquainted with the famous country place of General Mahlon Rives. The tall white sandstone towers make their appearance above a little forest of maples and beeches against the dark background of the Yonkers hills.

On the morning of Thanksgiving Day, the steady wheel horses of a canary-paneled coach sprang into a lively canter as they rounded a curve and dashed into the *porte cochère.* A fair young girl, dressed in russet brown, and muffled to the chin in a long boa, came out of the doorway and greeted the ladies who made up the coaching party with a pretty stateliness.

"Papa declares he won't go," she exclaimed dubiously. "He says that, having forbidden Jack to play, he does not think he ought to countenance the game by going to see it. Did you ever!"

Immediately a tall old gentleman, with rather a stiff, military air, followed the girl out upon the porch. General Rives had served in the war of the Southern rebellion with considerable distinction. He wore no medals, but his empty sleeve told a story not without a certain eloquence. He advanced to the coach and gave his right hand to a short, red-faced, red-bearded young man who was driving, another Yale man.

"General, we can't let you off, you know; you promised us——"

"Circumstances——" began the general, clearing his throat.

"But you are an old Yale man yourself," interrupted a bright black-eyed little lady, who sat muffled in her sealskins next the driver.

"Circumstances——" again began the general.

"You were in college once, and now Jack is, and not to see this important match—*the* match of the year—why——"

The little lady waved a flag of blue bunting inscribed with the letter Y, and gave a little cry of animated despair.

"Oh, do come, General Rives! What are we to do for beaux?" pleaded a pretty young woman, who seemed to have swathed herself for the day in bands of blue satin ribbon. She wore a stylish Rembrandt hat, and beneath the low brim her eyes glanced out at the gallant old soldier with an amusing coquettishness.

"Why, general, the coach is literally stuffed with good things," urged the gentleman who was driving.

"Papa—I—I—if you don't go, *I* won't!" exclaimed his daughter.

"I really don't believe in this sort of thing, Mrs. Telford. I—I do not wish to countenance it—for Jack's sake, you know," said the general. "In my day at Yale they did not have these *tremendous* athletic affairs. I confess they seem to me—er—er—very bad for the students—very harmful to their studies."

The black-eyed little lady addressed as Mrs. Telford gave a slight cough.

"But we shall be so disappointed," she exclaimed. "If you don't go——"

"You see, I have forbidden Jack to play," said the general quietly. "His mother—Mrs. Rives has always been an anxious mother—and Jack, with his boat crew, had a tendency to overexert himself, and when it came to football—we have heard such stories that we forbade him. We are very anxious to see Jack graduate, if not with honors, at least with the usual number of arms and legs."

GENERAL RIVES.

"There are occasions, general, when it is an honor to lose an arm, don't you think?" It was the pretty girl in the stylish hat who made this graceful speech. The general merely smiled and bowed in reply, and hesitated. "Of course," he said at length, "I believe that my dear old alma mater is worth fighting for"—a fine light spread over his grizzled old face. "If there must be fighting and Jack was in the fight—I—I—shouldn't want him to—I shouldn't care to see him show the white feather. Yes—I would rather see him"—then he turned away quickly and nervously. "Come, Bessie," he said, "don't keep Mr. Telford waiting."

Bessie petulantly leaned against the wall. "I know it's horrid of me," she said apologetically to the ladies in the coach, "but papa is behaving so badly. I—I shall not go, I shall stay and miss it." There were girlish tears in her eyes.

"Bessie!" said the general sternly. Then he appeared to relent a little. He could be severe enough with Jack, but he was more lenient toward his daughter.

"Papa is just——" she cried, stamping her foot, and then, filled with keen disappointment, yet amusingly willful, fled into the house to hide her tears.

"Come, general," said Mr. Telford, "it will be a fine drive. It will be a grand game, and for the championship, too! Although I'm not a college man *I* shall shout for Yale, and when you get there you will shout, too, I'm sure."

"Nonsense," laughed the general, "my days of enthusiasm are

over. Now don't let us keep you. The horses are restless. Very sorry that my wife feels too ill this morning to come down. I don't mind confiding to you that we received a very unwelcome letter from the faculty last night, about—about Jack. It seems— and I know how grieved all you neighbors will be to hear it—that he is in the first stage of discipline, and so won't be home this Thanksgiving." Lucky the general never found out about Jack's rustication the year before!

The general's words filled most of the party with a wholesome awe. Only the girl in the stylish hat and bands of blue burst out into the jolliest of laughter.

"Oh, how funny!" she laughed. "You know, General Rives, that I spent last Commencement in New Haven—and—I—I feel sure that everyone that I met who was at all nice was in some stage of discipline or being suspended or something."

"In my day," said the general gravely, "the 'nice' fellows were those who were most careful to conform to college rules."

Again the pretty young girl burst out laughing, as if this were a very odd, old-fashioned way of looking at the question. Mr. Telford looked at his watch.

"Good-by, and a pleasant day to you!" said the general, bowing. Telford gave the signal, the coach rolled away, and the horn sounded as it disappeared down the avenue of leafless maples. The general watched it for a moment and then entered the house.

He was obliged to encounter there a very pale, very *distraite* young woman, who stood with her wraps thrown back upon her shoulders, her hat hanging by its ribbon from her hand. She was tall, like her father, and possessed something of the general's erectness. As he entered she confronted him: "Does it seem like Thanksgiving Day?" she asked.

The general took her two soft little hands in his one hand very gravely.

"I had no heart to go, Bessie—Jack not at home. You see it is probable the faculty have seen fit to compel him to remain at New Haven over the Thanksgiving holiday as a punishment. It's his own fault, he has brought it on himself. He has probably been very wild and disobedient, but when a boy devotes himself as he has been doing to athletics instead of his studies, what must he expect?"

"We must expect that his father will cease to care anything about him, of course!" said Bessie defiantly. "We must expect that we must only mention his name with bated breath—that we must go about as if we were ashamed of him—although everyone says there never was such a bow oar on the Yale crew."

"But, my child, you don't appreciate; it is the gradual deterioration of his moral character. This devotion to sport leads to smoking, drinking, gambling——"

"Papa! don't you know they go into training and can't do these things?"

"I don't know—I don't pretend to know about all that they do. It has all come up since my day. In '46 we had no nines, no elevens, no crews—nothing of the sort; we had our books, our oratorical contests, our literary prizes. To be an editor of the Yale *Lit.* was our highest reward, and *I* attained that honor. I—I hoped that my son would follow in my footsteps."

The general turned into his library, and Bessie sorrowfully went to her mother.

Mrs. Rives was a delicate, refined-looking woman with a pale, sleepless look about her eyes. As her daughter entered the handsomely furnished chamber she looked from the couch where she was lying. "I'm sorry, dear, about the football game. I'm sorry you did not go without him; but your father feels Jack's disgrace very keenly. It would have been torture for him to try to be gay and jolly all day long, but you might have gone in spite of Jack's disgrace."

"Jack's disgrace?"

Bessie leaned down and kissed her mother on her forehead gently. "I just hate the faculty!" she murmured.

"You are a stanch little sister to Jack!" smiled her mother. "Yet I don't know why I say 'little,' for you are as tall as I am."

Then they heard the door bell ring, and in a few moments more

the general entered with a telegram.   His face had grown younger
by ten years.

"A telegram from Jack!" he cried.   " 'Be home to dinner to-
night; will bring a gang—JACK.'   He'll bring a 'gang'? "

"A lot of his friends—how jolly!"   cried Bessie, clapping her
hands.   "It must be the 'Gimly gang'!"

"Jack will be here?" said Mrs. Rives, sitting up.   "They will
let him come home?   Ring the bell for my maid, Bessie, quick.
If he brings his friends there is no time to lose.   We must have
his room and the spare rooms aired.   There are—we had better
prepare for at least nine—or eleven is it?   Oh, eleven at once!
What *shall* we do?"

The good woman rose briskly from the couch and was all happy
activity in a moment.   The whole household assumed an air of life
and gayety.   Bessie ran out to the kennel and told bounding
Pompey and fawning Carlo, "Jack is coming! Jack is coming!"
She danced across the lawn as blithely and as gracefully as a
Spanish *danseuse;* for Bessie was very much of an outdoor girl,
and could ride and walk and run like a young boy.   As she flew
through the light brown maple leaves she found herself suddenly
caught and held fast.

"Oh, papa! how happy I am!"

The old general winked mysteriously.   Then he cleared his
throat.   "Er—er, your mother—er—is upsetting the entire house,"
he said.   "There is so much noise going on I can't work.   It is
very embarrassing!"

"Poor papa!"

"Er—the 1.52 train—er—confound the boy! of course he'll be
there to see the game.   I—I——"

"You dear old thing!   You *will* take me after all?"

"Er—well—we will see—after lunch!" he said, laughing, like a
boy, to himself.   She threw herself into his arms.

No gathering of any kind is so gay with color and display, so
rich in lovely faces of pretty girls, so brave with fine-looking well-
dressed men, so noisy, so good-natured, so fashionable, as the great

Thanksgiving foot-
an annual event, this
in New York, be-
The following year
vard, won the right
The grand stand was
on either side were
and dotted
there, a bit
coaches bril-
ble people;
mothers,
cousins — all
to enjoy the
partisans as
  The rival-
universities
it is earnest.
rivalry has
opportunity.
fitted for
bats only
preparation,
less work
ing, by self-
and exacting. Triflers
to try for those three
binations of skilled
the crew, the nine, and
"It is character first
strength afterward,"
mous old Yale coach,
tedly taught his crew
rival university! No-
this deep-centered dis-
trust a greater oppor-

ball game, which began as
year, at the old Polo Grounds
tween Yale and Harvard.
Princeton, by beating Har-
to play Yale on Thanksgiving.
festooned with bunting;
dark masses of men,
among them, here and
of a girl in color;
liant with fashiona-
students with horns;
fathers, uncles, aunts,
not merely assembled
spectacle, but earnest
well.
ry between our
is as amusing as
In athletics this
its grand
Teams are
these com-
after years of
through end-
and coach-
denial, rigid
are not asked
great com-
strength—
the eleven.
and brute
said a fa-
who admit-
to *hate* their
where has
like and dis-
tunity than

MUFFLED TO THE
CHIN IN A BIG BOA.

the football field. Here is actual physical contact; here are blows and knocks, and falls and "tackles," and brawny men pressing the life out of each other till the cry comes—"Down, down!"

The Yale team were gathered in their dressing room beneath the grand stand some time before the hour appointed for the game, and yet the noisy, stamping feet of thousands of enthusiastic collegians could be heard through the well-lined ceiling above them. Hardly a man was there on the team who did not appear nervous, except the captain, who was busy talking to a reporter. There was old man Cushing, or "Cushion," as they nicknamed him, tall, broad, steady, perfectly cool, perfectly reliable, entirely brave; his hand trembled as he opened his valise and as he heard the noise beginning above. He had been through a dozen conflicts; he had not known defeat; he never expected to be beaten. Yet he experienced just then that dread common to all men, that secret preliminary spasm of weakness which often seizes great public speakers. He knew very well that on him, the "center rush," would come most of the tremendous strain. If he wavered, if he weakened or misjudged, every newspaper in every large city in the country would in its report of the great game hold him up to everlasting scorn. There was little young Bailey, who stopped at nothing—pale, yes, and worried. It is no child's play ahead of this young quarter-back. Bailey is not the only pale face. Football men are never ruddy, their paleness is the pallor of health, for these men are all trained to the very pink of condition. Bailey is worried and silent. He is susceptible to the various rumors he has heard and which always float about before a great game. He has overheard that two of the opposing team, whom he has fought and wriggled through and dodged in old games, have announced they will give him "particular attention." There is Dobson stripped, and the trainer is rubbing the knots of muscle on his back with rock salt and water. He strained his side in practice the other day, and *that* worries *him*. He bends over a chair, and the trainer puffs and blows with the rough rubbing and slapping he is giving his bare back. Everyone is rather silent.

Harry, by right of his being on the nine, and an athlete, is present and rubbing Jack's back with a coarse hand towel.

"Who is this Mr. Lansing?" asked the reporter, who happened to be an old college man himself. "He must be a freshman?"

"Jack, speak for yourself," called out the captain to a curly-haired, wiry fellow, who was to play half back that day.

"Why, it's Jack Rives!" exclaimed the reporter.

"Yes but don't give it away," said the captain—"a family matter. His father refused to let Jack play—went right back on his own college, too! But Jack won't have it, so he is playing under the name of Lansing."

"Lansing's father doesn't object, I suppose?" laughed the reporter.

The little joke livened up the team and the substitutes wonderfully. Everyone fell to chatting. Cushing, to try his back, playfully lifted Jack, who weighed about 150 pounds, and threw him over his head. He landed lightly on his feet.

"He was a substitute at first," whispered the captain, watching him proudly, "and he's the best dodger we've got now. I intend to work him. I intend to give him a chance to make his reputation."

Then the captain began to ask the reporter questions about Harvard's team, but as he had had his own private and confidential scout following the Harvard team about for two months and making careful notes of all their games, the reporter could tell him nothing that was new. As the reporter departed the captain turned and lectured the whole team and substitutes: "We are going in to break the hearts of those heavy-weight bruisers in the first half. We're going to make 'em work and 'wind' 'em. Tackle low and throw hard. Work will come easier later. They've got the weight in their rush line; you're going to see a good deal of end work to-day right at the start, and don't forget the signals."

So spoke the captain, a man famous in Yale football annals from that day to this.

A deafening volley of cheers, tremendous pounding of feet, a roar of the vast multitude announced to them the entrance of their rivals on the field for their preliminary practice.

"They're out!" cried the captain sturdily, "and that's bad luck for them at the start."

The team well knew the captain's methods of coquetting with the jealous Dame Fortune, and that it never was his policy to enter the field first. As the men got into their canvas jackets, and began to present, with their padded knees and mud-stained "britches," that terribly "hard," bruised-like appearance, the characteristic sign of a champion team—several friends entered.

"Every girl in New York is on the ground!" said one.

"My sister? Is Bessie here—and the old gentleman?" asked Jack.

His informant was not able to say.

"Ready, men!" called out the captain, who finished blowing up a pigskin football, and had his hand on the door. "Youngest first —here, Jack!"

Another sop to Dame Fortune!

A moment more and a second tremendous din of "Rah! rah! rah!" rent the air. All was noise and confusion.

Old college men stood upon their seats and cheered. The blue seemed to be everywhere. The entire eleven and the seven substitutes went to work kicking, punting, and warming up in the cool, clear air. Experts studied their score cards and wondered who that new fellow "Lansing" was. It was Jack Rives' first game before a great metropolitan audience. He was an "unknown." There was something about his handsome curly bare head that made him a favorite at once.

Suddenly Jack's hawk's eyes rested upon a coach drawn near the line, the canary body of which was draped in blue. He wasn't so very near it, but he got the ball and made a run nearly the whole length of the ground in the opposite direction. The captain was after him, but Jack kept away.

"Here! don't run your legs out; stop when I say it!" called the captain severely.

Jack stopped. "Do you know who is on that coach?" he asked, not at all out of breath. "The old man, with Bessie!"

"Rub some mud on your cheeks and come along," said the captain crossly.

Jack pretended to fall on the ball again. While down he managed to daub himself with more very neatly. He came up looking like a wild Indian.

In five minutes more the great game began—"the finest game ever played," as said the reporters.

The Harvard team was a magnificent one. Their rush line was tremendous. In the first five minutes "it all looked one way," as an old Harvard player said. Then his friend sitting near by observed:

"I don't know. The Yale men are so deuced tricky."

"But look at the ball on Yale's twenty-five-yard line!"

"Well, look at it *now!*" said the friend.

A kick from Cushing had sent the oblong sphere whirling two-thirds the way toward Harvard's goal. There appeared to be as many Yale men under it when it fell as Harvard. The grand work of Harvard's rush line had gone for naught.

Then, little by little, they went to work again. Superior weight told. They were crowding the lighter men from Yale off the field. Again they reached the twenty-five-yard limit. As if by magic the ball again was kicked down the field.

"I tell you they are trying to tire our rushers out!" insisted the Harvard expert. "It's as plain as dirt!"

It *did* seem rather plain, it must be confessed. Then, in the last part of the half, Yale began to take the offensive.

Gradually, by tricks, by feints, by massing his men at the wrong place and sending Jack Rives in the right place "for all he was worth," the skillful Yale captain got the ball where he wanted it, in front of Harvard's goal, and just inside the twenty-five-yard line.

Now came an exciting moment. The entire twenty-two men were nerved up to the highest tension as it was plainly evident that Godolphin, Yale's famous full back, had come up to kick a goal from the field. Godolphin appeared indifferent to what was going on, or what was expected of him. Months of training, long sleeps and autumn winds had braced his nerves to perfection.

He knew that he was to get the ball, instantly to drop-kick it, and immediately be hurled down by that terrible weight of Harvard's rushers and trampled—perhaps to be severely injured. Yet Godolphin sauntered up to just the right spot—just the right blade of grass, and waited. Yale had the ball and the captain was fiddling with it between Dobson's great legs.

Not a sound could be heard in all that vast auditorium of twenty thousand excited people. The Harvard men, in a great mass of red at one end of the ground near their own goal, looked on with a sickening sense of despair. It was like watching the deathbed of a friend. They had seen Godolphin do this same thing before. They knew that he had calculated with the cool precision of a mathematical savant the distance between himself and that terrible rush line which Yale admittedly could not hold. The little fraction of a second when the ball would arrive in his hands *ahead* of those maddened bulls was the time when the ball was to soar up above their heads and sail gracefully between the goal posts. The captain looked back, fiddled some more. "Steady, Lansing!" he called in a low voice to Jack, and Jack knew the trick. He went back a couple of yards.

Godolphin knew it also, and because he saw the change of tactics and knew the ball was not coming to him, he pretended to grow nervous, and rubbed his hands together anxiously to attract the Harvards' attention.

The captain still fiddled with the ball between Dobson's great legs. Then a flash—it was snapped back to Jack. A roar of the crowd followed. The crafty captain had fooled them well. Jack ran like a hare down along the right line, dodging a big brute of a man, tumbling over another, diving between the legs of a third, his face blanched, his teeth set, his eyes on fire, the whole pack after him. Courage? The boy would have charged up a hill under the raking fire of a hundred Gatling guns if he saw a goal in sight by so doing. He would have given his life then with just as glad good will.

Have you ever seen a great sprinter finish near the tape of a one-hundred-yards dash? If he is pressed his face is bloodless, his eyes have a most spiritual, unearthly look. The soul pervades, rides high over the earthly framework. It is *do* or *die*.

So Jack, clinching the ball under his arm, as in a vice, dodged and ran, was tackled, and at last was downed by a crushing weight full on the Harvard base line. It meant a touch down.

Mighty cheers went up. Mighty clappings and stampings and horn blowings for the pretty piece of strategy. Everything blue waved in the air.

Then, when the great pile of canvas, backs and legs and arms, rose and separated, one lay still on the ground. His head lay across the base line, the ball still held tightly in his grasp. His face had the pallor of death. Time was called. Two doctors ran out of the crowd.

"It has probably killed him," sighed a gentleman of science, who had calculated the weight which fell on him.

His remark made a sensation. Ladies stood up in their seats to try and get a better view of the fallen hero. One young woman fainted, and had to be carried out. The captain was kneeling at Jack's head.

"Oh! he's taking his last words!" said someone, and the vast crowd became still.

This is what the captain was saying: "You slung old Tobits like a lily! [Tobits was one of Harvard's "heavies."] Jack, you young limb of Satan, get up, bow to the crowd, and stop your gallery play!"

Jack: "Wait till I get more wind; besides—how about cooling down here, cap?"

"The goal is sure enough, and I pity you, you duck, after this."

Then slowly Jack got up. Cheers and horns gave him a tremendous applause. He had made a "star" play, and Godolphin kicked the goal with the air of a man who felt wearied and bored—he was simply playing second fiddle.

In the five minutes left of the "half" the Yale captain played purely on the defensive and gave Jack nothing to do.

On the Telford coach, which was drawn up not far from the Harvard goal, a rather amusing little comedy had been enacted.

Mr. Telford had espied Bessie and her father before the game, and had sent and had them come to sit on the coach. He was amused to see that the old general had been conquered.

The old gentleman at first, while on the train, had tried to read his morn- ing paper. Un- fortunately the car was full of people wearing the red of Har- vard and wav- ing, amid jolly laughter, flags on which were embroidered the letter "H."

JACK LANSING.

At the station some fakirs were selling and call- ing out "Har- vard red an' Yale blue — here yar' now! Flags! Flags!"

"I *didn't* mean to wear any rib- bon," said the general, "but— er—Bessie, get a yard of that blue satin, and I'll buy two Yale flags. I'll put a bit in my hat, too."

"I've got all my blue ribbon in my pocket," said Bessie, laughing. "I knew we'd want it when we got there!"

At the grounds the general would insist on buying a third and a larger flag, "in case we meet Jack—he'll want one," he said. "Of course *he'll* be on hand." On the coach the general began to show his interest in the game by asking a young Yale man, who was seated next the pretty girl in a Rembrandt hat, a number of questions. It was his first game, and it was all Greek to him. When the play began he thought that there was no ball to be used at all, as for a long time he could not see it. After a little he began to grow interested. As the game went on he began to cheer a little. "Hurrah! hurrah! hurrah!" he cried, standing up, as, after the ball had reached Yale's twenty-five-yard line, it came flying over the field from the famous Godolphin, Yale's full back. Everyone on the coach laughed. "You must say rah, rah, rah! papa," said Bessie. "Hurrah is played out; it's too old-fashioned."

Then the general tried to cheer in the modern fashion, but he got in ten "rahs" and made them all laugh again.

Again the ball went ramming down foot by foot under the crush of Harvard's heavy-weights to Yale's goal, and again came flying back.

"When Yale got the ball so near their own goal," he asked of his pretty daughter, whose face was now pale and her eyes strained with excitement, "why on earth didn't they toss it over?"

"Oh, papa! That is just what they are trying to prevent the Harvards doing!"

"Oh!" exclaimed the old boy, and again they laughed at his ignorance.

Then the two elevens surged and struggled near them. Lansing got the ball, but was quickly downed not ten yards from their coach.

Suddenly the general stood up.

"*Jack—it's Jack!* You rascal—confound you, my boy—lick them out of their boots!"

Then there *was* excitement. Lansing—was Jack!

Nearer, nearer the Harvard goal line they crowded and surged. Then came the wait for the expected kick from the field—and, instead, Jack's famous run.

While the boy lay there panting on the ground his father was down from the coach, walking to and fro behind it. Bessie was trying to follow him. "Papa," she cried, "he isn't killed, he isn't killed!"

"Killed!" muttered the general, looking very old and wretched. "The brutes! to fall on my boy that way, and to interfere with him that way! My boy is half their weight, I say——"

When they told him Jack was all right and playing again, he said, with a gasp, "What *is* that boy made of—rubber?"

And then, as the time was called, he started on a run across the field to the training quarters to find Jack. When he found him he gave him the severest lecture the boy had ever received. Then he broke down and cried like a child. "Jack," he said, "win this game and—I—I'll—there's nothing I *won't* do! I'm going off. It's too much. I can't stand it! I'm going home. We expect you, and bring 'em all along. *Only don't come unless you win!* It's a new thing to me to have to *fight* for my alma mater!"

The flashing eyes of father and son answered each other; there was a quick handshake, and the old gentleman left amid respectful silence.

The second half was played very hard and stubbornly. Both teams were now at their best. The perfect skill shown, the running, the tackling, the punting, never before had been equaled. Godolphin had more to do this half—he kicked a goal from the field. Then Harvard's big men, angered and raging, drove the ball down the field and made a touchdown against Yale and so secured a goal. The score was now 11 to 6. The last half—three-quarters of an hour—waned. Yale's captain saw, with the intuition of genius, that it was the Harvard plan to send Dale, their great half back, through the Yale line as a last resource. He spoke to Jack. "Watch Dale for a break," he said. The words were hardly out of his mouth when out of the Harvard "V" Dale sprang away with the ball like a deer. Jack, at the captain's words, had run back fifteen yards to stop Dale.

It was well he did so. The tall man, with a great burst of speed, was coming with a puzzling zigzag run, a trick they had learned from a Canadian lacrosse expert. Jack and Godolphin started for him and Jack lit on Dale's back. Dale fell and Jack got the ball and was away with a long run, and then the Yale captain played for time, going as slow as he could and advancing his five yards only on the third attempt. The Yale team had no appearance of being tired as had Harvard's heavy rushers, and Dobson advised rushing the ball down the field. The careful Yale captain, however, knew his game, and "played for no errors." He had no more call for "star" plays. The ball, after a dozen red-hot "scrimmages," slowly made its way toward Harvard's goal, and Jack was at last sent to run around their ends. He made a gallant run, but was cleverly stopped by Bostwick, who seemed to have a special grudge against him. As there were but seven minutes left of the half it was decided to try for a touchdown. The center rush, "Old Cushion," instead of passing the ball back, pushed forward and carried a Harvard man on his back for fifteen yards. It was a magnificent effort and might have been crowned with success had time allowed. As it was the game ended 11–6, with the ball three feet from Harvard's goal line.

Then came the shouts and noise and carrying the great victorious eleven off to their quarters. The Harvard captain shook hands with the Yale captain. Each eleven cheered the other. It had been one of the greatest games ever seen in America, and the defeated team had been beaten only by the most carefully concealed strategic play.

Jack brought his captain home—in ordinary life the Yale captain was a very mild, meek-looking individual, who had the greatest dread of being left alone with a pretty girl—and five other worthies, whose personal appearance had the effect of making one suspect they had recently been through a very severe sort of a cyclone.

"*Can* we eat a Thankgiving dinner?" they all shouted in glorious unison. Then Jack danced a clog and sang some doggerel verses of De Koven's about "Poor Harvard's Way."

They joked each other, they laughed at Jack's father and at Jack's playing 'possum. Jack was the hero of the eleven. What could they have done without Jack was the question of the hour.

When they got home they found that the general had literally hung the whole house in Yale blue bunting. There were blue lamps at the door, blue Bengal lights under the trees, and when Jack came home a cannon boomed out a salute from behind the stables. There was a grand dinner and a ball, for the general had hastily sent out messengers to all his friends and neighbors far and near. Harry and Kitty came up from New York. The Thanksgiving vacation had been a jolly one for the former that fall.

The general hugged Jack and forgave him, and after that game the boy had it all his own way with the "old boy" and, as well, his sister Bessie. It was a year after this that the captain—the famous captain—whose name was Stafford, modestly proposed for her hand. "Take him, Bessie!" said the old general, "take him and be glad; the man who could manage his team as he did will be perfectly capable of managing a wife!"

CHAPTER XXXVI

HARRY BECOMES A "DIG."

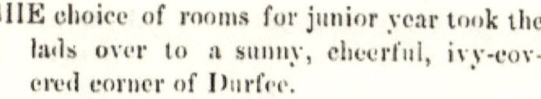

THE choice of rooms for junior year took the lads over to a sunny, cheerful, ivy-covered corner of Durfee.

Harry settled down to the quiet and repose of winter term, and for a time athletics ceased to interest. He kept up his outside reading which he began during the summer, and Jack, on the highest wave of popularity in college and society in town, went in for having a good time. Occasionally Harry would grudgingly drop his books—Jack called him now a "dignified dig"—and don his dress suit for a dance, but he had no heart in it and looked forward to the Promenade as a bore. Jack was chairman of the floor committee, and Harry, too, was first on the committee and then resigned. Miss Hastings, who was in New Haven for the year, went out a great deal, and she and Jack (in spite of her engagement) were great cronies; the handsome fellow was so profoundly insincere that every girl knew that he only made love *pour s'amuser*, and allowed him many privileges. He was constantly receiving scented little notes. He went into private theatricals a great deal; he was the delight of Phi U audiences that year. He was handsome, easy-mannered, jolly, all things to all men—a popular hero—and he loved to tease Harry over the regular letters he received on thin foreign letter-paper, postmarked "Roma." He wrote quaint little poems and *vers de société* for the *Record*. He ran down to New York for the Arion and the French balls, as did a round dozen of Umpty-four men. It annoyed Harry to see the number of photographs Jack had of actresses signed "Ever thine—Adele," or "Forever yours—Florine." This theatrical nonsense—Lester Wallack had actually invited him to see a play from the wings the Christmas vacation when Jack was in New York—angered Harry, and he lectured Jack well for it. He thought it was all Caswell's influence. Caswell was spending a tremendous amount of money now that he had passed the Charybdis of soph. annuals and felt assured of completing his college course. He lost two thousand dollars on the Saratoga race, which he won back at Thanksgiving, in New York. He kept a stylish pair of horses and drove pretty New Haven girls out tandem. Caswell and Jack were now always together. Clark told him it "didn't do his rowing any good," and Jack replied that "Rowing was played out." Clark himself had his tremendous ambition yet to satisfy, and he looked forward to a long season of training again without any qualms. His enmity to unfair Harvard and his wrath—equal to that *Mηνις* of Achilles of which old Homer sang so grammatically and poetically in the first line of the Iliad—at their crew for not daring to go ashore and be walloped, was still touching to behold!

Harry's room in Durfee, looking out on the new quadrangle, with a vista of the campus and the library building in the distance, was very charming, but it did not quite seem like being in college; it was so quiet, so elegant, and so cloisterlike! Everyone in their entry seemed to be studious. A professor roomed just above them. Nevers, who now roomed alone again two flights above them (for Grannis was still away, and Harry did not know whether he had found Ella or not), was busily putting the finishing touches on his essay for the *Lit.* prize which he succeeded in capturing. Even Coles was working pretty hard, and De Koven had taken to immuring himself in his elegantly furnished Farnam rooms and composing songs on his piano and verses for rejection by the magazines.

Somehow a great seriousness had suddenly come over the class of Umpty-four. Dear reader, these fellows were now no longer boys—they had become *upper*-class men. Life at college was now a serious business. No more rushes and street fights, if you please!

They now, too, came under the influence of a professor who had
the ability to inspire them with a desire to understand his subject
—political economy. It was a pleasant surprise to be actually
taught something in the class room. Hitherto it had been, apparently, an inspection, an examination with questions of a prying
nature directed to points in the lesson, calculated to make them
flunk and catch them unawares—minute rules as to the second
aorist, a dozen questions upon the accent of the article. It was a
Yale professor who, after a lifetime of laborious toil, brought forth
a work upon the "Greek Noun," but afterward sighed wearily and
exclaimed "Oh, that I had not been so foolish and given myself
such wide range—oh, that I had simply confined myself to the
ablative!" In spite of the class room, and with the encouragement
of Professor Growler, Harry's intellectual life had really begun
now at Yale.

He planned out his day methodically so that he could have his
evenings to himself for work. He sent regrets to everything that
went on in society until invitations dropped off. He did not wish
to meet Clara if he could prevent it, and there was no other girl he
fancied especially, in all the charming New Haven "set." He
counted on his weekly letter from Rome. This sufficed him. They
were not love letters—far from it. Daisy Stevenson affected to
despise love as much as she did religion or any other "emotion"
which disturbed the perfect use of one's faculties.

Jack openly revolted against Harry's becoming a "dig." As
for Stamp, the old dog had grown rather sour and solemn after
the last boat race at Saratoga Lake, and became a dig and recluse
himself, lying for hours at a time curled up in the corner of the
sofa, while Harry read Mill and Herbert Spencer and smoked a
long pipe, until at one of the wee sma' hours Jack and Caswell, in
their evening dress, would burst in upon him and tell of what a
glorious dance they had been having at Miss Mulford's, or the
Talmans', or elsewhere. Clara Hastings, although engaged to
Saxton of " '68," seemed to be going about having a very jolly
time of it. Once or twice Harry met her in the street, bowed
coldly, and walked rapidly on. Like many sweet young women

who had "erred" by breaking hearts, she began now to pity him. From the way she had succeeded in Umpty-four she began to believe she was irresistible. De Koven was her latest victim. He wrote her many pretty poems and sent her many bouquets. To what end? Although he *did* keep careful copies and sent them to the *Lit.*, afterward, they were rejected promptly, and did not even receive, most of them, the compliment of resting a moment in Purgatory.* The glum Saxton of '68 perhaps smiled over some of De Koven's efforts. But Jack and De Koven got even with him by speaking of him always as "the sexton," and Clara's marriage as her "funeral."

The Puritan estimate of a lady, which Clara pretended to admire so greatly, but which she hardly put herself out to conform to, frowned upon pleasure in the young, and persuaded some of them to suppress their youth, deny themselves, take solemn "views" of life, think much on the hereafter, and try always to be "serious." Clara was hardly of this kind. Youth comes but once. The years creep on fast enough. Very serious expressions were often on her pretty lips, but hardly put in practice! She was a gay, beautiful creature and she was bent on having a good time. Some might have called her a college "flirt;" probably this was rather too severe a term for the beautiful girl. She loved excitement and fun.

Clara admired Puritanism and bragged highly of her Puritan ancestors, yet allowed herself much material joy and many pleasures. Daisy scoffed at the Puritans and at religion, yet in her heart wore a crown of thorns and denied herself much. Both these fine girls were of New England stock. Which was the truer Puritan?

* The revered society of Chi Delta Theta, which manages the *Lit.*, has (or used to have) three places to which a contribution is consigned ; (1) Heaven, *i. e.*, on the table, denoting acceptance ; (2) Purgatory, under the table for a second reading ; (3) Hell, in the waste-paper basket.

CHAPTER XXXVII.

THE LOST UNFORTUNATE IS FOUND.

HARRY was sitting up rather late in his room on a bleak, stormy night in December. The east wind was howling across the Sound and striking full against the front of Durfee, piling little clusters of melting snow in the corners of the window-panes. Harry thought he heard a little low tap at his door. He listened. Then he credited the tapping to his steam radiator, the usual "detonator" of their new quarters, and turned to his table, drew out some note-paper from a drawer, and contemplated writing to his mother, whom he had neglected now for nearly a week. Just then his eyes fell upon the old freshman oar (hung above a picture of Thornton) which Jack had pulled with his sore hand at Saltonstall. Near it hung a base-ball, gilded, with the significant words, "Cambridge: Yale 16, Harvard 4," printed in blue letters. He could not write for some reason. He was weary with study, weary with theories of "silver and gold as a standard"—he laid down his pen. Then he thought he heard the gentle tap on his door once more.

This time he went toward the door and hesitated a moment. Who could it be? Jack would not be home till late. He was at a dance—he and Caswell with a number of his classmates. It couldn't be Jack—he grasped the knob and opened it wide.

Crouched in the narrow hallway was the slight figure of a young woman. Her face was buried in her hands. She was wet through to the bone. She was trembling with cold and wet and fear.

"Who are you?" he started to say. And the figure shivered and hid her head. Then, suddenly, she turned and looked at him. "My God! Ella!" he cried, "is it you?"

351

"Yes"—and she shrunk away from him, cowering.

Her face was wan and pinched. Her pretty mouth, her dark eyes, seemed set in the face of an old woman. It was the last of "Eline St. Pierre."

Harry did not hesitate now an instant. He caught her up, half lifted her in, and laid her, dripping and wet as she was, on his lounge.

"Tell me where you have been—and where you are going!" he cried, half dazed. "Do you know how late it is?"

"I don't know," she moaned. "I am going away. I'm going down to the wharves—before I went, Harry, I just wanted to see you once more."

He hurried to Jack's room and groped about in his closet for his brandy flask. His hand trembled like an aspen-leaf. So Ella Gerhart, whom Grannis was seeking for in California, had returned to her old home in New Haven and had sought out her old love! There was only one thing now to be done—bring her back to her father and take care of her as he would have taken care of his own sister. The brandy revived the poor girl, and she sought to raise herself and sit up.

"My poor, poor Ella!" he cried, the tears almost coming into his eyes, as he knelt by her side.

She put out her hand in a weak, groping sort of way, and he grasped it. This seemed to give her courage.

"I came to you," she said in a low voice. "I want to see you again. I shan't live long."

"Tell me—all—everything!" he exclaimed excitedly. "Do you know that Grannis and your father are seeking you in California?"

"Oh, I can never see my father's face again!" she moaned, and shuddered. "He will never forgive me—oh, it is horrible, horrible! I wish I were dead——"

"Nonsense, Ella!"

"I thought he was an honorable man, as God knows. . . He promised he would marry me. . . He took me to New Orleans —to San Francisco—I trusted him. He swore he loved me. He does love me—but he went away and left me."

Harry said nothing, and presently Ella began again.

"It was in St. Louis. I was dancing there. He sent me flowers every night. He was rich and handsome. He made love to me. I believed he was true. They all told me he was rich and that I had made a great capture, and the very girls I danced with helped him on. I see why, now—they hated me. I was dazzled—and then—he persuaded me and I ran away."

The heat and light of the cheerful room, and more than all, Harry's sympathy, encouraged her. She went on:

"He was good to me in his way. He gave me dresses, jewelry, diamonds, but when I urged him to marry me he got very angry. We lived in a splendid hotel in New Orleans—that was last May and June. Then we went on his ranch in Dakota. Oh, that was a beautiful place in the mountains! I was very happy then—hidden away there. I had my horses, my ponies. I was very happy. I was a sort of princess and all the men on the ranch were my slaves, and my husband——"

Then she burst into tears.

"It came to be September, and he went back to St. Louis and then came back to me again, but he was never the same after that. Then we traveled, and once, at Omaha, out of the car window, I saw Mr. Grannis walking back and forth on the platform, and I was frightened for fear he would see me."

"Yes, Grannis is out there now, in California, searching."

"But he will never find me, and I must go now. I feel better. I must go, Mr. Chestleton. I have some money yet. I have enough."

Then she gazed at Harry's face fully a minute in silence.

"Do you know there is only one place for you to go now?" he said gently—"that is, home?"

She shook her head.

"Your father is a rich man; his electric light has succeeded. Think, Ella, of your mother. They are nearly crazed by your absence. Don't you believe they love you? The very money you sent home to your father out of your salary enabled him to perfect his inventions and sell them. He will be worth—I don't know how much. They say it is already a hundred thousand dollars. Can't you believe that he will be glad to see you, to welcome you home—to forgive you?"

"*Ach, nimmer mehr!*" she sobbed.

Her hair fell down, and Harry saw that, with all her sad experiences, she still retained a large portion of her beauty. He argued and urged a little while, then he said firmly, "Ella, you have voluntarily come to me, and now, for the present at least, you must do exactly what I say. Will you obey me?"

There was a long silence, and finally she whispered, "Yes."

"Then I will take you to some friends of mine for the night."

"Friends?"

"Mrs. Gimly and Samanthy, where I used to board as a freshman. They will take care of you, and to-morrow I shall take you to Cleveland. I shall myself take you home."

In his agony over the poor willful girl, and the pain at his conscience that *his* first desertion of her had paved the way to her ruin, he would gladly have undergone any sacrifice, now, for her sake.

"*Home,*" she murmured twice over to herself. "I dare not go home."

"I will go with you. I will explain and prepare them all. Not one word shall be said against you. Oh, my dear girl, I myself have been to blame for all this!"

"Hush, Harry! I did not come here to disturb you, to worry you. I only wanted to see you and then go away—out of your sight forever."

"You did right to come to me, and to trust *me* to do what was right. Now just forget the past. It's done with—it's over. Can you get ready to start—it's only a little way over to York Street, you know. The Gimlys are kind-hearted folk; they won't say a word. To-morrow, or when you are stronger, we'll go away quietly—home. Poor girl—dear, dear Ella! Don't sob so. Your mother longs to see you; they are rich now. They—they'll take you to Europe, and you'll forget—yes, you'll be very happy, my poor—darling."

The word came out almost before he was aware of it. She stood up and he caught her tottering in his arms. His heart told him he could say anything—any loving words to persuade her. It was almost his duty. Oh, how he repented then the silly flirtation of his freshman year!

Ella perceived his motive.

A solemn-eyed professor roomed in Durfee, just over Harry's room, and he wondered just what would happen if he should venture down, hearing a woman's voice at that late hour in college. "Lord!" he thought, "what a row there'd be!"

"Let me slip this ulster of mine over you—there! and can you walk? let's start for Mrs. Gimly's. The first thing is to think of *you.*"

She was but a pretty child still. Her pale, mobile face, framed in her long, dark, luxuriant hair, which had fallen over her shoulders, was touching in its expression of helplessness. That *she* should have been forced to go out into the world and earn her living—to combat with fortune, to run the gauntlet of temptation and sin! Harry felt a tide of compassion well up within him and almost prevent his speaking coherently. The pathos of it! She had been so dutiful—had sent nearly all her salary home; had lived on the scantiest portion; had tried to do right, he knew—and at the wrong moment he had taken a prop from under her, and when this rich, unscrupulous St. Louis admirer came along and stole his perfidious way to her innocent, childish heart—she fell, because she needed love and kindness and support.

"Thank God!" he thought, "she has come back at last."

Fortunately it was very dark and rainy, and no one saw them as they passed, under an umbrella, across the campus by the library, toward York Street. Somehow Ella seemed to throw off her sorrow now in a light-hearted fashion. He secretly rejoiced. "She is not of the kind to let crushing despair haunt her very long," he thought, "yet—if she had not fortunately found me, what would she have done? Perhaps drowned herself."

Arrived at Mrs. Gimly's they rang half a dozen times before the good landlady arose and lighted her lamp. At last she peered out at them, after chaining the door carefully. It took Harry ten minutes to explain. As he was not now a wicked sophomore, but a mild and godly junior, a friend of freshmen, she finally (on receipt of ten dollars) let them in.

Harry did not tell Mrs. Gimly Ella's story, and he let the kind-hearted Samanthy believe that Ella was a Fair Haven young lady who was too late for the last horse-car. They bustled about in the warm kitchen. The fire being in a state so that it quickly started up again, Samanthy furnished Ella warm dry clothing, which she put on in the former's quaint little bedroom. As the fire grew hot Harry himself stirred the hot oysters and helped brew the tea, while Mrs. Gimly whispered in Ella's ear, as she sat silently by the stove:

"He's a good young man, to my sartain knowledge, bein' in my house, him an' a limb named Mr. Rives, a year as freshmen, both. Oh, I'd trust him with my darter Samanthy fer to go to—say a picnic or a clam-bake—any day; but he never ast her."

Ella bowed her head and smiled. Her eyes followed Harry around the warm, snug kitchen as a dog's will its master. More than any woman that ever lived she needed a strong, firm will to control her—to love her.

Poor, pretty, unfortunate! His heart yearned for her as she sat in Samanthy's queer gown, warm and dry, thank God! and with a smile of thankfulness on her lips.

Harry left presently. "See that she is made warm and comfortable," he said to Mrs. Gimly. "*Her parents are wealthy.*" He knew Mrs. Gimly would respect her charge after that. "She's got wet through, you see. Here's five more. Don't say a word. To-morrow I'm going to take her home."

"An' so you're good, too, Mister Chissleton, an' Samanthy says so, too. You paid us reg'lar fer things broke an' not broke, too—you, a friend of Professor Shepard's—an' if I can serve you, me an' Samanthy, waal, guess we'll try. She shan't be made uncomfortable, an' it's fortnit she happened along jest now, fer rent comes due next Monday week, an' the top front room's ben to let all the term. Of course if her parints cum to make inquiries, why

—shall I say you jest seen her a-walkin' 'long Chapel Street like, an' you jest fetched her in, say?"

"Oh, they won't bother." Harry ran out, and over to his room, in a happier yet tremendously excited state of mind. That night he could not sleep. He heard the chapel bell toll out the tragic hours till morning.

After chapel next morning he went straight to Professor Shepard with the whole story, and it wasn't long before he had his permission to absent himself from college for a few days. It happened to be at a time when he could get away over Sunday just as well as not. He telegraphed his mother to meet them in New York and go on to Cleveland with them. He telegraphed Grannis in San Francisco—and he told dear old Jack never a word about it all. He couldn't just then; he felt too deeply. He couldn't endure any chaffing.

"How the—what makes this sofa so damp?" growled the good fellow, who felt a little grumpy after his dance, the next morning.

"Oh—Stamp, probably!" said Harry, packing his valise for a Sunday home, as he said.

"Caswell and I are invited down to the Dolphins' for over Sunday, so we won't miss you, old dig!" said Jack laconically. "Come here, Stamp. I'll lick the hide off you, you dear old rascal!"

And so Harry said good-by and departed.

Mrs. Chestleton cried over poor Ella for an hour as they rolled up the Hudson in the easy drawing-room car, but she soon got over this. She saw that it was her duty, as Harry insisted—it was odd how she had begun to defer to this wise young man—to cheer the girl up; to take her mind off the past, and to prepare her for the trying meeting with her mother and sisters at home. She had not left her brother, Dick Lyman, at home in New York in an especially equable frame of mind. He had, indeed, openly protested.

"Who are these Gerharts?" he asked. "Who is this Ella? A pretty, sad face, no doubt—but has Harry wronged her in any way? Why, if he had ruined her, you two couldn't be doing more for her!" Yet the good fellow saw them off at the station, and acted toward Ella as if she was a princess in the land. Secretly he would not have liked it at all if his sister and nephew had acted toward her in any other way.

"Poor girl! poor girl!" he said to Harry. "Thank God, she was not led astray by any Yale man! But I think, if no one knows, it's right enough to *send* her home alone. I don't believe she will like to have you all standing around when she enters her father's house. But it's like you, sister, and Harry is like you. Egad! She's had a hard time."

Harry never forgot that trip to Cleveland. The Gerharts had, indeed, come up astonishingly in the world, and lived in a handsome house which the old man had purchased at a bargain—house, horses, furniture, and all. They took their good fortune modestly, and they were more pleased to get Ella home again than anything else that had happened to them. There was very little "forgiving" done. Mrs. Gerhart received her with open arms. All the sisters were at home now, and two were engaged. Grannis had become rich in a lesser degree with them, and during all his long summer and autumn quest after Ella, had kept himself at the control of the new company, pushing its interests with true Western grit in every city in which he temporarily sojourned. Grannis was an ideal business man—keen, alert, sagacious, and fond of making money. It was his management which had made the Gerhart electric patents as valuable as they were.

Harry and his mother drove about the most beautiful of Western cities and saw the stately home of Clara Hastings, on Euclid Avenue. The elegant house, with its gardens, its greenhouse, and its beautiful elms occupied an entire square.

"This is the home—a fit one, too, for your princess, Clara," said his mother. "It's an American palace."

Harry was silent. After a little while he said, "I shall never marry. I—I think I would like to go into the army. I don't think I'm fitted for girls—I either bring disaster in some way to them or I—I get left."

With what relief he returned to hard work in college! He had told no one of the secret remorse over poor Ella which had for a year been tormenting him. No wonder the poor lad was disconsolate!

A week or so later he received the following letter from Grannis, dated Cleveland:

MY DEAR CHESTNUTS:

God bless you and your kind mother ! so Old Gerhart and I both say every day. For some time Ella kept her room and would see no one outside of her family. But now she is willing to see me, and they have told her how I have been all through the West in search of her. It was while she was on the ranch in the mountains that I lost all trace of her. She says she wrote many letters home, but that villain never allowed them to go. She says she will never marry, now, and will simply live to take care of her old father. Sometimes she sits all day long silently crying. Her heart is breaking, and so, Harry, is mine. . . However, we hope things will change. The wretch sent her a check for ten thousand dollars, but she returned it at once. Next spring the Gerharts are going to Germany for the summer—partly business, too. There is another thing, you know we are making plenty of money. We both want you in this electric business. When you graduate we'll see you get a soft berth at once. Nevers writes you are getting to be a hard-working dig. That's right. Don't fool away all your time on athletics. Yale College is the place to learn how to work. Met Yale men all over the West. They are always the leading best citizens wherever you go. I delivered a lecture on Yale for a charity in Salt Lake City ! You can bet I always say the best word I can for the old college. Some day I am going back to graduate, but now I'm in my element—business. By the bye, I've placed old Hetherington, at last, in a small town where liquor is prohibited. He is doing very well, too.

Write me all the news, and give my regards to all the boys of Umpty-four. Has Bob Clark forgiven my desertion yet ? Poor Bob ! Harvard ought to have rowed that race over again at Saratoga. To my mind it showed she was a "leetel feared," as they say in Arizona. Regards to Jack and all. So good-by.

Your friend,

OLD GRAN.

P. S. Ella is going to let me take her out driving next Saturday. I'm going to be just friendly—that's all. You ought to see her ; her beauty is so delicate, so refined ! She is as lovely—more lovely than ever !

"Dear old Gran!" sighed Harry, as he folded the letter and put it away. "I think he's the noblest man in the world to still love poor Ella after all that's happened. She's learned a terrible lesson, poor, poor girl! and in fact so have I! But how glad I am Hetherington is going to get started again out West! He was simply going to the dogs here."

"Dear old Gran," he wrote in reply, "How much good you do in the world—and it seems to come so easy to you! You are a *man!* you quietly do what's right—and you don't seem to care what anyone else says. I think that's the diff. between a Western chap and an Eastern. We, here, dread too much what our neighbors will say and think. You first size up what your consciences tell you is right, then you bust right ahead. As for Ella—I felt for her a whole year as if she was my own sister—she's just as pure and good a girl as ever lived! She has been sinned against, and has been innocent through it all."

CHAPTER XXXVIII.

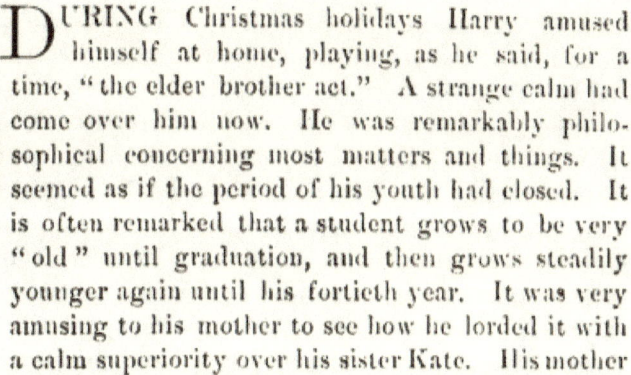

DURING Christmas holidays Harry amused himself at home, playing, as he said, for a time, "the elder brother act." A strange calm had come over him now. He was remarkably philosophical concerning most matters and things. It seemed as if the period of his youth had closed. It is often remarked that a student grows to be very "old" until graduation, and then grows steadily younger again until his fortieth year. It was very amusing to his mother to see how he lorded it with a calm superiority over his sister Kate. His mother felt sorry for him, but she thought, on the whole, his great disappointment and the Ella Gerhart affair had been a good thing for *him*. His trials had resulted in an unfortunate tendency to agnosticism, but on this head her brother comforted her a great deal by telling her that it was a phase which every thoughtful student had to pass through during some time of his college existence.

"Why," said Lyman, "when I was in college we were all howling atheists for a time ; but we soon got over it. Harry will outgrow it. Believe me, he'll see that the Church, after all, meets the needs of humanity more perfectly than any philosophy."

His mother sighed—and waited.

Meanwhile the great Umpty-four Junior Promenade, in February, drew on apace. No such elegant invitations had been gotten out before, no such magnificent preparations made, no such supper ordered from Delmonico's. Jack Rives and Caswell went in to make it the greatest ball New Haven had ever seen.

"Umpty-four is a great society class," they said, " and it's due to our friends to 'hump' ourselves." They went about and raised all the money they could in the class, and then Caswell's father donated five hundred dollars more. They were to have two New York bands, and old Music Hall on Orange Street was to bloom and blossom with flags, flowers, and decorations.

At length the night of the great ball arrived. The weather was clear and mild. The snow had not yet melted away. It was a perfect night. As Harry and Danforth walked over toward Chapel Street from Durfee, the moon threw a tender light on the snow through the elm branches. The long brick row was aglow with gaslight. Across College Street, the Greek Parthenon of a State House* gleamed out white and beautiful in the moonlight. There were closed carriages going and coming. Excitement, delight, jollity, was in the keen air. It was Umpty-four's accepted time of youth and love and merriment.

Never again—never again will a ball seem so glorious as then to these young Americans! All night long, while the moon swung over and dipped into the west and the gray dawn tinted the east, they danced and made love to the most beautiful girls in the world—for they were never to be so quite intoxicatingly lovely again, never so charming again in after-life !

To be sure, they would have their senior ball at Commencement—large, indiscriminate family affairs these, which never were known to contain very many pretty girls except by accident. They were always a sort of alumni gathering, similar to the president's reception at the Art Building—these hot senior "proms" in Alumni Hall.

But the *Junior* Promenade came at a time in winter when nothing else happened in college—when no one was racing, or base-balling, or studying, or—anything ; in the dull February, when it shone like a star by itself and kept hearts beating and life going until the Easter holidays. No wonder Yale men look back, at the distance of twenty years, and sigh over their experiences at the Junior Ball.

* The State House, once the most formidable stucco building on New Haven green, was destroyed in 1881, when Hartford became the capital of Connecticut.

SHE WAS PROUD OF HER TWO CHILDREN THAT NIGHT.

And with the girls! All their real life dated, to some of them, from that third or sixteenth or twenty-third Lander's waltz!

Harry and Dan strolled into the New Haven House and sent up word by the perennial fat-boy clerk, who from time immemorial seemed to haunt those pleasing shades, to Mrs. Chestleton and Kitty, that they and the carriage were waiting. It was now about ten o'clock. In the parlors upstairs they found dozens of becloaked and behooded girls, with chaperons and without, awaiting or chatting with their brothers and escorts, in readiness to leave for the the ball. Everyone was laughing and excited. "Ah, there, Harry!" called out a class-mate, as Harry and Dan bowed. "Oh, is that the famous battery? How *clean* they look!" from a pretty girl in a pink opera-cloak, who glanced at them saucily.

But just then Danforth violently gripped Harry's arm. A vision was coming downstairs, in white, with gorgeous blue ribbons, carrying her opera-cloak on her arm. The vision was followed by a tall lady, in a rich, violet-colored velvet dress. The vision was in high color as to its cheeks, and its pretty shoulders were just visible. Actually it seemed to be a tall confusion of lace and white mull and Jacqueminot roses, which Dan had sent.

"Kitty, how sweet you look!" cried Harry, astonished. He couldn't help it; he suddenly leaned forward and kissed her pouting lips. She was angry enough to have boxed his ears.

"How *can* you be so silly before all these people!" she cried, indicating the swell crowd in the hallway and parlor. Then turning, "How I do wish that Bessie Rives was here—wasn't it mean of the general not to let her come?"

"Isn't she sweet?" laughed and beamed Mrs. Chestleton proudly. Indeed she was proud of her two children that night. Kitty thawed a little. "I don't mean to be cross, Harry, but I— I'm no longer a little girl, you know; besides, you tumble my dress all up."

Danforth was all smiles and bows. She had given him the grand march in and the first dance, and Harry had sent her card around among the nicest men in the class.

Dan would not ride down in the carriage with them. "One of

his nonsensical notions," laughed Harry. "He always *will* put himself out if he can. He's afraid of crumpling you. Dear old Dan! Kitty, I want you to be just as kind to him as you can be to-night, for my sake. I would never have pitched a game if *he* hadn't persuaded Harding——"

Kitty made a face.

"He looks so ungainly in his dress-suit."

"Ungainly? Everyone thinks he's graceful," and Harry pulled on his white gloves.

Dan was there to meet them, at Music Hall, and there, too, was the gorgeous Jack, full of importance, with a long white satin badge in his lapel. Kitty, blushing furiously, gave her hand to Jack and was helped out by his strong, gloved hand.

"Kate! My stars, how we girls grow!" he laughed, and if he had kissed her she would have thanked him, he was so handsome —such a *preux chevalier.*

"Is this your sister?" he pretended, as he helped her mother out.

"Ah, Jack!" laughed Mrs. Chestleton. "Do you expect me, too, to fall in love with you?"

"I only expect—reciprocity!" he laughed.

All this, and poor Danforth stood awkwardly at one side looking on. They waited for them at the dressing-room again, and crowds surged past them. The ball was about to begin. Suddenly Harry was made aware of a presence near him. He did not turn.

"Will you allow me to pass, please?" It was the same old low, sweet voice. He bowed; Clara nodded lightly, gave him a swift glance, and passed him with her maid, followed by Miss Mulford, in lavender. Kate came out and said that, "Jack was to lead off the march with Miss Hastings; and, do you know, they say her engagement is broken, Harry—so there is hope yet!"

Harry started. "What's that to me?" he asked gruffly.

"Oh, nothing. I thought you might want to know; that's all."

The large opera-house was a mass of flowers, its ugliness and tawdriness well concealed even to the great chandelier which hung from the ceiling. There were shells and boats, flags and gas-jets of " Umpty-four " and " Yale," and long festoons of evergreen.

" Oh, there's Mr. Nevers! Do bring him up; I want to congratulate him on taking the *Lit.* medal," said Mrs. Chestleton.

Nevers shook hands with her warmly. " I've just heard all about Ella Gerhart," he said. " Grannis has written me. Of course Harry would never tell a soul anything. I think your going 'way out to Cleveland with that girl, Mrs. Chestleton, was the noblest thing I ever heard of. It was just as—as—fine as——"

" Silk ! " suggested Harry.

" Well, it was ! I wish I had a mother like you. My mother died years ago, soon after I was born. I'm so sorry for Harry to-night," he whispered. " Miss Hastings is, of course, looking her best. He has just heard she has broken her engagement."

" Has she ? " asked Mrs. Chestleton.

" A flirt, that's all she is," said Nevers, with a gesture of anger.

" Depend upon it, she will get him to dance with her."

" Oh, Harry is greatly changed. He doesn't care for girls now. I think he's entirely gotten over *that* affair now," said Danforth.

Mrs. Chestleton shook her head. Then, as Harry urged, they went down on the floor for the march. The music began. In walked Jack with Clara looking as stately and superb as a queen. The committee and their " girls " filed in after them—a splendid file of them !

" It's as bad as Yale and Harvard drawing side by side positions at Saratoga ! " laughed Nevers.

" Is there not sure to be a *contretemps*, Harry ? " asked Mrs. Chestleton lightly.

" Mother, dear, isn't she the most beautiful girl in the whole world ? " Harry's eyes were fixed upon Clara.

Around her white throat Clara wore one string of pearls. She wore a gown her father had sent over from Worth ; she was easily the loveliest girl at the Prom.

It was odd to see what a belle Mrs. Chestleton, too, became that evening. It was not solely because of Harry's great and deserved popularity, but because she was in herself pretty, graceful, and full of *esprit*. What her children liked she liked. She danced half a dozen square dances, and entered into the affair with the greatest zest. " Why should we old ladies retire ? " she demanded laughingly, and no one could answer her to the contrary. And there, too, was Uncle Dick himself coming up and pretending he was a junior too, with a B K E pin, his old trick, and asking to be presented to Kitty. He had run up at the last moment that evening from New York. Later they saw him devoting himself with all his old-time gallantry to Miss Walker, who was radiant in blue satin and old lace.

" Ah, let me see," they overheard him ask her, " This is your——"

" Twentieth Junior Prom. Yes, and I hope I may live to see my fortieth," she laughed facetiously.

" Bah ! Miss Walker, I used to see you trundling a hoop, in front of South, when I was in college—you were a child then—and that's not so many years ago."

She gave him a grateful glance.

" It's a terrible misfortune for a girl to live in a college town," she sighed. " Students come and students go, but *you* go on forever. Do you know this continuous pouring through of students wears out the brain after a time ? My father says it's like the precession of the equinoxes, only a great deal worse. There is no change, no cessation."

Presently a set formed for a quadrille—Harry and a Miss Dolphin, Jack and Annie Mead, Lyman and Miss Walker, and just then—to fill up—Caswell and Clara Hastings happened along arm in arm.

" Hurry up—here's your place—just waiting ! " called out Jack.

Before he knew it Harry found himself opposite the most beautiful girl of the evening, for Clara's appearance that night was simply overpowering. Miss Walker confided to Miss Dolphin—to whom Harry presented her—that " it was a real Worth creation," and purchased for the occasion.

There was something patrician in the elegance of her carriage. In a year of society she had acquired a manner. She was in command of herself—calm, beautiful, superb. At her corsage, in the fashion of the day, she wore a huge bunch of La France roses. Caswell had been trying to get her to sit out the dance with him, and was much provoked that she allowed Jack to inveigle them into a "stupid" quadrille. The chairman's command had to be obeyed, as it seemed. Caswell, pale and with a slightly dissipated, cigarette-smoker's complexion, concealed his vexation as best he could. It was awkward all around. Miss Mead of Stratford, one of Jack's rustication "adorables,"—and he still kept up an infrequent correspondence,—and Jack and Miss Louise Dolphin had only recently agreed to disagree. As for Harry and Clara—Caswell smirked and smiled under his long handsome mustache and wondered what Jack, who so generally kept himself wide-awake, *could* be thinking of.

The fact was that Clara herself asked the good fellow to bring it about. She bore no ill-will, and her conscience did not smite her for anything *she* had done. Indeed, what had she done? It was no fault of hers if half Yale College fell in love with her beautiful face!

The lively music began—an amusing quadrille written out by a musical genius in the class for the occasion. Every now and then there was a refrain shouted by the orchestra. It was a rollicking, jolly quadrille, full of life and motion. Everybody in New Haven was whistling it the next day. At the close the cry was *Facultee —facultee!* and everyone was called on to *Disperse! disperse!*

During the dance Clara, in passing Harry, whispered, "Why are you so cruelly unkind to me?"

He smiled bitterly, and the next time they cross over, said, "Because you are always unkindly cruel to me."

"I thought we were friends at least," she said.

"So we are," he replied, "I hope. Friends—at last!"

Then after "visiting" the opposite couples they came together again.

"Friends!" she smiled, so enchantingly that he felt his soul drawn from his very eyes into hers.

The next "crossing" she slipped her dance-card into his gloved

hand. "Do you see all those places reserved?" she whispered—
"For you!"

He glanced at the card. There were some three or four dances
left blank. In these he thoughtlessly scribbled his name. His
head was in a whirl. Were these blanks really intended for him—
or for Saxton? Was the old flame to be relit? Why did his
heart leap so at the touch of her hand? At the end of the quadrille he took Annie Mead to her seat, and left her rather abruptly.
He wanted to be alone. Clara's glance, and her word "Friends!"
had penetrated his very soul.

Could it be possible? He had thought all the year that he
would never speak with her again if he could help it. Now he was
wild for her dance with him to come.

"Clara is certainly very lovely," said his mother when he
rejoined her. "She has a good deal of manner for such a young
girl; she hasn't the rare sweetness of that wild rose, Annie Mead
of Stratford. I wonder you don't lose your heart to *her!*"

"Miss Mead is—I don't know—without any fire. I don't think
I like 'goodness' in girls. I'm afraid I like them full of high
crimes and misdemeanors!"

"Harry, what *sentiments!*" exclaimed his mother, aghast.

And he rushed off again to meet his engagement to waltz with
Miss Hargreaves, who was up from New York with the Columbia
"crowd."

"So Clara Hastings has broken her engagement," she said, her
head above his shoulder in the dance. "I knew it would be so.
She's a flirt. She always will be a flirt. One of those serious
flirts who always seem to have so much back of them, but are really
as silly as the rest of us."

"You are severe," Harry said. "It's the way with girls!"

"I'm not severe. Clara loves admiration, and Mr. Saxton got
tired of giving so much of it. He said she must choose between
him and all Yale College. She replied that if it came to a choice
between an undergrad and an alumnus, she preferred the student,
as at least *he* had some possibilities. They say that Will Saxton,
who was here at the german, and expected to be here for the ball,

packed his bag and left for New York. Clara is so high-spirited, you know, she boldly announced to everyone forthwith that the engagement was broken. She must have *hated* to send back that lovely diamond ring, though."

There was a distinct tone of spite in what Miss Hargreaves said. How he hated a spiteful woman!

At last the waltz was over, and he hastened across the wide ball-room floor to where Clara was standing surrounded by a number of seniors. The great swells, Bellamy Storrs and Holland, were vying in "airy persiflage and repartee" over her dance-card and begging for half dances. The great Bob Clark had just been favored. Guthrie, one of the big men of the senior year, physically and mentally, stood near her, playing with his *Lit.* triangle, and occasionally begging her to remember him in the "crush." She was in her element with these jolly, amusing young fellows—the *jeunesse dorée* of their time at college. Her eyes sparkled—she triumphed—she felt the joy, too, of drawing the lorgnettes in the gallery down on her.

" Ah, here comes Umpty-four," she laughed, as Harry approached. " And Umpty-four——"

" Takes the cake !" laughed Clark.

"Oh, it's the juniors' privilege, I suppose," said Storrs. "We seniors are getting to be too old. Youth and hope must win to-night. Take her, Mr. Chestleton. She's yours—because I see you've got your name down for this dance."

They danced the Redowa—then stopped—then walked slowly—then they sought an obscure corner beneath the gallery, where they sat earnestly conversing.

Holland : " Gad ! a man might go farther and fare worse. Lots of style, Bellamy ; she's to be at Newport this summer. De Koven says she'll be a belle. I think I'll look her up."

Storrs : " By all odds the prettiest woman here." It was the thing to use " woman " for " girl " in the swell set. " She's in great shape to-night ; but there's a Miss Hargreaves, of New York, here I like quite as well."

Holland : " Not in it !"

Storrs : " Who's that woman Caswell of your class has got on his arm ? "

Holland : " That's a Miss Mead."

Storrs : " I rather like her cut—simplicity is a capital thing in a woman. She has a charming color, too. I wonder if that young rascal isn't making love to her ! "

Holland : "Cassy, they say, is confining himself to actresses nowadays. Did you hear? He followed the Lydia Thompson troupe to Boston, and acted for a week there as one of the tin soldiers."

Storrs : " He's a great chap ! " (Mental note : He's not the right sort, quite, for senior year. He's too wild, too bohemian.)

Result : In the ensuing elections Caswell does not go, as he expected, to a certain senior society.

So the ball waxed and waned. The supper was grand, the champagne *frappé* to a nicety. Everything was just perfect. The chaperons felt better after supper, and the music seemed livelier and jollier. Kitty danced every dance, and would have gone on dancing to " Home, Sweet Home," at the end, as several jolly girls did. But at last the Junior Prom was over. Harry saw Clara Hastings into her carriage beside that grim old maid, her Aunt Mulford, as the sun was beginning to illumine the heavens for another day. What had happened between them? He could hardly tell. He let himself into his room in Durfee, and threw himself heavily, without undressing, on his bed. He couldn't sleep. His head was in a whirl.

What had happened? Simply this : in a dark passage-way, where no one saw them, she had thrown herself in his arms- the glorious young beauty that she was—and kissed him passionately, and breathed the hot words in his ear, which rang there forever, " *Now*, do you think that I care for him ? Will Saxton is nothing to me, Harry—I did not know my own heart. I love you—I have always loved you. Why do you make me go down on my knees to you ? "

He kissed her—blushing scarlet. " My—darling !—darling ! he whispered ; " is it true ? Do you really love me ? "

Those moments of first, sweet love—when *your* girl yields at last! They are God-given, holy, pure, ecstatic moments, and they should be held as sacred and as secret as the confessional of the Church. Neither could speak; they knew they must separate and

HARRY SAW CLARA HASTINGS INTO HER CARRIAGE.

go back to the ballroom. They were too full of emotion. Beside, this was not a place to linger. Already a man was looking for Clara for a waltz. Harry must hunt up Miss Walker. Yet they stood there, her cheek against his, *so happy!* while the moments fled, and the crashing music—yes, it was "Morgen blätter," which Jack was always whistling when he wanted particularly to study. *She was his!* and over them the large picture of St. Elihu—the same that gazes on us still from the cover of the *Lit.*—seemed to beam with joy and congratulations as they re-entered the great ballroom arm in arm—"the handsomest pair," as Mrs. Professor Shepard observed to Miss Mulford, "on the entire floor!"

Alas! how soon this perfect bliss of first love was to change for the distressing period—"Have we not both made a mistake?" which so often intervenes and spoils all in college love affairs. Perhaps it all began by Clara's insisting that night that their engagement, if such it was, should be held a "*mortal secret.*"

Days and weeks passed, and the secret engagement waned. A quarrel estranged them. Both were high-spirited—easily angered. College engagements are flimsy affairs. Clara's mother urged her to reserve herself for "higher things"—"perhaps," she urged, "a titled Englishman, as your sister in London has captured." Many influences were secretly brought to bear on Clara. The engagement was brought to an end for the time being.

Yet both surely knew that some day it would be renewed, and that the fires of love were only smoldering in their breasts.

Harry went out a little more than he had done, and Jack persuaded him without much trouble to take in Miss Walker's dance, the latter end of the term.

CHAPTER XXXIX.

MISS WALKER GIVES A DANCE.

T turned out that Miss Walker's dance was an exclusive one—only the particular "college set" being invited. In this set were chiefly the highly educated daughters of professors, who mostly preferred to sit out the round dances, and a sprinkling of New Haven girls who for some reason were invited because of their cleverness and similarity to the professors' daughters in wearing spectacles.

Professor Walker's house was a large roomy structure on Grove Street; the first floor was thrown open, and a skilled musician was thumping the grand piano as they entered. It was supposed to be a jovial galop, but no one was dancing although the rooms were full. They were obliged on entering to pass their overcoats through the hall and upstairs to the gentlemen's dressing room, and then to descend again, as if it was really their first appearance.

Several young ladies whom they knew cut them dead as they passed through upstairs, who, to their surprise, on their again descending, received them with radiant smiles.

There were many charming girls in spectacles—none *decolletée* of course, and none wearing very startling gowns. Jack, who was getting to be quite a "society" man, went up and spoke to many of his acquaintances. Everyone seemed to know the handsome fellow.

Miss Walker came out on the arm of a tall senior also in spectacles, flew at Jack, seized upon him, and dragged him away to be presented to "a most charming, lovely creature—her dearest friend"—a dumpy, fat, jolly old spinster, Miss Crimsy.

Poor Jack bowed and said he was "so very happy." Miss Crimsy was supposed to be very bright and clever. She had

374

written a book of poems. She would doubtless have a career—but all this went for naught with the handsome devil-may-care young junior. Her wit was lost on him. "You have the air of wanting to escape," she laughed. "Fly then! I don't find under-class men particularly amusing, if caged; they are like flowers——"

"You cut them, I suppose, generally? Please don't cut me."

"Oh, I prefer them wild." She gave him a meaning glance.

"That *is* my reputation—undeserved," he laughed.

"Yes; wild and *unstudied?*"

"I shan't try for the valedictory, yet I study hard enough too—and as I am always in training I'm not *very* wild. I see I shan't suit you, Miss Crimsy—not the kind of flower—so good-evening!"

"No, for I'm a great wall-flower myself," she laughed. At least she was good-natured. "But I've heard Miss Walker speak of you so often. She likes you. When they rusticated you, Mr. Rives—you haven't any idea how she *insisted* that you had a good true heart."

"She ought to know—she's had it long enough for examination!" he laughed.

Miss Crimsy laughed, too, loudly. "She has dissected it then—and she finds you true blue! It must be a satisfaction to you. It's like going to an insurance company and finding nothing's the matter with you and you're a good risk. If Sarah Walker takes up a student—there *must* be something to him."

His eyes wandered off to the three homely, scrawny daughters of Professor Winkelmann, a German instructor, as he answered, "I don't flatter myself that, like Elijah, I've been taken up. I admire Miss Walker exceedingly. I feel that she's been like a good elder—ahem—a sister to me. To know her, as one may say, is not only a liberal education but a post-graduate course. Last week we had a moonlight sail of ten of us which she organized—she entertained us by reciting four cantos of 'Childe Harold.' Miss Crimsy," his fine eyes were twinkling in merriment, "I'm *sure* she's *full* of poetry!"

Again Miss Crimsy laughed very loudly, and protested that he was a very wicked person to talk so about her dearest, oldest friend!

His eyes wandered again. This time he saw Miss Sanger, in eyeglasses, a pretty girl with high domelike forehead, who preferred to talk of the modern scientific leaning of religion, but who danced very well. He bowed to Miss Crimsy and asked Miss Sanger to dance. "I've had a horrible day," she exclaimed over his shoulder as they whirled about. "I've been reading Amiel's 'Journal'—it's undermined me."

"The *what* newspaper?"

"Amiel's 'Journal.'"

"Oh! I didn't know Amiel had let anyone read it, let alone publishing it."

"You are flippant, Mr. Rives, as usual," said Miss Sanger, and they stopped dancing after a moment and sat on a sofa and watched the dancing.

Harry had possessed himself of a girl who towered high above him like a graceful elm. She was pretty, however, and had the quaintest, queerest little old-fashioned ringlets. She was the youngest daughter of ex-President Waring, who had a family of ten girls, who, like him, overtopped their compeers round. Harry liked her because she knew all about baseball!

"Tell me, Mr. Chestleton, doesn't it frighten you to death to know that all depends on the way you throw in the ball?"

"No. I get used to it," said Harry drearily.

"Suppose you should miss the catcher altogether?"

"That would be a wild pitch, an error."

"Wouldn't it be dreadful!"

"It sometimes happens, of course."

"And oh! suppose you forgot when you struck the ball, and ran as hard as you could to third base?"

"That would be out at first, and you wouldn't do it," he laughed, "unless you went crazy."

"But in the *excitement?* I was reading in the 'Life of Hume' the other day—no, it was in the 'Life of Kant'—that one day his house got on fire and he threw open a window and carefully let down the tongs with a rope. And in baseball I should think that the strongest mental endowment would at times be inadequate?"

"Oh, we sometimes get rattled, but we soon pull ourselves together," he laughed.

"And why can't you run to first base when you make a foul?"

"Because it's against the rules."

"Is it considered unfair to foul?"

"No, but——"

"I think it *ought* to count, don't you? It's a hit."

"No." He couldn't explain it to her exactly. He felt hopeless.

"I'm so interested, although father says it's not the best thing for girls to be going to ball games. I want to see the next game with Harvard. I feel *certain* we are going to win if you pitch."

She took off her eyeglasses and wiped them gently, and a junior came up, and asked her to dance. Harry stood alone for a few moments, hoping the next girl wouldn't talk baseball to him—a subject, somehow, with girls, he felt he knew nothing about. He amused himself for a little while looking vaguely around and observing certain grave and reverend seniors, ablaze with golden senior society badges, cavorting about in as lively and youthful a manner as if they had been merely juniors themselves. There was Brown, chairman of the *Lit.* board; what awful secrets were concealed in *his* brainy looking head! *He* knew well enough the Umpty-four juniors who were going to Spade and Grave—and in a few weeks more the whole college would know it. There was Tom Bixby, who condescended to nod to him now. There was Paton, laughing and chatting with Miss Winkelmann like an uncouth freshman. Yet he certainly seemed older, and more *awful* to him than did Professor Walker himself, who came in and stood by his good wife and interesting daughter for a little while. Professor Walker came in, looking upon the innocent amusement of the young people with a wise shake of his Ptolemy-like head. Harry was struck then, more than ever, as he saw the professor in a formal dress suit, by his resemblance to an Egyptian sculpture—his hair carried up over his forehead and down behind his ears in true old Nilean style. He went over and talked with him.

His hand was icy cold as he shook his feebly. He seemed to be looking on at the dancing and the entire *ensemble* as if it were a hopeless, foolish performance. Around the wide hallway and in the large drawing room were many stiff portraits of his ancestors— an old well to do New Haven mercantile race. Fine old Puritans they were, with their solemn heavy faces, thin nostrils, deep, sad, puritanic eyes and starched ruffs.

Mrs. Walker was a short, brisk, chubby woman with pretty gray hair. If her husband looked bored, she was on the contrary all liveliness.

The professor said, as if coming out of a reverie, "About these curves now, in which you succeed in turning and twisting a baseball; has anyone succeeded in calculating a formula for them—the relation of the resistance of the air, and the spinning quality which you give with the hand?"

"No, sir," said Harry, desiring to make himself agreeable. "It would be a good thing if someone would."

"A simple question in physics. Let us see if we cannot calculate it now in our heads. Consider the force you drive the ball as 1. We will then call the resistance of the air n."

But Harry was hardly in the mood, with the piano thumping in his ears, and in the confusion of the "dancers dancing in tune," to pay any close attention.

"Do you follow me?" asked the professor. "One nth of x will equal the cosine of a circle whose diameter——"

"Certainly, yes," said Harry, losing the rest of what the professor was saying in the rush past him of two couples in the waltz.

"And applying the rule of physics, bodies move inversely as the square of their distance——"

"Yes, sir," said Harry, wishing he was well out of it.

"We equally must remember *one-nth* of x into the square root of the——"

"Mr. Chestleton, you're not dancing! come with me at once!" cried Mrs. Walker as he gave her his arm, and she rescued him. The professor didn't seem to notice his departure, but when he went off was evidently still calculating his problem in great shape, as he

wore a smile on his lips. His hostess presented him to a nice
looking girl, a Miss Brown, who, rather singularly, was without
spectacles. Harry danced with her until she began to turn pale,
gasp, and breathe with some difficulty as if quite pumped, and he
took her to a seat.

"I've been working very hard lately," she said, "and I'm tired
out. I'm attending the Art School this year, and we are all painting
away for dear life for the prize to be awarded in June. But it's
the funniest thing, you know, the only paintings we have to speak
of in the Art Building are the Trumbull gallery and the Jarves
collection. Therefore all our 'styles' are founded on Trumbull or
on Cimabue. I prefer Cimabue, and my figure of 'A Woman Washing,' is the scrawniest, sourest looking dyspeptic you ever saw.
Have you seen the Jarves collection? Have you seen Giotto's
'Head?' Oh, it is wonderful! But it's making most of us Pre-
Raphaelites. I wish they *did* have some more modern paintings.
A woman always imitates in art, and it's a pity we have to be so
Trumbully florid, or so ascetically Jarvesian ; is it not so?"

"It's a shame!" he laughed. The girl was going to be good
fun, he thought. She reminded him of Daisy Stevenson. "You
ought to be allowed to visit some of the saloons in New York."

"*Salons*, I suppose?" She gave him a quick glance.

"No, saloons ; art galleries—the depositaries of modern art in
the Metrolopus!" and they both laughed.

"Can you keep a secret?" she asked.

"What is the secret?"

"The article on 'Mediævalism in Modern Art' in the April *Lit.*
is by me, and it's a joke. It's signed 'S.' Read it, and see if it
isn't stupid, solemn, deep, and incomprehensible like every other
Lit. article you ever read."

Harry laughed. "I think the *Lit.* is very fine," he said ; "a
friend of mine, Nevers, writes for it."

"Don't tell *him* or anyone. My brother would murder me!
But you see the *Courant* and *Record* will speak of my article in
highest praise. They won't understand it, nor will anyone else.
Women at least know how to imitate, and I've imitated the regular

standard *Lit.* article in fine shape. It's all a burlesque, though—a joke on my brother and all the *Lit.* board. I did it for fun, but it's an awful secret. I don't know why I tell you, Mr. Chestleton, except I will say, you have the most sincere, truthful looking eyes I ever saw."

"Do you ever use what is commonly known as a mirror?" he asked. She took her seat in an antique chair and he stood leaning over her. "By Jove! this Art School girl is great fun!" he thought.

"No—have I a black india ink smudge on my nose?" she asked innocently. "I generally *do* have. But you will keep my secret?"

"Inviolate——"

"*Sub rosa* will do!" She looked up, punning. She was fair, and her light hair was distinctly charming, this Miss Brown!

"It's a good joke—but it will leak out, won't it? and when it does! Oh, Miss Brown, you will then need a champion—then my strong right arm will be needed——"

"Yes, but your strong right arm is needed to pitch, and to beat Harvard."

"But if Chi Delta Theta* dares to haze you for what you have done!"

"Oh, *would* they?" She looked up at him fearfully.

"No telling. It's a secret organization armed with terrible powers."

"Oh, you frighten me to death! And my nerves are all shattered anyway, working for that horrid prize in the Art School."

"Well, supper is announced. Take my arm and we'll eat a salad or ice, or something; and perhaps your nerves will recover. But to tell the truth I wouldn't be in your b—boots—slippers, for ducats. Chi Delta Theta—three Greek letters meaning '*Death to Traitors*'— has a terribly bad reputation around college."

"But my brother—he would die, if necessary, for me?"

"Not if he's like most brothers."

"I don't care. My brother is so proud of being on the *Lit.* board

* The society which edits and publishes the Yale Literary Magazine.

that I wanted to take him down; and I'm glad I did it; I don't care what happens. They can eat me up if they like, with their Chi Delta Theta—and the article will show the powers that be that art students ought to be fed on stronger art food than Jarves collections * or Jonathan Trumbull !"

They went out to supper, and she asked if he was fond of riding, and that if so, she might possibly give him an invitation for the day following.

Harry dove into the crowd for a plate of ice cream, and when he came back, in the course of time received his invitation in due form. His extravagant praises of riding as a form of exercise did not mislead the clever girl. She frankly told him she saw through him, and she felt highly flattered that he should want to go on her riding party. "However, we shall want another girl," she mused. "Miss Mulford's niece is in town over Sunday. Do you know her—Miss Hastings? she's a stunning beauty. I'll ask her."

"Yes, I know her," said Harry, reddening. "I've known her a long time."

"A victim?" asked the girl, amused. "You look so *very* demure !"

"I've known her two years."

"Oh, this is delightful ! I want to show her some attention because her aunt has been so kind to me ever since I've been in New Haven. I've been up there with my brother a great deal in the old house on Hillhouse Avenue; but that's the *only* place I have been to. I have not gone out at all. I have taken Lord Eldon's advice to those studying law—fed like an insect and worked like an ox; and now my doctor says I must 'let up' a little, so I've taken to riding. My aunt Miss Donald has asked me to bring out my friends once a week and take tea or lunch, and to-morrow it shall be only Umpty-four and *one* other. Miss Walker says it's the

---

*Since the time of this story a very fine collection of modern paintings has been added to the art collections at Yale, and the value of the Jarves collection, contrary to Miss Brown, the flippant art student, has only grown the more apparent.

nicest class in—I don't know how many years! And oh, pray! keep my secret, won't you, about the *Lit.?*"

" Yes ! I swear it ! "

" Then *au revoir* till to-morrow. Mr. Rives will explain where and when."

She gave him a sweet smile and left the room. Instantly, when she left, the whole affair became a deadly bore to him again. There was Jack dancing away, and Nevers sitting on the stairs with a girl in spectacles, and he wanted to go home. After a few minutes the music stopped, and Jack *had* to stop. He went up to him with a gloomy look.

" I'm going," he said. " Meet me at Mory's; I want a rarebit and something cheering."

" No, Harry," said Jack. " Wait a second and I'll get Nevers, and we'll go along with you."

Then the music struck up again, and there was the faithless Jack prancing around the room again with another girl. Harry went and collared little Nevers and dragged him away with him. An hour later, as they sat chinning in the Quiet House, over their third mug of Burton, Jack, singing a jolly air, turned up. It was one o'clock then, in the morning. So ended the dance in the " college set."

" It was hardly a *joyous* affair, was it ! " laughed Jack. " Perhaps I had better say spectacle ! "

CHAPTER XL

MISS FANNY BROWN'S horse was awaiting her, as was Miss Walker's, in charge of a groom. The art student looked a little pale and weary, and as if a little country air and brisk riding would do her good. When the "men" came up to the stoop of the house where they were sitting, she became pert and chipper enough. Harry thought she was very "interesting." She was not pretty, but she had a great deal of expression and feeling, and a sense of humor, rare enough in girls, he found. While they were waiting, her brother, Brown, of Umpty-three, came up, holding one of the new *Lits.*, just out, in his hand. He was introduced, and bowed with a lofty condescending air to the juniors.

"Oh, the *Lit.!* *Do* let me see it !" cried Miss Brown, making a grab for it out of her brother's hand. He handed it to her gravely. Before the juniors he was on his good behavior.

"Oh, how interesting ! 'Mediaevalism in Modern Art !' I must read *that*, and get some ideas," she cried, with a side glance at Harry. "Who wrote it, Will ?"

Brown of Umpty-three shook his head solemnly. "We must not reveal the grim secrets of Chi Delta Theta !" he laughed pleasantly.

"It's very profound—starts off with Adam—as all good college essays do. Hum—hum—tell me, Will, did a mere student really write this ? "

"We consider it one of the greatest essays the *Lit.* ever published. By the way, I don't mind saying that the author's name is unknown, but we think we know pretty well it is David Alum of Umpty-four, a very high stand man."

"Yes, he lives with his aunt, who is going through college to herself in private," said Jack. "A queer couple as I ever saw."

"She's a rustler herself, a towering intellect, yet a good fellow," said Nevers.

"My father says she is a wonderful mathematician," said Miss Walker, rising.

Someone was galloping up the street, followed by a groom. Harry went with her out to the gate, and all followed.

"Doesn't she look stunning!" exclaimed Fanny Brown, as Miss Hastings, on a handsome chestnut, brought her lively steed to a standstill, bowing right and left to her friends. Harry hurried out and grasped her gloved hand.

"I was afraid some accident had happened, and you weren't coming!" he said, as their glances met.

"Indeed I wouldn't miss going to a tea at Sedgewood Farm for a good deal!" she replied.

It was proposed to ride out Hillhouse Avenue, then by way of Whitneyville around in a *détour* to Sedgewood Farm at five o'clock. Brown helped his sister to mount, and Jack mounted Miss Walker. Their horses were fresh and all pretty good. The day was cloudless, and not too warm. They turned into the beautiful concrete of Hillhouse Avenue at a brisk trot.

Though not great in extent, what more beautiful avenue of pleasant American homes exists than this famous little street? The slope up to the stately old Hillhouse mansion on the hill, the double row of magnificent elms, the aristocratic exclusiveness of the gateway at the entrance, the perfectly kept lawns, everything tended to remind them of some old cathedral town in England.

"I always feel as if I was in the presence of royalty in Hillhouse Avenue," remarked Fanny Brown, in a hushed voice. "Everything—including the elms—is so high and mighty."

"This is your aunt's house, it looks like a Grecian temple," she said to Clara Hastings, who was riding at her side. The house was a stately, solemn mansion with high white pillars in front of it. Miss Mulford was at a window and Clara bowed affectionately to her as they passed.

"My aunt has five cats," said Clara. "Do you like cats, Mr. Chestleton? Come up to-morrow and play with the cats!"

He felt, that, with the lovely girl at his side, he never could resume relations *exactly* where he left off. To-day she was rather distant and cool to him. He became silent and depressed in the thought that, after all, she did not care for him, and would never really love him, in spite of all her kisses and all she had said.

All that glorious afternoon, as they rode—and Fanny Brown set them a hot pace—Clara seemed to keep at a distance from him. She kept Nevers by her constantly. "Was she jealous?" he asked himself. "What curious creatures these girls are!"

At an old-fashioned little inn at Whitneyville, Jack prescribed milk punches, which the girls drank without dismounting. Already a healthy glow was making itself seen on Miss Brown's face. She was of a stylish figure, jolly, a "companionable" girl; and Harry found himself drinking his punch at her stirrup, instead of Clara's.

"I am in fear and trembling over that *Lit.* article," she said. "If you ever tell!"

"I shall be silent as the grave. I haven't been in secret Delta Kap, and in mysterious Delta Beta Xi for nothing. I know how to keep a secret!"

"Well, secret societies have *one* good effect then."

"I've heard my uncle say—he was a Yale man—that they were the one institution left to man that woman could *not* pry into."

"Woman *pry* into those silly little college societies? as if any one of us cared to know *what* goes on in those places!"

She gave a quick toss of her head.

"Ah, yes, you shall never, *never* know—*never!*" he said teasingly.

"There is *one* thing I see—you are trying to be provoking."

"I? how so?"

Clara Hastings overheard the remark.

"How is he trying to be provoking?" she asked, coming near them, glass in hand. He thought she never looked so beautiful.

Miss Brown gave her a glance as much as to say, "This is my *own* little funeral, don't *you* interfere!"

"I was saying, that you poor girls could never, never know what goes on in our secret societies."

"We know that if everything was as it should be, you students would not be ashamed to let everyone know what you did inside of them."

This was a staggerer; Harry could not retort as he would have done to the same remark coming from Miss Brown. He meekly swallowed the last of his milk punch in silence.

"It's the pin, the chief joy of secret societies, I believe," said Fanny astutely. "How they love to disport themselves covered over as to their waistcoats with badges of all the letters of the Greek alphabet!"

"And what do you say of the senior societies?" asked Harry.

Miss Brown said nothing; even she was aware of the atmosphere of mystery and respect which in New Haven surrounds the societies of senior year. Yet after they had ridden on a mile or two she turned to Harry, and ventured, "There is a Latin motto which applies to senior year—*ignotum pro magnifico.*"

"Hush!" cried Nevers. "Let us not speak of senior year—'lest the very air carry tidings' and our 'chances' are hurt."

And so, laughing and joking, they came along a winding gravelly ascent, 'tween hedgerows fresh scented, and covered with climbing vines and flowers, to Sedgewood.

They passed between two high posts covered with ivy; on the top of one was a motto:

"*Leave all care behind, ye who enter here.*"

Their genial host came out and greeted them. And they dismounted, and sat about on the wide veranda listening to his genial reminiscences of his days at Yale long before the war. A number of agreeable people drove out from New Haven, and tea was served on the smooth lawn before the pleasant country house. The talk fell upon the deplorable lack of a "literary atmosphere" at Yale, and Mr. Donald seemed to be of the opinion that in time this would all change for the better. "Look at our famous Yale authors and poets," he said. "What a list they are from Morris and Willis to Stedman! It's a pity the college does nothing to honor them—but what can they do?"

"Harvard made Longfellow and Lowell its professors," said Nevers.

"Well, give Yale money and time to develop out of its provincialism and puritanism. It's growing fast. The time will surely come when an author of celebrity will be as highly honored as a back country minister or a politician!"

"Why was it she captured Nevers and hung on to him, and would hardly say a word to me?" asked Harry that night, as he sat smoking—Harding allowed one cigar a day for his nine that year. "Jack, I don't believe she cares the snap of her fingers for me. In spite of all her professions, at Sedgewood she would hardly let me pass her a bit of cake."

"Yes, and you devoted yourself to Fanny Brown; laughing and talking all the whole time, made a dead set at her. No wonder Clara 'kicked'!"

"And how about you and the Walker?"

"Old friends, that's all." Jack looked around furtively. "In the garden, walking among those rose vines in the dusk—I asked her to marry me—I did—by Jove!"

"Good Lord!" Harry was thunder-struck.

"And she let me kiss her—dear old thing—and she cried, and she told me how many men had asked her, and how she had hesitated and questioned her own mind so much and often, and talked with her father, who is such a 'nice' discriminator—that she never could quite make up her mind. 'Now, when I am old,' she said, 'I see my mistake: I should have followed my heart, not my head. It's too late now for me to marry.'"

"I suppose she went to her father the professor, and he sized up all the different students one after another according to stand since—who was it? Dingley, now U. S. Senator, of '63?—and pointed out some unfitness. But you'd be safe enough, Jack; he'd easily point out *your* unfitness! You're only just above average!"

"Sarah! I love you, dear old thing! I'd leave college and marry you! She's got splendid principles. She confessed her age to me—thirty-one—*and she refused me!*"

Harry breathed a sigh of relief. "You're a good fellow, Jack," he said. "But don't do it again."

"No, my sense of honor is satisfied; I mean to be simply good friends. That's all. There is going to be a german at Governor Talman's next week, and I m going to be her partner."

"Yes, and I Fanny Brown's."

Jack whistled. "Well, I should think Clara *would* object," he laughed.

Harry didn't say anything for a few moments; then he observed casually, "I thought you considered yourself engaged to that Dolphin girl in Stratford?"

"Hang it, I'm engaged to three besides that," said Jack. "I do it because I like to do what the girls like. Girls like sincere, honest fellows who come up to the scratch and ask them to marry. That's what the girls want—to marry!"

"Sincere and honest rascals!"

"I'm engaged in New York, one; in Charmington, one; in Mitford, one; and it would have been in New Haven one, too, if Miss Walker had not been so sensible. I tell them all that I can't write but once in two weeks, as the faculty forbid it. I am under the *banns,* you see!"

"You'll get your name in the newspapers as breaking the record in hearts," laughed Harry, as they blew out the lamp and got into their separate, narrow little beds.

Harry lay awake a long time; many things worried him. The ball nine seemed to be falling off. Amherst nearly beat them (to be sure he was not in the box). Dan's fingers were sprained, Harding's knee troubled him. But aside from that he had an undefinable sense of regret over Clara Hastings, she treated him so like a perfect stranger. He would go up and see her in the morning to-morrow, and try and find out whether she really intended, as he for some reason supposed, to wholly throw him over.

But when the morning came it was Saturday; he was busy running about for Harding, who was nursing himself in his room, and trying to get his knee "limber," as he said. They were to play Brown in the afternoon, and Brown had come very close to beat-

ing Harvard. Harry was to pitch, although his " understudy "—
Stickney, the freshman—begged very hard to be allowed to " down "
Brown. He had no time to run up to Hillhouse Avenue, and back
on the green lawns of the Mulford place, and play with the cats.
He sent a note up by a messenger boy that he was so busy over the
details of arranging the game that afternoon that he would not be
able to call.

In the afternoon before the game, which proved a surprise for
Yale, he went up to the Mulford carriage, in which Miss Crimsy,
with her homely but good-natured face, made almost too much of a
contrast to Clara Hastings' beauty. A very dashing looking young
man had ridden out on a fine thoroughbred horse, and was standing leaning over her carriage and talking to Clara beneath her
white sunshade. It was a man of over thirty, with handsome
eyes and long dark mustaches. Harry, as he came up in his ugly
baseball suit, wearing his large shoes, his dingy blue-and-white
uniform, felt rather out of place. Clara introduced him to " Mr.
Clayton of Umpty-one." Why did Clara, who had confessed her
love for him at the Junior Promenade, wish to flirt so with every
handsome graduate who appeared ? " Confound these good-looking old grads," said Harry to himself, " they don't let a man have
half a chance ! "

All through the game with Brown Mr. Clayton flirted and
chatted with Clara to such an extent that everyone noticed it.
Harry began to pitch in the wildest and most unreliable manner.
How she loved to tantalize him—the exasperating, dashing, wicked
little Puritan ! What was the reason of her capriciousness ?

At all events, to Harry's chagrin, Brown beat Yale that day,
7 to 6.

CHAPTER XLI.

THE GAME AT CAMBRIDGE.

THE last Saturday of that beautiful month of May brought the first Harvard game of the season at Cambridge. Captain Harding took his nine, with the four substitutes, followers, scorers, officers of the Y. U. B. B. C., to Boston on the day before the game. Harding himself was in a state of tension the moment the Boston and Albany depot was reached. He admitted he felt as though they were now on the enemy's territory, and that their path was full of pitfalls. All the Boston world was excited over the coming match. Great red and blue posters, announcing the game, adorned every available wall space and fence. Harry felt that the eyes of the universe were upon him. He expected to win, but baseball is mighty "onsartin!" Suppose the nine should get rattled by the tremendous shouting of all Harvard and Boston combined !

"I'll tell you how to keep down the yelling—the only way," said Harding, who was cool as an iceberg. "You can't expect to shut off all the noise, but it's my experience there's one infallible way of keeping things decidedly quiet on the enemy's ground."

"How ?"

"Why, start in and get a winning lead the first inning!" he laughed. "You'll be surprised how it quiets things down ! All this talk about winning on the shouting is rot. We've got to expect it. Don't think of the crowds. Play the game." And Harding distributed to each man a stick of chewing gum. "Nothing like chewing gum to keep one's nerves down," he laughed.

The next morning the nine went out to the professional "Bostons'" grounds for a little light practice. Every man was

very confident, and the professionals who were not practicing told
them they had what is known as a "cinch." "The Hayverds is no
good this year," said the famous pitcher Mike Stacy. "Dey
aint no better'n last year. I've heerd yer was quite a twister, Mr.
Chissleton. I'd like to observe some o' them curves, if ye plase."

To oblige the great professional pitcher, Harry threw in a few
to Danforth, while Mike Stacy stood behind Dan and got his eye
on the line of the ball.

"Ye've got a mighty pritty command o' the ball, youngster,"
said the veteran. "Now, here, I'll show you anither thrick. With
the same motions ye can sind in the ball fast or slow. See?"

"That's old," said Harry, and he proceeded to pitch the ball to
show that he was familiar with the trick. Mike smiled. "Ye do
that well," he said. "But the best of all is to sind the ball close
to the striker. The more I contimplate the philosophy o' the subject the more sure I am it's putting in the ball, high or low, close to
the body as is the hardest ball to hit—except fer Misther Anson
mebbe—fer there's some as kin hit ennything, an' him's wan o'
them."

"Don't pitch too long," called out Captain Harding, and Harry
stopped, and went in to bat. After half an hour's further practice
they went back to the hotel and read the papers. There were long
columns on the abilities and chances of each nine. The Boston
papers expected Harvard to win—"because they had never yet
been beaten by Yale until last year"—and there was a great deal
of talk in the way of "rattling" a green nine in a tight place.

When they arrived in their stage at Harvard Square, it seemed
as if the entire university was out to welcome the team. Harding
jumped down and shook hands with Captain Byng; nearly all of
the Harvard nine were there, also, and as it was an hour before the
game was to be called at Jarvis' Field, every one of both teams went
over to old Massachusetts Hall, where Captain Byng threw open
his room and entertained them. There was not much said, and
each camp seemed to eye the other with some jealousy and suspicion. It was the first time Harry had ever been in Cambridge,
and he and Jack strolled about the beautiful college yard under

the escort of two or three of the Harvard nine. The great Memorial Hall was just completed, and the Yale contingent were much interested in the capital idea of all the classes dining in the same great room together. They went over to the boathouse on the Charles, but the 'Varsity crew were not on exhibition that day for the benefit of Yale men, of whom the beautiful old town by this time was pretty well filled.

"It's a delightful old place to spend four years in," said Jack admiringly. "And if one cannot have the privilege of going to Yale, I suppose a fellow can worry along here in this little village pretty comfortably, with Boston in sight."

"Do you notice that no one wears a badge of any kind?" said Harry. "At Yale everyone sports some sort of a sign and declares what he is—but here—how can you tell who's who?"

"Oh, we brand our men as they do cattle out west," laughed a Harvard junior. "Did you ever see a Dicky man's arm? He doesn't need a badge to remind him he's 'in it'!"

"I wish you would explain your society system—it seems so complicated," said Jack. "I understand that a man is elected to a senior society in freshman year; and after that, if he wants to go to the Hasty Pudding club, he has to be initiated into the Institute in sophomore year and so enter the A. D. Club, vulgarly known in every other college as Alpha Delta Phi, or he joins the Dicky—also vulgarly known as the D. K. E., and then he may stand a show of getting into the first twenty of the Pudding—a man just explained it to me——"

The Harvard men laughed. "You are hopelessly mixed," they said. But as they were at the entrance of Jarvis' Field by this time, the society system of Harvard remained a mystery to Jack for some time thereafter.

A train full of Yale men had come up to Cambridge to back their nine, and the rah-rahs had already begun before the nine came out on the field. The Harvard crowd was entirely confident of victory, and Stamp, who wore three yards of blue ribbon around his neck and body, had all he could do to stem the tide and keep spirit in his men. When they began playing, and for three innings not a run had been scored on either side, there seemed to be a growing uneasiness on the grand stand. In the fourth inning the tide turned. Danforth hit a scorcher to short, which Harvard fumbled. Harry knocked out a clean two-base hit to left, and Dan stopped on third. Harding batted out a high fly to right, caught—but Murdoch hit safely, and Dan scored. Devine cracked out a liner to right after that, and brought in Harry and Murdoch. The inning closed with Yale 4, Harvard 0.

Harry, feeling confident, let up a little next inning, and tried all his fancy tricks: result, Harvard made one run. But Yale was certain of the result as if the ninth inning had arrived.

Yale had now got on to the Harvard pitcher, and banged the ball all over the field. The game turned out a Waterloo. Intense gloom filled the air to all except the jolly Yale men, who sang and danced and offered any imaginable odds and found no takers. Victory had consented to perch on the Yale banners, even on Jarvis' Field! The score rose to 9-3. The Yale nine felt "chipper," and went at the ball with a confidence which precluded a mere strike, and they played almost faultlessly in the field. It was a glorious day for Yale! The bright sun beamed upon them with a cheerful sympathy. How beautiful the trees looked against the turrets and towers of the college buildings! How *easy* it seemed to play a "gallery" game and win! The Harvard crowd had an indignant, sullen air, as if they thought the Yale team highly impudent to come over and beat them on their own campus. "Oh!" cried one pretty young lady in red, "oh, for one half hour of Archie Bush!"

As they approached the ninth inning Yale went in to make the score as large as possible, in the same provoking way a crew that is ahead will pull for all they're worth to humble their rivals, and succeeded in making the final score 17-5.

The team, after cheering the vanquished, took the first express for New Haven, where they arrived about ten o'clock that night with the Yale contingent, flushed with champagne and victory. The whole college was waiting for them. A band was ready at the depot. The nine was mounted on a coach, and red and blue fire burned galore all the way up Chapel Street. As Harry rode up with the nine, holding Stamp in his arms, and the shouts and applause and cheers greeted his ears, he wondered if Clara Hastings had heard the news, and whether the fact that he had struck out ten men would have any bearing on her supposed regard for him. Even in the supreme moment of victory, victory was robbed of its grace unless he could hear words of delight and congratulation from her lips.

But nevertheless it was a glorious celebration. A great bonfire was built out under the elms before South Middle. Around it hand in hand danced a ring of jolly students, the fire flashing into their faces, singing, "Here's to good old Yale!" Rockets shot up through the elms with a rush and a roar which frightened the poor theologues, over in Divinity Hall, out of their wits. The band played till long past midnight at the fence, and the entire freshman class got very jolly on beer, and made the rest of the night hideous for those who tried to get a little sleep. The next day being Sunday, early chapel was very thinly attended. And the "sick excuses" handed in Monday for absences from church (and marks) were as thick as leaves in Vallambrosa!

CHAPTER XLII.

N spite of considerable opposition Bob Clark had succeeded in getting "on" an eight-oared race with Harvard at New London.* "Eights," were then a new departure in American college rowing, and a departure which was destined to be followed, each succeeding year, on the American as on the English Thames. Eights made a finer show, a greater contest, and interested more men in the crew. Besides, we naturally wished to be on a par with our English cousins from whom all our rowing comes. Yale, as the originator of the English stroke, naturally followed this up by wishing to imitate the English system throughout. English ale was first used in training by Yale, and the English system of keeping a man a trifle undertrained and fat rather than overtrained and stale. In the English stroke the back was kept straight, the head thrown back, the body brought to hardly more than a perpendicular position at the end of the stroke, and the chief work was done by means of the sliding seat and the legs. The old-fashioned "Ward Brothers" stroke (Ward trained Amherst for two wins, and Williams for a sixth place) was at the time generally regarded as the best "winner." It was similar to the stroke used subsequently by the Sho-wae-cae-mettes of Michigan; in other words it was a "git

* We are fully aware that the first "eights" rowed in 1876 at Springfield, when Yale won; and we are merely taking a liberty with boating history which is warranted by the desire to describe a New London race, the usual annual contest at present.

thar" stroke. The reach forward was hardly as far as the toes, the back, arms, and legs moved simultaneously, and the body at the end of the stroke was at a slight angle forward of the perpendicular. It was a difficult stroke to pull effectively for any distance beyond three miles by any except very strong and well-seasoned athletes, the reason being that the swing of the body was so great as to "pump" the oarsmen, without any corresponding increase of speed. To this day there are old professional oars who claim that this stroke is the best for the strong man.

Oh, alumnus! now just blossoming forth in the coming generation with a son a freshman, and a daughter pretty, plump, and debonair and crazy over Yale athletics—it won't do for you to say you're getting old, or to depend upon the New York morning papers for your accounts of the great race. Go to New London race week—go, sir, and don't hesitate an instant! Take Mrs., your wife, and Miss, your daughter—the freshman will take care of himself! It wasn't so many years ago that Mrs. Brown or Smith or Jones was getting in her early work on you with her pretty eyes at Springfield, when lowly Amherst, who trained on beans, prayers, and oatmeal, came spurting in to victory. Can you forget those glorious days in '73 when Yale won? Well, then, take that lovely duplicate of your good wife—that blue-eyed, sweet daughter of yours, and go and see Yale win again at New London!

The Caswells came up from New York, and went on to New London in grand style this year. Mr. Caswell, Sr., had been a Spade and Grave man in his senior year at college, and he felt deeply Teddy's not being elected. He didn't run or guy the young man on this subject, and Teddy was grateful to him. It was too bad—but Caswell had been a little too "gay." He had got on several wild sprees, and had shown up on the campus, singing maudlin songs and daring various members of the faculty to "come on!"—and that he would "disperse" for no man! He had had narrow escapes at these times, but had never been caught by anyone save kindly Tutor Dilworthy, who never appeared to see anything that went on, to the students' detriment. Caswell *ought* to have gone

to a senior society. So *ought* about a hundred more of his classmates, but where there is room only for fifteen or so—how are you
going to crowd in the rest of the class? My good friend whose
luck has been unfavorable, especially along in May term junior
year, don't feel too much grieved over your fate. Go to work;
show the world that you deserve a high place in it. Let not the
gall and wormwood of this disappointment unfit you for life. Caswell made enemies in his own class, and when the time came for
his friends to elect him, he was defeated by a man who cherished
a grudge against him for some reason since sophomore year. It
was a good thing for "Cassy"—it made a man of him afterward,
sobered him up, and for two or three years after leaving college
no man worked harder for a reputation than he. And to-day
what man has made a greater success in his Western railways than
that harum-scarum chap, oh alumni of Umpty-four? But it was
a bitter, bitter disappointment at the time. To look forward
through all the first three years—in his case four—for the "sure
thing" which in his cups he confided to everyone who happened to
be near, and then slip up—well, poor Caswell nearly went crazy!
He talked of going around the world in a year, and getting a pledge
from every man in the Umpty-four "crowd" before he went.
But he gave this up. Senior societies are *the* great crowning gift
of Yale, but if one does not receive the gift fairly in turn, is it so
much an honor? and is not some equally deserving man in the
class unfairly bereft of *his* chances?

Perhaps it was because he was so sorry for his son that his father
made extra preparations for the race week. He had sold the
famous old *Tarquin* and bought a new roomy fast steam yacht, the
Alcazar, and he gave "Teddy" full control for the race week as
to guests and equipment. "Invite your friends," said the old gentleman. "Invite those you liked best in college—and their cousins
and their sisters and their aunts!"

So Caswell made out a list. It included Uncle Dick, the
Rives family (Bessie was said to be engaged to Stafford of Umpty-
three, captain of the football team), the Chestleton family (Kitty
was growing to be a "raving beauty"), Clara Hastings and

her aunt Miss Mulford, Miss Walker, Miss Mead, Fanny Brown, Daisy Stevenson and her brother, who had just returned to America from abroad for the summer and were visiting in New Haven— making a " jolly crowd for a three days' trip from New Haven— and afterward to Newport " ; the plan being to wait till the next day after the race, then end up the trip over Sunday at Newport, at the Caswells' country place.

Kitty and her mother went on to New Haven with Uncle Dick Lyman the Saturday preceding Commencement week. The last ball game of the year took place on the new Yale Field, a few miles more or less out of New Haven, and possibly not any further from college than Hamilton Park. At the time the field was hardly ready for occupation—the outfield was rough—but the grand stand was in order, and they had enjoyed seeing Harvard laid low in the dust, by a score nearly as good as the game at Cambridge. There followed, that night, the jolly Glee Club Concert, and Sunday they had all been to chapel—held there for the first time in the new and beautiful Battel building at the corner of Elm Street. Kitty in her pretty, large, summer straw hat made a sensation in the gallery, by her beauty, which was of a dazzling and dynamic quality ; Sunday afternoon—a drive about New Haven ; Sunday night—a tea at Harry and Jack's room in Durfee. When she got back to her room at the New Haven House Kitty sat down and wrote a letter to an old school friend in New York, and we have been allowed to transcribe it in full :

NEW HAVEN, June 24, 18—.

DEAREST FLORENCE :

I promised you I'd write and so I'm going to *try*, but it's *so* hard to find time! Here it is Sunday night, and yet everybody is walking about the campus in the moonlight, and they are singing hymns over on the fence. Where shall I begin? Oh, the ball game! to *see* Harry cool as a cucumber and Mr. Danforth standing up so *close* behind the bat, I was sure he'd get hit; only he looked so funny in a mask, a great wire thing like a dog's muzzle. But *such* a game! and I felt *so* sorry for Harvard. They hadn't any chance. And once Mr. Danforth turned around and smiled up at us, and mamma and I bowed to him; and Mr. Rives said he was the best catcher Yale ever had, and I was *so* proud of Harry I couldn't speak. And oh, it *was* such a sight! carriages four deep all around the grounds, lots of smart girls too. And *such* men! oh, I've got *lots* to tell you. Mr. Nevers I like *so* much; very quiet, a literary light and all that; but I think I like dear Jack best. So handsome he is now with his brand-new mustache, and *so* clever. And you ought to see their room in Durfee; just as pretty as it can be, ever so much prettier than the one in South Middle last year. They have Jack's 'Varsity oar over the mantel, and lots of flags and trophies, and gilded baseballs, and dance cards, and photographs of actresses—they're Jack's, poor Harry has only *one* girl in *his* eye; and no one can tell, they are so mysterious about it, whether they are really engaged or not. I was *sure* they made it up at the Junior Prom; but since then they say Clara has been flirting desperately with Mr. De Koven and several others. To-day we went to chapel to hear the Baccalaureate sermon, and *such* a lecture those boys got! Probably it's the last sermon a good many of them will listen to for many a long day. And this afternoon we drove all over New Haven, and up to see the soldiers' monument. Oh, the view is *grand*, almost as beautiful as Mt. Desert. And to-night the boys had us to tea in Durfee; issued cards and had twenty people there jammed into their little parlor. And *such* a beauty as Clara Hastings is this summer! no wonder she flirts her head off. I would too, and have a good time before I settled down to stupid marriage.

What do you think they gave us to eat? Lobster *broiled* and Bass' ale and coffee; and then Welsh rarebits, which Jack and Clara made in a great chafing dish, while Harry stood off silent, and looking so sort of lost. Oh, the Glee Club concert was just *sweet!* such a nice set of men. So funny, too—the songs. Mr. Danforth sang "Peter Gray." Do you know it? Then, to-morrow—oh, I've forgotten lots of things to do. See the buildings for one thing. And I've made more than twenty engagements and have forgotten all of them. Oh, now I remember, we are to have a swell lunch at the Mulfords' on Hillhouse Avenue, and a sort of lawn party after it; and to-morrow evening a dinner and a german at the Talmans'. I've met Daisy Stevenson, whom we all liked so much at Mt. Desert last year. Back for good, they say—will study art in New York now. And there was a jolly girl, Fanny Brown, who they say is the most popular New Haven girl in college. She's a round, rosy, lively, witty sort of a girl. Do you know we're invited by Mr. Caswell on his yacht for the races; and are going to New London Wednesday afternoon, just giving me time to look in and see the Commencement at full blast! and then, ho for New Lunnon!

Ever your

KATE.

P. S. Jack says that he's engaged to three girls already, and to-night he had the *impudence* to ask me if I didn't want to make a fourth! He says it keeps him pretty busy buying presents, and not getting his correspondence all mixed up! and he'd like to turn the literary bureau over to me.

Kitty's letters to her schoolgirl friend are so perfectly *naïve* and fairly descriptive of what a "sister, a cousin, or an aunt" sees in New Haven at Commencement time that we'll insert another, (always with the reader's kind permission).

WEDNESDAY.

DEAR FLORENCE:

We are just about to go aboard the yacht. Let me see, when did I write? Was it Sunday? Well, Monday the fun began in earnest. The first thing that happened Mr. Danforth presented himself as we came out from breakfast, bearing the most elegant basket of "Jack" roses you ever saw; he just handed 'em to me in the parlor in an offhand way; said he thought it would make our room seem more homelike. Well, mamma just went crazy over them, they were so beautiful. She loves flowers—and so do I—who doesn't? The dear, sweet, silent things! and Jack says roses are full of love—and nonsense! Mr. Danforth says such snippy things of Jack, it's real mean of him. And Jack *always* speaks so kindly of Mr. Danforth. Well, Monday went in a sort of a whirl. Oh, I met so *many* men! They all flatter you to death. If I *believed* everything they said, you wouldn't know your vain Kitty! Well, Monday, let me see. Oh, we went all over the buildings, Peabody Museum and Library (N. B. Elegant place to flirt in, as says Jack); saw several girls I knew in New York, Bessie Hargreaves, for one. Her father has just given her a diamond star to wear at the Senior Prom, which we are not going to stay for to-night. I'm fagged out and glad to rest. I know we had a ride in the afternoon and went in to Mr. Donald's place, ten in the party. Evening, dinner at the Talmans' and a german; then, what do you think? It was a glorious moonlight night and they teased us so we all went out sailing at twelve o'clock! Oh, that moonlight sail—perfectly heavenly! with the singing and banjos, and guitars and our poor, poor chaperons! We got back at four in the morning at early cockcrow. Mamma let me sleep till ten, then up I got and went down to Mrs. Moriarity's with Harry and Mr. Danforth—"Just to see it, you know," but *sub rosa* I drank a Toby of ale! Tuesday afternoon being class day, Jack and I endured a little of it and bolted. Where *do* you think we went? Why we drove down to Savin Rock and had an oyster supper, he and Mr. Nevers and Clara and I, and Clara confided in me that she didn't know what had got into Harry; he was of late *so* offish and jealous.

"Clara," I said, "isn't it true that a college town is the worst place in the world for a girl?"

"Yes, it *is*," she said. "Oh, there are so *many* men, and such nice ones!"

"It is hard to choose?"

"It is hard not to choose every day!"

Tuesday night, what? Why, a party at the Pillsburys'—great Hillhouse

Avenue swells, grand old house; I never saw such a jam, everybody there. But *we* kept together, I mean Clara, Fanny Brown, Daisy Stevenson, and Bessie Rives, and I. I went to bed at one and got up again to listen to the most beautiful serenade you could ever imagine—the entire Glee Club! given to all the girl guests in the hotel. It lasted an hour. *Oh*, so heavenly! with the soft moon trickling through the graceful old elms and a great crowd on the fence singing. I think that Latin song of Horace, *Gaudeamus igitur*, as *they* sing it, is a perfect college hymn. I felt so stirred, as I knelt at the window, that I cried. Oh, it was so sad, and I thought how soon all this dear old college life will be over for my dear, dear brother and Jack! Well! you've no idea of the effect of night, and the dim outline of the distant college buildings and the songs out of the deep stillness floating up—then what do you think? Some wretch let off a dozen great cannon crackers! I shut my ears and went to sleep as best I might!

But I can scarcely write another word. Commencement to-day, you know, isn't what it's cracked up to be—as they say here, "It's awful slow." I peeped in and saw enough to satisfy me that I'd prefer my cool flannel yachting suit, a biscuit, and a glass of champagne, and a good talk with Daisy Stevenson, who is going with us, on the *Alcazar*. Mr. Caswell met us and took us off with Harry and Jack. We expect a jolly trip of it, and Yale *sure* to win. Rah! Rah! Rah!

Your

KITTY.

CHAPTER XLIII.

ON THE YACHT.

EVERYONE on the *Alcazar* had felt sure that Yale would win, but when the yacht arrived about 8 P. M. off the Pequot House, the terrible news was rumored from shore that Bob Clark had broken down.

"Don't believe a word of it," said Mr. Caswell, Sr. "The old Yale joke, but played out!"

"But, father, Bob is overtrained, and they say the boat doesn't suit the men, and each man has a felon."

"Bosh! I say, bosh! Teddy, go bet every cent you can place. The Pequot House is the great rendezvous; go skirmish about and scare up some Harvard men there; bet anything, give odds on Yale, back up the old college!" The old gentleman grew red with anger.

"Thanks, I guess I'll stay aboard and wait over till to-morrow."

"Why, Teddy!" His father gazed at him, astonished.

There was a mournful air, a quietude about Ted Caswell, which was unnatural. It had been so since senior society elections were given out. He somehow hung back now, and seemed afraid to put himself forward. To Jack and Harry his changed demeanor, his quietude, seemed pitiful, and made them both feel very uncomfortable. The way, too, General Rives and Mr. Caswell talked about Spade and Grave made their hair stand on end! as though there was no secrecy at all! no mystery! Being old Spade and Grave men themselves, they felt that their open talk of old times in the society's halls was both natural and eminently proper!

"Do tell us all that goes on in Spade and Grave!" cried Clara wickedly.

Jack and Harry tried to turn the subject.

402

"Why, Jack, what *are* you winking so hard at me for?" asked the old general, with a twinkle in his eye.

"Oh, nothing, sir."

Clara and Harry were in a relation of "strained feeling," at present. During the term they had had not one, but several "lover's quarrels." For a few weeks after the Junior Promenade they had been very happy. Everything went smoothly. They agreed to a secret engagement. Clara went out a great deal, passing Easter again in New York, where she went demurely to church with the Chestletons at St. George's. Mrs. Chestleton treated Clara affectionately, as she treated all her children's friends. But she could not honestly tell her son she "took" to her very heartily. To Kitty she once spoke of her as a spoiled child. The truth was that Clara was, like many girls, super-sensitive over the question of her relation to Harry. She "vowed and declared" that she would *not* have a long engagement, and she knew it would be several years before Harry could think of marriage. After Easter holidays she went home to Cleveland, where influences decidedly opposed to our hero were brought to bear on her by her family. A "great" match was talked of. Her mother wished her to have a London season as her sister had done, and to see something of the world and society. "Who is this Chestleton boy, who is so ridiculously fond of you, Clara? Is his family in society in New York? Has he any money?"

"Not very much," she replied faintly, and as far as Mrs. Hastings was concerned his doom was apparently sealed. But her mother's opposition to Harry strengthened the fair girl in her determination that she *would* eventually marry the handsome pitcher of the 'Varsity. When she came back to New Haven for the Commencement festivities she signified to Harry that, whatever happened, she would be true to him. But then she flirted so desperately with Blakely, a rich New Haven graduate, that Harry began to despair and get angry again. Jack laughed and counseled patience. "She is so lovely that she can't help being a college belle," he said, "and she is used to being adored, she's so very adorable! That's the worst about a college town, a girl is spoiled by too much attention, but, dear old boy, she'll get over it ! She'll make the best of wives; don't be too severe with her now." Then he gave him a piece of worldly advice : " Pitch in and flirt like the mischief yourself, and devote yourself to some other girl—Fanny Brown, for instance—then see how quick she'll change her tactics."

Ted Caswell got his party on board by four o'clock that Wednesday afternoon—all but his father and General Rives, who were down to speak at the dinner in Alumni Hall, and who had not long to be waited for ; and the voyage up the blue Sound had been, as the pretty girls aboard said, "Simply gorgeous !"

"Is life worth living?" asked Daisy Stevenson of Harry as he stood moodily leaning against the cabin door, smoking. "You seem not to think so now, Harry, and yet your letters when I was in Rome have been so invariably cheerful. To me life *is* worth living if I am rich."

"Heresy ! It's peace of mind—if you're rich it's only amusement you seek, and suppose you *can't* enjoy ? "

"You can always choose your environment—how delightful this yacht is—and how pretty the lights ashore ! The Pequot is a blaze of red lights—Harvard's quarters, I suppose ? "

"Oh, no ; not the quarters of the crew, you know. They are 'way up the river somewhere."

"Doesn't the moonlight, the little lights of the yachts—the feeling of excitement in the air over the race to-morrow, exhilarate you ! "

" No, not an exhilarate ! "

"Brute ! " she laughed. " You *blasé* at your age ! "

Daisy Stevenson, after her year abroad at Rome, had returned to New Haven almost completely cured of her early infatuation. She had seen more or less of the gay society, American and English, which every winter makes its headquarters in the Imperial City. At first she, like *Hilda* in Hawthorne's famous story, had worked hard at her favorite pursuit, but latterly, in the warm sunny spring days, it had been one continual succession of social engagements. She had had many men at her feet. She read and studied and developed. At that distance the world seemed very large and Yale

College and its jolly students very small indeed. She had a serious flirtation with an English artist, a man of celebrity. She grew handsomer, more womanly, more mistress of herself. At the time of the yachting trip she was meditating a favorable reply to the English artist, who offered her his hand—and a delightful home in London and a place in the brilliant London world of art and letters.

"What?" cried Kitty, overhearing them, and coming up to her brother, she put her head down affectionately on his shoulder.

"Call my be—rother a brute?"

"He won't enthuse!"

"He will to-morrow! Poor boy, he's tired! Is his arm all right?" she asked. "The arm that beat Harvard?"

De Koven, always the immaculate, joined them. Although Caswell had handed out yachting caps of the same degree of gold lace and elegance all around to the men, nevertheless De Koven's had the neater, jauntier air; it looked better on him somehow. He offered his arm to Kitty and they strolled off toward the bow, laughing and chatting.

"That young man ought to be a diplomat," said Daisy—the same wise Daisy as of old; "the way he *does* things is enchanting."

Harry was silent. At the stern, beneath a wide awning to keep off the dew, and beneath a dozen Chinese lanterns, nearly all of the party was sitting. It was just after dinner. Mr. Caswell was extremely fond of music and in the large cabin of the *Alcazar*, he had a fine upright piano carefully covered with rubber cloth. Mrs. Caswell went in and played a lively waltz for them, and presently everyone was dancing on the deck. Boatloads of people appeared out of the darkness from neighboring yachts, and there was more dancing, and now and then an ominous popping in the cabin below indicated that Teddy was playing the host in his old style. With considerable personal inconvenience Mr. Caswell started a blue Bengal light at the bow, and presently four red lights burned brilliantly near them, and a

"Rah, Rah, Rah—Harvard!"

was heard in the distance, coming over the water. They felt as if the enemy was upon them! A few moments later and a bevy of girls dressed in red appeared at the yacht's companion way, and were invited aboard by Mr. Caswell. They were New York girls, and their escorts were old school friends of Harry and Jack who had unwittingly gone to Harvard. A jolly dance followed. The *Alcazar* was a large roomy steamer, with plenty of deck room, and the music was furnished by guitars and banjos.

Clara danced with Jack, and then with Harry. "Why are you so odd—so distant?" she murmured.

"Clara, you know that my heart is like lead."

"Then *do* be careful about falling overboard, dear."

"Perhaps it will be the best thing for me. Life is unendurable to me, when you seem to care so little for me."

"Please—please don't go on spoiling all my fun. Are you always going to be a 'killjoy,' standing about with grewsome face? Do cheer up a bit, Harry. You act so like a—chump!" and she burst out laughing.

"Tell me one word, and I will."

"What is it?"

"Tell me you love me, as you did the night of the Junior Prom, last February."

"I *did* then."

"And now?"

"Well, I don't care for anyone else. No one shall ever, *ever* marry me but you. But I don't think I want to marry at all—I hate to lose my freedom."

"What do you mean by freedom—opportunity to go on flirting with every man you see?"

"Harry, how dare you!"

"Well, I'm dreadfully tired of things as they are!"

"Don't think there is any tie between us that *I* shall hold you to, Mr. Chestleton."

Her voice was so cold and distant it almost made him feel ill.

"I am not willing to go on in this way," he said sternly.

"Either you are engaged to me or not. Say the word, Clara, and end my misery."

"If you cannot let things go on precisely as I choose to have them, then good-by!"

"But——"

"I want no 'buts.' You're at the end of your junior year. Are you prepared to marry now?"

"Yes. I'll jump in a boat, row you down to New London, hail the first minister we can find, and be married. Come! I'm ready!"

Clara, looking as beautiful as excitement, a glass of champagne, and the lamplight and moonlight in her face could make her, hesitated a moment.

"If I dared, Harry, it would show your jealous heart, once for all, that I would sacrifice *all* for you. If we could carry it out, I'd do it—yes, yes—I know it's best! I know that I deserve to be thrown over a dozen times for the way I've acted all through, but what's a girl to do in a college town? I love to be amused."

"You love to flirt!"

Her eyes fell before his, and she reddened. "I'm not going to confess *anything*," she laughed. "Besides, it isn't my fault."

"Whose, then?"

"Why are students so deceitful?" she asked, bridling. She looked doubly pretty to him when she put on her little airs and graces of high dignity.

"That has nothing to do with it."

"Ah, yes! if men were only more truthful, it would be impossible to flirt with them."

Harry was silent. He gave her his arm and walked toward the bow. On a yacht near by a crowd of Harvard men were singing that beautiful Eton boat song:

> "But we will still swing together,
> And cheer for the Harvard crew," etc.

and at the Pequot they were letting off some bombs in honor of the freshman victory of the day before. The graceful elmlike rays of red fire rose high above the trees and went out in a gorgeous mass of color against the sky. The Fort Griswold hotel across the harbor, not to be outdone, shot up a dozen rockets.

"Isn't it beautiful, Harry, dear?" She sought his hand. "The moon, everything."

"It might be, if——"

"If what?"

"We could come out—announce our engagement."

"Harry!"

"Is it too much to ask?"

"I *despise* an engaged girl, she always looks so conscious."

"It would make me *sure* of you."

"Isn't my word enough?"

"Does it keep off the crowd?"

"Students! You are the first and only student who ever seemed the least bit in earnest, to me. Even Mr. Saxton, to whom I was engaged before you, I never thought was wildly in earnest."

She was dressed in her white yachting suit with brass buttons. The neat costume set off her exquisite figure to perfection. Clara was tall, graceful, dark-haired and starry eyed. She was his goddess and she knew her power. They passed and repassed Miss Stevenson on De Koven's arm. For the life of her, as they met, she couldn't help catching De Koven's glance and smiling. To flirt seemed to be the life of this girl. She loved admiration. It was her food and drink.

"Are you ever in earnest?"

"I confess I'm not half so solemn as I used to be at school in Charmington. The world is not half so sad as I used to think. But in the serious matters I'm in earnest; of course I am!"

"Then, dear?"

"I'll tell you. The race is doubtful to-morrow, let it depend on that. If Yale wins—then we'll announce our engagement. I'll paste a label on my back, 'Beware—she's private property!' I'll go about with a long face, and I'll never, never, never speak to a man again, as long as I live. I'll just say 'hands off!'" She caught herself. "Of course I *always* said *that*, I should *hope!* and I'll say yea, yea, and nay, nay, and talk about political economy, and if anyone mentions your name I'll blush and look conscious and pleased."

" If Yale wins ! "

" Yes. But if Harvard (oh, how I hope she'll just beat by three inches !)—then I shall have just as good a time as I know how ! and when the time comes for us to be married——"

" Married ! do you think then that I'll care to marry after you've broken my heart to pieces ? "

" Why, Harry ! Of course, you don't mean you would not, in the end ? "

" What can you think me made of ? "

" Well, I *have* heard it said you had a good deal of Yale sand in your composition." She looked away demurely.

" Can you be a Puritan—you, with such light notions ? "

" A Puritan ? No. Puritanism I renounce once and for all. I don't believe in it. I think my ancestors were all deluded. They meant well—but the world is given us for a purpose, to amuse us. But, come now, let it stand on the race. Engaged or not engaged. To marry or not—to marry ! Heigho ! I *did* long to have Yale win."

" But now ? "

" I'm a Harvard girl—just for to-night ! "

With that she left him, and Harry lit a cigar cheerfully, and strode about less silent and thoughtful.

CHAPTER XLIV.

THE race! The race is the thing! All other college events grow small in comparison with that great and glorious June day at New London. The crowds that gather about a ball field will disperse to gather again next week, but the vast outpouring at New London comes but once a year. Alumni may forget the nine, or may know little about football, but when, at what age, does interest in the boat race die out?

At forty, fifty, or sixty years? We saw an old Harvard graduate last year at New London, at least seventy-five years of age, white-haired and bent, yet with red ribbons in his buttonhole and waving a red flag like some antiquated auctioneer. His grandson had just entered college. He was still able to be jubilant over his boy's victorious crew, and will be so until he dies. When Harvard crossed the line a winner, amid the booming of cannon and the crackling "'rah, 'rah, 'rah, Harvard" of the undergrads, we heard him shout a quavering "Hurrah, Hurrah, Tiger!" just as he used to do on the Charles in 1843. Enthusiasm for one's college is a good thing, and we in America love to brag of our successful Alma Mater as we do of our successful business. We love to meet our opponents later on cool summer hotel piazzas and rub them the wrong way. If we lose at New London the joke is on us. We submit to harmless teasing, and say hopefully: "Oh, just wait till next year!" It is a part of our interest in life.

The general accommodations for sightseers at New London are good. Those who devote a week to idling at the Fort

Griswold House at Eastern Point or at the Pequot enjoy the gayety of the week at its best. Old classmates meet and shake hands on the broad piazzas which overlook one of the prettiest marine views on our coast. What continued interest there is in this busy harbor! Here flashes past one of Herreshoff's smart little steamers; there goes the new Government vessel, the *Vesuvius*, with her three pneumatic guns at her bow. Here is one of the crack cutters darting by, with its decks crowded with "swagger" girls in red and blue. The very air is keen with excitement. There are plenty of college fathers, mothers, sisters, aunts, and cousins. There are plenty of other people who care not for the races, but who love the delicious liveliness of the great aquatic week—the stir, the fun of it. We may be all landlubbers the rest of the year, but we are all watermen at New London. We roll in our gait, we hum airs from "Pinafore," which is sung by a company of amateurs, appropriately, the night before the race, at the opera house. We live on the water, talk boating and recall old boating days. There is a dispute between us. Is a girl prettier in her yachting dress or in a ball costume? We insist she is at her best in her charming white yachting cap, her gold lace, her blue and white flannels; *certes* she never looked prettier in her life than when she (in red) fairly danced about to the imminent peril of her life (for she would go overboard were she not so light and dainty) when she saw her Harvard crew dash away with a lead and victory again, apparently, at the first mile perching on the crimson banners of Cambridge! My dear old college grad, you cannot do better than to take the girls down to the New London race week. Go down and stay through the entire week from Sunday to Sunday. Take in the beautiful sea pictures before you. Sit a little back from the crowd. Let the girls "go it," if they want to. There is dancing in the parlors of the Pequot and Fort Griswold every night. There are plenty of handsome, sun-browned cavaliers, mostly in sailor-like flannels. They are "just off the yacht" and white flannel prevails. It is the great aquatic week of the year, and—ah! well we have lost our heart to one of some other fellow's sisters for the thirty-third time.

There is plenty to do. If one is an old oar, he may visit the
"quarters" and be invited to dine with the crew. It is something
like feeding so many "cattle." It overpowers one. Huge
chines of beef disappear off the table like magic, and great
pitchers of milk, tobies of ale, and loaves of stale bread are quickly
devoured. Here be hungry men, their brown skin like satin, their
eyes clear and white like porcelain. It is forty "feeding like
one." At the head of the Yale table sits the great coach, Captain
Clark ; and to-night the table is graced by a bevy of pretty Yale
girls from New Haven—not allowed *often*, but this year " Yale is
sure to win," and so, having a "snap" on Harvard, as the saying
is, a little laxity prevails at headquarters.

The party on the *Alcazar* spent the morning of race day steam-
ing up the beautiful Thames River, and taking a peep at Yale and
Harvard's quarters far up on the left bank by Gale's Ferry. The
race was to be rowed at five o'clock. Yet already, by noon, the
town was full; every train brought crowds of "sweet girl graduates" and noisy throngs of students. Four great Sound steamers
are moored at the docks. They are crowded to the water's edge
with sightseers from the neighboring towns. The yacht has some
difficulty in getting up to the wharf, where a number of Yale notables
await it. Old grads, old oars, and old "coaches," whose interest
never flags. Yes, there is Grannis talking with the referee, and
the *Alcazar* is selected as the referee's boat—to follow the crews
from start to finish. Harry welcomes Grannis on board, and
introduces him to all his friends. His presence is a surprise. " I
couldn't keep away," said Grannis, " and as ' Yale is sure to win,'
I thought I'd come down and help the shouting." Grannis had a
great deal to tell him about Ella Gerhart—how lovely and how
subdued and quiet she was, and how he loved her and saw her true
worth more than ever. He told him about Hetherington too, who
was making a great reputation in the Western college where
Grannis' influence had got him installed. " He doesn't drink—and
he's so glad he went West he writes me an ode once a month in
Greek hexameters to tell me so ! "

Clara had never known about Ella Gerhart, and her story was

generally unknown in New Haven. Indeed very few knew it
except the gay members of her burlesque troop, who made little to
do over what they called her "love affair."

All the way to the starting point at Gale's Ferry, that afternoon,
Grannis told them of the great future of their electrical lighting
business and how he had "roped in" Miss Hastings' father to the
extent of fifty thousand dollars. Whereat Clara laughed and
Grannis said they intended to rope in her "fancy" next—he
probably meant *fiancé*, but he put on the western pronunciation
with a bold face. "Oh, there's millions in it for all of us!" he
laughed.

"Well, it all depends," said Clara enigmatically from beneath
her blue sun umbrella.

"How so?"

"Well, Mr. Grannis, perhaps Harry will tell you. I certainly
will not."

"I don't mind Gran," laughed Harry. "But don't tell anyone.
If Yale wins we're engaged, out and out, up and down, official. If
Harvard wins then it's off—Miss Hastings will choose some other
student—a Harvard man presumably, at some watering place this
summer. As for me, I'll enter a monastery."

"Do you really mean—you're not joking?" asked Grannis,
amazed.

"We are perfectly serious. You see how important an event
it is——"

"Will you two let your entire future lives, your happiness, turn
on such a slight point?"

"Why not?"

"I think it's wicked!"

"Oh, but 'Yale is sure to win,'" Clara said, with a smile at
the Westerner's earnestness.

"Suppose she breaks her rudder—an oar—gets stuck in the eel
grass—a thousand things?" cried Grannis earnestly.

"Oh, we've considered all that, Gran," said Harry. "And Clara
has practically given me the best crew and boat. It is perfectly
fair."

"Fair? Why, either you two are in love or you're not. The race? Ridiculous! There will be a thousand races where there'll be but one real true honest love match!"

Harry endeavored to change the subject, but Grannis kept harking back to it and urging his friend to withdraw from such an absurd wager.

"You are Western, Gran," said Harry, with a sardonic smile. "You appear to have queer notions out there. Can't one bet on love as on everything else? Can't we toss up a cent—and trust to luck? I'm sure a great many marriages might have been warded off if the contracting parties had been as level-headed as we are about it."

"Yes, indeed!" said Clara imperturbably.

The *Alcazar* gave three loud long whistles, which had the effect of cutting off all further conversation. Kitty and General Rives were promenading to and fro, the general now anxious as he ever was before a battle in the Civil War, discussing the chances of the race. Miss Garland had come aboard, and a party of Charmington girls. From that time till near the end of the race Clara and Harry became separated.

They passed by a hundred yachts, anchored along the line with their gay signal flags flying. The referee and timekeepers were up in the bow, and it was nearly five. They were passing the Harvard's quarters. Not a sign of life was visible. Apparently no one had ever heard of a boat race in that pretty little red-roofed cottage on the bluff over the river. The boathouse looked deserted. Presently one or two men, naked to the waist, and wearing very abbreviated white trousers and canvas slippers came on the float, bearing oars the blades of which were painted red. In this country we paint our oar blades red or blue, and row nude. Even the coxswain strips with the rest. There is no need to row in dress suits, but there should be seemly clothing. How it has come to be the fashion in America to adopt the prize fighter's "buff," we do not know. Old prints show us Yale crews of '52 in white uniforms (college colors were not chosen until 1865). It is to be hoped that the crews will in future make an effort to remedy this custom,

We are proud of your muscles, oh, 'Varsity oars, but, with our wives and sweethearts, we prefer to see you clothed and in your right minds as all oarsmen row in England !

The referee bawled out certain instructions. As the *Aleazar* steamed away more naked men appeared, bearing more oars which they laid down in order on the float. Presently the cedar boat appeared, upside down. How thrilling it was to see that ship which was to bear them to victory or defeat, handled so tenderly, and dropped into the water ! No. 2 and No. 5 got in, and then the *Aleazar* lost sight of Harvard round a bluff, and a puffing tug, dragging an enormous coal barge, came straight down over the course. The *Aleazar* darts up to the captain of the slow, panting little tug, and the referee shouts :

"Get off the course, won't you—and wait till the race is over !"

"Go to thunder ! This is a free river, aint it, boss ?" shouts the captain politely.

"No punishment is too severe for such a scamp," said the referee, "but under the present law he cannot be punished, for he has as much right in the river as anyone. It ought to be possible to lock him up and fine him, and it ought to be possible also to do away with 'suction' by regulating the distance of the steamers ; but a statute is first necessary to attain this object."

Now all eyes are turned to a little craft which has crossed the river further up and is quietly coming leisurely down the stream by the right bank. It is the Yale crew. There seems to be no "snap" to their stroke. They row listlessly, but how smoothly the boat slips along ! They arrive first at the start, generally considered a misfortune. There are shouts of a thousand voices from the "moving grand stand" which comes up from New London just then, and the shouts are doubled as the Harvard crew crosses the river, looking bigger and heavier than Yale, and rowing a "snappy" stroke which makes their boat "lift" at every stride. At last the two ancient rivals are lying side by side, boatmen holding their rudders at an equal distance. It is a moment of great tension and anxiety. The *Aleazar* steams up as close as the shallow water under the bank will permit, and more orders are shouted over the water. From the deck of the yacht it seems almost a straight four-mile course to the great railway bridge piers at New London. Not a course which requires very great dexterity in steering, nor which permits of any great display of watermanship. It is simply ding-dong pulling from start to finish—four miles.

The narrow streams of England furnish more excitement in racing to on-lookers than does this broad lakelike expanse of water. Sharp turns, shoals, and narrow bridges give an English coxswain something to do. With us he is simply an interested passenger, entirely useless, and only carried in imitation of the English system. The steering of an "eight" could be as well done down that straight wide four miles of river, as the steering of a "six," by the bow oar.

After a brief silence, both crews are "set," reaching forward at arm's length. "Are you ready? Go!" A pistol shot follows, then the cry of relief and excitement:

"They're off!"

Instantly shouts, rah-rah-rahs, and insane yellings begin. The steamboats flounder along, following the *Alcazar*. Yale and Harvard are rowing now side by side. Each crew is in perfect form. There is no splashing, neither gains. The two styles of rowing can be easily compared. The Harvard boat "jumps," the Yale boat "moves"; so it goes until the half-mile flag is reached, and the *Alcazar* has to make a turn to avoid the coal barge. Then, oh, woe to dear old Yale! Harvard forges a little ahead. Then a trifle further. Then clear water between Harvard's little rippling rudder and Yale's brass-tipped bow. "*It's Harvard's race!*" shout a boatload of reds, as they pass. It looks so.

Harry, glass in hand, stands at the gunwale, the picture of utter woe. The race is life or death to him. At a little distance near him stands a girl crying as if her heart would break. She tries to conceal her tears from him. *He* shan't see her weaken!

"I wouldn't have supposed that Miss Hastings cared so much to have Yale win," said Mr. Caswell. "What a tender heart the girl has! and they say she's such a coquette!"

At every stroke now it seems as if Harvard was adding to the "clear water" between the two boats. The *Alcazar* is in the rear of both crews, and appearances from this point are deceptive.

Harry quietly put down his glass, and went into the yacht's elegant cabin. He was alone. He threw himself on a divan, and gave himself up to bitter musings.

"So Harvard wins—and Clara will claim that she is free," he said to himself. "I don't want to see the finish. It means too much to me. She doesn't love me—she never will. It was a ruse of hers to make an excuse to leave me. All that she said at the Junior Prom was mere nonsense, the result of the lights, the music, the excitement."

Suddenly he felt a soft touch on his shoulder.

"Harry!"

He looked up. Clara had sought him out. The traces of tears were in her eyes.

"Well?"

"I—I—don't care if Harvard does win—I—I can't. I won't—I'll do just—just as you please."

But he put her away with pretended sternness.

"Perhaps this, too, is only a momentary, a temporary feeling. Do you remember the Junior Prom?" His heart was beating wildly.

"Harry, forgive me!" She was in tears.

He could no more resist her than he could fly. He took her in his arms.

"Whoever wins, *you're my girl?*" he cried joyously.

"Yes, yes!"

"Everyone shall know it?"

"Yes."

"If Harvard wins by ten boat-lengths?"

"By a hundred!"

Suddenly they hear a great shout outside. On their own yacht there is comparative silence, as it is not considered decorous to take sides very strongly while the yacht is performing her mission of "referee's boat." But they are evidently passing an anchored Yale yacht, for they hear someone shout the words "*Yale's gain-*

ing!" and hand in hand rush up on deck. They tell their tale in their happy, radiant faces—but who looks at *them* now? The race is the thing! Harvard is still ahead, but rowing a trifle ragged.

Yale is rowing well and pulling every stroke through; not so Harvard. They are spurting, and look already half pumped, but they are strong, and keep up their work and so maintain their lead. Great overloaded steamboats at anchor are passed; everyone is on one side and the great tubs careen, and look as if they were going to capsize; vast volumes of roars come from these boats and from the moving grand stand, on the shore. The two and a half mile flag is passed, Yale is now slowly creeping up. As her men are close under the *Alcazar's* bow, it is easy to study them. Everything is quiet in the boat. Bob Clark at stroke is cool and well "within himself." He is setting 32 strokes a minute, and he has not varied this so far. Old Harvard oarsmen on the *Alcazar* groan at the even and perfectly businesslike way the Yale crew is working; while everyone's heart is in his mouth with excitement. An old Harvard oar whispers to a friend in Clara's hearing, "It's all up with us" and she believed all was lost! She is clapping her hands, now, and crying—happy tears running down her cheeks, as Yale with that beautiful smooth movement, as a fish swims, creeps up. No excitement whatever in the boat. It's the same killing smooth stroke, same time, well pulled, though! The men themselves know Bob's policy. They've expected Harvard to jump away with the lead, and now they know as they begin to hear the desperate "swish" of Harvard oars again, that "Bob" is right! Slowly, slowly, Harvard drops back. The three-mile flag is passed. The two crews are as even as at the start. But now glance at the difference in the rowing! No. 3 in Harvard's boat shows signs of distress, No. 6 pulls half his stroke, No. 7 is pulling out of the boat. The crew are in a desperate fix. Their struggle is awful! Nos. 4 and 5 row "out of the boat." The face of their famous "stroke," who is pulling each stroke as finely as the first at the start, is stamped with terrible agony. Oh, it is so hard, so *hard* to win—to believe the race over—and then to lose! In Yale's boat the men are rowing as if at their ease. The water roughens a little and a new danger arises; suppose they get water-logged? But though they carry a number of extra pounds of H_2O, it seems to make no difference. The race is theirs. Each man knows it. They keep up perfect form, the $3\frac{1}{2}$ mile flag is passed. Yale leads by a half-boat length, and *now* Bob calls in his men for a spurt. He quickens to 38, the Yale boat slips away, and the race becomes a procession. Cannon boom, whistles shriek. The line is crossed, and Bob stops rowing, his crew not at all pumped. They wait a minute for Harvard to pull up. As Harvard rests, No. 3 falls over in a faint, and they dash water in his face. As the *Aleazar* approaches they ask the time, which is 21:42. The race is over for the year!

> Rah—rah—rah!
> Rah—rah—rah!
> Rah—rah—rah!—Yale!

Harry looked down into Clara's beautiful eyes.

"You darling! you came to me when you believed you were free."

"Yes, dear."

"Now I've won—you shall do exactly as you please. I'm a jealous old fool!"

"Harry!"

"You shall flirt all you please!"

"How noble we *both* are!" she laughed.

But on the way to New Haven that night everyone on the *Aleazar* had laughed over and knew their story. And from that great 'Varsity race day Harry never had cause again to complain of the pretty college belle's behavior.

CHAPTER XLV.

THE summer vacation with the Hastings family was the most delightful one of Harry's college days. Clara's father had returned from abroad and chartered a steam yacht which was large enough to accommodate a dozen guests. After the season's yachting Harry went home with them to Cleveland in September. While in Cleveland, at their beautiful home on Euclid Avenue, he called upon the Gerharts. Ella was living alone in the large house with her father. The rest of the family were still on a visit to Germany. She would not leave him, and he told Harry that he was glad she had not, as she had nursed him through a severe illness. The faithful Grannis was away in New York on business when Harry was in Cleveland. Ella's father could not say enough in praise of his daughter when Harry called on him. "She goes about among the poor," said old Gerhart, "and she stints herself, poor girl! Ach, himmel! it's sad to see her. She gives everything to the poor, all that she has. And she especially befriends poor working girls. And every night and day she prays for you, Harry. And she's glad you're happy and are to marry rich Mr. Hastings' daughter, but she won't see you ever again, so she says; but dear me, she's only twenty, you know."

Clara spent the fall of Harry's senior year in New Haven. She was undoubtedly now very much in love. Those who had doubted it and had questioned her fidelity believed when they saw how little she went out, save in Harry's company.

Meanwhile, senior year, the loafing year, sped on with a solemn and a serious tread. It is not a picturesque year at Yale. Even society life in New Haven "drags" a little. One knows all the girls. There are no surprises. Yet many claim that senior year is the pleasantest of the four. The struggle of the low-standers to " stay in " is mostly over. The senior society men are no longer discussing " chances." It is like a safe harbor after a stormy sea.

In old days seniors, all that were able, took up their abode near the fence in " South." The old dormitory is gone now, to make way for the " greater Yale." It has followed the fence. But in those pleasant old days of Harry and Jack, in old South, college life, mellowed with three years of " hard grinding," was now lightened into scholastic ease. It was a year of " calm delight " like Heber's Sabbath. Solemn thoughts of what was expected of them in life by parents and guardians now occasionally haunted them. The top-heavy old *Lit.* was burdened with their Addisonian essays upon such serious topics as " Life's Highest Aim," " What four years have done for me," " Yale and Harvard compared " (to Harvard's disadvantage).

The Townsend prize essays and the De Forest gold medal occupied the thoughts and attention of many, but clever diplomacy with Harvard and Princeton over athletic questions absorbed the best talent and most of the time of the " knowing ones."

The diplomacy, reader, required in arranging modern college ball games, boat races, football games, or intercollegiate sports, requires talent of no mean order. The ordinary old-fashioned college grad may wonder, " What on earth has got into those fellows ? " but he must be told that diplomacy must and shall have its day. It's the same when Oxford or Cambridge, England, arrange a race with us. They always try to win on paper. It's so in the grand international yacht races: clever men try to leave nothing fair undone that will tend to bring victory their way. So we have letters from captains, college meetings to protest, counter letters, meetings of captains, and what not; each college is trying to suit itself. One year Harvard " won't play " Princeton, or Yale, and all because some little point is refused. It looks rather silly ; it is really not so in the least. These college games have assumed a national importance in the sporting world and everything, forsooth, must be carefully arranged by diplomacy !

With Harry—especially under Professor Growler—it was a year of hard work. He had stood pretty well up in the first division all junior year, and now he "let up" a little in his studies, but read history and "outside" books a great deal. His future began to trouble him. Clara wished him to become a lawyer. So did his mother, but hard-headed Mr. Hastings said: "Go at once into that electric business in Cleveland with Mr. Grannis, and make money. You can study law afterward—but my experience is, Harry, that to *practice* law, a young man needs a good income!"

This was what Harry himself wanted to do. After his long hard studying year he came to the conclusion, like so many young Americans, what is it all worth unless you have money? Money was his chief object now, yet Clara wished him to be a lawyer. So did his mother. He did not wish to disappoint them.

Since that moonlight night in New London Clara had been a different girl. She *felt* she was Harry's wife, she often said. She received no one. She gave the wealth of her heart and sweet young girlhood to him. She leaned on him, trusted him.

As our hero's character and mind expanded under his earnest, studious college life, hers expanded also. She learned that beneath his intense earnestness of purpose he had a fine high spirit. He was unselfishness itself, and when he came to trust her, his moroseness and moodiness disappeared.

At last the closing college days came at Yale. The class day, with its jokes and jollity, the ivy planting, the Senior Prom, Commencement, with "Old Andy" leading off in the Salutatory and David Alum, pale, and already ill with the fatal disease which soon after carried him to his grave, ending all with the Valedictory. What a proud, sad day it was for that quaint, faithful Aunt Sarah, who sat sobbing with a queer, lean old man in a front seat in the gallery. The queer, lean old man was David's father, the Rev. Cyrus Alum—a rural Connecticut clergyman, who had graduated at Yale in the remote past, had himself stood at the head of *his* class, where David now stood, but had since scarcely been heard of—the way of so many valedictorians!

Harry was not to make his last appearance as an orator in midday, in that hot, crowded Center Church, in a dress suit. The unkind fates did not grant him an appointment, and he was only one

unusual thing—the audience applauded the famous pitcher who had only once been defeated by Harvard.

"Oh, you're so silly!" cried Kitty, as her mother's eyes filled with a proud delight and the tears rolled down her face. "The idea of *crying* over Harry when everyone is just crazy over him!"

Clara Hastings looked on with a fine light in her eyes.

She was proud of him, and so too were her own father and mother, who came on to attend Commencement. Harry was the most sincerely popular man of his class. He was quiet, modest, yet greatly liked. "If you *must* throw yourself away on a student," exclaimed her mother, who had been completely captivated by Harry, "he's the pick of the flock! Ah, well! I don't know, Clara, but it is just as well. I believe in youthful marriages. So I hear you began your acquaintance in the drawing-room car when Harry first went on to New Haven as a freshman? and you followed it up by being upset by him at Lake Saltonstall! Well, he's a fine looking young man. Your father quite takes to him. But he's got a will of his own."

"Yes, but I'll control that!" laughed Clara gayly.

"I'm not so sure!" said her mother. "But I prefer a young man who is in earnest, as he is. There are too many shambling, easy-going, pleasure-loving young men nowadays. Yes—I like his soberness, his earnestness. He will make a fine man."

Miss Mulford gave them a luncheon when Commencement was over, and Jack made them all very merry again with his gibes and wit over the laborious years, and the "little to show for it."

"Thank Heaven we got out of college when we did," he laughed. "The way buildings are going up the campus will soon be nothing better than a stoneyard. Everyone seems kind enough to die at once and leave Alma Mater a dormitory! When I die I shall leave some money to increase the professors' salaries. Dear old Yale! Dear old faculty! They've been square to me, as they are to every mother's son of us! We've had a jolly four years of it—haven't we, Harry? We never really had a serious row, had we?"

"No, you always yielded to my superior judgment!" laughed Harry.

"And now *we* are going off the stage so soon," sighed Jack. "Others are going off too—did you hear of Daisy Stevenson's engagement, Harry?"

"She wrote me; to her English artist who has a gorgeous house in London."

"And Fanny Brown's?"

"To whom?"

"To Daisy's brother! Oh, by the bye, Stamp is engaged too."

"To whom?" laughed Clara.

"Engaged to end his days at Yonkers at the old place. The governor has engaged him—but he'll be on hand as mascot every Harvard or Princeton game *sure*—he has behaved gloriously. Did you ever hear, Miss Mulford, of his great fight at Mitford? No? Well, you see——"

And Jack, in spite of all they could do, went on and narrated all about Stamp and his three conquests, and the wicked Bridgeport dog they "rang in" on him. Miss Mulford always delighted in Jack; was secretly grieved that Clara did not prefer him. He amused her. She loved his wild stories. Harry she thought a little too self-contained. He took things too seriously. She laughed till she nearly had a fit, and they were obliged to give her a swallow of water, over the diploma and degree of C. I.—*Canis Illustrissimus*—which Jack had written out in Dog Latin, and hung on Stamp's collar.

After lunch on Hillhouse Avenue they drove to Alumni Hall in time to hear the speaking, and in time to hear General Rives thrill the audience of old grads with an eloquent appeal for Yale and its future needs—a trite and familiar subject at Alumni dinners, but in this instance made effective by the old general's enthusiasm.

Harry, at Grannis' request, and after many tears on Clara's part—tears which were turned to joy afterward as she realized that Harry would not now have to be separated from her—went to Cleveland and into the electric lighting company. For a year he worked very hard and faithfully. He had good judgment and a sound business head. Grannis watched over him like a father. Mr. Hastings bought more stock and went into the concern as an officer. From the first Harry became self-supporting, and refused to receive from his mother or uncle a cent from the estate. Grannis thought this a wise step, and everything that Grannis said, he did. It made Clara provoked. " You never think of *us*," she said, with a pretty pout, which Harry laughingly kissed away.

" You see," said old Gran, " you'll work the harder if you are just fighting it out on one line for yourself. You'll have enough and to spare. Then, you know, your mother—why, she's a woman. I—I hate to be supported by a woman."

He could say no more.

But a year later Clara put *her* foot down, and presently there was a gorgeous wedding, and half of Umpty-four came to attend it from all over the country. And Dan came. Dear old Dan and dear old Jack—Harry's groomsmen—and as one wedding always makes another, and as Jack and Kitty had gotten over their little affair by this time (whoever expected Jack to be serious in these matters?) and as Kitty and Dan were thrown much together, why —was it odd that their engagement was announced in the following fall?

For six months Harry and Clara traveled in Europe. They rode bicycles in England through the Lake Country, they boated on the Thames, they rode to hounds in Surrey and Shropshire, went fishing in Wales—visiting some old friends of the Hastings, at their fine old country seat. Ah, what a delightful six months they had ! And they learned to love England as a mother ! and Oxford seemed a second alma mater.

After Danforth's engagement to Kitty Chestleton was announced, and after the good fellow had buckled down to hard work in the Columbia law school, her mother took Kitty out of school and went abroad, meeting Harry and his lovely wife in Mentone. One day in January Harry received the following telegram from Grannis at Cleveland :

" *You must return at once. Important matters call me away. Expect to be married myself. Two can play at that game.*"

They knew that the good fellow had obtained Ella's consent at last.

L'ENVOI, AFTER FIFTEEN YEARS.

A year or so ago Harry spent a week at New Haven with his wife and his two boys—sturdy young rascals whom he was already inculcating in early lessons in baseball—and went over the old days from that first morning when he was a lad conning his Vergil, and smiled upon by Ella Gerhart and the pretty shop-girls. Jack was there with them, and the two old friends were wandering about the campus, looking sadly around for the fence "that is no more."

"What old fogies we are," said Jack Rives (the distinguished and very *rising* young lawyer, now of New York). "Is it possible we've been out of college fifteen years? How the old place has changed!"

"*Eheu fugaces!*" said Harry, forgetting the rest of the Latin. What has a busy, money-making, business man to do with Latin, anyhow?

"Yes, *Eheu—eheu, labuntur anni!*" laughed Jack. "The old place is not the same. There are a lot of strangers here now, Harry. Dear old Professor Shepard has passed away. Who are these boys one sees—not students? How young they look! even the seniors! Could *we* have ever been so ridiculously green and youthful looking when at Yale?"

They agreed that they felt, both of them, exceedingly old.

A voice called out of a doorway:

"Mannin', Mas' Rives and Mas' Chestleton!"

It was Alston! He was the same old, dingy sweep, with the ring of brass keys about his neck, as of old! *He*, at least, had not changed.

It is a singular touchstone, going back to college. The world is so large—it's so hard to become anywise famous. Hopes were so grand in those days! How far any of us have come from fulfilling them! The great men in college days fill such small niches in life! That high-browed, fine-foreheaded Smith is now a little pettifogging attorney somewhere in Pittsburg. Ormsby, the college poet, is—alas, shall we confess it?—a country dentist. The great man—Stonley—the genius of his class, is teaching in

a ladies' seminary. For a genuine attack of the blues, go back
alone, oh, alumnus, and wander about those classic shades once

" MAUNIN', MAS' CHESTLETON."

again, solus! Ah, the ghosts of the fading past! They haunt
every elm, every doorway, every window, crying continually, " To
the few shall come success, to the many failure ! "

They went back to their hotel fairly depressed. "We amount to nothing—we have done nothing—we feel ashamed!" they said, "after fifteen years!"

"Nonsense!" cried Clara, looking up with her fine, beautiful eyes in Harry's face. "You have married *me!*"

"Well, *I* haven't!" laughed poor Jack. "I think I'm left!"

They sat out on the balcony of the New Haven House that evening, smoking, and looking across at the beautiful new Osborne Hall, and talking of old times.

"Our days were not these days, Jack," said Harry. "The college is grown great. Life here is different now. Why, they even have an illustrated comic paper, the old *Record*, you know—and they are much greater swells than we, in our simple times, ever thought of being. But the spirit is the same. *Yale sand!* that's it! Yale pluck, not luck, wins now, as it used to do. Yale men out in the world get ahead in the same way, by work and energy—that's what Yale teaches."

"A material sort of teaching," said Clara.

"Yes, that's so, it *is* material, the money-maker's philosophy—American doctrine. Not a bit of literary *finesse* or poetry or romance, but dogged work, and success to crown it, that's Yale—and always will be, I hope!"

"As a young millionaire—it behooves you, Harry, to have such sentiments! But, for me—a starving lawyer——"

"Oh, you must marry a rich girl, Jack," laughed Clara. "Come out and make us a visit—we'll soon marry you off, you dear old boy!"

Jack, the rascal, shook his head. "No marriage for me! Thanks! Ted Caswell isn't; Nevers isn't—lots of us are left. I—I wonder if Miss Walker would have me now? She must be very—*ripe*. What a dear old thing she was—and is!"

THE END.

2

Outing ◉ Fiction ◉ Library

Contents Volume One.

A Comedy of Counter-
plots. *Illustrated.*
EDGAR FAWCETT.

Bear's Head Brooch.
Illustrated.
ERNEST INGERSOLL.

Pastelle. *Illustrated.*
CLARA SPRAGUE ROSS.

The Flagellante's Sin.
Illustrated.
THERESA M. RANDALL.

A Very Strange Case.
WM. HINCKLEY.

A Two-year-old Hero-
ine.
FRANCIS TREVELYAN.

The Deserted Kingdoms.
FRANK C. BRUMBACK.

ATTENTION IS INVITED to this series of Short Stories, beautifully illustrated, attractively bound in permanent form, issued quarterly by

The Outing Company, Ltd. 239-241 Fifth Avenue, New York, N. Y.

Each volume contains Short Stories, by well-known authors, told with graphic force, sure to command the interest of the most cultivated reader.

The publishers of OUTING take pride in being able to furnish this new series, so attractive in style and convenient in form, at a price far more reasonable than any hitherto offered.

SHORT STORIES IN POPULAR FORM.

Single Numbers, 25 cents each.

Issued Quarterly.

On all news stands, and by mail.

Price $1.00 a year, postage paid.

www.ingramcontent.com/pod-product-compliance
Lightning Source LLC
Chambersburg PA
CBHW031057110726
47900CB00003B/966